✪ THE WATCH

Also by Dennis Danvers

Time and Time Again
Wilderness
End of Days
The Fourth World
Circuit of Heaven

The
WATCH

Being the unauthorized sequel to Peter A. Kropotkin's

MEMOIRS OF A REVOLUTIONIST—

as imparted to

Dennis Danvers

by Anchee Mahur,

traveler from a distant future,

or

A SCIENCE FICTION NOVEL

An Imprint of HarperCollins Publishers

EOS

EOS
An Imprint of HarperCollins*Publishers*
10 East 53rd Street
New York, New York 10022-5299

ISBN: 0-380-97762-1

Library of Congress Cataloging-in-Publication Data

Danvers, Dennis.
The watch—being the unauthorized sequel to Peter A. Kropotkin's Memoirs of a revolutionist—as imparted to Dennis Danvers by Anchee Mahur, traveler from a distant future, or, A science fiction novel.
p. cm.
ISBN 0-380-97762-1 (hardcover)
1. Time travel—Fiction. I. Title: Watch—being the unauthorized sequel to Peter A. Kropotkin's Memoirs of a revolutionist—as imparted to Dennis Danvers by Archee Mahur, traveler from a distant future. II. Title: Science fiction novel. III. Kropotin, Petr Alekseevich, kniaz', 1842-1921. Memoirs of a revolutionist. IV. Title.

PS3554.A5834 W38 2002
813'.54—dc21
2001040224

First Eos hardcover printing: January 2002

Eos Trademark Reg. U.S. Pat. Off. and in Other Countries, Marca Registrada, Hecho en U.S.A.
HarperCollins ® is a registered trademark of HarperCollins Publishers Inc.

Printed in the U.S.A.

FIRST EDTION

10 9 8 7 6 5 4 3 2 1

www.eosbooks.com

§ In Memoriam:

Peter A. Kropotkin

1842–1921

Contents

§ Men passionately desire to live after death, but they often pass away without noticing the fact that the memory of a really good person always lives. It is impressed upon the next generation, and is transmitted again to the children. Is not that an immortality worth striving for?

—PETER KROPOTKIN, *Memoirs of a Revolutionist*

§ When we got home, we laid the foundation of two large cities: one at Shacco's, to be called Richmond, and the other at the point of Appomattox River, to be named Petersburg . . . Thus we did not build castles only, but also cities in the air.

—WILLIAM BYRD II, founder of Richmond, 1733

§ THE WATCH

1 ⑤ I Am Reborn

I was suddenly struck by an extraordinary spectacle; on the
dark vault of the sky I saw an immense meteor with a long tail
and dazzling green light which lit up the sky and the earth. It
fell slowly and disappeared on the horizon. I had never seen
anything like it in my life. We stood as if fixed to the spot. It
seemed to us that there was a mysterious relationship between
the falling star and the dying revolutionary.
                                  —BORIS LEBEDEV, *Kropotkin's son-in-law,*
                          in his account of Kropotkin's death February 8, 1921

[In prison] I asked, of course, to have paper, pen, and ink, but
was absolutely refused. . . . I suffered very much from this
forced inactivity, and began to compose in my imagination a
series of novels for popular reading. . . . I made up the plot, the
descriptions, the dialogues, and tried to commit the whole to
memory from the beginning to the end.
                          —PETER KROPOTKIN, *Memoirs of a Revolutionist*

Since my death, I've thought a good deal of my
childhood in Russia, when I was "Prince" Peter Kropotkin, a title
I renounced at twelve. These recollections serve to remind me
that I have always been—from my earliest memories to this moment (some hours into my new life)—very much the same. It's
remarkable when I think on it: seventy-eight years, and the same
earnest fellow all along. It makes me wonder if I'll change this
time round, or whether I'll keep working for my heart's desire—
that the world should change instead.

My mother died when I was not yet four. I must confess, being
so young, I did not really know her. I have of her a mere hand-

ful of memories—each one too grand and charged with emotions to be entirely trusted even if I could manage to disentangle
reality from legend. But there was nothing illusory about the effect of my mother's memory on those servants entrusted with
raising my brother and me. Even if they had not repeated it on
every occasion, I would have known from the care and concern
lavished on her sons that they thought my mother a fine woman
indeed. Their kindness to me can never be exaggerated, nor their
wisdom rivaled by later, more sophisticated teachers. As for inherited traits, I attribute to my mother whatever characteristics I
possess of a worthwhile nature.

My father incarnated the man I did not wish to be. With such
a father's shadow over me, I could never subscribe to any form
of genetic determinism. As for his living presence—the parent's
guiding and shaping hand—he little influenced my elder
brother Sasha and me, for he largely ignored us.

He was a gentleman soldier, an officer naturally, like most of
the lesser nobles of his generation who could imagine no greater
contribution to the world than fine uniforms and close-order
drills, a ballet without music or joy. He was as stingy as my
mother was open-hearted; as dull as she was lively; as vindictive
as she was loving. He was rich, however, master of twelve hundred serfs, human beings he presumed to own, tending to land
he presumed to own. There was no end to his ownership and
presumption.

I remember one night at dinner—I was eight or so—he told
Sasha and me that he had been awarded a medal for gallantry
because Frol, his man, had rushed into a burning house at great
risk to himself and rescued a doomed child. My father's commander, witnessing these events, gave my father the Cross of St.
Anne straightaway.

"But Father," my brother and I objected, "it was Frol who
saved the child!" Through my childish mind flitted the fantasy
of a just ceremony—complete with military band and a goodly
number of horses—Frol on a platform bearing up bravely beneath the burden of an armload of valorous trinkets.

But Father soon chased that illusion from my brain. "What of that?" he replied. "Was he not my man? It is all the same." He believed it, you see—that a man such as himself could possess a man like Frol, when the truth is my father did not possess the tenth part of Frol's virtues.

As always, Frol was present that evening, standing in his usual place like a pillar, and just as likely to move from his post at our father's elbow. Every evening, with near-invisible signals and gestures, Frol directed the throng of fifty or so men and women who labored to serve us dinner, who would see us into bed and tuck us in like tiny infants. It was a form of suicide, such wealth—the complete abdication of all responsibility for one's own life.

My father paused in his tale to make some complaint about the meat, and I attempted to catch Frol's eyes, but he avoided my gaze and looked darkly out the window into the night. I looked at my father and thought, without quite knowing what I meant, *Someday Frol will toss you out that window into the snow. Someday it will be your house ablaze with no one to rescue you.*

I hated my father. I have never publicly confessed that fact before. In an effort of fairness I can allow that my father was far from the worst of the serf owners—that even though he forced dozens of young women to marry young so that they might breed him new "souls," he never personally raped a woman to my knowledge;—that even though, on a whim or for some imagined slight, he was in the habit of condemning young men to a quarter-century stint in the army (a death and torture sentence rolled into one), he never murdered a man outright. Even on the battlefield.

There were worse men than my father, certainly.

I can further allow that he was a product of his time, an ordinary man who by all the standards of his class and kin was a good enough fellow. In the terribly conventional neighborhood into which I was born there were hundreds of fine houses, nearly as many princes decorated for gallantry, but scarcely two or three opinions to go round. Those who thought otherwise could live somewhere else, preferably in another country. Be that as it may, he was *my* father, and I wished that he were better than the times, better than his peers—wished it in vain with all my heart—and I never forgave him for being what he was.

In a sense, I suppose, I dedicated my life to *not* being my father. In that much, at least, I succeeded.

But what does that matter now? That life is over. My father died in 1871. I died in 1921. This is 1999, almost the end of the millennium. Surely, I can forgive him now.

I have been raised from my deathbed and given a new life by a strange benefactor from the future named Anchee Mahur. I'm resurrected full-grown like a character in a novel. I've kept my name, Peter Alexeivich Kropotkin, no reason to take another. As Anchee explained, no one is likely to mistake me for a man who's been dead for seventy-eight years. According to the papers Anchee gave me, I'm from Dmitrov, a sly irony since that's where I died. But instead of my old birth date of 1842, I have a new one, 1967, even though it seems to me I've only been in this new time a matter of hours. In this life, I start at thirty-two and have no childhood to recollect. At that age in 1874, I was in jail for the first time, and anything is preferable to that, even if this future, or rather, this present in which I find myself, is thus far a terrifying place indeed.

I sit inside an enormous airplane. It's the size of a country house. A nervous glance out the window confirms that this behemoth is miles above the surface of the earth. Rationally, I should not be alarmed: I am a man of science. I understand the principles of flight. But still, even though I've been here now for some hours, a terror lingers like nothing I've ever felt before, and it won't listen to reason, as if I were some wretch out of the Stone Age, cowering before the magic of my betters. The image annoys me, and I grow impatient with my fear.

When I asked Anchee what future age he came from, he said it was so far hence—thousands and thousands of years, that a date would be meaningless, and his science would seem like magic to me if he attempted to explain it. He quoted some fellow named

Clarke to back him up on this, which meant little to me. And I objected that perhaps I was not as dim as he supposed. But even now, in this time, a mere lifetime into the future, I must face my humbling ignorance. The sentence Anchee gave me to answer all inquiries—"I am flying to America"—is like some incantation out of *1001 Arabian Nights* or else the ravings of a madman.

But it is not *magic* quite yet. I understand the airfoil well enough to know that it is physics and not magic that holds this huge airplane aloft. I hypothesize that the propellerless engines roaring outside the window work by propulsion, like a rocket. Perhaps most important in quieting my fears, however, is the demeanor of my fellow passengers—who look no more alarmed than if they were aboard a slow steamer floating down the Mississippi. This airship, however, is a good deal less sociable than any vessel of my acquaintance, much to its detriment. I attempt to entertain myself with the fantasy of someday plying the Mississippi. I have a great fondness for rivers. But the image will not hold, as if borne away on a current. There is more to my fear than this airplane.

I am an immigrant, my papers say. They make no reference to the fact that I have visited America twice before; nor should I, Anchee advised. Soon, in a few hours I gather, I will arrive in Washington, where I will get inside another airplane and proceed to my ultimate destination. RIC, the papers say. An official of the airplane company, Alicia—a striking young woman with a warm smile, dressed in a military-style jacket and dark trousers—explained that RIC is a code for Richmond, Virginia.

What an odd choice, I thought immediately.

The Capital of the Confederacy.

When I was last in America in 1901, by a coincidence I met Varina Howell Davis—widow of Jefferson Davis, the late president of the rebellion—in New York City. Booker Washington joined us, and they spoke briefly of Richmond. Neither had the fondest memories of the place. For the former slave, it had been a leading center of the slave trade, for the former first lady, it was a test of her self-proclaimed abundance of patience. "I could please no one," she declared. "I have never been anywhere quite so concerned with questions of etiquette and breeding when there seemed, to an outsider such as myself, so little of either to be found within the city limits." I gathered that an anarchist, even a well-mannered one such as myself, would not have been welcome there.

But that was almost a century ago. Whatever I might find in Richmond, I doubt its choice is random; it, too, is part of Anchee's design, whatever that may be.

"Tell no one you are an anarchist," he advised. "They will not understand what you mean."

"That will be easy," I joked. "That's the state of affairs now."

I close my eyes to the frantic images of a color motion picture flickering everywhere I turn, but I can still see it on my retina like bursts of flame. When it began, I forced myself to watch for a while, to see if I could sort out its constantly shifting perspectives—by my calculations, the product of no fewer than half a dozen cameras going all at once and spliced together in a furious montage. But I could make no sense of it, and my head throbbed with the effort. Everyone else stares at it transfixed, tubing snaking out of their ears. I can hear a faint sound coming from the tubing of the man seated beside me. Voices? I can't be sure. He showed little enough interest in my voice when I attempted to engage him in conversation. Earlier it was his "laptop" which gripped his attention. I was curious about the device, but his tone when identifying it was such to discourage further questions.

What have I done? What am I doing here? I've made a terrible mistake. *I'm* alive, but everyone and everything I've ever known are gone. Why didn't I just die and be done with it?

But as I draw in an apprehensive breath—a strong, clear breath, free of the bronchitis that has plagued me since my years in prison—it doesn't *feel* like a mistake to be alive. I squeeze the arms of my seat, made of a curious pliable substance like a stiff clay, and there's no pain in my hands or my joints. It is good to live. Life is good. I have always believed this, regardless of the circumstances.

When Anchee came to my deathbed, I already knew I was about to die, even if he had not told me. He knew the time by heart, it occurs to me, the day and the hour. *Three o'clock in the morning, February 8, 1921.*

Sophie, my dear wife, was with me. Sasha, my daughter, and her husband, Boris. Earlier there had been another voice, Atabekian, I thought, but couldn't be sure. My consciousness came and went, I daresay, at least as often as my caretakers.

Boris and Sasha were talking excitedly about the most re-markable meteor they had just seen blazing across the sky. Boris babbled some superstitious hokum trying to implicate me and my ill health in the business of the cosmos. I wanted to inquire further concerning the shade of green light the meteor em-anated, but it was too much effort to speak, had been for days. And with speech came the coughing, and life itself had come down to *not* coughing if one could help it, knowing that soon, very soon, I couldn't help it, and I would die coughing. I couldn't imagine any other death.

They thought I slept, but I was awake, listening. It was my last connection with life—their voices. Certain profound moments of complete solitude have touched me in the way, I imagine, that mystics claim to be touched by God. But for me the voices of those I love, or even the memories of them, are a sufficient rea-son to live. I listened. Even when my inner eye could no longer mount a reliable image of the speaker, I listened to their words.

So when there was silence, an absolute silence, I forced my eyes open to see what death looked like.

To my surprise, even without my eyeglasses, I saw perfectly, something I hadn't done in years. There were a trio of lights by my bed—the flames of the candles—but they didn't move, didn't flicker. Their light was unnaturally steady. With surpris-ingly little effort, I rolled over onto my back, and there was Boris standing over me, frozen in mid-sentence, his hand poised in a passionate gesture. The tears on the cheeks of Sasha and Sophie didn't flow. Atabekian stood motionless, the poker in his hand thrust into the fire. A cloud of sparks hovered above the grate.

The only movement of any kind other than myself was a man, a black man in a white robe or gown, watching me intently, his eyes blinking. When I caught sight of him, he stepped forward and sat on the edge of the bed, Boris looming over him like a statue in a park. "Peter Kropotkin," the black man said. "Do not be afraid. I am a friend. I have come a long way to see you. I am from the future. My time owes you a great deal. I have stopped time so that we may speak. You are about to die . . ."

I stopped listening to his precise words—for they scarcely made any sense to me—and attempted to fathom what was going on. It was quite the speech, rehearsed I would say, but well delivered. Everything about him bespoke a sense of purpose. Is he an angel? I asked myself. Does his presence mean there is a God after all? The thought so distressed me that I felt a wave of revulsion and anger—to have been so wrong about such a fundamental question right up to death's door. Worse to imagine a God who would willingly preside over such widespread suffering and inequity as fill the world. No. No God. I refused to believe it. No angels either.

"Who are you?" I interrupted in English, for he was speaking English, though in an accent strange to me.

"I am Anchee Mahur," he said, then summarized his recitation in slow and precise syllables: "I've come from the future to offer you a second life. By scientific means, I'll restore your body to what it was in younger and healthier days, then transport you to a different time and place, where you may live out the balance of a new life. If you so wish it, that is. We force no one."

I was vainly trying to comprehend what on earth he could be talking about when he laid his hands on my head, and said, "Allow me," and all came clear like a sudden burst of inspiration when the most incredible things seem as if they have been obvious all along. Of course: my body restored to youth and fitness, transplanted into some future time like a cutting from an old tree.

But I am *not* a tree, and there was still much I wanted to know. "A time machine?" I asked, and it was then he claimed his science would seem magic to me, magic he could not explain in anything less than *hours.* "I wouldn't even know where to start," he said. "You don't have a grasp on the most basic principles involved." How odd, I thought. He can stop time, but still be in a hurry. Eager to get on with things, I would say.

But did it matter, I asked myself, whether I understood the science or not? More important (presuming this wasn't just some deathbed delirium) was whether he was telling the truth and whether he could be trusted—reminding myself they weren't always the same thing.

He was very handsome and very dark. Also quite young, maybe twenty, with a bit of that cocky brashness about him, but so old in his bearing—a great dignity that was no mere haughtiness—that I had no idea what to make of him. I'd never met anyone even vaguely like him before, and I have met a good number of people from all over the world. It was easy to believe he came from the far future. Much easier than believing him an angel.

"But what of them?" I asked of the frozen mourners, for it was as mourners that I thought of them even before Anchee showed up. "Mightn't they be alarmed when I vanish altogether? That sort of thing could arouse the most ridiculous rumors. I don't wish to be the cause of any new religions sprouting up. There are quite enough already."

He laughed heartily, and I was glad the future, even his magical future, still possessed a sense of humor. It was that discovery more than anything else that decided me. (That and the likelihood the entire experience was hallucinatory). There was no way to know if he was trustworthy. Whether he spoke truth or delusion would be clear soon enough. "No one here will know," he reassured me. "When time resumes you'll still be here just so, but you'll go on to live another life unknown to them, in the future."

"When in the future? In your time?"

He found this amusing, with a little laugh and a big smile.

"No, not nearly so far. You couldn't possibly adapt. You would say the year 1999. April 8. A lifetime from now."

"My lifetime, to be exact."

"Yes."

"Is there some scientific reason for that?"

"Hmm. More aesthetic I would say."

"Why do you do this? What possible reason could there be for making an old man young again and inflicting him on future generations?"

"I don't know if you can understand."

He was beginning to annoy me. "Try me," I snapped. "I'll concede the science, even the aesthetics, but not the ethics."

"I'm sorry. I don't mean to condescend."

"Comes naturally, does it? Take your time. I gather that as long as you stay, I don't cough, I don't die." I tested this theory by sitting up, planting my feet on the floor, standing up effortlessly.

"You don't want to die?"

"Most definitely not."

This apparently encouraged him and gave him renewed patience to answer an old man's questions. "Time isn't a single stream," he said, "but an infinite number coexisting. We've learned to . . . weave them together by transplanting lives from one time to another. In this way we make new times, new realities. We move among them, experience them, learn from them."

"An experiment?"

He made a face. Tact did not come easily for him. "In a sense. Zola, I believe, spoke of his novels that way. You love the opera, I believe. It's more like that. An *experience*. A work of art."

"With real people. You are tampering with reality itself." I gestured at our frozen witnesses as evidence of my accusation.

"No. We're making new realities. 'Reality itself' doesn't exist." He held out one hand and then the other: "There's the time when Peter Kropotkin is reborn in America, and there's the time he isn't. Each is as real as the other. Each is its own time." He weighed the imaginary times in his hands and held them out as if I should choose.

"Once upon a time," I said.

He laughed again. "Yes! Exactly! You're just as I imagined you."

I gathered I was to take this as a compliment. He had the unsettling look of a disciple about him. "How do you know so much about me?"

"In my time you're a famous man, Peter Alexeivich Kropotkin. I have studied your life and your works. That's why I've chosen you. Once we're under way, I'll answer any questions you ask. But before we go any further, I need to know: Do you want another life in America on the eve of the twenty-first century or not?"

He spoke as if offering me a pastry or a chop, while for me there were still questions within questions, so many I couldn't begin to fathom them all, but at the heart of them stood one question, alone: Life or death? The answer was simple.

"Yes," I said.

The next thing I knew I stood fully clothed in a cavernous building he called the Moscow Airport. It, too, was frozen in time, but it was packed with hundreds of people. Their unmoving aspect was too terrifying to behold *en masse*. I looked high up into the rafters to avoid their dead gaze. A finch, trapped inside the building, caught in a moment of terrified flight, hung over my head like some parody of the soul. Anchee stood at my shoulder reciting instructions, counsel, warnings, strictures— like a priest reciting a catechism. I only half listened.

Any questions?

Is that what Mephistopheles asked Faust? I thought, almost giddy. At least if he were an angel or a devil I would know what he was up to. Of course, he could have told me he was an angel, and I would have had little choice but to believe him. It wasn't real to me. How could it be? Dead one minute, alive the next. Not the next minute, almost the next century. This, all around me, was the future. Everything—the colors, the surfaces, the smells—all were different.

I heard the crinkle of paper and realized I held some documents in my hands. I was in a queue of people with documents in their hands. My hands—I couldn't quit staring at them—were young and strong. I made and unmade a fist, touched the smooth, taut skin of my face. I looked around for a mirror, but there was none to be seen.

Any questions?

"No," I said impatiently, and the life and the noise and time started up again, and Anchee had vanished. In the wake of his departure, I had my first realization of a question I wished I had asked: Am I the only one here in this place like me—a transplant from a different time? Am I the only variable in this experiment? The only role in this play?

Overhead the panicked finch scrambled desperately for a purchase on a steel girder, screeching . . .

"Mr. Kropotkin! Are you all right, Mr. Kropotkin?"

I must have let out an involuntary cry and alarmed Alicia. She stands over me with a look of such heartfelt concern that I momentarily feel as if I am back in my deathbed. I look around and see that a few of my fellow passengers are regarding me with alarm as well, though most are still transfixed by the motion picture. The man who was sitting beside me has gone. I spot him loitering in the aisle. He looks away, embarrassed for me.

"I'm fine," I reassure Alicia. "Just a nightmare, an undigested bit of beef. Thank you for asking."

"Is this your first time flying, Mr. Kropotkin?"

"Yes. Yes, it is."

This seems to please her immensely. "Somehow I thought so. Would you care for something to drink, Mr. Kropotkin? We have Russian vodka."

I start to tell her I no longer drink because of my age and my health, but realize my error. "That would be lovely," I say. "And please, call me Peter."

2 ✍ I Learn the Alphabet

Is there a higher aesthetic delight than to read poetry in a language which one does not yet quite thoroughly understand?
—PETER KROPOTKIN, *Memoirs of a Revolutionist*

Over and over again in my life I have heard complaints among the advanced parties about the want of money; but the longer I live, the more I am persuaded that our chief difficulty is not so much a lack of money as of *men* who will march firmly and steadily towards a given aim in the right direction, and inspire others.
—PETER KROPOTKIN, *Memoirs of a Revolutionist*

"And what is your job with the airplane company? What are your duties?" I ask Alicia, who will not join me in a drink because she is "on duty." The vodka is really quite good and comes in tiny thumb-sized bottles. I'm drinking the contents of two such bottles over ice in a vessel made of some sort of flexible glass. Alicia is young and pretty, and I try to calculate the last time I sat and chatted with a pretty young woman, not counting the pilgrims who came to see the anarchist prince in his dotage, rather like motoring out of Cairo to see the tombs. *I have studied your life and your works . . .*

"I'm a flight attendant, Mr. Kropotkin."

"Is that like a porter on a train?"

She smiles at this, amused. "Yes, like a porter. It's my job to see that every passenger on board is safe and happy."

I'm quaint, old-fashioned—*the silly old man*. Then I remember—I'm not old to Alicia, only to myself. She sees a boyish-

looking man in his early thirties. Earlier in the lavatory of the airplane, a devilishly confusing place if there ever was one, I finally
found a mirror. There I was, only younger, my hair red again, my
beard trimmed to an absurd neatness, suiting Anchee's tastes, no
doubt. But that wasn't the only way I wasn't simply a replica of
the man I was: There wasn't a scar on my body, even those I'd
gotten as a boy. I notice a tiny crescent-shaped scar beside Alicia's left eye and realize I've been staring.

"That's a good job to have," I say. "And you are quite good at
it. When you saw that I was not only unhappy, but sharing my
unhappiness with everyone inside the airplane and for miles
around, you distracted me from my distress with vodka and conversation. A most effective strategy I would say. I must inquire,
however: If I were to reassure you that I am completely cured of
my unhappiness, may we still continue our conversation?"

She laughs. "Of course. At least until the movie's over." She
settles more comfortably into her seat. She has installed us in the
back of the airplane, beside what she calls the galley, as on a
ship. An airship. The other flight attendants hurry about attending to the other passengers. I am Alicia's responsibility apparently—keeping the anarchist quiet. The others smile at me as
they pass, glad to see I'm not bellowing anymore. I feel light-
headed and smile back. "Try to look a *little* unhappy," Alicia suggests. "I don't want the others to think I'm having a good time."

I laugh along. "Will frightened do? I'm really quite terrified."

"There's nothing to be afraid of. The airplane is perfectly
safe—"

"No. It's not the airplane that frightens me. I understand the
airplane. The airplane is simple physics. It's everything else. I'm
a . . . a stranger. There's so much I don't know. I don't know anything about . . ." I don't even know where to start. I raise my
hands in frustration, and my vodka lists dangerously close to the
lip of its vessel. The ice clatters dully like pebbles on wood, but
flatter in tone, and I can feel the impact in my fingertips. I set the
vodka down on the tray, and the surfaces click together. I rub my
fingers on the tray. I must start somewhere.

"What's this?"

"You mean the tray?"

"The material, the substance of which it is made. What do you call that?"

She is perhaps a little scared of me at this moment. My ignorance is frightening. "Plastic?"

"Plastic." I tap it with my fingernail. I tap my nail against the side of my vodka. "Plastic?" She nods. "I have heard of plastic. Baekland's Bakelite. But nothing like this."

She's fascinated by someone so unfamiliar with plastic. "Most of the plane is plastic," she says, pointing here and there. I can see she's right. "It's just simple physics, too," she says reassuringly, "or chemistry, I guess. Most of *America* is plastic, as you'll soon see."

I try to imagine this. I want to pursue her remark about chemistry. My guess is that this plastic—and there seem to be several different varieties—is a synthetic substance conceived in the laboratory. But my scientific curiosity will have to wait. Clearly I'll have much catching up to do before I can call myself a scientist again. Other matters are more important now. "Would you be so kind as to tell me about America?" I ask.

The question seems to surprise her. She positively beams at me—no mere duty any longer, if ever I was. She likes to help, as most people do in my experience. She takes a moment considering her answer, clowning with a pantomime of concentration and tortured thought only to mask how seriously she takes my question.

"You know the America you see in American TV and movies?"—she begins—"it's *almost* like that—not as good in some ways, not as bad in others. You know what I mean?"

"I'm sorry. I don't know these things."

Her question was rhetorical. My ignorance stops her in her tracks. "American TV and movies? You don't know American TV and movies?"

I shake my head no.

"Where are you from? I've been *all* over the planet, and I've never been anywhere they didn't have American TV and movies."

"Dmitrov," I lie. "Outside Moscow." Seventy-eight years ago.

"So they *must* have TV there. I've watched TV in Moscow. You're pulling my leg, right?"

Fortunately I know this expression. But not this word she keeps using. I hesitate to admit to further ignorance, but see no way around it. "What is TV?" I ask.

She claps a hand to her chest, genuinely alarmed. "You don't know what *TV* is? *Television?*"

"I have heard the word 'television.' I am familiar with the concept."

"But you've never *watched* television?"

"I have been out of touch lately. . . . Working. I write books." I hope that's something people still do. I shrug and smile. "I've never seen a television."

"Movies?"

"Yes. I have seen movies. I like Charlie Chaplin very much. I like . . . old movies."

"Is someone meeting you in Richmond, Mr. Kropotkin?"

"Peter, please. No. I know no one there. But I'll be fine. I'm quite resourceful. I lived a number of years in Siberia, traveling thousands of miles, with little more than the bare necessities." I hope to distract her from my present ignorance and my uncertain future with tales of my exploring past. Now that I'm young again, they seem more appropriate. They had grown too wistful in my old age.

But she is wide-eyed. "Siberia? You lived in . . . Siberia?"

"When I was young, yes. Five years, beginning when I was twenty."

"You poor, poor man."

"Oh no! It was beautiful, breathtaking. I learned so much there—the land, the people. They were, in a way, the best years of my life. It was good to be young in the wilderness."

Something in what I've said touches her in some way I can't imagine. Her eyes fill with tears, and panic overtakes me.

"America," I blurt out, "tell me about America!" And that seems to steady her, to bring her back to her duty.

"It's busy," she says. "Go, go, go."

I think of Wordsworth—*The world is too much with us late and soon.* . . . "Industrious?"

"No. It's not work or play. It's everything. Everything's in a rush." My confusion must show on my face, and she bites her lip in frustration, reminding me of my daughter Sasha when she was wrought up about something. "It's like . . . like . . . a *train*—you know trains—it's like a runaway train." She laughs. "There's a song I like called that, as a matter of fact."

I imagine American culture as a train rushing out of control, jumping the tracks. Perhaps this is why Anchee has put me here. "Might there be a revolution?"

She laughs out loud. "In *America*? No way. People have it too good."

"They *like* everything in a rush?"

"Not exactly."

"But all the people have their needs met?"

She finds my question odd, I can tell. I'm used to that. "Well . . . no," she says. "Not everybody."

"There are poor people?"

"And homeless people, and old people, and . . . gangs and violence . . . drugs and AIDS . . ." She gives me a wry smile. "It's better than most places. My neighborhood's okay."

"What city do you live in?"

"DC," she says. "Arlington actually. I like it there. I like working the overseas flights. I was working out of New York for a while, but I hate JFK."

"JFK?"

"I'm sorry. John F. Kennedy. One of the airports in New York City is named after him."

"He is an important American?"

She stares at me, searching my eyes. "Yes," she says softly. "A president." She gives me a big smile. "Let me get you another vodka, Mr. Kropotkin—*Peter*. They're on the house."

"That means free of charge, doesn't it?"

She laughs again. "Yes it does."

I laugh as well, trying to lighten things up. "That's good. Because I have no money!"

She is concerned again. "None? Not even any Russian money?"

"Not a ruble," I say cheerfully. I made this discovery while still in the queue at the Moscow Airport and thought to make an inventory of my strange pockets. Anchee has dressed me in clothes of his choosing, suitable, I assume, for the times—blue dungarees, a cotton knit shirt, and a blue denim jacket. Eight pockets in all. Besides my handful of papers, there's my new passport and a plastic card that says RESIDENT ALIEN and has my picture on it. The only artifact from my old life Anchee left me, tucked away in the smallest pocket, is a watch I used to keep in my dresser drawer underneath the socks. I'll have more to say about this troublesome watch presently.

But he gave me no money. I hoped at the time that perhaps the future had done away with the need for money, but Alicia's concern makes it clear matters are not so fortunate.

"Do you have an account somewhere?"

"No. I have no funds at all."

"A credit card?"

I show her my empty hands without confessing I don't know what she's talking about. She thinks me addled enough as it is, and I can imagine what she's talking about—some quick easy way to live on account at some usurious rate.

"Peter, how will you get by?"

"I will work. I have many skills—surveying, carpentry, journalism." *I have written books in Russian, French, and English,* I want to boast to her. *I am a famous man!* This fit of pride repulses me, and I say to myself, *Peter, you're a pompous ass!*

"You're most kind to be concerned," I reassure Alicia, who looks none too convinced. "But really, I'll be fine." I laugh. "After all, I survived Siberia."

"But Peter, the immigration people might not let you in without some 'visible means of support.'" She gives me an apologetic smile. "I used to date an immigration lawyer. He talked shop all the time—which is why we broke up actually. But I'm pretty sure you need money or a job waiting for you, unless you're seeking asylum." The word hangs in the air; the same look "Siberia" conjured earlier transforms her features once again. She places her hand on my arm in the kindest way. "Is that what you're doing, Peter—seeking asylum?"

Asylum. I've been through that nonsense before—begging one bully to protect you from another. I couldn't begin to answer the questions involved—*Well you see, sir, I can't possibly return to my country of residence because I've been dead there for seventy-eight years. . . .*

"No. I am . . . I am just an immigrant. But I cannot go back to Russia, under any circumstances." There would be no record of me there, Anchee told me, and I would risk arrest if I tried to return. In this life, I have vowed, no more prisons.

She nods thoughtfully and rises from her seat. "I'll get you that drink now. Sounds like you're going to need it."

From a cart in the galley she takes three more tiny bottles, placing one on the tray before me and slipping a couple more in my jacket pocket. Promising to return, she hurries down the aisle, where I can see her conferring with her fellow flight attendants. I'm only a little bit drunk. Apparently Alicia seems to think I should drink myself into a stupor. It's tempting. I take the bottle on the tray and put it with the other two in my pocket. For now, I want my wits about me. Later, perhaps before a cozy fire, I'll savor these at my leisure.

No money. This *is* a problem. I can't deny it. But nothing new.

Born a prince I might have been, but I never lived off my father since I left home. I've always lived simply and poor, sometimes cold and hungry, but supporting myself by my own labors. As an impediment between me and what I hoped to accomplish, money or the lack of it has only once been truly significant: I was crossing a tumultuous river in a tiny boat, waves like mountains rising on either side threatening to capsize us, and I tossed a heavy sack full of copper and silver overboard so that I and my companions might live.

There's a stack of reading materials in the galley, and I pass the time by reading the publications of the day. *USA Today*, *Business Week*, *Cosmopolitan*, *SkyMall*, the *Wall Street Journal*, *Time*. There are the usual wars and such that sound discouragingly familiar except for the weaponry. There's much I don't understand, but this much is clear: I find myself in an age of capitalism triumphant. The theory which maintains that men can, and must, seek their own happiness in complete disregard of other people's wants is now the accepted wisdom. The ideal, apparently, is relentless and sustained consumption, a sort of conspicuous gluttony, while the rest of the world goes a-begging.

The apparent guiltlessness of the privileged is what I find truly appalling—for they don't seem to be uninformed about the economic realities of the rest of the world. In one grim piece about child labor in Asia, the facts of the case sound like something out of Dickens, but instead of that fine novelist's moral outrage, this writer seems chiefly concerned that the controversy might "negatively impact" on a certain shoe manufacturer's profit margins producing "widespread fallout in the marketplace." I'm not sure what all that means exactly. But the gist is he doesn't give a damn about children, poor ones at any rate.

America is doing very well, spectacularly well—and seems almost drunk with wealth. There's a tone throughout rather like a chorus of roosters who've slain the fox. Russia is not doing so well, is doing horribly, in fact. The "collapse of the former Soviet Union" is spoken of as fairly recent history, though I haven't been able to pin it down precisely. I confess to a certain delight in the failure of the Bolsheviks, whose authoritarian ideas and hoodlum tactics finished the revolution, but to find themselves at the mercy of an international capitalism the likes of which I could only imagine in my worst nightmares—I can take no pleasure in that!

I set aside my stack of reading and turn off the light overhead. My brain aches from taking so much in. I wish I had Sophie and

Sasha here to thrash it out with. I miss them terribly. But I've missed them for months, haven't I, lying in bed, little more than a bag of bones? Now they'll be able to get on with their lives.

Not now, *then*, I correct myself. Their lives, like mine, are long concluded, their grief long spent. I imagine my own funeral, all my old friends wishing me well. I hope the damn State didn't stick its nose into the arrangements. Lenin and his cronies must've had all they could manage containing their glee. Those bastards . . .

And now, this moment, my heart full of venom, I realize that Lenin, too, is dead, that everyone I knew is most likely dead, and I am deeply ashamed. And alone. May they all rest in peace. I wipe my eyes, grateful the lights are low.

The movie ends, the lights brighten, and the other passengers blink like miners emerging from the earth, stripping the tubing from their ears, filling up the aisles. I gather from their excitement and conversation that this air voyage will soon be coming to an end. The captain's voice from nowhere—one of the bits of magic I've grown accustomed to—confirms that in an hour we will arrive in America.

My seat is close to one of the lavatories, and there is a queue at the door for some time. I eavesdrop on the conversations to learn about American language and culture. Two men discuss someone named Skywalker or Vader—I can't decide whether this is two people or one—when one says, much to the other's envy, "I have a Skywalker at my mother's place must be worth a couple hundred by now—still in the original packaging." I decide Skywalker must be an artist of some sort whose fortunes are on the rise. The man with the Skywalker goes into the lavatory and the second man strikes up a conversation with the next person in line about some ongoing event they call "The Bombing." I listen intently, but they never mention where this is taking place. I assume they mean the trouble in the Balkans, but they never so much as mention the name of a city or a country. The man who envied the other his Skywalker thinks it has something to do with "Monica." Several others in the queue spontaneously agree, and the discussion moves up and down the line. One is of the opinion that "Hillary" is the key to understanding the whole business. I have no idea what they are talking about, but still it gratifies me to hear strangers conversing about matters of the day, to see that man is no less a sociable species than he has ever been. I feel a fresh pang of loneliness, for my ignorance is a gulf between myself and them. But I can cross it I'm sure. Class and distance and custom couldn't sever me from my fellow humans in my old life, and neither will time in my new one.

Alicia makes her way down the aisle, telling all the passengers to return to their seats, herding them like a skilled, patient sheepdog. She kneels in the aisle beside me and presses an envelope into my hands. "I took up a collection from the crew. It's only a hundred dollars. Nobody carries any cash anymore."

There was a time when I wouldn't have accepted her kindness, but such pride is hurtful. Was she to make the rounds on my behalf a second time, saying I was too good to take their money? It sounds an enormous sum to me, but she insists it will only get me through a day or so. "You are too kind," I say. "I will repay you somehow."

"Never mind that." She kisses my cheek and squeezes my hand. "I have to get back to work now. When we land, don't go anywhere. I'll come get you."

At the airport, I stand before an official, a perfect example of the universal species, and hand over everything in my possession (save the watch and the money) for his quick perusal. He asks me a series of questions, which I answer with strains of the theme Anchee suggested: I have come to America because it is the land of opportunity, in order to make a new life for myself, to be free and prosperous. I don't voice my doubts concerning

prosperity and freedom for the few at the expense of prosperity
and freedom for the many. I don't voice my beliefs that a capitalist economy and a strong state combine to crush all possibility
of a just prosperity and freedom. I lie shamelessly about the extent of my monetary assets. The official's only true concern is
that my documents be in order. Anchee's forgeries are apparently flawless. The official never looks up from a machine with a
keyboard like a typewriter where he records my answers, a
larger version of the *laptop* device. "Welcome to America," he
says. "Good luck. Next."

Alicia, who has been waiting for me during this interview,
identifies the machine as a computer as she hurries me along to
the Richmond airplane, and introduces me to a young man
named Chris, a flight attendant like herself. "Take good care of
him," she tells Chris. "He doesn't know anything."

I know she doesn't mean it literally, but she might as well. I
hadn't expected time travel to be so humbling. Alicia gives me a
card with her name, address, and telephone number. She points
to another code of some sort: "That's my e-mail for when you
figure out the computer thing. Gotta run." She hugs me and
kisses my cheek again. This time I return her embrace. She hugs
Chris as well, pounding him on the back. "Thanks," she says,
then she's gone, receding at a brisk clip down the long carpeted
hallway filled with hundreds of people; even the walls are carpeted, and seem to swallow everyone up. *Go, go, go.* I have a
glimpse of what she means.

Chris says, "She called the airport and found out who was
crewing your flight, saw my name, and called me at home to tell
me about you while you guys were still in the air." There's no
trace of Alicia now down the long hallway. Chris and I face each
other. "She likes to take in strays," he says. "We went to flight attendant school together."

"She is most kind."

"The kindest."

On the much shorter journey to Richmond, Chris, too, is kind
and helpful, and I succeed in not shocking him with my igno-

rance. I have many questions about all sorts of things, but I've had enough of feeling stupid for a while and confine myself to questions anyone who is a newcomer to the country and the town might ask.

From him I obtain the name and location of an organization that helps refugees and immigrants settle in Richmond. That there is such an agency I take as a hopeful sign. He knows of it because a neighbor of his works there. He and his "partner" live across the street from her.

"Your wife?" I inquire, not sure I understand what he means by his "partner."

"I'm gay," he replies, without answering my question. I am further confused by his tone, far from gaiety, more as if he were apologizing for something, with a touch of anger.

"That's good, isn't it—to be gay?"

He laughs. "You're all right, Peter."

"It's some sort of slang, isn't it? What does it mean?"

"Homosexual," he says.

"Oh," I say, for I don't know what else to say, and that seems to suffice. That he should be so candid about such a matter certainly speaks to a less prudish America than I recall, though I gather from his initial defensiveness that things are not completely free and open.

Upon landing, Chris, without my realizing what he's up to, hurries me to the baggage claim area, where I must explain that I have no baggage to claim. Churning metal conveyor belts make a terrible racket so that we must shout at each other to be heard. He shakes his head in disbelief. "You have nothing? Nothing at all? You brought nothing from Russia?"

"I have some money," I say.

That reassures him, I think, more than it deserves, and he checks his watch. "I wish I could help you get into town and everything, but I have to catch a flight. You going to be okay?

You can catch a limo into town right out there. Just show them the address I gave you." He points out to the street through a wall of glass. It's dark and hazy, an odd hue as if a storm approaches.

The conveyor stops and everything is unnaturally quiet. "I'll be fine," I say. "Thank you for everything."

As I approach the glass doors, they open of their own accord, and I realize all the glass is tinted. Through the doorway it's incredibly bright, the sky almost white, heat rippling from the ground. The airports and airplanes have provided a seamless cocoon up to now. Out there is the new world, the future, my new home. I hesitate and find myself rammed from behind by a valise on wheels, a well-dressed man at the helm, and I scurry out of the way into the open air. I can tell by their clattery pitch when they hit the sidewalk that the wheels are made of plastic.

3 ✵ I Make My First Acquaintances

The next day, and the next, we rode and walked about [Richmond], which is delightfully situated on eight hills, overhanging [the] James River; a sparkling stream, studded here and there with bright islands, or brawling over broken rocks. Although it was yet but the middle of March, the weather in this southern temperature was extremely warm; the peach-trees and magnolias were in full bloom; and the trees were green. . . . [But] I . . . went upon my way with a grateful heart that I was not doomed to live where slavery was, and had never had my senses blunted to its wrongs and horrors in a slave-rocked cradle.
—CHARLES DICKENS, *American Notes*

Men are often better than the institutions they belong to.
—PETER KROPOTKIN, *Memoirs of a Revolutionist*

Outside it's even hotter than I imagined. The air is nearly palpable with moisture. I take off my jacket, and squint in the glare. A broad-brimmed straw hat, such as I've seen in sketches of old Virginia life, might yet be a wise purchase. It must be well over eighty degrees Fahrenheit out here. This is the first time I've been out of doors since my new life began. It smells different, distinctly different. I don't know if this is Virginia or the end of the millennium I'm smelling, but suspect it's the latter. It's all these automobiles. They are literally everywhere, seem, indeed, to almost outnumber the people, if such a thing were possible. Their exhaust is what I'm smelling. The autos are long and low, smaller versions of the airplanes that screech by overhead, unremarked by everyone but myself and children.

I approach the glass booth and walkway Chris pointed out to me and discover a busy man working there. He strides up and down the walkway steering travelers into automobiles that line the road. He is portly, and moves with a rolling motion, his arms out from his sides as if to keep himself from tipping over. When he's not walking, he bounces up and down on the balls of his feet. He carries a silver clipboard he refers to occasionally, though more often he uses it to point the way or hurry someone along, slicing the air with it like a metal semaphore. Should a conflict arise with passenger or driver, he clasps it to his chest like a breastplate and wags his head in steady refusal until the conflict withdraws, vanquished.

The drivers largely ignore him until—after some quick official squiggle that could just as easily be made, I imagine, by a pen thrown at the page from across the road—he tears a sheet from the clipboard and hands it to one of them. Even then the driver doesn't really look at him but takes the sheet from his hand (without looking at it, either), and greets his new passengers, welcoming them to the city, loading their luggage into the back of the automobile with what seems to be genuine friendliness. These drivers are mostly black men, most of them with gray or graying hair. They talk, read newspapers or small paperbound books, though they usually don't have long to wait between fares. The busy man is younger and white, and probably makes more money strutting around in his officious way piloting that clipboard than the drivers do actually getting people where they want to go, though I imagine passengers and drivers would muddle along just fine without the services of the busy man with only the slightest application of common sense.

But the busy man apprehends me in the act of loitering, and demands to know, "Where ya headed?"

"I'd like to go here," I say, and show him the address Chris wrote down for me.

"Zone one," he says decisively. "That'll be nineteen fifty."

"Is this a long journey?"

"Twenty minutes, maybe less this time of day."

Almost a dollar a minute. I took note of the prices of things in the publications on the plane, and this seems no trifling sum. A month's subscription to the Internet could be had for that, and although I've no clear notion of what the Internet *is*, it costs as much as the new John Grisham novel, an author much in demand judging from the size of the advertisements trumpeting his latest book. From the prices I saw in my jaunts through two American airports, I would judge that one could eat three or four times on such a sum. I suspect a swindle, but no matter. Spending almost a fifth of my money merely getting into the city does not sound like a prudent plan. "Is there a cheaper means? Can I walk?"

The busy man laughs at the suggestion. "It's miles and miles. There's no bus or train, if that's what you mean." He sneers at the very notion that such conveyances would be allowed anywhere near his airport. "You by yourself?"

"Most decidedly."

"Too bad. Group rate's twenty-three dollars for two, twenty-six for three, eight each for four or more. Maybe you can hook up with somebody. You know Richmond?"

"No. I have never been here before."

He checks the address again. "Down by VCU. Maybe some students, faculty, or something."

"VCU is a university?"

"Yeah. Look, you stand over there, and I'll try to hook you up with somebody." He looks around at my feet. "Hey, where's your luggage?"

"I have none with me."

"Damn airline lose it for you?"

"Yes, something like that."

"Had a guy out here couple weeks ago—they sent his luggage to Richmond, *California!*" He spots a man and a woman on the other end of the platform and bears down on them. "Where you folks headed?"

I take in my surroundings. Everywhere I look are automobiles, every color imaginable. There must be thousands and thousands of them. The publications I read on the airplane were filled with advertisements for automobiles—appeals based shamelessly on vanity, snobbery, power, even sex. Most people pass the limousines by and proceed to this sea of machines. I witness several persons getting into automobiles and driving away, usually one, sometimes two people per vehicle. I can only assume that's what the rest of them are doing as well. It strikes me as a terribly wasteful system, a triumph of what capitalists like to call individualism, a notion that ensures a good deal of excess consumption so that each individual gets the chance to express himself to the extent of his assets and beyond. The air is fusty with this self-expression.

Many, however, come seeking a limousine, and though the busy man occasionally points me out to various travelers, they decline my company and drive away without me. Apparently the prospect of riding with a stranger is less attractive than the monetary savings. Between waves of arriving passengers, my host talks with me. "Name's Buddy Showalter," he says, shaking my hand, bouncing on the balls of his feet.

"Peter Kropotkin," I say.

"You Bosnian?"

"No, Russian."

"You visiting somebody?"

"No, I've come here to live."

"We've gotten lots of Russians in here last few years. Guess everybody has. We get all kinds now. Too damn many Haitians, if you know what I mean."

I don't get a chance to ask him what he means, for three young men approach and divert his attention. "Jeez," Buddy mutters under his breath. "Would you get a load of these guys."

Although I am new to this time and place, I am no stranger to young people who strive for novelty in their appearance. But these three are indeed startling. One is short and heavyset, with a ring in his nose. Atop his shaved head is a tattoo of a spider the size of my hand, its web covering the rest of his skull. He wears

high boots with silver spikes bristling from the toes. Another is
tall and rail thin with hair dyed bright blue and brushed to a cot-
tonlike loft. His eyes are made up after the fashion of an ancient
Egyptian in a shade of blue to match his hair. They are both
dressed in long black coats like villains in a melodrama. The
third one, the obvious leader, is the most ordinary-looking,
dressed in a short brown coat, blue denim pants, and a leather
collar around his neck that looks as if it were made for a mastiff.
From a ring attached to the collar, a broken chain dangles before
him like a necktie. His close-cropped reddish brown hair has the
look of an African's, and his features and skin tone belie the fact
that he is a mulatto. His bright, intelligent eyes are a pale violet.

I stand close by as Buddy negotiates their passage, stowing
their substantial luggage in the back of the limousine. In addition to large canvas knapsacks, they carry several hard cases that
likely contain musical instruments. On one a cartoon has been
painted of a white-haired man with a maniacal grin dressed in
ancient Greek attire. He holds a stem glass aloft in a toast. The
words HEMLOCK COCKTAIL are written across his chest. I smile in
recognition at this playful portrait of Socrates. They are most certainly students.

"Three for Zone 1," Buddy says. "That'll be twenty-six dollars."

The three young men pay their fare, but Buddy neglects to ask
if I may join them. I lean around him, and inquire, "Are you
bound for the vicinity of the university?"

Buddy takes my arm and pulls me aside before they can answer. "Look, Pete, you don't want to ride with these punks," he
says. "Give it a few minutes. Somebody else'll come along."

He has spoken loud enough for the trio to hear him. The mulatto's violet eyes meet mine. "You're welcome to join us punks,"
he says with quiet dignity.

I take out my money, count out eight dollars, and hand them
to Buddy. He shakes his head as he peels off two of the bills and
practically throws them at my Samaritan.

"Suit yourself," he says to me. "You're not in Russia anymore,
you know."

I have no idea what he means, but if I did I'm sure I would be offended. I enter the limousine with the three young men, and we drive away. I see the driver's face in a mirror suspended from the ceiling, and his broad smile is studded with gold fillings.

"I want to thank you for sharing this vehicle with me," I say to my companions. "The fare seems quite high to me."

"It's a fucking ripoff," the fellow with the nose ring says.

I take this to be agreement. "I am Peter Kropotkin," I say.

"Peter Kropotkin the anarchist?" he asks.

Before I can reply, the blue-haired one laughs at his companion. "No, you fucking idiot. That Peter Kropotkin's been dead for a hundred years or so."

"Somewhat less," the mulatto says blandly. "We all took that course, Dave. No reason to sound so superior. You can't even *spell* anarchist."

"Course?" I inquire.

The mulatto turns his intelligent violet eyes on me. "*The History of Anarchy: Godwin to Chomsky.* We're all students at the university. I'm Mike Cole." He extends his hand, and we shake. "We just got back from a gig in Providence. We're a band." He nods toward nose ring: "Brad Speeks." And blue hair: "Dave Aikens." I shake their hands in turn. "What brings you to Richmond?" Mike asks me.

Magic, I am tempted to say. "I am an immigrant from Russia."

"Cool," says Dave.

"You any *relation* to Peter Kropotkin the anarchist?" Brad asks.

I start to say yes, but fear contradicting history. I have only a daughter and don't know what descendants my nephew Nicholas may have had. Best not to claim a lineage one can't recount. "No. I have heard of him. But no."

"You look just like him," Mike says. "Are you familiar with his work?"

"Yes, somewhat."

"Mike's a big anarchist," Dave says. "Thinks we should shitcan all government."

"Not government, the State," Mike replies calmly, and I am impressed he can make that distinction.

"Whatever. What do I know? You're the philosophy major. I bombed that fucking course. Ditameyer didn't like me." Dave turns his attention to me. "So you teaching at VCU or something? You look like the professor type."

"No, I have no employment at present. Do you know of any work?"

"The place I work's looking for dishwashers," Brad says. "They're always looking for dishwashers."

Dave laughs derisively. "Does he look like a dishwasher to you, butt munch?"

"Fuck you," Brad says.

"I am not afraid of manual labor," I say. "And I need a job right away. Could you give me the address?"

Brad borrows a pen and a small pad of paper from Mike and writes down the name and address of a restaurant.

"All work is honorable," Mike says more to himself than to the rest of us, looking out the window at the hot, hazy day. It's difficult to determine his tone, for there's always at least a trace of irony. "Give him our address, too." He turns to me. "Come over for dinner tomorrow at six. It's my turn to cook."

"Why, thank you very much."

Dave laughs. "Don't thank him. You haven't eaten it yet. Hope you like tofu."

The address Chris gave me, a redbrick row house, is on the edge of the university on a corner across the street from a small park. The sign beside the door identifies it as the Refugee and Immigration Assistance Agency. There are other notices posted on the door. One in Spanish is addressed in particular to Guatemalans, Hondurans, and Salvadorans who meet certain criteria, spelled out in the universal language of government regulations. Another, in English, is a call for volunteers to work in the agency and "make a difference." When I voiced some hesitancy at putting myself in the hands of the State, Chris expressed immediate understanding and reassured me that this is not a government agency, but a charitable one. I have decidedly mixed feelings about such organizations.

So-called charity, with its implicit assumptions of high and low, is no remedy to injustice, but its willing accomplice. Charity allows the privileged the opportunity to buy the silence of their consciences for a few coins (with the added bonus of much to-do being made of their philanthropy)—rather than wrestle with why, in a world of plenty, they wallow in pampered luxury through no particular virtue of their own, while most of the world is in rags, starving, and living in shacks. Jesus advised the rich man to sell everything he had and give it to the poor. The numerous charities operating under his name ever since have set a significantly lower standard.

Those who actually labor in charitable organizations, however, almost as poor as those they serve, are usually, in my experience, the best sort—good-hearted, willing to help, and unlikely to turn me in to the authorities, in any event. Perhaps I have broken no laws. Who would have dreamed up a law covering the facts of my case? I have appeared as if out of thin air, where I don't belong, bearing forged documents from a country that has forgotten me. I once spent three years in a French prison for supposedly being an active member of a defunct organization, so I have no trouble believing I could go to jail for the crime of not existing.

But I have to get help somewhere. It occurs to me that I would not be nearly so needy if Anchee had provided me with funds as easily as he gave me documents. I can only wonder why he didn't. Was it a matter of principle or sport? What is he up to anyway? I have chastised myself a thousand times over for not pressing him harder about his intentions, so eager not to die that I forgot to think. But it's pointless to waste my energies on him now. When I have food and lodging, I'll put my mind to other matters.

Across the other street is a handsome cathedral facing the park, its back to the ugly, factorylike university. The cathedral's copper dome is struck by the golden rays of the late-afternoon sun, and its green patina glows like a glowworm. How rich life is. Inexhaustible. And here I am, in a new life, with a lead on a job and the prospect of a hearty plate of tofu tomorrow evening. I should be full of hope instead of trepidation. All I lack for the moment is a place for the night.

I'm lucky to be alive at all, I remind myself, *damn lucky*, and boldly step inside the place whose name I've already forgotten.

A flight of stairs ascends in front of me. A long hallway stretches to the back of the building. Upstairs and down, the place is a bustle of activity, alive with the pleasant rumble of several simultaneous conversations in diverse languages. Directly before me, a brown-skinned family—a man and a woman and their three young children—are engaged in Spanish conversation with an American woman. She is trying to explain some bureaucratic rapids the family must navigate to obtain unspecified aid. Her hands and sentences are full of government forms with alphanumeric names so that she sounds as if she is speaking in code as she delivers each form into the hands of the patriarch who in turn entrusts it to the matriarch. The American woman is patient and kind and genuinely helpful, the sort of person who exudes trustworthiness, and I take an immediate liking to her.

I'm not quite sure what to do with myself. What little room there is to stand by the door is greatly diminished with computers, or parts of computers, piled chockablock along the wall and down the hallway for as far as I can see. My way forward is effectively blocked by the Spanish-speaking family whose business I do not wish to interrupt. From the sound of things, they have enough obstacles placed in their path without having to worry about a crazy Russian coming up the rear. But the business of my entrance—the banging of the door and the blast of hot air from outside—has roused the sleeping boy on his mother's shoulder. He opens his eyes, sees what the devil's blown in, and wails with unbridled alarm. I back away and stumble over the computers, which shift and clatter in the now familiar sound of plastic on plastic, as one heap cascades into another, and the floor is covered in coiled wire and slabs of plastic. One of the things like a typewriter keyboard flies out, lands on end, and sows bouncing letters across the carpet like dragon's teeth.

"Are you all right?" the American woman asks me.

"Yes, I'm fine. I'm terribly sorry." I look down at the sprawl of beige plastic at my feet and feel as if I'm standing in a boneyard.

"Don't worry about those damn things. They were supposed to be out of here weeks ago when we got the *new* ones that don't work. You can kick them once for me while you're at it. I'm almost through here. If you'll wait in there, I'll be right with you. I'm afraid everyone is busy right now."

She points out a waiting room to the left, and I take a seat beside a stuffed bear the size of a two-year-old child. There's a desk here, but no one is manning it. A clock on the wall behind the desk reads 4:45; the hours on the door gave closing time as 4:30. Above the cold hearth is hung a large banner made of pieces of brightly colored felt which says—amidst an array of symbols (a dove, a torch, a bridge)—WELCOME TO RIAA!

What is a Riaa? I wonder, then realize it's an abbreviation for *Refugee Immigration Something Something.*

There are magazines on a low, round table, but they're all filled with photographs and gossip of people who mean nothing to me. *People* one is called, which I hope will be about *The* People, the great mass of humanity, but it concerns itself only with rich people. Rich people in skimpy "swim wear." Rich people getting in and out of automobiles. Rich people in milling herds of rich people. I toss it back in the pile.

There are yet more computers piled along the walls. I wonder what is wrong with them. They don't appear to be broken. In the corner behind the door, a clearing has been made to park a bicycle, quite different from the one I rode in England with its enormous wheel in the front and tiny one in the rear. This one splits the difference with two of equal size. I study its wonderfully complex but elegant system of gears. One could ride a bicycle like that up the side of a building, I imagine.

The American woman doesn't keep me waiting long. When the Spanish-speaking family leaves, she locks the door behind them and beckons me up the stairs with a friendly swing of her arm and an open smile, and I realize she's the first person I've met in my new life who doesn't seem to be in a great hurry. A stream of her coworkers pass us on their way down the stairs, wishing her a good evening, confirming that the office is closed for the day. Her name is Rachel, I discover. She leads me into a small office with three desks and a half dozen chairs jammed into it. "I'm Rachel Pederson," she says as we sit down. "How may I help you?"

Her desk reminds me of mine, stacks of books and papers slowly shifting into a single mound, overflowing chairs that get too close. A framed photo stands in this moraine, Rachel with two men who are unmistakably her brothers.

"My name is Peter Kropotkin," I say. "I am pleased to meet you. I have only just arrived in America from Russia, and I am looking for a place to live. Perhaps you could help me secure some lodging for a day or so until I can get on my feet? I was told that you help immigrants here."

"You're not claiming refugee status?"

"No."

She makes a regretful face so I'll know where I stand up front. "Our primary mission is helping refugees. We provide advice as well as language and citizenship classes for immigrants, but no housing assistance, I'm afraid. Who was it who referred you to us, Mr. Kropotkin?"

"Chris. Let's see." I take out my collection of paper, and fish out the slip Chris gave me with his name, address and telephone, and the agency's address. "Chris *Billings*. He was the—what do you call them?—*flight attendant* on the airplane, the second airplane. He said his neighbor works here." I look at the paper again, and there's his neighbor's name, *Rachel Pederson*. "You're his neighbor," I say stupidly. "I'm sorry to be so addle-pated. I've had quite the day. Just this morning . . ."—*I was dying. I was a sick old man, and I was dying*—"I . . . was in Dmitrov."

I feel a giggle building up inside me and tell myself to shut up, to quit babbling, to calm down. I smile desperately at her. She is a very attractive woman with dark, short hair, and large, intelligent eyes, and she makes me uncharacteristically nervous. There's a self-possession about her I find most admirable. My friend Emma Goldman used to speak of a "woman of the future," and here she is before me. I blush to realize I'm strongly attracted to her. I'm not only alive again, I'm young again. I hadn't exactly *forgotten* what that experience entails, but memories of desire were all I had, and memories, in the case of desire, don't do it justice.

She gives me a cautious smile. I suspect she's not entirely pleased that Chris is sending strangers to her doorstep. "I'm sorry," she says. "I was a little thrown. I wasn't expecting a referral from my neighbor. How did that come about?" She laughs. "I wouldn't have thought he would remember what I did."

"I think he was particularly keen to help me for Alicia's sake—the flight attendant on the first airplane. They went to school together, he said. I believe she was quite a good friend to him at one time."

"And she is a friend or relative?" She is trying to puzzle me out. I only wish I could tell her the truth.

"No. We met on the airplane. I had a nightmare. She was kind enough to sit and talk with me a while." I smile trying to lighten things up a bit. "She gave me some excellent vodka as well."

"You seem to have quite a way with flight attendants, Mr. Kropotkin."

"And they were my very first ones, too," I joke, and she rewards me with a smile.

"You seem to have some documents there?" she prompts, pointing at the official-looking papers Anchee gave me.

I hand them over, glad to be relieved of them. Maybe she'll understand them better than I. Anchee's explanations, I'm afraid, went in one ear and out the other.

She scans them expertly. I imagine they are like most government documents—the important information is concealed in a thicket of rubbish, enough to fill the paper to the margins in a font too small for the naked eye. "You're a lottery recipient," she says. "You must have a green card."

Now I recall that Anchee explained that in the future a certain percentage of immigrants to America are selected by lottery. An odd system it seems to me. Nonetheless, his forgeries attempt to pass me off as one of the winners. But apparently he has neglected some important detail in the ruse. I haven't laid eyes on a green card. I shake my head and try to keep my voice steady. "I have no green card."

"That's odd. You should have gotten it from the American Embassy. It's about this big and has your picture on it?" She holds her fingers in a rectangle. Her hands are small, her fingers . . .

"Oh *that*! The one that says RESIDENT ALIEN?" I unearth it and my passport from inside my pocket and hold them up.

"Yes. It's called a green card."

"But it isn't green."

She laughs as she takes my card and passport and examines them. "It used to be," she explains. "In the seventies. Now it will always be the green card. There's a toll bridge here in town still called the Nickel Bridge even though the toll's five times that now." As she talks in this friendly way, she copies down my name and the multidigit numbers from my passport and green card on a yellow pad in front of her. She looks back and forth from the passport to the green card, smiles upon them, and hands them back to me. "You take a nice photograph, Mr. Kropotkin."

"Thank you," I say enthusiastically as I fumble to stow the counterfeit images away, neglecting to mention I never sat for either flattering portrait, that they're another fiction of Anchee's devising.

"And what made you decide on Richmond as a destination?" she asks. "Do you have friends or relatives here?"

I shake my head.

"Then do you have employment here?"

"No, not yet. But I have a lead on something. A young man in the limousine knew of an opening where he works." I hold up my last slip of paper, Brad's swirling letters snaking across its surface, to demonstrate I have the matter well in hand.

Clouds of concern are forming on her brow. "In the limousine. So you had no prospects before you arrived? I don't mean to pry, but I'm a little puzzled why you've come to Richmond, Mr. Kropotkin. Did you just choose it at random?"

"I . . . I . . . read about it."

She's perfectly willing to believe this lie. "Oh really? Where?"

I am seized with panic. I can make something up, I suppose, but then I have to keep lying about it. I desperately dash about my memory searching for anything I've ever read about Richmond. Anything good, that is. I reach it like one breathless at the finish line. "Dickens!" I announce. "*American Notes* by Charles Dickens. I read about Richmond there. Do you know it perhaps?" *Surely not*, I'm thinking, *must be a hundred and fifty years old.*

Her eyes widen and contract, and my heart sinks. "Oddly enough, I *do* know it. I was a history major. As I remember, Dickens hated the place when he visited. He deplored slavery." She is eyeing me suspiciously, as if I might have taken leave of my senses. "You actually came to Richmond because of what Dickens said about it?"

"He spoke most admiringly of the James River, as I recall, that it was an exceptionally lovely river. I like rivers," I offer lamely.

She stares at me a moment. "Me too," she says, then looks at the yellow pad again, more, I imagine, to avoid looking at such an odd duck than to read anything there. "I'm afraid I can't be of much help, Mr. Kropotkin. As I said, as far as housing assistance goes, we mainly serve refugees. Immigrants are usually, well . . ."

"Better prepared?"

"Yes."

I should just thank her and leave, but I find that I want terribly for this woman to understand me, or at least not to think me an idiot, and I have to speak up for myself. "When I said 'I like rivers' I meant that I'm a geographer. I can rattle on about watersheds with the same enthusiasm my father reserved for racehorses. Living on the banks of a river, for me, is like a painter living in a city with first-rate museums. Do you understand? I know no one. Not here, not anywhere. I have no reason to come here, but here I am. I know of no other place to go."

"I'm sorry, Mr. Kropotkin," she says quietly.

"No, don't misunderstand me. I am not complaining. I like meeting new people. Like you, today." I smile, and she smiles back.

"It's a beautiful river with acres of public access. It won't disappoint you." She seems genuinely concerned that I not be disappointed. She likes me, I think, or wants to at least, if I don't prove to be a complete lunatic.

"I'm sure it won't," I say. "Could you, perhaps, recommend an inexpensive hotel?"

"You don't have a car, right?"

"Right."

"There are places on the other side of the park where you might be able to get a room for, oh, fifty dollars?"

"That's too much, I'm afraid."

She nods with a slight sympathetic wince. "There is a shelter close by, but . . ."

A beeping sound starts up, and she says, "Let me get this. I'm expecting a call." She answers what must be a modern telephone. "Rachel Pederson. How may I help you?"

Her end of the conversation consists mostly of affirmative noises. Then veers to, "I understand that, Mrs. Charles, but . . ." She closes her eyes and massages her forehead with thumb and forefinger. "But the class is already enrolled with a dozen students. . . ." Her hand contracts into a fist as she continues to listen, her jaws clench. "I assure you it's perfectly safe down here, Mrs. Charles. There's a lighted parking garage. The class meets

in the university library. The security is . . ." I recall the bottles of
vodka in my pocket and imagine offering her one, massaging
her temples for her. "I understand. Yes. Yes. Not at all. Thank
you, Mrs. Charles. Good-bye." She hangs up the telephone. It,
too, is plastic. Her eyes are still closed. "Shit," she whispers, a
tiny puff of air. She raps on her forehead three times as if it were
a door and opens her eyes.

"Bad news?"

"Oh, one of our volunteer ESL teachers has canceled on us at
the last minute. I thought she might. Wouldn't want to teach an
ESL class would you?"

"ESL?"

"English as a second language."

"Ah! I *would* be glad to teach such a class, as a matter of fact.
It sounds delightful. Just the thing."

"I was only joking, Mr. Kropotkin. Your English is very good
indeed. But this is a volunteer position. It doesn't pay anything."

"I realize that. But I would enjoy it nonetheless. I speak and
write English, German, French, Russian, Spanish—*pero mi es-
pañol es muy malo*. I speak Italian, Dutch, Norwegian, Finnish,
Mongol, Manchu, and get by in a few others. I'm sure I could be
helpful. I've taught languages before." I don't tell her yet that I
taught them in jail to my fellow prisoners in exchange for tute-
lage in their languages. She might get the wrong idea.

She seems a bit overwhelmed by my enthusiasm. "I'm delighted you want to help. But you don't even have a place to live
yet, Mr. Kropotkin."

"I'm sure that will sort itself out. It always does. When does
this class meet?"

"Sunday afternoon, three o'clock."

"And today is?"

"Thursday."

"Sunday sounds splendid."

"But I couldn't possibly agree to let you teach a class . . . under
these circumstances."

I bristle at the cowardly phrase. "Circumstances? You mean

because I'm poor and have no place to live? I've been poorer, believe me, and lived worse places than no place. The sign on the door asks for volunteers. I am volunteering. These people coming to this city without the language—do you think they care about my 'circumstances'? Mrs. What's-her-name—*Charles*. Her circumstances are none too shabby I'll wager. Why don't you give *her* a ring?"

Miss Pederson is taken aback by my outburst, but she doesn't show me the door. In fact, I seem to have elevated her opinion of me. "I'm sorry," she says. "That was terribly rude and insensitive of me. Forgive me?"

She's quite serious it seems. "Of course, certainly."

"Good." She takes a form out of her desk and hands it to me. "We do need to have some information from you, however. Fill in what applies and bring it in tomorrow, okay?"

"Certainly."

"Mr. Kropotkin, are you sure . . ."

"Yes?" My returning gaze leaves no question whatsoever of my absolute surety.

"Nothing. Would you like the address of the shelter?"

"No, I don't think that will be necessary. I'm young and fit, and the weather's fine. Can you tell me somewhere in the vicinity I might purchase supplies—a blanket and such? Someplace inexpensive."

She starts to say something, but doesn't. "There's a thrift store west on Main Street at the corner of Meadow," she tells me.

"That way?" I point in the direction I believe to be west.

"Yes."

"And which way is the river?"

She nods, expecting this. "South. If you go south on Meadow you'll see signs directing you to James River Park."

"Thank you very much." I rise to my feet and offer my hand.

She shakes it, all business at first, but she can't help herself, and her face pinches with concern. "Mr. Kropotkin, I feel I should tell you there's no camping allowed in the park. You could get in trouble with the law."

"And would there be many policemen hiding in the bushes enforcing this ordinance?"

She laughs. "Not so very many."

"I'll keep a cautious eye out. West you say, then south?"

She's still smiling. "Would you like a map, Mr. Kropotkin? We have them in the orientation packages for the refugees. Someone donated a case of them. I don't see why I can't give you one."

"If it wouldn't be too much trouble."

"None at all. They're downstairs in the waiting room. My bike's down there anyway."

"That's your bicycle?"

"Yes," she says.

"What a marvelous machine!" I exclaim.

"I'm glad you like it," she says, laughing, and I suppose my enthusiasm seems excessive, but why should I contain it when I am rewarded with such laughter?

I follow her downstairs into the waiting room. She goes around behind the desk, kicking the scrapped computers out of the way with what I take to be relish. I wonder what there is about these machines that invites such ill will. I suppose I'll have the chance to learn firsthand. She finds a large envelope, takes out a map, and spreads it out on the desk. "We're here." she says, and points. "The thrift store is here. The North Bank Access parking lot is here."

I turn the map to get a better look. All the streets are listed at the bottom with a letter and a number keyed to the grid, and I locate her address. "And you're here," I say, giving her a big smile, thinking she'll be pleased, but she's definitely not. All of a sudden, I am acutely aware—as, no doubt, is she—that we are alone in the building together.

She folds up the map and hands it to me as one might deliver an eviction notice. "Good night, Mr. Kropotkin. Good luck."

In no time at all she has ushered me out the door, and I hear the clunk of a lock behind me. I seem to have frightened her or committed a horrible breach of decorum by the mere fact of knowing her address. Am I as odd as all that? I recall the air-

plane full of people, their ears plugged, their eyes straight ahead
pummeled by flashing images—all, it seems to me, so they could
avoid each other until they reached the anonymity of their personal automobiles. Perhaps I'm too sociable for the times. I could
find this a lonely world indeed.

As I descend the steps, I admire the cathedral awash in a
golden glow. The street is filled with sleek, quick automobiles,
glittering, brightly colored, as if the contents of a kaleidoscope
had been shaken out of the sky. But along the walkways, throngs
of university students make their way to evening classes with
the familiar loping gate of youth. Smiling to myself, I plunge
into the thick of them, walking briskly into the setting sun.

Alive again.

I proceed at a lively pace, and years stretch before me. My old
life, mostly gone before I left it, now lies unreachable across a
gulf of time—everyone and everything I've ever known, utterly
unreachable, immutable. But every hope, I find, remains alive.
Every mistake calls out to be rectified. Every resolve is strength-
ened. Here I am, old enough to take not a second for granted,
young enough in body and soul to accomplish anything I set my
mind to. I can't imagine a happier state of affairs, like a lucky
prince in a fairy tale. I smile at the irony—I suppose I shall have
to renounce my title all over again!

And then there is the lovely and amiable Rachel Pederson,
whom I shall see tomorrow with as properly a filled-out form as
I can manage, and perhaps a bath, and a change of clothes as
well. I fancy her more, I daresay, than anyone I have met since
Sophie many, many years ago.

Just as I am thinking of her, out of the corner of my eye, I see
her; and I turn to watch her sweep past on her bicycle, sleek and
strong and beautiful; and I recall the goldfinch in the Moscow
Airport, desperate to reach the sky. In my mind, steel and
glass—and plastic too, no doubt—are swept away, and she and
I are flying.

4 ॐ I Secure Lodgings and a Fishing Pole

My extensive journeys . . . taught me how little man really
needs as soon as he comes out of the enchanted circle of conventional civilization. With a few pounds of bread and a few
ounces of tea in a leather bag, a kettle and a hatchet hanging at
the side of the saddle, and under the saddle a blanket, to be
spread at the camp-fire upon a bed of freshly cut spruce twigs,
a man feels wonderfully independent, even amidst unknown
mountains thickly clothed with woods, or capped with snow.
　　　　　　—PETER KROPOTKIN, *Memoirs of a Revolutionist*

Every injustice committed against one individual is, in the end,
experienced by humanity as a whole.
　　　　　　—PETER KROPOTKIN, "Prisons and Their Moral
Influence on Prisoners"

The thrift store proves to be where the "all kinds"
Buddy Showalter spoke of shop, and I don't feel quite the oddity. There is as much variety in the clientele as in the merchan-
dise for sale. I catch phrases of three or four languages, and the
racial diversity is like nothing I've ever seen before in an inland
city—though the majority here appear to be of African descent.
Everyone is friendly as we navigate the crowded, cluttered
aisles, and I feel as if I'm at some exotic crossroads where conti-
nents meet. It's been years since I could make it into town under
my own power, much less travel to a distant land and wander
through the marketplace, and I wish to relish the experience. Unfortunately, I had best get settled by dark—no more than an hour

away—and I don't have time to linger. But as I hunt for supplies I manage to make the acquaintance of several people—a black woman, herself outfitting a new kitchen, who points out a lightweight pot that will best serve my purposes; two Cambodian youths looking through a bin of plastic contraptions they tell me are games one plays on a television, though none of the ones in the bin are worthy of purchase by discriminating buyers such as themselves; a middle-aged couple from Bosnia looking for lightweight clothing for their sons that complies with the dress code at their school; and an old man from Guatemala who looks exactly like a Mayan deity I have seen in drawings, and I tell him so—which pleases him no end.

All together, I purchase a knapsack, a wool blanket, a change of clothes, a pot, a cup, a plate, a fork, a spoon, and a pocketknife with an amazing diversity of blades. The whole business costs me just over twenty dollars. I would buy more clothes, but until I actually have a job in hand, it's best to keep some cash on hand. Money is an evil system, but when it is the only system, one ignores it at his peril. The clerk, a kindly Chinese woman who indulges my dreadful Manchu, directs me to a small grocery nearby where I purchase bread, coffee, and canned meat sufficient for a few days . . . *travel* I start to say . . . and after some consideration, decide the term is apt. I have traveled in time, place, and culture. What does it matter if I now stay put? I'm traveling just the same. As a last-minute indulgence, I add what I consider an American delicacy, a jar of peanut butter and a box of crackers.

The grocer, a Pakistani, explains the difference between instant and regular coffee to me after breaking the news that, alas, there is no good, black tea. He recommends the instant coffee because you can make it as strong as you like one cup at a time, and I adopt his suggestion. "Soap?" he inquires. Certainly, I say, and buy a bar of Irish Spring. He gives me handfuls of book matches for free. I request candles, but he suggests an electric torch instead, since it won't blow out in the wind, and sells me one quite as bright as any candle for ninety-nine-cents-batteries-included. It takes us some time to straighten out this mysterious price because he says it as if it were all one word. "But what is the price?" I keep asking. We both ache with laughter by the time the deal is concluded, and I'm shining the tiny torch about his shop, bouncing beams off a parabolic mirror he has mounted on the wall to catch thieves. We have no languages other than English in common, but he teaches me hello and good-bye in Pakistani and "flashlight" and "batteries-included" in American.

After a grim stretch on either side of a bridge spanning a canyon-like road where automobiles whiz by like enormous bullets, Meadow passes through a handsome neighborhood of modest clapboard cottages, with gardens blooming all around. I've never been in a city more in love with spring than this one, and it makes my heart glad. Most of the residents here are of African descent, taking advantage of the waning light to tend to their gardens or relax on their front porches. I greet them as I pass, and they return my greetings with enthusiasm.

The entrance to the park is at the end of Texas Avenue, and I stop here to consult my map, which includes some helpful information on local sights. I'm just west of Hollywood Cemetery—where Varina Davis's late husband and other dignitaries are buried. Across from it lies Belle Isle, a large bean-shaped island in the middle of the river. I struggle to recall why Belle Isle is familiar, then it comes to me. Prisons, unfortunately, are a subject to which I've devoted some years of study. Belle Isle was a particularly gruesome prison camp during the American Civil War. Thousands of Union soldiers died there from the horrible conditions. I see from the map, that it, too, is now parkland accessible by footbridge. I wonder if any of these public lands are set aside for cultivation, but don't find such a designation on the map's legend.

The trail descends rough stairs fashioned from railroad ties to

an iron bridge spanning at treetop height an abandoned canal
and a pair of railroad tracks. It then descends a concrete-and-
steel staircase. A few enigmatic words and symbols are painted
on the walls of the echoing shaft, but I don't pause to interpret
them. At the bottom I emerge into the comforting gloom of the
forest and the sandy soil of the floodplain. Some time ago, perhaps transplanted from a fine estate upstream, English ivy took
root here, carpeted the forest floor, and wrapped the tree trunks
in dark green shawls. It gives the wood a quaint feel to be done
up so fine amid the general chaos of a muddy, debris-strewn
floodplain, rather like those dowagers of "reduced circumstances" who populate the novels of Jane Austen.

A fence of heavy iron mesh separates me from the railroad
tracks. I'm pleased to see that someone has cut the wire and
folded it back. But I don't go that way today. I want to go where
most of the trails lead—to the river. I wind through the dark
woods to the banks of the James, and it's just as wonderful as
Dickens described it. Even now, though I can see upstream and
down for a couple of miles, there is little evidence I am in the
heart of a city. An osprey dives for fish. A heron wades in the
shallows. Dozens of geese dot the water. Sinking into the river
upstream is the last of a fiery sun. Only downstream are there a
few boxlike buildings peeking over the top of Belle Isle, intrud-
ing upon the illusion of wildness.

Would you like the address of the shelter?

No, I don't think that will be necessary.

I head downstream until the trail gives out, then make my
way to a small island by hopping rock to rock and wading across
a shallow channel, my shoes hanging from my neck and my
pants rolled up to my knees. A beaver already has a fine residence here, but I don't imagine he'll mind the company if I don't
burn up all the tasty saplings. There is a nestlike depression between snagged logs where I take up residence. I build a tiny fire,
dining on a meal of bread and sardines and weak coffee. As
night falls, I settle in to watch the stars coming out on a moon-
less night, one of the great pleasures in life. At first I despair that

the lights of the city will blind me to the heavens, but eventually I'm rewarded with the sighting of Arcturus, and the Big Dipper tilting on its handle. The stars, at least, have not visibly altered. I take out one of my tiny bottles and drink off a toast to the familiar stars.

As I look up at the vast sky, something in the way it makes me feel brings to mind the time I stumbled upon my mother's things in a storeroom of our country home. They'd been there, I suppose, undisturbed since her death years before. I had the vague sense that I was doing something wrong and locked the door behind me so that I might not be discovered as I mined its secrets. At that time in my life I was near obsessed with learning who my mother was—what she cared about, what she believed in, and, most of all, what she would have thought of me had she lived to see me almost a grown man, or so I thought at the time. And here were her books and her paintings, signed in her tiny hand—romantic watercolors of lakes and mountains and mown fields and rivers. Here were ribbons she wore in her hair, gowns she danced in.

By candlelight, I read her diaries, poring over those sections where she spoke of her sorrows and her thirst for happiness with heartbreaking intensity. She'd copied poems dear to her. I was particularly affected by the Byron, transcribed from some book of English verses. I had not yet loved, much less imagined its passing, but my mother had, and copied these lines in her firm but pretty handwriting:

So, we'll go no more a roving
So late into the night,
Though the heart be still as loving,
And the moon be still as bright.

For the sword outwears its sheath,
And the soul wears out the breast,
And the heart must pause to breathe,
And love itself have rest.

Though the night was made for loving,
And the day returns too soon,
Yet we'll go no more a roving
By the light of the moon.

I cried my eyes out when I read that, vividly imagining my
mother's unhappiness—even while I was incapable of understanding the heartaches of a woman I'd never known. My
mother was said to be a passionate woman with an artist's temperament. She used to take great pleasure in watching the peasants dance and would often join them as the night wore on,
much to my father's disapproval. It was during such a bout of
dancing that she caught the chill that killed her.

Or so the story goes. It used to haunt me—that story, the
poems, all of it. And there was no escaping it, no putting it to
rest. She was like a heroine in a tragic opera—larger than life, un-
bearably sad, too passionate for this world. Doomed. That was
the opinion of sympathetic and unsympathetic recounters of the
tale alike: Doomed! I and my brother Sasha were the only other
characters in this drama as far as we could tell, the Motherless
Children. Our older siblings were largely invisible to us. It was
impossible for me to believe that my father had ever been the object of her passion, and once he remarried, he scrupulously ignored her memory in any event. Sasha used to tell me his
memories of her over and over again at my prompting, for he
was older and had a larger store of them than I. After my brother
shot himself, I was the sole survivor. The moral of the tale always seemed clear: An excess of passion is so exquisite, it can
kill you. Perhaps in this life I can finally bring down the curtain
on that grim little drama.

Not surprisingly, passion came late to my own life. It was
there all right, there all along, frightening the daylights out of
me. It had, after all, broken my mother's heart and brought her
low, made of her a woman doomed by nature instead of someone who died of consumption—a disease, not an edict from the
gods. Before I met Sophie, it was as if I'd never let myself out of

that locked storeroom, lamenting a lost love I never had. Sophie dragged me out into the sunlight. I was thirty-six; she was twenty-two. We had a "rational marriage," we called it, a contract up for renewal every three years. It seems laughable now to think we would have ever considered parting from one another. I'd gladly sign on for three more centuries.

We used to watch the stars together, she and I, and I tell myself there's no harm imagining her here beside me. In recent times I've often done as much as I waited for death to come, remembering our life together.

Are you quite warm enough, Peter? she asks.

"Yes, my love," I say, tucking my blanket around the both of us, imagining her head cradled in the hollow of my shoulder.

As a young man, I dreamed of becoming an astronomer. It was my scientific first love. I plunged into astronomical reading, especially during the last year of my stay at school. The never-ceasing life of the universe, which I conceived as *life* and evolution, became for me an inexhaustible source of higher poetical thought, and gradually the sense of Man's oneness with Nature, both animate and inanimate—the Poetry of Nature—became the philosophy of my life. I later abandoned astronomy for the more down-to-earth sciences of geography and biology—for revolution is very much a down-to-earth affair (or better be, if it hopes to succeed). But someday, comes the revolution—I used to tell Sophie—when the world has come to its senses and given itself the peace, freedom, and justice it *claims* to want so badly, I'd like to take a good, long look at the stars.

Look, Sophie whispers, and a meteor streaks across the sky east to west, shattering my illusion. *This is not a dream,* I realize, and for a brief moment I am filled with terror. I clamp my eyes shut, and soon I have fallen into a deep sleep.

I wake to the sound of geese overhead calling to one another, and open my eyes. The sky is overcast; the sun lies just below the

horizon at my feet. I sit up and scrub my face with the dew from
my beard, stand and give my clothes a shake to wake whatever
boarders I may have taken in overnight. There's a bit of a chill in
the air now, but it's going to be another hot, humid one, I'm
guessing, and this is only April. What must the summers be like
here?

The kindling I set aside last night is damp, but I manage to get
a fire going with the cardboard from the flashlight package and
the receipt from the thrift store. I'll have to remember to keep
some kindling dry inside the plastic bag I obtained from the grocer.

("Plastic?" I asked the grocer, pointing at the bag, merely to
verify another manifestation of this versatile substance.

"I am so sorry," the grocer replied. "I have no paper."

I had no idea what he meant, but we'd only just managed
batteries-included, and other customers were waiting.)

Once the water's boiled, I sit down with my back propped
comfortably against a mossy log and have my breakfast. The
grocer was certainly right about the instant coffee. I find that
three spoonfuls in a cup of hot water is absolutely delicious. The
bread is soft and lifeless—the crust breaks without a sound—but
it is filling, and I spend a good while reading the package (another plastic bag) for it is covered with text and symbols. The
bread itself was baked in Georgia, and here it is in Virginia, unnaturally moist. There's a short but enthusiastic treatise on nutrition illustrated by The Food Guide Pyramid. "Visit our web
site for more information," it concludes. Below that is a numeri-
cal code under a rectangle of parallel lines of various widths. I've
noticed similar markings on the flashlight package, the coffee,
and the sardines. But nothing matches the bread for sheer volu-
bility. From a complete nutritional analysis followed by a dizzying list of ingredients to a "limited warranty" promised by
something called *Good Housekeeping*—there is no end to its mysteries. What sort of entity might call itself *Good Housekeeping*? Is
it some sort of National Nanny? I can't figure it out. I find a tri-
angle formed by three bent arrows, the number 4 inside, the let-

ters LDPE under the base. I give up. Even a package of bread is beyond me. How will I ever manage to get by here, now?

I have another cup of coffee and another piece of bread, setting aside my bread-wrapper studies for the moment, taking in the life and beauty of the rolling river. *I can do this*, I tell myself, not quite knowing what I mean, but what sort of anarchist would I be if I always had to know what lay in store? If you want certainty, try prison. There's certainty for you, dead certain.

I rinse and stow my cup, strip, and wade slowly out into the river with only my bar of soap. The water feels a good deal colder than it did last night. But I have bathed in colder, have even developed something of a technique. When I'm calf deep, I scoop up handfuls of water and splash my face and body mercilessly; when the water's to my knees, I set to lathering like a madman, wading on in jerks and starts into deeper and deeper water; and when the water's thigh deep, and I look, I suppose, like a crazed redheaded snowman, I fling myself backwards into the current, its chill embrace immediately propelling me out of the water with a roar and a shake as if I've been shot from a cannon. Any further traces of drowsiness and ill temper are jolted out of me, and I stride ashore sputtering, letting the wind dry me for all of a minute before putting on my new clothes, new to me at least—tan trousers and a collarless white shirt—and they feel fine. A great blue heron, croaking like a disgruntled anarchist first thing in the morning, flaps by no more than a dozen yards away.

I can't imagine a finer place to be.

But as I transfer my things from yesterday's pockets to today's, there's another enigma I must ponder, one a good deal more mysterious than a loaf of lifeless bread. I make myself comfortable and take out the only possession Anchee granted me in this life besides the clothes on my back and my forged documentation—the watch he placed in my pocket.

It's running, the second hand marching round the dial a tick at a time like a good soldier walking the walls. The right time by the look of it, seven o'clock. I've put off confronting this watch—

too scared on the airplane, too bone-weary and light-headed by the time I reached town—for a good reason: It isn't just any watch; it's the watch that saved my life, or one that looks just like it.

In 1876, I was in a prison hospital in St. Petersburg, not likely to survive my sentence. An elaborate escape plan had fallen apart, and a new plan had to be communicated to me immediately by my accomplices. The new plan—a successful one or I would not be alive today—came written in code on a small piece of paper hidden inside this watch, or its twin. I am drawn up short, for I have just misspoken: Watch or no, I would not be alive *today* if it were not for a series of miracles beyond my control. No. This watch saved me once, but what is it doing here *now*? Why, out of all my possessions, was I bequeathed this lone artifact?

It had no practical utility in my former life. I hung on to it for years as a reminder of the time I spent in prison and of the terrible risks taken by others to set me free. It was a symbol, a touchstone I kept in a dresser drawer to give me courage when I needed it. But I hadn't carried it or even wound it to my recollection. And here it is in this life, polished by the look of it—made new again like me. The paper, originally inside of it, I read and ate in 1876.

I open up the back, and I have to laugh out loud, for there *is* something there all right—not a piece of paper, but a tiny square of *plastic*. I hold it up to the light. It's transparent, marked with the tiniest writing imaginable. I can't possibly read it without a magnifying lens. Perhaps I can borrow one at a library or a jeweler's. But it's hard to mount much enthusiasm for such an expedition. I'm not sure I want to know what it says. I'm not sure I want it to exist at all. I wanted life. I wanted freedom. This watch and its contents that demand I solve their mysteries make me feel, in spite of Anchee's denials, like a subject in an experiment.

No mere souvenir, this watch demands that I fathom its *meaning*. On the face of it, by conveying this watch to me, Anchee is implying by analogy that he regards my so-called new life as a prison, an image that in itself doesn't bother me—death's a wall as good as any other—but that he's tossing *messages* over that wall fills me with foreboding. Little bits of plastic or stone tablets—it's all the same to me—I want no correspondence with the gods. In my former life, I lived free of the superstition that a deity runs the world like some good-intentioned landlord who'll fix the pipes if you petition him in the right tone of voice or cross his palm with money or favors. The opera that is my new life, however, is apparently not without a script, an author, a director—a god, in short. And gods are notorious enemies of freedom. I have half a mind to see how far I can throw this watch and its plastic cargo upstream before it hits the water. But my curiosity has the better of me, and I have to have a look at it.

A more thorough examination reveals it's not the watch of former days, despite the resemblance. It makes not a sound, and, no matter how hard I try, I can't remove the crystal. There doesn't actually seem to *be* a seam where metal meets glass—if it is glass, since it won't take a scratch from any rock on this island. Neither will the metal. Maybe it's all another exotic form of plastic. The stem is a mere working ornament, for while it turns and pops in and out just as a watch stem should do, I can neither wind nor set the damn thing with these operations; still, I suspect it keeps perfect time, and will continue to do so, without any meddling from me, whether I toss it in the river or bludgeon it with a rock. I stow the square of plastic in its compartment, put the watch back in my pocket, and try to put it out of my mind. For now, all it's good for is telling the time, and the sun's quite adequate for my present needs. I'm not so foolish to think I've heard the end of this damn watch or the fellow who slipped it into my pocket, but unless I pawn it, there's little it can do to address my immediate concerns. First no money, and now this watch. My host from the future is beginning to try my patience.

I stand up and let out a startled cry, for directly across the channel from me on a large boulder no more than five yards away sits a man cross-legged, as still as a statue. And still he remains, in spite of my shout, and so I study him. He is gaunt and sinewy, with an untrimmed beard too erratic to have been grown by choice, streaked with gray, but as sparse as a young man's. He wears a dark wool business suit—sizes too large and out at the knees and elbows. He is not, I gather, the original owner of this suit, a giant apparently. The sleeves and pant legs have been unceremoniously trimmed (with a knife by the look of them) to accommodate my neighbor's shorter limbs, though he himself is as leggy as a spider. Beneath his coat several garments compete for attention. A ragged yellow collar spills out of a faded black knit, itself torn open above the heart to reveal a red woolen oval the size of a fist. A plaid scarf, mostly pink with some gray, is tied around his waist. There's a green cap on his head—COUNTRY CLUB OF VIRGINIA, it says—and rubber boots on his feet. He holds a long bamboo pole planted beside his knee like a triton. It is tied with line—plastic, it seems—and a hook. I was apparently so immersed in my investigations, I took no notice of his approach.

He stirs, pointing at the pocket where I put the watch. "Nice watch," he says.

"Thanks," I say. "Beautiful morning, don't you think? My name is Peter Kropotkin."

"No names."

"Too late," I say regretfully. "You already have mine. Don't worry. It's on the house. I have a patronym—a middle name, if you like, though Peter will do just fine. Or what is it you Americans say? Pete."

"*You Americans.*" He mimics my accent. "Where are you from?"

"Russia."

He laughs. "Russia!" He laughs again. He talks to himself, facing one way and then the other, using his accent, then mine: "*Where are you from? Russia!*"

"Where are you from?" I ask.

He quits laughing and eyes me carefully. He points downstream toward Belle Isle, still a hulking shadow on the water, blocking out the sun. "Over there," he says quietly. When he turns back to me, his face changes like an actor putting on a part. Only I don't know which part, if either, is real. "You want to buy a fishing pole?" he asks.

"What do you want for it?"

"How about that watch?"

"The watch isn't for sale. Besides, why should I buy a pole? I can salvage the tackle same as you—it must be everywhere in all these trees—and I can cut my own pole."

"Not a pole like this one, you can't. You won't find bamboo like this anywhere around here. This bamboo's imported, harvested special, at least three or four miles from here, and none too easy to find either. But suit yourself. There's cat big as your arm in this river, you know. Bass. Crappie. Course, maybe you don't like fish. Maybe you never run out of rations. Maybe you never been hungry."

"What about the winters hereabouts?" I ask, ignoring his pitch if not his theme. "What are they like?"

He looks up and down the river, squinting. He's not having any of my neighborly overtures. "The winters are bad enough. You want to buy a pole or not?"

"All right. How about some spirits for it? Some good Russian vodka."

"How much?"

"Two full bottles."

"Damn! Two bottles? You got yourself a deal."

I take the bottles out of my shirt pocket, and my scruffy entrepreneur shrieks with laughter. "*Those* are the bottles?" He almost pitches over into the river. "What are they? *Russian* bottles?"

I roll up my pant legs, wade across, and exchange the tiny bottles for my new fishing pole. My neighbor conducts the business with good humor, holding up the bottles to the light, reading the label aloud. The bamboo does indeed have a nice spring. As I'm bouncing it over the water, getting the feel of it, an enormous catfish glides by. "I have to go into the city today. Do you think my things will be all right on this island?"

"You mean, will I *steal* anything?"

"I should think with the bargain I just struck, it would be you worrying about me. No, it wasn't you I had in mind. Any police about?"

"Not usually. Police after you?"

"Not that I know of. You?"

He laughs, looks over his shoulder. "Maybe they are. Maybe they aren't. Hard to keep track. More's the merrier, my daddy used to say." He looks quickly over the other shoulder as if he hopes to surprise an inattentive pursuer, but this performance strikes me as more comic than mad.

"Where was your daddy from?"

He hesitates a moment. "Tennessee. Sullivan County." He ducks his head and squints his eyes shut. When he opens them, he's looking past me at my gear, and he waves his hand at it. "Your stuff'll be all right if you just cover it up and keep it out of sight. Boats come through here sometimes, but they're just passing through, having a high old time of it. Playing." He sways with an idiot grin on his face as if riding in a tossing boat, then scowls at this character floating by. In spite of myself, I halfway expect to see a boat when I follow the direction of his gaze.

"Cover things up though," he says. "It's going to rain, near certain. Maybe a little today, definitely by tomorrow."

We discuss meteorology, an interest of mine, and he points out particular cloud formations, enumerating the conditions that lead him to predict rain, and I can find no fault with his logic. From his several references to previous seasons, I gather he's been living off this river for a few years and draws on a stock of experience. He's probably mad as a hatter, but he's a good-hearted fellow nonetheless, with, I suspect, more than a common education.

I stow my new pole and my other gear, pack my knapsack with supplies for the day, and follow him to the north bank. His route is far superior to the one I took going out. "Thanks for everything," I say and offer my hand. "You've been most kind."

His hand is like a bundle of cautious sticks. "Earl Hollander," he mutters. "Folks call me . . . Call me . . . Earl."

"Pleased to meet you, Earl."

"Same here, Pete. You be careful there in the city, you hear? People there aren't quite right."

5 ⑤ I Find Employment and It Finds Me

... the modern ideal of a workman seems to be a man or a woman, or even a girl or a boy, without the knowledge of any handicraft, without any conception whatever of the industry he or she is employed in, who is only capable of making all day long and for a whole life the same infinitesimal part of something: who from the age of thirteen to that of sixty pushes the coal cart at a given spot of the mine or makes the spring of a penknife, or "the eighteenth part of a pin." Mere servants to some machine of a given description; mere flesh-and-bone parts of some immense machinery; having no idea how and why the machinery performs its rhythmical movements.
—PETER KROPOTKIN, *Fields, Factories, and Workshops*

Anarchy is the political philosophy of skilled artisans and farmers who do not need a boss; of men in dangerous occupations, like miners, lumbermen, or explorers, who learn to rely on themselves and one another; of aristocrats who can afford to be idealistic and who know what is behind the show of power; of artists and scientists who respect the facts but are not timid about inventing something out of their heads. Kropotkin was all of these.

—PAUL GOODMAN

The restaurant where Brad works is in the heart of a district the map identifies as The Fan, obviously named for the shape of it. With the tiny park across from Rachel's office as the fulcrum, several streets fan west for about twenty blocks to an eight-block width. The shaded avenues are lined with handsome two- and three-story residences built around the turn of the century. Several have shiny brass plaques announcing the construction date with the blessings of some historical society; 1897 is the oldest date I see, and I have to smile to myself. Even if I hadn't traveled in time, I would find it mildly comical for a hundred-year-old house to be considered old. It's one of the charms of America, to be like a precocious child who doesn't realize how very young he is, because he's ever so clever. "When I was a lad," I often prefaced my astute observations on life when I was a man of twelve or thirteen, and understood only years later why such an introduction prompted a fit of coughing among adults even before I could deliver my seasoned opinion.

There's no plaque on the restaurant door, however. It is a straightforward establishment with a plain facade. The message

BREAKFAST LUNCH DINNER
6–11 7 DAYS

is painted on the glass. A battered cardboard HELP WANTED hangs from a string under that. I'm directed to William, the owner of the restaurant, who is seated at a back table with coffee, cigarette, and newspaper. He has an unfortunate smile that brings to mind a dog baring its fangs. Not a vicious dog, but a mean one possibly, and dim. He is about my size with dark hair swept back on his head and secured with oil, or perhaps plastic. I tell him that Brad referred me, but it takes some time to establish Brad's identity.

Finally, it comes to him. "Brad, Brad. You mean the fat little fuck with the nose ring?"

"He does wear a nose ring, yes."

"I didn't even know he still worked here." He calls to a drowsy woman polishing the bar. "Does Brad still work here?"

She answers in a machinelike monotone. "Tuesday, Thursday lunches. Monday, Wednesday dinners. Sunday brunch when his band isn't playing out of town."

But my references are not an issue. As Brad promised, the only qualification for the job seems to be the willingness to do it, but for some reason William is hesitant to hire me. Finally, as I'm in the midst of telling him what a rich and varied work experience I've had, I realize my mistake. He wants somebody to work, not to think. Moreover, he recognizes a fundamental conflict between the two. Hiring an intelligent dishwasher would be like recruiting a kindly soldier.

I deliberately lose my way in the sentence upon which I've embarked and shake my head. "English not good," I say, seized by an attack of stupidity. He smiles understandingly. I lay my palms on my chest and grunt pathetically in a thicker-than-mud accent, "Need job today. You have job?" Once I limit myself to three-word sentences, he starts taking me seriously, asking me questions. I shake them off like a horse shaking off flies. No, I have never done this. No, I have never operated that. I have no experience, no references, no car, no driver's license, no social security number, no telephone, no address, no wife, no relatives, no past, no future, no will of my own. "I learn quick," I say. "I work hard. You have job?"

Since you put it that way, yes. Could I possibly start today? Would I mind being paid in cash "to make things simpler for everyone"?

Today is good. Cash is good. Whatever you say.

He likes the sound of that. "Put on this apron," he says. "Follow me."

In the very back of the restaurant is a small windowless room with a door standing open onto the alley. A sagging screened door pretends to keep out flies. Beside a sink with a sprayer dangling over it, sits a big shiny metal box. This is the dishwasher. I might be more properly described as the dishwasher's assistant. I take dirty dishes out of plastic tubs, dump the mounds of wasted food down a hole into a large plastic cylinder, and load the dishes into racks (plastic of course—one kind for plates, another for glasses and cups). I then spray them with water, slide them into the box, close the door, push a button, pull them steaming out the other side, and stack them up. Cutlery accumulates in a trough of blue liquid until there's enough to fill its own rack. I'm to be ever mindful the cutlery doesn't get pitched into the garbage. Every once in a while—"when the wash water looks gross"— I open a baffle and drain out the water. As it drains, I lean against the sink and watch my young coworkers through the screened door as they have a smoke in the alley, talking about what they're going to do later or what they did last night. I can't actually hear what they're saying over the roar of an exhaust fan in the wall above my head. When the dishwasher is drained, I spray out the reservoir, close the baffle, run fresh water, turn back to the tubs and the sink, and keep washing. A fellow worker has left a mascot in the form of a plastic frog on a noose hanging from the spring that holds the sprayer hose aloft. It dances before my eyes as I work.

At first no one speaks to me. Busboys come and go bringing in tubs of dirty dishes, carrying out racks of clean; rolling away cans full of garbage, leaving me empties to fill. A waitress named Deidre asks me if I speak English, and when I say yes, she asks me to please, please, please save food for her dog, so I fill several plates with bacon, sausage, eggs, muffins, steak bones, and potatoes. When breakfast is over, she shovels it all into a plastic bag and thanks me profusely. She introduces me around, telling everyone what a splendid fellow I am. Being a Russian seems to lend me a celebrity beyond the simple curiosity toward the foreigner I would expect. Everyone does a double take when Deidre announces with a dramatic flourish, "Peter is from *Russia*!" Several consider this "awesome." I can't imagine why.

A pen I rescued while excavating for cutlery writes perfectly well, and I use it to fill out the RIAA application for volunteer service as I eat my own fresh plate of bacon, sausage, eggs, and muffins prepared by Pierce the cook. Pierce is also a musician and an acquaintance of Brad's. He talks to me about music as I eat. There is always music playing, and he answers my questions at length, identifying the different exotic instruments—electric guitars, synthesizers, drum machines—commenting on the music or the musicians or both. He is quite discriminating. Of the dozen songs or so that play during our conversation, he finds only two worthy of praise. I gather some sort of rivalry exists between his musical group and Brad's, but my total ignorance of what he is talking about allows me the luxury of blissful neutrality.

I improvise freely on the application. Now that I have both a job and a fishing pole, perhaps my other shortcomings will be overlooked. For teaching experience, I pass off Russian and French prisons as universities, and such all prisons are—universities of crime maintained by the state. For work experience, I tell the truth—I was a freelance science writer, and I list some of my publications—but I must lie about the dates. Three personal references pose a problem, but since I know the first and last names of only eight persons in the world, it's not difficult to narrow the field. I don't consider Buddy Showalter. I have Earl Hollander's name but no address. I settle on Alicia, Chris, and Mike, leaving out Brad, Dave, and Rachel herself. I consider Rachel's inclusion, but fear she might not think it funny. When I ask Pierce for William's last name so that I might name him as my employer, Pierce tells me to put down Doris Bates, the drowsy woman, instead. "William's a dickhead," he informs me. "Doris is okay. She's the one who really runs the place."

I work through lunch until midafternoon when Doris summons me out front, and we sit on a pair of stools at the bar. She lights a cigarette with the same weariness she brings to all her actions and hands me an unsealed envelope with my name on it. I peek inside and find money. "Usually, payday's Saturday, but I thought you might want today's money today. How much work do you want?"

I ponder this. I have a lot to learn. Already I'm brimming with thousands of unanswered questions. I can't squander all my time laboring for money. "Work four day."

"Can you work weekends—Saturday and Sunday?"

"Saturday, not Sunday."

"How about Saturday eleven to eleven; Wednesday, Thursday, Friday seven to two?"

"That is good." I open the envelope and count my pay as she writes down my schedule on a piece of paper for me.

"Is the money all right?"

"It is money," I say.

It's midafternoon as I head east toward RIAA, plenty of time to make it there before it closes. A light misty rain is falling. Perhaps it will help wash the smell of food and soap from my clothes, but it would take a downpour to accomplish that, I imagine. The apron I was issued—one per shift, little more than a towel with strings—ceased to be effective in the first hour, and I set the sodden thing aside after two. I will obviously need more clothes for work, perhaps something in plastic, or a diving suit. Even if the sun comes out, these clothes will still be wet tomorrow. My shoes and socks are soaked through, and my feet ache from being planted in one spot for the better part of eight hours. My spine also is stiff and sore, and I can feel each aching muscle in my shoulders. I haven't felt this good in *years*. Far better the young man's pains from honest work, than the old man's grim attendance at the relentless decay and collapse of his lifelong home.

Even better, my work is done for the day, and it feels delicious to walk, to move, to be out of doors, taking it all in. With these lungs, I do believe, I could walk around the world without coughing once. I take in a deep breath, and I don't want to feel it, but I do—*gratitude*—to Anchee—like Adam in Eden, I suppose, the first pitiful wretch beholden to his Master, not a myth I wish to emulate. But what's the alternative? *Ingratitude? Curse you for giving me life?* No, it's when matters turn to Obedience, to Master and slave, that the tale turns sour for me. Put me in the Garden, you'd need no snake to persuade me—I'd eat the fruit straightaway. I would "disobey" in order to deny the category had any relevance to my dealings with anyone who would purport to be my friend. So far Anchee has only failed to be considerate and shown a flare for the enigmatic; he hasn't tried to order me about.

There are few people out and about on foot—and the oddest thing—the majority of them are running, some of them dressed as if for a field event. At first I think there must be some cross-country race in the area, but the runners pass in all directions, quite independently it seems. They generally have a purposeful look about them, almost driven, but what they are about I can't imagine.

But we pedestrians—slow or fast—are far outnumbered by automobiles. Automobiles line the streets on both sides, parked nose to rump for as far as I can see on each and every street. They zip by at incredible speeds, their fat tires hissing loudly on the wet road. I learn quickly that I'm as good as invisible to the operators of these vehicles, and I cross the broad streets with the utmost caution. Now that I'm in the heart of the residential area, I seem to be the only soul on foot.

The light rain stops, and the air almost immediately grows hotter, thicker, heavier. My soaked clothes seem just the thing. The plants and blossoms in the small front gardens luxuriate as if in a hothouse. As I readjust my knapsack, the lightest breeze blows at my back, and I'm grateful for the shirt's wet chill. The day has gone well, I think, as well as can be expected. If I just take things one step at a time, I'll be all right.

Finally, I spot someone else walking—a young woman approaching in the company of a lively dog with a magnificent white coat. He pulls her along as if she were an Eskimo sledding across the ice, instead of someone whose entire efforts are consumed in a fruitless attempt to restrain his forward progress. I've always liked dogs, such sociable creatures, and this one is irresistibly drawn to the smiling man who smells like a platter of chops. As I scratch his great shaggy head and attempt to exchange a good afternoon with his human companion, he takes it upon himself to lick clean some delectable deposit on my right thigh. It is with much difficulty that the woman drags him off me and away, his great tongue lolling longingly over his shoulder. His name—she repeats it with all manner of inflection from stern to pleading—is Brutus.

I close my eyes, imagining Sophie here beside me, sharing this comedy, and I can hear her husky laugh, feel her hand squeezing mine. In our old life, *The Woman, the Dog, and the Tasteful Trousers* would have found a place in our personal anthology of comic tales—unpublished, unspoken, perhaps even unintelligible, to others—like a secret language, a secret world of our own. I imagine us in some playful tussle in our younger days, her shrieking in mock alarm, *Brutus! Brutus! Stop that at once!* I laugh out loud here and now, imagining it. Our most intimate moments were filled with such whimsy. Age and disease and dashed hopes have made such joy scarce in recent years.

Do you miss me? she asks.

"Terribly," I say aloud.

And she's gone.

The illusion collapses, leaving behind a terrible void. My chest constricts, and I stumble to a stop, my eyes wide-open. Sophie is gone. *I left her*, I left everyone, to come here. *I left her.*

When in the future? I asked Anchee. *In your time?*

No, not nearly so far, he said. *You couldn't possibly adapt.*

Maybe *this* is too far. Maybe I can't adapt to *this* life. Maybe I don't *want* to adapt. What then? What choice do I have?

I sit down on a low garden wall and stare at the street, feeling more alone than I've ever felt in my life. In my *old* life, I remind myself. This one's young yet. I stare at my hands, now puckered and pale for having been in water all day. I'm still not used to them—so young and strong they frighten me. I face them only because I have to. I avoid mirrors—full of young Peter looking back at me. He makes the present seem like a memory, as if I don't exist in this moment, so that I'm frightened, almost literally, of my own shadow.

Another runner pounds by, and I start like a scared rabbit. *Where are you going? What are you doing?* I want to call after him, but I only watch him recede down the long street—a man, maybe fifty or sixty, dashing about in little more than boxer's

trunks on some mysterious mission. Beside me, planted in a
stand of tulips that would've cost a fortune in my day, is a hexag-
onal blue sign reading, SECURED BY ADT. *Where in the hell am I?
What do I think I'm doing?*

I've gone from old sage to young fool in a heartbeat. There
was a certain freedom I relished in being the sick old crank.
Some thought me brave for standing up to Lenin and his barbaric ways—me a feeble old man—but what could he have done
to me that a strong wind or merely another day's passing might
not accomplish? Why would he bother? Now, young and fit, I
talk like a simpleton to win the favor of—what did Pierce call
him?—a *dickhead*, for the privilege of wallowing in his garbage. I
started out this life lunging like Brutus for the mere aroma of life.

Here boy! *Fetch!* I take the watch out of my pocket, take out
the little square of plastic inside, hold it up to the light, and
squint at the miniscule text—a message for the prisoner. What
does it say? I wonder. Does it tell me where the guards are
posted? Does it tell me who's a spy? Is it written in plain English
or in code? Does it tell me where to tunnel to reach a different
life? Does it tell the truth, or does it lie? Does it tell me not to eat
from the Tree of Life? It's too late for the Tree of the Knowledge
of Good and Evil.

"I learn quick," I say, mocking myself. "I work hard." Toward
what? What is it I'm doing here? Now that I've saved my miserable hide—pale and puckered as it may be at the moment—what
is it I'm supposed to set these hands to *do*? I scowl at the plastic
square. *Not* what I'm instructed to do. I put the plastic square
away and heft the watch in my hand. Why *this*? Why *me* for that
matter? What is his stake in this, my new life? To what extent
then is this life not my own?

I look up and down the street. A storm drain gapes at the corner. I consider pitching the watch into it, striking out on my own
to someplace of my own choosing.

An automobile slides to a stop in the road directly in front of
me, and I look over. I must look odd, poised at an imagined
crossroads, hefting a watch as if it were a baseball. The driver

leans out his window and smiles. "You okay?" he asks. "You want a ride?"

He's an ordinary-looking fellow—freckle-faced, middle-aged, probably not too prosperous. His automobile's older, rustier, a bit noisier than most. There seems something auspicious in his coming along at this moment that lifts my spirits. I slip the watch into my pocket, walk across the road, and get into his automobile. The inside smells like machine oil and cigarettes. "Tim Binder," he says. "I'd shake your hand, but I'm a mechanic." He holds up a battered, grimy hand. His fingers tremble slightly.

"I'm Peter Kropotkin," I say.

"Nice to meet you," he says, not looking at me, and we start moving down the road.

"I was lucky you came along," I say.

"Yeah," he says, his eyes on the road, and I wonder why someone so unsociable would stop and offer a ride. We've gone at least four or five blocks now, and still he hasn't asked me where I'm going, though he seems intent on some destination ahead of us. He notices I'm staring at him and flashes a nervous smile. "We'll be there in no time."

I get a sinking sensation in the pit of my stomach. "You can just let me out at the next corner," I say.

"But it's just a few more blocks to the cathedral."

"I didn't say I was going to the cathedral. Anywhere here is fine."

"But we're really *close*."

I start hunting for the door latch, ready to jump out if I can get the damned thing open, and he swerves over to the curb and stops. I find the release and fling the door open.

"Please don't go," he says. "I can really use this hundred dollars. I did everything just like he said."

I freeze. "What are you talking about? Like who said?"

"You don't know? This guy came into the shop. He said you'd be needing a ride down to the cathedral, and if I just got you there it was a hundred bucks for me. He told me what you looked like, what you'd be wearing, told me the time and the place. That was it. Said I didn't need to know any more than that, swore it was nothing illegal. He said I had to get you all the way there, though, or I got nothing."

"When did he hire you?"

"Yesterday morning. I come this way every day at this time anyway. It was like getting paid to drive home. I swear I didn't mean to make any trouble for you or anything. I thought he was a friend of yours."

A busy friend, apparently. A friend who knows what I'm going to do before I do it, knows the clothes I'll be wearing before I've even purchased them, knows where he wants me to go, and when. My friend the magician. "He described *these* clothes to you?"

"Yessir. He said they'd be wet and dirty. That's why I got a towel on the seat there for you."

There is a plush green towel underneath me. "Thanks," I say. I absentmindedly dab at the spot Brutus found so intriguing. "What did this fellow look like?"

"Young black guy, tall, good-looking, like a movie star or something. Funny way of talking like he's from some other country."

I have been in several prisons but never felt so thoroughly trapped as this—placed in a life of another's devising, so that simply to be *alive* is to be imprisoned with no possibility of escape. I settle back in the seat and close the door. I have to find out what's so damned important about my completing this pilgrimage. The only way I can understand the game Anchee's playing is to play along, at least for a time. "All right, Tim Binder. Give me a ride to the cathedral. I wouldn't want to stand between you and a hundred dollars."

Tim needs no second invitation, and we lurch into motion again. He's content not to speak of our business, whatever it is, probably figuring quite rightly that the less he knows the better. I have no reason to doubt Mr. Binder. He seems to be the hired hand he presents himself to be. It's his employer who concerns me, a concern that grows the closer we get to the university, and there are more people on the streets, any one of them hired, perhaps, to play some role in my life according to Anchee: *See the bearded chap over there? Go sing an aria for him, will you? Here's a bow and arrow. Shoot this apple off his head. He took a bite out of it, you see, and must be punished.*

I have to find him, speak to him face-to-face, put a stop to this nonsense. He offered me a life, not a role in a play. "I don't think my friend wanted me to *know* he was doing this favor for me," I say to Tim. "I won't tell him you gave away his secret if you won't."

"Fine by me," he says.

He pulls up beside the cathedral, and I open the door. "By the way, where are you supposed to get your money?"

"Here, I guess."

"You're supposed to meet him *here*?" I ask, thinking *this is too easy*.

"No. He said you'd give it to me, said it'd be in an envelope in your pocket." He cautiously points to my pay envelope, sticking out of my shirt pocket.

There's a tingling at the nape of my neck as I pull out the envelope, open it, and look inside. In addition to my pay are five crisp twenty-dollar bills that weren't there half an hour ago when I counted this money. With trembling fingers, I take them out and hand them to Tim. "Thanks for the ride," I say, and get out of the automobile. I hesitate before closing the door. "You're not supposed to meet him again, are you?"

"He said I'd never see him again—made a point of it because he said you'd ask about that. How do you suppose he knew?"

"It's just a guess, but I'd say we've taken this ride before some other time."

"I don't recall it."

"It was a different universe, apparently. Did he say whether he'd be seeing *me* again?"

"No, he didn't say a word about that."

I close the door gently, and he drives away, accelerating rapidly, glad to be done with me I suspect. I'm still standing in the street, staring after a car that's well out of sight. I look the other way and notice a policeman in the park, watching me. I turn and mount the curbstone, and there's Rachel, coming toward me. Her eyes light up with recognition, she smiles, and I'm at once delighted and horrified. She must be the reason Anchee has maneuvered me to this place, this moment.

6 ⑤ 1789 Texas Avenue

> And really, it is one of the two; either the moral conceptions of man are merely the further development of the moral habits of mutual aid, which are so generally inherent in social animals that they may be called a *law* of Nature,—and in that event our moral conceptions, in so far as they are the product of reason, are nothing but the conclusion arrived at from man's observation of nature, and in so far as they are the product of habit and instinct, they constitute a further development of instincts and habits inherent in social animals. Or our moral conceptions are revelations from above, and all further investigations of morality become merely interpretation of the divine will.
>
> —PETER KROPOTKIN, *Ethics*

"Mr. Kropotkin, is that you? Are you all right? You look awful."

I want to tell her: *I am awful, horrible, to be avoided at all costs. Whatever you're thinking of doing, do its opposite. Ignore my existence. Someone from the distant future has contrived for us to meet. Run for your life!*

I want to tell her all this, but I can't, because I am, in spite of everything, so very glad to see her. "I'm fine, thank you. I was on my way to see you. To bring you this." I hand her my application, somewhat damp and crumpled from its sojourn in my knapsack.

I study the top of her head as she gives the application a cursory glance and hands it back to me, and I wonder, *Does she know? Is she too a spy in my life?* My instincts tell me she's not, perhaps only because I *want* them to deceive me. My instincts haven't expressed themselves so forcefully in quite a long time.

"I was just leaving the office," she says. "If you'll give this to Nancy at the front desk, she'll make sure I get it. I'll contact you after I've had a chance to look it over." My disappointment is like a stone sinking through me. She looks away, clearly wanting to go.

I must look like a madman in my current mental state—I certainly feel like one—a filthy one to boot. I should walk away, tossing this application she doesn't want anyway and Anchee's blasted watch into the nearest trash bin. That would be a fitting end to the Adventure of the Abducted Anarchist: Anchee maneuvers me here with the clumsy contrivance of Tim Binder, as if life itself depends on this meeting, and I sabotage the whole business, like Huckleberry Finn, by simply allowing the current to sweep me away downstream.

But I can't bring myself to simply wish her farewell and walk away. That would be its own unendurable defeat. "How will you contact me?" I ask.

She touches her forehead with her fingertips. "Oh that's right. You don't have a phone. Maybe you could come by on Monday?"

"The class begins on Sunday, does it not? Perhaps I could walk along with you, and you could look over the application, and I could answer any questions you might have. I have a job now, by the way. I just got off work." I gesture at the Tasteful Trousers apologetically. "As you can see." I screw up my face in exaggerated disgust, and she smiles at my antics, though I suspect she's trying not to.

"What kind of work are you doing?" she asks.

"It's really quite invigorating. Not too far from here there's a frog pond where huge quantities of garbage are dumped by a band of wasteful gluttons. It's my job to dive in, fully clothed as you can see, and rescue the dishes and cutlery and bring them to shore safe and clean. Wonderful job really. Gets me out in the world, doing my part. Keeps me fit." I come up on my toes and throw out my chest like a preening lifeguard. I can't stop myself. I desperately want to charm this woman even though it doesn't seem wise. When she rewards me with a laugh, wisdom is sent packing.

"You're washing dishes?" she says, placing a comforting hand upon my arm. "I'm sure it'll only be temporary."

"I don't know. It's a pretty large pond." Our eyes meet, and she withdraws her hand and looks away. "But I'm sorry," I say. "You were on your way somewhere, and I'm keeping you." I take a step backward and almost tumble into the street.

When she rescues me by seizing my arm, and I've managed to right myself, she acknowledges for the first time in the look she gives me that I'm a man clearly attracted to her—acknowledges but regrets, perhaps rather deeply, but regrets nonetheless. She would probably at this point have to push me in front of a speeding automobile to be quit of me.

She steps back, putting a little distance between us, as I'm still teetering on the curb. "Actually," she says. "I'm headed over to a food cart by the library. I missed lunch, and I have to stay late to meet with a new Cuban family. This is my only chance to get a bite. You can walk with me if you like, and I can look over your application. How's that?"

"That would be wonderful." I offer my arm, but she plucks my application from my hand. She's all business, reading as she walks. She doesn't comment on the lack of an address, but she comments approvingly on the rest. "You wrote for *Nature*? I'm impressed. . . . All these languages . . . The Geographic Society." But when she comes to more delicate matters her tone grows cautious. "These references—Chris Billings and Alicia Cykowski are your helpful flight attendants—but who is Mike Cole?"

"He's one of the three young men I met at the airport. He struck me as the most intelligent and responsible. They are students at the university, musicians."

"You met them yesterday sharing a limo?"

"That's right."

"Is Mike the one who told you about your job?"

"No, that was Brad."

"I'm surprised you didn't use me as a reference."

"I considered it, but I was afraid you wouldn't find it funny."

She winces. "Do I seem as stern as all that? I'm sorry. It's this job." She doesn't explain her meaning, but she does seem sorry. She likes me, I think. But . . . There is a "but," clear enough. Whatever it is, it can't be any more off-putting than the truth: An escaped lunatic from another time shows up in your life and becomes terribly infatuated with you.

Now that she's finished reading the application, she quickens our pace, and the silence builds. When the food cart is safely in view, she waves my application in the air and says with some force, "I think it's a terrible waste that a man of your abilities is washing dishes. I'll talk to the employment specialist, informally of course, and see if he can't come up with something better."

Whether she's trying to distract me or herself with this *non se-quitur*, I don't know. I stop walking. "But I don't want something 'better.' " She stops a pace and a half ahead and turns around. "I *want* to be a dishwasher. I want to swim in the pond. I understand it. No subtleties elude me. I come out of the garbage, wash up, change my clothes, and my life is my own. I can spend my time learning about more important things. I know I'm odd, that I'm not quite like other people. I have been away a very long time in a very remote place. I need to catch up. If I have a 'better' job, I will be running faster, but I will *never* catch up. Do you understand?"

I hadn't intended to get so carried away. She is looking at me very intently. "More than you can possibly imagine," she says, then smiles and shakes her head, pointing at my clothes. "Now when is it you get to the 'wash up and change clothes' part?"

We both laugh. "I was afraid I would miss you if I took the time to wash and change before I came here. I knew the class starts on Sunday, and I didn't want to miss you."

I would've missed her, actually, if Anchee hadn't intervened. I was on the verge of turning around and heading the other way, someplace out of town, a place of my own choosing, a place far away from her, into the past, into my memories, anywhere but here. In spite of myself, in spite of all common sense, I'm glad I didn't. In this life, I have no past.

We have reached the food cart. The woman serving the food is as self-promoting as the bread wrapper, with a constant chatter that sounds almost religious. The word "organic" keeps cropping up, but with an indeterminate meaning I can't sort out. As Rachel endures the sermon stoically, I study her striking profile. It seems clear that Anchee wants me to carry out my intention to call on this woman, going so far as to enlist Mr. Binder to make it so. I can't imagine why, and I would rebel with every fiber of my being against being so manipulated, if I weren't so taken with her, if I weren't so curious to discover what happens next.

When she has her food, we sit down at an open-air table, and I allow her privacy to eat her meal while I observe the students coming and going. The day is still warm, and many of them don't wear much, just like the people in the magazines. Somehow I'd assumed ordinary people would be more modest. I find it somewhat unnerving, though Rachel doesn't seem to pay it any mind. Looking past such surface differences, however, these could be students in St. Petersburg or Zurich a century and a half ago. Except for the number of women, of course, and blacks. In this, I suspect, Virginia, not so long ago, would be quite like Russia—a bunch of fellows who look like me.

Rachel wads up the paper wrapper that contained her meal and tosses it in a trash bin. "I inhaled that," she says. She places her fingertips on my application. My interview has begun.

"That is the university library?" I ask, pointing behind her. "Where the class is to be held?"

"Yes. They're letting us use one of their conference rooms."

"Can anyone use the library, or only students and faculty?"

"You can't check anything out, but you can use the materials there. The public library is three or four blocks east. What do you want to research?"

"Everything."

"I'm sorry. I don't mean to pry."

"Oh no, no. I didn't mean to imply any such thing. I'm just so ignorant. Politics and science, I guess you would say. History as well. Literature. Music . . ." I laugh at myself. "Everything."

"Somehow I doubt your great ignorance. But why do you want to teach this ESL class when you have so much you want to learn yourself?"

"I will help them learn English. They will help me learn about everything else. They won't take so much for granted as people who've lived here all their lives."

She smiles at that, studies me, approvingly, I think, then looks again at the application, but she's not actually reading anything there. She sighs. She has a job to do, unfortunately, unpleasant duties to carry out: "Do you have a place to live, Mr. Kropotkin?"

"A very nice place as a matter of fact. Scenic. Lots of fresh air. I've even met one of my neighbors—one of the human ones, that is. I purchased a fishing pole from him."

"Mr. Kropotkin, you really should be careful down there."

"Would I be safer and healthier in the shelter you spoke of?"

"Well no, probably not. But you wouldn't be breaking the law."

"The law is my least concern, particularly such a stupid one. I'm as careful as I can afford to be, Miss Pederson. When I have enough money, I'll find a cheap room. How much is a cheap room, would you say?" My tone is a bit combative, I'm afraid, but I want to quash this assumption that I long for a better job or a better dwelling.

"I prefer Ms.," she says.

"I beg your pardon?"

"You called me '*Miss* Pederson.' I prefer to be called *Ms.* Pederson."

"I prefer to be called Peter, Ms. Pederson. So what do you think? How much would a room cost me?"

She smiles warmly—at my persistence, I suppose. "All right, Peter. One fit to live in, more or less safe?—three hundred a month, at least, I'd guess. Maybe including electric, maybe not."

"Some don't have electricity?"

"No, I meant . . ." She gives me a quizzical look and seems to lose her train of thought. "I'm sorry. I don't mean to . . I'm just concerned is all."

"Don't worry about me. I can have three hundred dollars saved in a couple of weeks or so. I'm in no hurry, to tell the truth. As long as the weather is so mild, I like it where I am. As you promised, it has not disappointed me in the least. I believe you expressed a fondness for the river yourself, Ms. Pederson?"

"Yes, yes I did."

"I have all day Sunday off from work; I made a point of it because of the class. I was planning to explore Belle Isle in the morning. Do you know it?"

"Yes, it's very nice." She looks away. She knows where this is going.

I go there anyway. "Would you be so kind as to join me for an outing Sunday morning?"

She looks at me oddly. "Where did you learn to speak English, Mr. . . . Peter?"

"Did I misspeak?"

"No, no, not at all. You just have a way about you—kind of old-fashioned, I guess. Are you old-fashioned?"

"I've always fancied myself a radical—a good, old-fashioned radical." She laughs and smiles at me. There is no question that she likes me. "Sunday then?" I ask, surprising myself this time. But what have I to lose?

"You seem like a very nice man, Peter, but I can't go out with a client."

"But I'm not a client. You said yesterday there was nothing you could do for me, and I've just declined your kind offer to inquire after a better job on my behalf. I gather from your doubtful tone that even my status as a volunteer is highly unlikely, if not impossible. So we have no professional relationship whatsoever—*and* share a fondness for rivers. And I know no one in this city but the names on that paper, almost strangers, as you know."

Her distress is manifest, her lips compressed, her head wagging. "I'm sorry. I can't. I don't think it would be a good idea."

"It's not just because I'm 'a client,' is it? May I ask what makes me not 'a good idea'?"

She sighs. "You seem . . . I don't know how to put this. You seem . . . I don't know . . . so . . . intense. So . . . needy." She gives me a look both searching and apologetic. "Are you recently divorced, Peter?"

I'm stunned by the question. Sophie and I never considered such a thing. It takes me a moment to recall the word for what I am, longer still to say it. Finally, I manage, "I'm a widower, Ms. Pederson."

She draws in a breath, equally stunned by my answer. "I'm so sorry," she says. "I had no idea. How long has it been?"

The question dizzies me. *For whom?* I want to say. *For whom?* I don't know how long she survived me, mourned me. I don't know how she died. I don't know where she's buried.

"Peter?" Rachel gently prompts. "Are you all right?"

"Two days," I blurt out. "I lost my wife two days ago." For me, at least, it's the truth.

"Oh my God," she whispers, taking my hands. "You poor man."

My life with Sophie flashes through my memory like the crazy patchwork of the airplane movie, and I feel as if I'm falling out of the sky. I don't know how I've held in these sobs so long, but I can't stop them now that they've started. Rachel keeps hold of my hands, squeezing them tight. "Go ahead and cry," she whispers. "It's all right, Peter. Just go ahead and cry."

I have no choice but to obey.

By the time I've cried myself out, I see matters more clearly, much to my shame. If only I'd seen them before I dismissed Anchee's *Any questions?* with a resounding *No!*

Sophie was quite young when I met and fell in love with her, even though, as we used to say, she was old for her years and I was young for mine. When we were first married, we had many discussions to the effect that the fourteen-year difference between us was totally without significance, though mysteriously we continued to talk of it for many years. But somehow, even so, we grew old together. Always *together*. Even when I was in prison in Clairvaux, she sacrificed her health and studies to be close to me, visiting daily. Those visits, I do believe, saved my life. For several years now, I have been saying a long farewell to her, knowing I was soon to die, soon to leave her—herself grown old and unwell. But now I'm young and fit, and she is the one gone—dead and buried.

It's a bitter irony my host has made of us.

He's raised me from the dead—me alone—but if we're canceling death, why not the two of us, together?

Sophie didn't have to die.

Perhaps one word from me—something like a prayer on bended knee, an earnest appeal to his aesthetic sensibilities— would have saved her. I'll never know.

I didn't ask.

I've been reborn, it seems, with a sin on my head. But even if it's true, as Anchee says, that reality itself does not exist, that there are infinite realities (littered like a minefield, no doubt, with his interference) they have as much bearing on the conduct of my life as grains of sand in the Sahara or on the far side of the moon. I can only make my way in this *one* reality, this *one* time and place—this *one* life. And sadly, I know only one way out, and it was to avoid that dark passage that I was in such a hurry to come here in the first place.

I'm dead. You can visit my grave somewhere, I'm sure. Lay some flowers on it for me, if you like; or on second thought, put the soil to some good use and plant something there—whatever will grow. I'm dead, but I haven't *died*, an experience I am willing to postpone indefinitely.

As I say, all this comes to me during my good long cry, rendered longer, no doubt, by the impossibility of my sharing a word of these insights with Rachel.

"Are you all right?" she asks me quietly. Such is her sympathy for my bereavement that she has warmed to me considerably, sitting beside me, her arm around my shoulders. But I try not to put too much stock in it. What is she to do—her shoulder still wet with my tears—say *Kropotkin, quit your whining or we'll ship you back to where you came from?*

"I'm feeling much better, thanks," I say. "I'm terribly sorry for falling apart on you like that. Now you've squandered all your time on my difficulties, and you'll surely be missed at your office."

She smiles. "A nice thought, but not likely. If I fall asleep at the staff meeting—*then* I'm missed." She gives my shoulders a hug and releases me. "You didn't fall apart—you cried. You have good reason. I do need to be getting back though. I'm supposed to meet a new family. Are you going to be okay?"

"Never better."

She looks at me differently now. I'm strange, without a doubt, but she has set my strangeness aside. She believes she's seen the essence of me, the sort of man I am, and I believe she has.

As a very young man in Manchuria I spent the evening in the company of a hundred Chinese soldiers who earlier in the day with great good humor helped me free a barge my incompetence had stranded upon a rock. As we smoked their tobacco and communicated by pantomime only, they regarded me, a total stranger in every way, much as Rachel regards me now. I was a crazy young Russian, to be sure, but more importantly, I was a decent fellow down on his luck.

"I appreciate your kindness more than you can know," I say to her, and—I swear I can't help myself—I rise, give a little bow, and offer my arm. "Perhaps I might accompany you back to your workplace?" I can't imagine what she must think of me— pursuing her on the heels of my wife's passing. How can I explain that not only did Sophie die, but Sophie's husband as well? *I was older then,* I wish I could tell her, *much, much older. This fellow who courts you now wasn't even born yet!*

But my fears prove groundless. She presses her hands against her chest and smiles at my proffered arm as if it were a precious child. "What is it you'd say?—'I would be pleased and delighted if you would escort me hence.' " She mimics me with charming skill, smooths imaginary skirts as she rises, and takes my arm in hers. We walk a ways in silence, comfortably close, our trouser legs brushing against one another. She gives my arm an affectionate squeeze. I suppose I should be analyzing the chain of events that has brought the two of us to this moment, but instead I wonder what Rachel might be thinking and feeling as we walk along entwined—while I imagine she wonders much the same about me. It's a most pleasant sort of wondering—and quite unchainlike—though I confess myself tangled in it like a kitten in a ball of yarn.

And if I could tell her what I'm thinking, what I'm feeling, it would simply be this: *I'm alive! I'm blissfully alive!* In some ways livelier than is altogether convenient, perhaps, but I'm helpless to do anything but rejoice in it. I smile at her, and she smiles back at me, and I am flooded with goodwill for the whole world, in this time, or any other, for I believe her to be a true friend. Someday, I realize, I hope to tell her the whole truth about myself. Someday, I try to imagine, she will believe me.

As we near her office, she asks, as if we've been discussing the issue the whole time: "You have your heart set on teaching this ESL class, don't you?"

"Yes, I do," I say enthusiastically. "I love that phrase *to set your heart on* something. English is such an evocative language, don't you think?"

"Yes," she says sadly. We stop at the bottom of the steps to her office. She turns her back on them and faces me, taking in a deep breath. I know what this means: *Application Denied.* "I have to be honest with you," she says. "I can't take on a homeless man as a volunteer teacher. I should be referring you to another agency, not putting you to work for this one." She speaks in confidential tones, though the only other people about are whizzing by in their automobiles or sitting well out of earshot in the park. Once again I wonder about spies—but the only secret I have is that I have absolutely no idea what is going on!

Declining to follow Rachel's example, I speak at a normal volume, or perhaps slightly elevated. "I wouldn't *go* to another agency. I'm not homeless. I was homeless yesterday—up in that airplane without a friend in the world. All told, I'd say I'm doing rather well at the moment—a job, a neighbor, a dinner engagement . . ." Our eyes meet. "A friend."

We hold our gaze for several moments, then it's several more before I can find my voice to go on. "But all those things came to me because I speak the language. The people in this class—maybe they have an apartment, maybe even a house, which is to say they have a landlord or a mortgage—but when they go to the store they can't talk to the clerk; when they pass a newspaper, they can't read the headline; when they are lost, they can't ask directions. And when they have a grievance with their precious landlord, he'll shrug his shoulders and walk away, making little or no effort to understand their foreign speech—though he'll hold *them* to every word of the contract they signed but cannot read. The way it seems to me, they are more homeless than I."

She is staring at me with rapt attention. She shakes her head, her face creased with regret, and sighs, running her hands through her cropped hair. I wonder what it would feel like to touch her hair . . .

"I know, I know," she says. "Everything you're saying is absolutely true, and you'd be a *wonderful* teacher, but when I turn in your file, Nancy must enter it into the computer. When she sees there's no address, she'll ask for it. When I tell her you don't *have* one, my boss will hear of it just as surely as if I'd put your occupation as drug dealer or thief, and *that* will be the end of your application. All files, without exception, must be complete, she'll tell me. The grant requires it. We have reports to make. I'm sorry. We could lose our funding. I am really and truly sorry. But I can't give you a class until you can give me an address. We have classes starting up all the ti—"

"So all you need is an *address*? A number and a street?" She doesn't answer, stopped midword, looking as if she doesn't understand the question, but then I see in her intelligent eyes that she understands perfectly, and is deciding her next move. I take the application from her hand, and my pen from my pocket. "May I use your back as a writing desk?" She hesitates only a moment before turning her back to me. I spread the paper across her shoulders. She is lean and strong; the smell of her hair is intoxicating; the proximity of her bare neck makes my fingers tremble as I put pen to paper. *1789 Texas Avenue*, I write on the application and hand it to her over her shoulder. "I wouldn't want you to lose your funding," I say.

She reads it and turns to me, her conspiratorial smile warming my heart. "*Texas Avenue* is the park entrance; *1789*—what made you choose that number?"

"It's a year."

She laughs and shakes her head at me. "The French Revolution?"

"Exactly."

"I've never met anyone like you, Peter."

"Nor I like you, Ms. Pederson."

"Call me Rachel, please."

"So do I get the class, Rachel?"

She searches my eyes and seems to find what she's looking for. "Of course."

"You won't regret your faith in me."

"I know. They're getting a wonderful teacher, and you've rescued them from my teaching. I arrange all these classes, but I'm terrible at it myself." She sticks out her hand, and we shake. "I'll meet you in front of the library a little before three on Sunday, and get you started with the class."

I'm a dozen paces away when I remember and make an about-face. She's still standing where I left her, watching me go. "Belle Isle on Sunday morning?" I ask.

"I'd love to," she says immediately. "What time?"

"Nine o'clock."

"On the island by the footbridge."

"I'll look forward to it."

7 ⑤ Dinner with Hemlock Cocktail

At the university I had not friends, properly speaking; I was older than most of my companions, and among young people a difference of a few years is always an obstacle to complete comradeship.

—PETER KROPOTKIN, *Memoirs of a Revolutionist*

I used to stay with them at Harrow and though I think they were very poor then, they always had friends staying or visit ing them. . . . Madame Kropotkin was kindness itself, but was of a somewhat melancholy temperament and even as a child I was conscious of it, whereas Kropotkin was gay and brimming over with life and interest in everything—very warm and affectionate. His vast knowledge, his vast experience and his great powers of thought, I was quite oblivious of them. It was enough for me to listen to his stories and play the delightful game he taught me, where he was a bull-fighter and I the bull, hurling myself in vain on him.

—MISS E. M. HEATH

After leaving Rachel, I go to the thrift store to purchase additional clothes. A round-trip to the river would make me late for dinner, and besides, the dungarees I have stowed there are too heavy for this weather. It's still an hour or more until sunset, and the temperature must be approaching ninety degrees. I consider purchasing short pants like everyone else seems to wear, but in the end can't do it, selecting the lightest weight trousers I can find—they are muslin and tie at the waist. The simplicity of their design appeals to me, and they weigh next to nothing.

While searching for a short-sleeved shirt, I hold up one—more to take in its bright splashes of color than to consider its purchase—but when I start to return it to the rack, a fellow customer takes up its cause in the friendliest way. He calls it a Hawaiian shirt and claims its particular mix of colors is quite striking with my red hair and beard. He's a thin black man, perhaps sixty years old. He's with his mother, he explains, nodding toward an ancient woman moving glacially among the dresses. He seems to me to be a gentle man and quite sincere. I wonder idly if he might be another of Anchee's employees, but I buy the shirt anyway. Its colors may brighten the banks of the frog pond, and its garish pattern should tolerate any number of stains. Besides, one must choose his battles, and wardrobe hardly seems to be a matter of sufficient gravity to warrant manning the barricades just yet.

I change into my clean clothes—stowing my soiled ones in my knapsack inside the plastic bag intended for the new—and they cheer me up considerably. Standing in front of the mirror in my new outfit, I feel like a new man. Not only are they clean and dry and comfortable, but they are clothes I would never have worn in my old life, and that fact alone pleases me. Perhaps because it makes me feel free—rather like my young friends putting rings through their noses and spiders on their heads, dyeing their hair blue or shaving it off—it makes us feel free, even though we're not.

I arrive on time for my dinner at the residence of Mike, Brad, and Dave. I pause after my brisk walk and make a survey of the neighborhood. The houses are high and narrow three-story affairs, aging none too gracefully. While a few sport shiny plaques confessing their age just like their betters a couple of blocks west, the buildings in this area are seedier, more fecund—habitat for students and artists and others with little money. I feel right at home.

It brings to mind my days in a sparsely furnished room writing propaganda for students and workers, stirring calls to action, attacks on the wage system, war, and other rituals of capitalism. I have to smile at how little progress I made—ending up my life in a sparsely furnished house with two rooms, writing books for . . . posterity, I guess you would say—the people living on this street. I was writing my *Ethics* when I died. I can still recall the last sentence I wrote:

The fact is, that while the mode of life is determined by the history of the development of a given society, conscience, *on the other hand, as I shall endeavour to prove, has a much deeper origin— namely in the consciousness of* equity, *which physiologically develops in man as in all social animals.*

Perhaps you might think it odd that I can recall the sentence, but not the moment I wrote it, or why it was exactly—a fit of coughing, a faint, a seizure—that I failed to write the next one. I wrote it, and there it turned, pirouetting in my mind. The next thing I knew Sophie was bending over me, reassuring me I was fine in tones that told me I certainly wasn't. I never wrote another word after that, though the sentence continued to turn and turn in my mind, awaiting a partner. I couldn't say how long I lived after I wrote it. Not long, I think. Not long at all.

I always wrote. My brother wrote poetry, beautiful poetry. I tried my hand at it, but made a poor showing. The two of us collaborated on several dramas—based on the gorier episodes in the saints' lives. We specialized in depictions of the sufferings in Hell, with every candle we could find blazing and smoking as we delivered lines consisting almost entirely of bloodcurdling shrieks. I penned several childish journals, with Frol a regular and discriminating subscriber. But my true literary ambition was to write novels, like Turgenev or Tolstoi or Dickens—I attempted my first at twelve—but set such aspirations aside when I found my political calling. Perhaps, like my Hawaiian shirt, I will take it up in my new life.

Most of the porches here are in need of paint and are cluttered with something—furniture, cardboard cartons, machines, beer bottles, flags and banners of various allegiances. The porch I seek is crowded with potted plants—perched on the railing, hanging from the ceiling, sitting on the windowsills and steps. A row of tiny cacti stand along the porch's edge as if upon the rim of a desert canyon. In the midst of this greenery Dave's bright blue hair is an exotic bloom. He and a young woman lounge upon what I believe to be a seat from an automobile. They are smoking cigarettes with a heavy Turkish aroma in the company of a number of cats—precise calculation is impossible—who might all appear dead if it were not for the slow sway of one fluffy calico tail, rather like a cobra in furs.

"Whoa! Peter!" Dave exclaims, calling into the house through the open window behind him—"Check it out, everybody: Peter's just back from the islands! You bring back any *ganja*, mon?"

"Don't be a dick," the woman says to Dave. "I'm Caitlin," she says to me. "You must be Peter. Mike's in the kitchen—all the way in the back." She gives me a friendly smile, but doesn't move, not to disturb the cats I suppose. Her hair is unnaturally black and cut straight across at her shoulders and just above her eyes. Her eyes are done up in the same Egyptian motif as Dave's, and I speculate she may be the artist for both. She could easily mount the stage in the role of Cleopatra, especially with all these disciples of Bast piled about her. They emit a soft choral snore.

Plants, cats, humans—no one stirs as I mount the steps, flanked on both sides by pots of basil and rosemary. As I reach the door, Brad's smiling face appears on the other side of the screen. The gauzy mesh filters details so that his face is a fleshy circle, a smaller silver circle (his nose ring) at its center, and a crescent of white teeth below that. "Cool shirt, Peter." He holds open the door, and behind me a pride of paws hits the porch in a cascade of soft thuds. A feline torrent flows round my legs and into the house, and I follow them inside only to find they've vanished without a trace.

Brad gestures at the mismatched armchairs, sprung love seat, and carpet from the threadbare and faded Orient that comprise the room's furniture, and says, "Here's the place." A place Sophie and I might have decorated ourselves. Entirely catless.

"Where did they go?" I ask. "The cats."

"They heard Mike using the can opener. Only one kind of food comes in a can around here."

That they could hear anything is remarkable in itself. A rattling electric fan sweeps the parlor, music thumps from the back of the house as if a tuba band is trapped inside an elevator. "I've never seen such solidarity among cats before."

"They grew up in the house together. TJ—you'll meet TJ—he and his uncle decided the place needed some cats and went down to the shelter and took a dozen home. That was five years ago. There's eight left. They're totally cool. They're like in their own world next to ours, you know? You totally blew everybody away at the restaurant, by the way. Doris called to *thank* me for sending you in. Even Mr. Doris liked you, and he hates everybody."

"Mr. Doris?"

"Sorry. William. Everybody calls him Mr. Doris. His wife does all the work and pays all the bills; he has all the problems and spends all the money."

"Those two are *married*?"

"Weird isn't it? Don't expect them to tell. They don't let on. I've worked there over a year, and I've never seen them touch each other. If you even mention one to the other, they like change the subject immediately. They're worse than my parents. Come on back. Mike's in the kitchen. He's totally wound about having Kropotkin for dinner, even if you're not really the Dude himself."

I follow Brad down a hallway made narrow by coatracks and a bass viol and several bookcases stuffed to overflowing. There's a large photograph of a man in wire-rimmed glasses, a very interesting-looking fellow I take a strong liking to. I also like the poster's single word text, IMAGINE. At the end of the hall, a row of wooden African masks gives off a distinct sympathetic buzz to the bass tones of the music—much louder here, throbbing like a pulse through the soles of my shoes.

Future music excites me—its abundance and variety, its brashness and energy. I am ignorant of its nuances, of course. But this piece seems particularly complex, multilayered—the tone alternately angry and hopeful. The melody, if such it can be called, takes wild, unpredictable turns. I rather like it.

Brad opens a swinging door, and music gushes out, filling the hall with sound. I imagine, across this threshold, a great hall filled with musicians, but guess I will likely find the same electronic reproduction I've heard everywhere, but writ larger and louder.

I follow him into the room, once a dining room it appears, and let the door swing shut behind me. It's as if we've stepped into a crashing surf. Like the masks, I vibrate—every inch of me a part of the sound itself—though I can't distinguish a single instrument, a single note, a single word in what seems to be a song. It's not entirely an unpleasant sensation, but I keep moving, my eyes on Brad, my unlikely Moses in this Red Sea of sound. Somewhere in the stacks of electronic machinery that tower on either side of us is the source of the music, though it seems to be welling up from the earth itself like magma erupting. I imagine the nails shaking from the floorboards, the paint showering from the walls and ceiling in flakes, my soles bursting into flame.

At the far end of the room, we pass through a swinging door and enter the kitchen as if washed ashore. The music swells and fades with the interval of the door's swinging open and closed, open and closed, open and closed. I can more clearly distinguish a voice in the music, now that it's muted by the door, but the words, heavy with rhyme, come too fast and furious to disentangle the sense:

 . . . *greed*
 . . . *speed*
 . . . *feed* *

. . . consume

. exhume

. . . bridegroom

Mike is at the stove working over a sizzling pot. Pungent oriental spices fill the air. A middle-aged black man sits at the table. The cats fill a corner, gathered around a single dish like eight petals on a daisy from which four have been plucked. Every variety of the feline tribe from Tabby to Siam is represented in their number.

"Hey, Peter! You made it!" Mike shouts to be heard over the music's thumping rumble, and the explosive sound of double handfuls of broccoli hitting smoking-hot oil. He gestures with his head as he stirs the pot, tossing in a flurry of additional ingredients from a row of little dishes beside the stove. "Peter, this is my Dad, Robert Cole. Dad, Peter Kropotkin."

Pleased to meet you, Robert mouths, as he rises from his seat at the kitchen table and shakes my hand, making no attempt to be heard over the bedlam. He smiles proudly. *My son,* he seems to say, *is quite the character, isn't he?* He remains standing, and so do I. He looks a good deal like his son, only older and heavier and darker, with a silver moustache I envy for its neatness. I smooth mine with my fingertips, my beard with my palms. Brad opens the icebox, taking out two bottles of beer, giving me one and sitting at the table with the other.

The music has reached an intensity reminiscent of driving rain on a tin roof. And then the instrument Pierce taught me to recognize as an electric guitar plays a staccato sequence of chords, and the music stops. Mike ceases his clatter and empties a cascade of spicy vegetables into an enormous crockery bowl with a pleasant slosh. And then out of nowhere, the singer can be heard to say quite distinctly, *No morals without justice, no justice without equity.* Other voices take this up, weaving it into a round, switching the terms back and forth, creating a tumultuous chant that builds in intensity until, like the guitar, it comes to an abrupt stop with all the voices shouting in unison: *Justice!* The song is over.

The ensuing silence is enormous. No one speaks. No one moves. I'm reminded of the moment Anchee stepped into my bedchamber and stopped time.

"Sounds good, Mike," Robert Cole says, breaking the silence. "I think it's your best song yet."

"That was *your* song?" I blurt out.

"Yes," Mike says. "Did you like it?"

"Yes, I did. Very much. The ending particularly."

"It's from Kropotkin's *Ethics*."

"I know."

"I thought you might."

Robert Cole laughs. "Well, I can see you two have a lot to talk about. I was just leaving, Peter. Nice to meet you. Enjoy your dinner."

"Will you and Mom make it to the show tonight?" Mike asks. "We're playing a bunch of new stuff."

"I'll try to make it. No promises. Your mother is flying to Seattle tonight." I gather from the way he says this, and the way Mike reacts, that there's nothing unusual in Mike's mother flying across the continent. It seems that a good number of people nowadays spend the majority of their lives in some conveyance or other—when they're not running about aimlessly.

Robert starts to leave out the swinging door at the same time that Dave and Caitlin arrive from the front porch, and four more people file in through another door at the other end of the kitchen. A general hubbub ensues as everyone exchanges their farewells with "Mr. Cole," while I—"Peter Kropotkin From Russia"—am introduced all around by Brad who seems to have taken me under his wing. Meanwhile, the young people mill about the kitchen in seeming chaos fetching plates and silverware and tumblers and such, laying out the meal in the most agreeably informal way. The swinging door seems to come open of its own accord, and I'm not surprised to see the cats pushing the door—too heavy for any one of them to manage—in concert, so that they might depart the kitchen *en masse*.

Everyone takes a seat, and Mike steers me into a place between someone named Sondra and himself. The other newcomers are Zipper and Wendy and TJ. I ask the latter fellow if he is
related to TV, and that draws a laugh from all but Sondra, who
seems to be in the midst of some conflict with Mike. The nature
of the relationships among these young people (except for Dave
and Caitlin, who are clearly a couple) I can only guess. Most
likely they are in a constant state of flux.

Sondra has straight white hair she seems to use to obscure her
features—perhaps because she is angry—and a low, quiet voice.
Wendy is quite striking, with a shaved head and large almond
eyes and a playful, ironic way about her. Zipper is a small, precise young man with Latin features and a thin moustache. He reminds me in appearance and manner of a cowboy I saw in the
West performing deft tricks with a bullwhip. TJ is a dreamy fellow, smelling of turpentine, with shaggy brown hair brushed
back like Lizst, an amiable smile, and slumping posture.

The table, which might comfortably seat six, is snug with nine,
but it feels good to be jostling up against my fellow creatures like
a pup in a litter. They are a boisterous lot, and it's all I can do to
keep their names straight and to follow the general topics of
their slang-laden, telegraphic conversations—often three or four
at once—but when they laugh I join in whether I "get it" or not,
and if I can make some contribution to the various discussions
that surround me, I offer it whether I'm certain of its relevance
or not. And I think to myself, *this* is why I chose to live again—
to be among my fellow creatures exactly so.

The food—broccoli and tofu in garlic sauce over mounds of
steaming rice—is so delicious I eat as if possessed, transported to
another realm. I almost cry for joy. I have not eaten so well in recent years—and could not have tasted such vibrant tastes if I
had. These young taste buds, however, are like an enthusiastic
multitude set on overwhelming me with sensations. I compliment the cook profusely as does everyone else. Brad tells me,
"We all trade our turns cooking with Mike because he's a better
cook than we are."

"The fucker never washes a dish," Dave comments, not without admiration.

"Or cleans a toilet," Wendy adds.

"Turns?" I ask. "You share the household duties?"

"We live communally," Mike says.

"All eight of you?"

They look at each other askance in mock surprise and burst out laughing. "The whole fucking crew," Dave says.

"Dave's the mascot," Caitlin says.

"I've never seen these people before in my life," says Zipper.

"I was here, and they just kept moving in," says TJ.

"That was your old girlfriends," says Wendy.

"No," TJ laments. "They kept moving *out*."

"Don't listen to them," Brad says, in case I don't realize they're just having their fun. "It's really wonderful."

"How splendid," I say.

And it is—a long and leisurely meal with friends such as were the joy of my old life, and I grow sentimental, and drink, perhaps a bit too much. Whenever my beer nears empty, another full bottle appears courtesy of Brad, who can reach the icebox from where he sits by leaning back in his chair until it is almost to the point of pitching over—a calamity which (owing to his great skill acquired no doubt through long evenings of practice) never befalls, in spite of the catcalls and heckling from his companions.

It is perhaps to his good offices I owe the decision, at a particularly raucous point in the proceedings, when I've been toasted and officially welcomed to the table and cries of "speech! speech!" are ill-advisedly offered in my general direction, to rise and propose a toast to the very fine Kitchen Table around which we are so companionably gathered. After Brad ensures that everyone is properly provisioned, I begin:

"To me," I announce with a loving stroke of the table's wooden surface, "the Kitchen Table is more truly a noble and sacred place than any monument or shrine ballyhooed for our edification by Church or State."

(*Applause*)

"The Church would have you visit, at no small expense and discomfort, the moldering bones of some pious ascetic at the site of his gruesome death at the hands of infidels (who more than likely merely wished to be left alone) in order to pay homage to the dead fellow who, never having much enjoyed his own life, saw fit to inflict this wisdom on others by quashing joy wherever it might rear its laughing head—including, I must point out, the sort of frivolity that goes on at this fine Kitchen Table around which we are gathered here this evening!"

(*Applause and table banging and a chorus of Rock of Ages*)

"The State—"

(*boos and hisses*)

"Thank you, thank you. The State, not to be outdone, transforms some innocent cow pasture into a Hallowed Battleground by the generous application of the blood of Common Men who fought and died so that the rich might continue to thrive and to deliver fine speeches about Sacrifice—a ritual known as Patriotism—as essential to the State as miracles to the Church—inspiring others to take up the Hallowing trade, when, if the truth were told, all the Common Man holds dear could be found around his Kitchen Table where he, sadly turned Patriot, will sup no more!"

(*Loud applause and diverse impressions of explosions and whistling shells and battlefield deaths*)

"The Kitchen Table, on the other hand, is the site of all that's best in Man—his sociability, his intellect, his good humor, and his generosity—not a monument to death but a celebration of living, not the theft of life but its sharing, not the jingoistic cant that generally passes for history but here and now, together in solidarity, *this very moment!* I give you: *The Kitchen Table!*"

(*A bedlam of hurrahs and table banging the likes of which would reduce a lesser table to kindling*)

We drink off a toast to Kitchen Tables everywhere to consecrate the matter, and I settle blissfully into my seat, basking in the approving smiles of my young hosts.

As Mike serves coffee, Zipper rolls a cigarette and lights it, passing it to Brad on his left. I catch a whiff of the smoke and realize it's not tobacco but cannabis. I have smoked hashish a couple of times, but usually shied away from such indulgences. I watch the cigarette move from hand to hand and decide that perhaps tonight I will indulge. The second time it reaches me I am struck with a fit of coughing, and I decline it thereafter, though it has already accomplished its purpose in spectacular fashion.

Meanwhile, they explain the workings of their commune to me—how jobs are determined and rotated, how grievances are settled, the history of their experiment. TJ, somewhat older than the others, is one of the original founders of the household. He has lived here almost six years. Sondra is the most recent arrival, having lived here eight months. Most have been here two or three years.

They have a greenhouse and a garden in the small backyard from which they harvest a variety of vegetables, canning the surplus for the winter months. Herbs are their principal cash crops, restaurants their principal customers. The potted plants on the porch (they fill the kitchen windows as well) are also a source of revenue, sold wholesale to various merchants around town. Everyone in the house works five hours a week in the gardens, and the profits cover all household expenses. The discussion of gardens soon has me describing the various gardens Sophie and I tended with much success and affection. This time when the subject comes up, I find it somewhat easier to say I'm a widower. At least I don't break down in tears. But I unearth memories that leave me pensive and silent.

But not for long. Like a child, I am brought out of my funk by the serving of dessert—an ingenious treat I recall from my last visit to America—the ice-cream cone—though my hosts insist with some force that it is *not* ice cream but something called to-futti. Specifically, Fudge Ripple.

"We're vegan," Caitlin informs me. "Do you know what that is?"

"I have several friends who are vegetarian," I assure her, lick-
ing my cone.

"In Russia?"

"In England." The melting of the ice cream—tofutti—has
reached the point that it requires my constant attention.

"You lived in England?"

"Mmmhmmm."

"Where else have you lived?"

I rattle off all the countries I've lived and traveled—showing
off a bit, I suppose—as I try to subdue the remainder of my cone.
"France . . . Switzerland . . . Italy . . . Belgium . . . Siberia . . .
Manchuria . . . Spain . . . Finland . . . Sweden . . . Canada . . ."

Caitlin is quite impressed, but so, I notice out of the corner of
my eye, is Mike, who has been listening to our conversation. I
turn, and he looks away guiltily as if eavesdropping on some intimate revelation. How odd, I think. It occurs to me that if he is
familiar with my biography, he might note the coincidence that
I have lived and traveled all the places the "Anarchist Prince"
did. I chide myself for being so indiscreet.

Fortunately, the conversation moves on to other matters. But I
continue to question my anxiety over being discovered, my secret revealed. How will I go through life without being able to
answer the simplest questions about my past? Not that I haven't
had to conceal my identity before. But there can be no "among
friends" here. I am, as far as I know, a faction of one.

But more disturbingly, how can I possibly be discovered
when no sane person will believe the truth should they discover
it? I could tell the whole tale now and not a soul at this table
would believe it to be anything other than another H. G. Wells
scientific romance. The beer and the cannabis combine to render
this latter paradox with particular clarity, as well as its corol-
lary: Since I am clearly impossible, the real risk I run is to be
found out to be *someone I'm not*—a much worse fate it seems to
me—too common among men as it is without my adding to the
store. And already it's true that I'm not who I am—for even as
gregarious a fellow as myself is effectively silenced by such de-

liberations, and I sit as silent as a saltcellar for what seems an eternity.

But no one notices, for they are passionately arguing some controversy involving the university art department—something to do with requirements and credits, tracks and programs. Most of them seem to be artists of one sort or another, though I gather Wendy is not since she shows her boredom with the subject through a delightful repertoire of exaggerated yawns. I find the discussion difficult to follow and wonder what it has to do with the making of art. But after a while, when the names of faculty are used as shorthand for the various factions as if they were the commanders of contending armies in pitched battle to the death, it all starts to sound familiar. I have heard this sort of talk before, in one context or another, only to later come upon the supposedly warring commanders in a pub commiserating over their woes and a few pints, denouncing the various potentates above *them* in much the same terms. Thus many a splendid evening passes, but no one is a step closer to freedom, for all accept the hierarchy and their places in it, and never come together to resolve their common difficulties.

Caitlin thinks to ask my opinion. "Perhaps, art does not need a department, a track, a requirement, or a credit," I say. "I should think it might prefer its freedom."

"That is so true," Caitlin says, and she and the others talk unabashedly of freedom. That's why I like young people. They'll still talk about freedom. They haven't resigned themselves to bondage or, worse, deluded themselves into believing it's freedom.

I notice Sondra staring at me. She has secured her hair behind one ear so that she may accomplish this feat. "How old are you?" she asks.

"Thirty-two," I say, a lie I've sufficiently rehearsed by now to half believe it myself.

"I've been watching you," she says. "Sometimes you seem like an old man. Other times you're like a little boy. You don't seem like some guy in his thirties. Do you know what I mean?"

"Yes, I do."

"Is that a Russian thing?"

"I don't think so."

"It's interesting," she says. "It makes you seem . . . complete—wired and smooth at the same time."

"This gathering has cheered me considerably."

She nods soberly. "I don't think anything just happens, you know? I think things happen because people want them to happen. Like you coming here tonight for dinner. You *wanted* to be here, or otherwise you wouldn't be." She watches me carefully for the least sign of disagreement.

"That is undeniably true," I say.

Her eyes narrow as she poses her question, *the* question it would seem by the way she asks it, "So why did you want to have dinner with a weird bunch of strangers?"

It seems a sincere question, prompted by an insatiable curiosity, without any intention of rudeness. "I am a stranger myself."

She studies me for a moment. "But we could've been like Manson or something. I live with these people, but still, you know, they are truly strange."

I don't know who Manson is and decide not to ask. "But Mike and the others had just done me a good turn by sharing their limousine. Their eccentricities mattered little. I'm sure I seem equally odd to them. In any event, this evening has certainly turned out well, so I am confirmed in my trusting ways, however unusual they may be."

"I guess so," she says, though she hardly sounds convinced. "I hope you don't mind that I ask so many questions. I'm a poet. I try to understand people, you know?"

"A splendid goal. My brother used to say that poetry requires a discriminating mind as much as a way with words."

"I like that. Is he in Russia?"

"He is dead."

She flinches ever so slightly at the word. "You said . . . about your wife earlier. Is anyone still living, in your family I mean?"

"No. No one."

She stares at me. I fear she might start crying, but she does not. "I'm twenty-two, and no one close to me has ever died."

"Don't be in any hurry for that experience," I say.

"See?" she says, attempting a smile. "Just what an old man would say."

Shortly thereafter, when I'm occupied in another conversation, she leaves the table. "Has Sondra gone?" I ask Mike when I discover her absence.

"Who knows?" he says with a scowl. "She's probably holed up in her room writing about the *moment*." He packs as much dismissal into his utterance of this phrase as he possibly can, and I realize that despite his talent and intelligence, Mike is nonetheless a *young* man. Emma used to say that it was a rare man who could accept a woman as his equal, and I'm saddened to find it may still be so.

"It's her turn to do the dishes," Dave comments, as if that explains her absence.

Just as spontaneously as it was set, the table is cleared, and the dishes are stacked in the sink. This time I take part in the labors. All but TJ (who is waiting to meet a friend) and Sondra are going out to a club (I gather they mean a nightclub) where Hemlock Cocktail will be performing. "You want to come hear us play?" Mike asks me.

And up to that moment, I no doubt would have said yes, but suddenly I'm aware of how tired I am, that night has fallen, and that I must make my way home in the dark. With pleasure I recall a bit of American baseball slang I learned my first time in America: "I'll take a rain check on that. I have work in the morning, and I want to go to the library beforehand."

I thank everyone profusely and wish the band a successful performance. I linger until it's down to me and TJ (and Sondra up in her room writing). I ask TJ if it would be all right if I washed the dishes.

"That's awful nice of you," he says. He points out soap and sponge, and leaves me to them. I have long been an advocate of the benefits of labor-saving machinery, but after a day with a dish-washing machine, I confess a certain pleasure in washing these dishes the old-fashioned way. There's a window above the sink where I can see my face reflected, and it's not so bad as before to see the redheaded fellow there. It is I, Peter Kropotkin, thirty-two years old, a recent immigrant from another planet, in all important respects not so very different from the one where I was born.

8 ॐ Accidental Encounters

If two hours after sunset of any day a slave be found in this city absent from his owner's or employer's tenement without such pass in writing as is herein after mentioned, he may be punished with stripes.
—From An Ordinance concerning Negroes, Richmond, 1859

Now, *here*, you see, it takes all the running *you* can do, to keep in the same place. If you want to get somewhere else, you must run at least twice as fast as that!
—LEWIS CARROLL, *Through the Looking-Glass*

I walk into the muggy night headed west. While it is not quite raining, the streets are slick from the moisture hanging in the air, condensing on every surface. The streetlamps are haloed in mist, and the smells of automobiles and animal urine are borne through the air as if a dirty rag were being held beneath my nose. Keeping to the quieter residential streets, I meet no one. I'm a few blocks east of Meadow, which I'll have to take across the canyonlike road between me and the river, Caitlin referred to as the RMA, but for now I prefer this quiet street to the lights and traffic of the more heavily traveled thoroughfare.

I enjoy the solitude. No one else is out of doors at what strikes me as an early hour—ten o'clock I'd say, but don't bother to verify it with the watch in my pocket. The leafy canopy blocks most of the light from the streetlamps and dapples everything with shadows, muting even my riotous shirt, so that I feel almost invisible, like a ghost. But I am real. I am here, *in the future*. I lived my whole life wanting to reach the future—a just and equitable future. I haven't reached it yet, obviously, but it stands to reason I'm that much closer, or so it seems to me.

The powerful revere the past and distrust the future, for it's the past that's yielded them power, and it's the future that will take it away. So they try to put a stop to the future where it begins—in the minds of men. In '86 my brother Sasha committed suicide while exiled in Siberia for a "political offence"—the crime of wanting a future better than the past. Sasha was exiled for his thoughts, for the mere dream of that future. He was no revolutionist, a much more moderate man than myself, and yet his life was wasted in exile. When he shot himself, it was because he despaired of that future ever coming to pass in even the smallest, most personal way.

One of the last times we spoke before his exile, he was in a dark mood. *Comes the revolution,* I used to say, to preface any evocation of a better world. He stopped me midsentence just as I uttered the catchphrase to ask if I really *meant* it, or whether it was just a metaphor, like a liberal Christian's "Second Coming." Did I really *believe,* he wanted to know, in that revolution, in that future? It was a question I had asked myself a thousand times, and I was ready with an answer. "I couldn't ask men to risk arrest or death for a metaphor," I said. "I couldn't dedicate my life to a metaphor."

He placed his hand on the side of my face as if we were boys again, and he the consoling elder brother. "Don't despair," he said, though it was clear that *he* was the one despairing, and it wasn't until years later, when I heard of his death, that I understood he wasn't offering encouragement, but a warning.

"Don't despair," I remind myself now. The future is not what I thought it would be. In some ways, perhaps, things are worse. But comes the revolution, the future will be better than the past.

I am joined in my ruminations by a belled cat who follows me, hops atop a low brick wall, then quickens his pace, drawing abreast of me at hand height so that I might scratch his head if I like. I oblige him, and he purrs a pleasant rumble—of his own free will. We part at the corner as I turn south toward the river; I hear him jingling off to the east to await the next passerby.

In some of the homes I can see people about their business, often lounging before a flickering glow. I stop and stare into one of these parlors as I see the glow for what it is. It's television. An enormous automobile is rumbling up a beautiful mountainside to no apparent purpose except to demonstrate the sheer power of the thing, spewing rocks and gravel in all directions, bouncing over boulders. The geographer in me is horrified. Is there no concern of avalanche or erosion? What havoc might these behemoths wreak on a watershed? In the center of the image the word MUTE in red hovers mysteriously. I feel a chill.

"Ugly, isn't it?"

I'm not entirely surprised to find Anchee standing beside me. I suspected he couldn't manage to stay out of things and would show up sooner or later. With his long white robes, he would appear quite the oddity if anyone were to turn away from the TV and look out the window. He doesn't appear concerned, however, even though time is clearly flowing: The treetops rustle in a light breeze; images continue to spew from the TV like rocks and gravel.

"It's worse than ugly," I say.

He looks doubtful whether anything could be worse than ugly. "It's an infestation actually. The carcasses will endure for millennia. But I haven't come to discuss cars. You're not happy with me. I thought we might talk things over." He puts his arm around my shoulders, and I shrug it off.

"What if I don't want to talk with you?"

He shrugs. "Then I'll come back in a minute, five minutes, or five minutes ago. Or five years from now at midnight. It's all the same to me. Some moment I'll catch you in a talkative mood. It might as well be now."

Accept your fate, the oppressor says. He is showing his true stripes, this "benefactor"—just another bully, just another braggart. I should've known from his talk of magic, not to trust him, for he fancies himself a magician, a wizard, a philosopher-king.

"I have only one thing to say to you: Leave me alone. I intend to lead my own life without any interference from you."

He looks as if I've hurt his feelings. "'Interference.' You're still mad about Tim Binder, aren't you? I agree it was clumsy, but nothing more subtle would work. At first I tried steering the dog and the woman away, but there's a cat down the street, then some hunk of stained glass, or the direction of the wind—who *knows* what—but *always* with the same result: If left alone with your thoughts, you pine, you despair, you take off. Several different destinations, interestingly enough. One dismal failure after another. Only when a fellow human shows up and offers you a ride could I get you to the cathedral." He speaks with the conviction of a hardworking dispatcher entrusted with getting the trains to run on time without smashing them into each other.

"And why was it so damn important that I reach the cathedral?"

"I think you know."

"I want to hear you say it."

"So that you could run into Rachel."

"And why does that matter?"

"You don't think she matters? I thought you were quite taken with her."

I am not a violent man, but I consider strangling Anchee and am dissuaded only by the fact that he's a foot taller than I. "Does she know about this?"

"Well, you're not too subtle . . ."

"I don't mean *that*. I mean you and whatever the hell you're up to. Does she know about that?"

My tone doesn't seem to register with him. He, in fact, seems amused by it. "No, she doesn't know about me. And what I'm 'up to,' ultimately, is trying to make a better world, Peter, just as you always were."

"And how will using people like puppets accomplish that?"

"I haven't forced you or her or anyone else to do a thing. She likes you, Peter. She really does. She's a closet radical living in Richmond, Virginia. You can't imagine what a godsend you are."

"You've manipulated—"

"I've merely created fresh opportunities."

"'Fresh opportunities'? And how do you do that?"

"I revise. I stop time, change a variable, try it again."

"Until I do what you want."

"No, no, no. You misjudge me. I have no fixed agenda. My interest is more . . . how shall I put it—"

"Aesthetic," I suggest dryly.

"Yes, you could say that."

"You'll allow me that line, will you? How kind. What about ethical? What is your stand on slavery, exactly?"

He makes an apologetic face. "This isn't helping, is it?"

"You deceived me."

"What did you think? That I would give you a new life and not take an interest?"

"An *interest*?"

"Think of it as a helping hand—mutual aid. Besides I didn't have to let you know anything was going on at all. I could've worked entirely behind the scenes. But when Tim proved to be so chatty, I thought I'd just have fun with it."

"That's why you came up with that nonsense of the five twenties?"

"Yes, exactly. I rather liked that, didn't you?"

"I most definitely did not. I felt like a mouse batted about for a cat's pleasure."

He rolls his eyes. "I did it to *intrigue* you, to get your juices flowing. And it worked too. Admit it. Would you *rather* have remained in bored ignorance?"

"I would rather you left me *alone*!"

"But no one's 'alone,' not like that anyway."

I recall the question I wished I'd asked before. "Are there others here like me?"

He feigns confusion rather badly. The distant future, for all its accomplishments, apparently lacks acting classes. "Like you?" he queries.

"You know what I mean."

He shrugs off the pretense. "No, you are unique. This is *your* time, Peter, as I said before. Only *you* are aware of that fact; only *you* have that perspective. There are what we call accidentals, but they don't matter—merely a side effect."

"Accidentals?"

"This place is particularly prone to them. It's obsessed with the past, constantly suppressing it, resurrecting it, worrying over it, opening old wounds, so that the past is always close to the surface. If the balance is upset, sometimes it breaks through."

"Breaks through how?"

"I believe it was *who* we were speaking of. Accidentals are people displaced in time with no control, no perspective. They can't figure out where they are or why. They're totally lost."

"Is my neighbor Earl one of these 'accidentals'?"

"I thought you wanted me to stay out of things. Now, you'd have me answer all your questions. Which is it going to be, Peter?"

"It's going to be *both,* Anchee. Well?"

His eyes dance with delight. "You're just as I imagined—spirited, smart. Yes, of course. Earl is one."

"And what has upset this 'balance' you spoke of?"

"You," he says, pouncing on the question as if he's just been waiting for me to ask it. "The effect of transplanting someone like you into a place like this can be enormous. Like tossing a boulder in a still pond."

"And Earl?"

Another dismissive shrug. "He got caught up in your current, you might say. Earl went to sleep in 1864 and woke up in 1995 without a clue."

"But that's four years ago."

"Yes? You have a problem with that? You still don't get it, do you? Time isn't a string of beads. An event at the equator might wash debris ashore at any latitude."

He wants to talk about this sort of thing, how his magic works, not mundane details like Earl; but I feel as if I'm discussing Newton with a hangman while he knots his rope. He might talk as if Earl just happened to show up here, but I strongly suspect Anchee put him here deliberately. Here's a man in control of time. He can hardly plead ignorance of consequence.

"Look, Anchee. I don't care at the moment what time is or isn't, whether it's a string, a ball, or a bloody jack-in-the-box. What I want to know is *why* you've brought me here."

He crosses his arms and sniffs. "But only moments ago you said you wanted me to leave you alone, so that you could live your own life. If I tell you what you want to know, that knowledge *alone*—whether I 'interfere' or not—is bound to affect your actions. Are you sure you *want* to know? Aren't you concerned for your *freedom*?" It's all a bit too theatrical and posturing, as if we were characters in one of Wilde's plays, and it occurs to me that all his bad acting might be intentional, part of the pose, whatever it is.

I'm not a crude man, but I have just spent an evening with Dave, who would know exactly the un-Wildean reply this sophism deserves, and I decide to employ it. "Fuck you, Anchee. Just tell me the truth."

He smiles. "It's like this: I brought you here because you are, in several important respects, the exact opposite of this place. It's obsessed with the past and slavery. You're equally obsessed, but with freedom and the future. This place loathes change; you live for it. But you get the idea." He holds his fists facing each other and hits them together like contending rams. "I want to see what will happen."

It occurs to me that he may simply be insane, some sort of rogue from the future wreaking havoc throughout time. "So you've brought me here to stir things up, to make a mess, to throw a few bombs and assassinate a few people? If that's what you intend, you don't understand me at all."

"Maybe *that's* the point—to understand you, I mean. I've studied you, read everything you ever wrote, but still, there's always a limit. Only in your actions will I understand—but I'd be very much surprised if you threw any bombs or harmed a single soul. I'd be equally surprised if you didn't manage to stir things up."

I decide to voice a growing suspicion concerning his motives. "Is this a race issue for you?"

"You learn quickly: All issues are race issues here. But as for *me personally,* as they would say it these days—no. My appearance has misled you. I don't really look like this." He holds up his fists again. Only now one is black and one is white. He strikes them together, and in the blink of an eye, his appearance has changed: He is identical in all respects except his white robe is now black, and his black skin is now white.

I'm not sure why such a simple transformation is so terrifying, but I find myself a bit wobbly in the knees, and it's all I can do to put up a brave front. "I don't care what it is you want me to do," I say. "I won't do it."

He opens his palms to the sky, the soul of innocence. "But all I want you to do is simply be here, to do whatever you want. That's all. I won't 'interfere' anymore. I promise."

"If all you wanted was for me to 'be' here, why did you go to such lengths to arrange a rendezvous with Rachel?"

"She'll be good for you. You'll see. You'll be happier."

"I'll decide that."

"Yes, you will. But I've seen the future."

I close my eyes in exasperation and heave a sigh, and when I open them, he's gone. I sincerely hope I never lay eyes on him again. I draw up short of wishing I had never seen him in the first place—for then all wishes would be moot—and I have to ask myself: *Are you still as afraid of death as all that?*

I hurry over to Meadow and the lights and the traffic. There are several people on foot here, mostly on the move, though a few hang out on the corners engaged in some clandestine business or other. A woman offers to sell me some "flag," and I decline without lingering to inquire just what she means. Nearly everyone on foot is black but me, and it's almost as if I can see the links of the chains that anchor this place to the past wrapped around their ankles.

At night, the grimness of the area is rendered more vividly by the harsh glare of electric lights from all directions—streetlights, automobiles speeding through, blazing bright businesses, traffic signals. This place must never sleep—and looks it. Even though these tired buildings are at least as old as those in the Fan, there are no proud plaques here, only NO TRESPASSING signs. Flyers proclaiming NO MORE PRISONS! festoon one of the light poles. Even the newer buildings are a pitiful sight. As I approach what is by far the finest building in the area, obviously new and faced with polished stone, I'm not surprised to see that it's a police precinct station.

I cross to the other side of the road and pass an old black man sitting on a crate in the middle of a side lot littered with broken glass, in clear view of the station house. He must be near eighty years old—the age of old Peter, wrinkled and dying in Dmitrov. I wish the man a good evening, but he looks right through me with half-blind eyes, muttering quietly to himself. On the steps of the police station, an officer smokes a cigarette and observes my passing. I wonder if he can see the old man any better than the old man can see him. *There's a crime for you*, I want to shout at the policeman, *this poor old man!*

But I don't imagine policemen have changed much since my day. To want the job they must, it seems to me, either be cynical opportunists or true believers in the State, though I've known many to be both. *We don't make the laws*, they will tell you. Nor do they question them. The law comes down to them like Moses off the mountain, and they obey. So that the simple human compassion the young policeman might feel for the wasted old man sitting in filth not a hundred yards away from him is eclipsed by the State and its laws. Let this old man somehow manage to break laws and not hearts, and he'll suddenly become visible.

In prison there were old men who'd been there since childhood or early youth—of whom it was often said, "once in prison, always in prison." When one died, four fellow prisoners would carry him to the common grave, the graveyard warder and his black dog being the only two beings to follow him; and while the prison priest marched in front of the procession, mechanically reciting his prayer and looking round at the chestnut or fir trees along the road, and the four comrades carrying the coffin were enjoying the momentary freedom from confinement, the black dog would be the only being affected by the solemnity of the ceremony.

I lower my head and hurry through the dark, down to the river, the sound of that dog's plaintive whimpering resounding in my memory, in my breast. Prisons don't require walls—only laws and prisoners, guards and graves, and a priest to bless the whole business. As for me, I'll cast my lot with that black dog.

The iron stairs down to the river, while spooky during the day, are positively terrifying at night, at least in my current frame of mind. Only the pencil-thin shaft of light from my flashlight marks my slippery-footed way, and the accelerating echoes of my footsteps simultaneously rush to meet me from below and descend upon me from above. At the bottom, I burst into the night, almost knocking over a trash bin, thrashing the darkness with my flashlight beam, my heart racing.

My hoped-for refuge—the charming, ivy-clad woods—offers nothing but murky, rustling shadows. A light gust stirs leaves and limbs to hiss and creak and groan, while a chorus of frogs and insects sings an unvarying anthem. An owl is the occasional soloist, a great horned if I remember the call correctly. I smile at my own fears. This is nothing but a night in the woods, a welcome companion in times past. Have I come to the future so that I might learn to fear the dark? After the day I've had, it's my fatigue I should fear. As strong and fit as my rejuvenated body may be, I am completely exhausted.

I find the way and plunge into the woods, keeping my light

trained on the path to avoid pitching over roots or twisting my ankle in a hole. A dozen yards down the trail I walk into a spider's web and feel the panicked fellow beating a hasty retreat across my beard. I assist his flight with the back of my hand. To fend off any others of his tribe who might be lying in ambush, I take up a stick and advance as before but with a wooden foil thrusting and parrying gossamer attacks.

But while my way is clear, there is still a great dark night all around me. And my light doesn't banish the shadows at the periphery of my vision, shadows that sometimes move inexplicably, shadows that vanish before I can find them with my beam of light. *Shadows*, I scold myself, *of your exhausted brain!*

But try as I might, I cannot shake the feeling that I am not alone. I have had no small experience at being followed. The authorities—always certain I was up to some mischief or other, plotting some anarchist madness—dispatched hordes of spies to follow me about wherever I went. I *was* always plotting, it is true—where I did all my plotting—in my head, whether I was in Piccadilly or the greengrocer's. It never occurred to the authorities that it was my *ideas* that were dangerous, and no army of spies could render them any less so.

But this shadow behind me now is of a different order from those old spies. They used to keep a prescribed distance, no doubt recommended in some memorandum, so that when I stopped, a clump of them would accumulate across the street or down the block like crows on a fence. This shadow, however, comes ever closer by degrees. It might only be curious, wanting a better look, or it might be stalking me. Or it might be my imagination. It's time to settle the matter, in any event. Fear is fear and must be faced.

Ahead of me lies a break in the tree cover, a ten-yard stretch of sandy trail before the woods again shroud it in deeper shadows. I hurriedly develop a plan. If it's mere foolishness, at least there will be no witnesses.

As I enter the clearing, I look behind me over my shoulder, careful to keep my flashlight pointed down the trail, my wooden foil wagging. I count my paces as I trudge on without watching where I'm going, peering into the darkness at my back. I have not counted five paces when I see a shadow following me that is no tree—unless it walks on two roots. At the count of ten, I stop, and he keeps coming for a couple of paces before he realizes his mistake and stops himself. I turn my light upon him and see that he is black, lean and wiry—dressed in rough peasant trousers cinched with a rope, nothing else. His face is creased with fear and pain and desperation. He raises his hands to block the light, and I lower it from his eyes. His bare feet are heavily callused.

He is no more of this time than I—I'm certain of it—not only because of his old-fashioned dress, but because of the look I saw in those eyes—like Coleridge's Mariner adrift on a wide, salt sea. I recall Anchee's description of the accidentals: *They can't figure out where they are or why. They're totally lost.* That I should encounter two of them in so short a time cannot be mere coincidence. Either there are a legion of them, or, as I strongly suspect, Anchee has literally placed them in my path to see what I'll do.

"I am Peter Kropotkin," I say. "I am new here also." I drop my stick in case he might think it pretends to be a weapon. I offer my hand.

I think it's the hand that decides him I should be avoided at all costs. What sort of white man offers his hand to a runaway slave in these dark woods in the middle of the night? One not alone, perhaps, or concealing a pistol or lash. His pain doesn't give him the luxury to ponder such questions. Saying not a word, he wheels about and bolts into the woods. I shine my light after him, and the beam falls square upon his back, slick with blood. His dark skin is striped with scars both old and fresh that could only have been made with a lash.

I don't recall when it was I first learned what such scars look like. I already knew, when, still a boy, I happened upon Frol in the heat of a summer's day kneeling by the river with his shirt off.

"Frol!" I whispered in shocked surprise when I saw his heavily striped back. Somehow my childish mind had exempted the dignified Frol from such humiliation.

He knew immediately what I was speaking of. "Don't mind those, Petya. Trophies of youth." He put his shirt on even though he was still dripping wet, and the fabric clung to him. My eyes went to his stripes, clearly visible through the wet cloth. "As we get older we take our blows to the soul and spare the flesh," he said. The flash of his sardonic smile broke my young heart. *You will do the same*, it seemed to say. *You'll be your father someday, Little Prince.*

This memory washes over me as I watch this man retreating into the darkness like a wounded animal, and I dash into the woods after him. I have the advantage of the light, and for a time I gain on him, but the light also makes me more cautious, while he never slackens in his headlong charge into the darkness. He runs like someone running for his life, which, I imagine, if he were in his own time, he would most certainly be. Try as I might, throwing caution to the winds, I cannot keep up. Soon I lose sight of him and slow to a walk, when I hear a crash up ahead and imagine he has fallen. I put on a burst of speed and almost trip over the same root that must have been his undoing. He is on all fours in the sand, blowing like a winded horse. His body is wet with sweat and blood, crusted with sand. As I approach, he rolls over and springs to his feet, crouching in the trail.

"Come near me, white man, and I kill you, I swear, with my bare hands!"

"Then I shall not come near you," I say with conviction, taking a generous step backward, hoping this is a successfully negotiated treaty. "You need a shirt." I start unbuttoning mine. "You should have those wounds looked after as well." I take off my shirt and offer it to him. He suspects a trap, so I toss it on the ground at his feet and retreat another step.

"What do you want with me? You the law?"

I cringe at the thought. "I am no law of any kind, I assure you. I was wondering if you could tell me the date?"

His head snaps back at this *non sequitur*, and he looks a little less like a panther poised to spring. "The *date?*"

I am calm, pleasant, nothing at all like a policeman. "The date."

He peers at me. "Why you ask?"

I shrug. "Why won't you tell me?"

"Thirtieth. August."

"And the year?"

"You don't know the *year*?"

"I know. You must listen to me: *You* are the one who doesn't know what year it is. This is not your time. *You have traveled to a different time.* Surely you've noticed. Does this feel like August in Virginia to you? How long have you been here? Long enough to see that things aren't right?"

We have run far enough east so that one of the automobile bridges is within earshot a few hundred yards away. The droning of the machines' passage testifies to the truth of what I'm saying, and I can see he listens carefully to every word, even though his face is contorted with pain. He listens, but he has no reason to trust me, to believe my incredible nonsense. I offer a deal: "I'll tell you what year it *really* is, if you'll tell me what year you think it is."

He wipes the sweat out of his eyes with a trembling hand, licks his lips. He's in a very bad way. "All right, then. What year you think it is?"

"It's 1999. What year do you think it is?"

He gives his head a harsh shake. His breath comes in quick pants. "*Nineteen ninety-nine!*" he shouts and straightens up, wincing from the effort. "What kind of fool you take me for? It's *1800*, and you be *crazy*, so I let you go." He sways back and forth, almost dead on his feet. "Just take this shirt here, and be on my way." He bends to pick up the shirt and crumples to one knee, then pitches forward, rendered unconscious by loss of blood, his terrible pain, and the truth he must know in his bones—however much he may deny it—that this is not his world.

I check him for symptoms of shock, and cover his back with

my shirt to staunch the bleeding. We are close to the road. I could easily climb the embankment, flag down a vehicle, and seek official help, but I am loath to turn this poor man over to the authorities. Two centuries ago, he was a slave, and freshly beaten by the looks of it. If he wakes up in a modern hospital with no one in the world to speak up for him, his wounds may be tended to, but he would soon be branded a lunatic—and would no doubt become one. I can't let that happen.

Anchee said these accidentals have *no control, no perspective*, implying that if they can somehow acquire control and perspective, they might keep a grip on their sanity. I am the only person, if Anchee is to be believed, who can provide a sane perspective for this man, the only one who will do him the simple courtesy of believing he is who he says he is, that he knows what he says he knows, and feels what he says he feels. As for control, once the State gets ahold of him, he might as well never have left slavery behind.

I peel my already blood-soaked shirt from his back and examine his wounds more closely. They want cleaning and dressing. Some could use stitches, though he's had worse in years past that went untreated. I think I'm up to the task. Fortunately, he's not a big man. I manage to hoist him onto my shoulders, stagger down to the river, and set him down on the beach, careful not to let his back touch the ground.

From the debris deposited by the last flood, I extricate four modest-sized limbs and lay them side by side next to the water. With regret that their hard day's service should end so, I remove Tasteful Trousers from my knapsack and cut them into long strips with my pocketknife, then use the strips to lash the logs into a raft. I slide it into the water, and it does indeed float. I find a plank that will serve as rudder and oar, then lay my passenger on board, propping his head up on my knapsack to keep his head above water. I shove off, jumping astride the stern as if it were a broad-backed horse, intending to float downstream to my island, where I can make a fire, boil some bandages, and bind his wounds.

My raft is not a nimble steed, and it proves to be a bumpy ride, careening from rock to rock, and I fear I will dash out my patient's brains or drown him in the river before I can attend to his back. But eventually we beach on my island with a reassuring crunch of sand. I dismount in the water and push the stern with me as I wade ashore. Crouching by the raft, I pull my patient onto the island. The unburdened raft buoys up and catches the current, slipping down the channel before I can stop it. I half carry, half drag him to the nestlike depression where I slept what seems ages ago, but was only last night.

But this is no time for reflection. The river has chilled me, and out here on the water there is a stiff breeze blowing. A fit of shivering overtakes me, and I hurriedly strip off my wet trousers and pull on my dungarees, knit shirt, and jacket, dancing around to warm myself up. I'll be no good to either one of us if I catch a chill.

I kneel down beside him out of the wind, wring the blood from the Hawaiian shirt, and lay it over his wounds again for the time being. I pull off his wet trousers and cover him with my blanket. I drape our wet clothes over a bush and wash my white shirt in the river. Once I boil it thoroughly clean, it is destined for bandages.

I set about building a fire. There is plenty of driftwood, and the beaver has been kind enough to leave a few uneaten sticks beside his lodge. The kindling and matches I stowed inside a plastic bag are dry, so the business goes smoothly.

As I kneel before a tiny pyre, feeding it beaver sticks, my guest lifts his head, looks all around, taking in everything—me, the island, the river, the horizon. His eyes focus for a considerable time on the enormous brightly lit buildings downstream. His head drops, and he is out again, but with a more serene look on his face, it seems to me. It's not hard to imagine reasons why: Crazy I might be, but I'm no overseer; there are no whipping posts and shackles on this island; and those impossible buildings—as frightening and inexplicable as they are—must reassure him that he's very, very far from home. Perhaps far enough to be free.

I put water on to boil, and, as I watch the pot, I tear my white shirt into strips for bandages. Somewhere I imagine, Anchee watches and smiles.

All I want you to do is simply be here, to do whatever you want. That's all.

But what is it I "want" under such extraordinary circumstances? What is the right thing to do? If Anchee may be believed, I am responsible for this poor fellow's finding himself lost in a strange new world. Technically, he is no longer a slave, but what good will freedom do him, if this world drives him mad?

They don't matter—a side effect, Anchee says of the accidentals.

And I, apparently, am the desired *effect*—a unique class of one. I'm familiar with the rhetoric of oppression: This class, this race, this party truly matters; all others are secondary. All the indignities this man ever suffered as a slave were mere *side effects* to those who beat him and prospered from his labors—their prosperity being the positive *effects* of their unquestioned privilege. When I met Varina Davis, I expressed the opinion that a great injustice was done when the slaves, though proclaimed free, were given for their subsistence, not even an inch of the soil that they had cultivated. She told me that in the eyes of the South (by which she meant the eyes of upper class white racist Southerners) the great injustice was that the slaveholders had not been adequately compensated for the loss of their legal property—*the slaves!*

What does one say to such a stubborn hold on bigotry? I asked her whether she thought the rapist should be entitled to any offspring that might result from his assault upon an innocent woman, and she told me, quite forcefully, that she certainly did not, and why on earth would I ask such a horrid question?

But that's old history. This poor wretch faces a whole new set of difficulties. Twice, it seems, his life has been stolen from him—while I—through no virtue of my own—have embarked upon my second. I must do what I can to restore the balance.

I'm not so naive as to accept Anchee's haughty dismissal of

the accidentals' importance at face value. It may very well have been a means of predisposing me to the exact course I've adopted, deliberately playing upon my sentiments, manipulating me. He did promise not to interfere any further, but what possible meaning could "any further" have for Anchee? He can "promise" not to interfere, because the job is already done. The spies have all been hired and have their instructions, innocent people have been tossed about in time like ninepins, and here I sit—right on cue?—tearing my clothes to shreds. The whole business could be arranged as nicely as a clockwork automaton in a shop window: *Kropotkin on the James.* Does he charge admission, I wonder? *I've seen the future,* he says—he who won't even admit of *reality.*

But if anything he's said makes any sense at all, then he misspoke, for he should have said he's seen *a* future. To which I reply, *well so have I!*

Enough. I have been tearing my shirt with increasing force. A pile of white strips fills my lap. Anchee doesn't matter, the future either. What would I do differently? Would I send this man to an asylum or abandon him in the woods? Shall I roll him into the river right now to show what a free man I am? No. I can't concern myself with Anchee's madness. I have to muddle along with my own!

"Do you know what you're doing?" a voice speaks to me out of the darkness, and I jump a foot into the air. It is Earl, standing on the same rock he occupied when first I met him only this morning. He points to the future bandages, my former shirt, now scattered on the ground at my feet.

"I have treated wounds before," I say, sounding more confident than I have a right to.

He grunts a doubtful response and wades across the water with something cradled in his arms. He sets it by the fire, and I see it is a doctor's case, an old one by the look of it, without a trace of plastic in evidence. DR. EARL HOLLANDER in a florid script is engraved upon the brass nameplate. "I am a doctor," he says lest I doubt it. He opens the case, and there are gleaming instruments inside. He kneels beside the patient. "You have a light?"

I hand him the flashlight.

"Boil those," he says, meaning the strips I'm gathering up from the ground.

"That was my intention," I say, depositing a handful into the pot.

He removes the Hawaiian shirt from the patient's back and drops it in the sand with a plop. While Earl lays out his instruments on a strip of red velvet beside the patient and examines the wounds, I retrieve the Hawaiian shirt and wash it in the river. Even in the dark of night I can see the river cloud with blood and then run clear. I'm sure it has seen such blood before, more than its share. I wring the shirt hard and hang it with the trousers.

Earl beckons me. "Come and hold the light."

9 ✆ Effective Medication

[We are suffering with] very cold weather. Four or five men chilled to death last night. A large portion of the prisoners who have been in confinement any length of time have been reduced to skeletons from continued hunger, exposure and filth. No wood tonight, and it's very cold. The nights are long and are made hideous by the moans of suffering wretches. . . . Men are too weak to walk nights to keep warm and sink down and chill to death . . . from 15 to 20 and 25 die every day and are buried just outside the prison with no coffins—nothing but canvas wrapped around them.

—JOHN RANSOM, prisoner on Belle Isle, 1863

Most of all, Richmond was a slave town. Slaves and free blacks numbered just above half of the roughly 5,700 residents in 1800. In nearby Henrico County, out of which Richmond recently had been carved, 4,600 more bondpersons toiled in the tobacco and wheat fields; there too . . . whites were a minority. . . . Standing at the heart of Richmond itself was the "public Whipping post," where squeamish whites could send their human property to be disciplined.

—DOUGLAS R. EGERTON, *Gabriel's Rebellion*

For over an hour, I shine the flashlight on the poor man's back as Earl expertly cleans and sutures the wounds. Neither one of us speaks except of the task at hand. There is simply too much to say, too many questions. We owe it to the patient not to distract ourselves until we have done all we can for him. It is hard to contemplate his wounds for such a long time, and it takes its toll on both of us. It's not merely the gore, which one grows used to, but imagining the hand that held the lash and tore the flesh over and over again, the mind behind the hand, the society that would have it so, and the State that would make it law. *All issues are race issues here,* echoes through my thoughts. How large is that "here," I wonder—this city, this state, this country, this time?

The light grows dim, the batteries included apparently failing, but Earl is almost finished. At his suggestion, I turn the flashlight off and put some more wood on the fire. My hand is cramped from holding the light, and my legs are stiff. It feels good to move about. The fresh wood catches, and floods our little island with warmth and light. Earl and I glow like a pair of demons or ghosts haunting the river, attending to a fallen comrade.

"Were you a doctor on Belle Isle?" I ask.

"I'm a doctor wherever I go," he says. He nods at his patient. "Runaway?"

"There is no more slavery here."

"Tell that to him." He cuts the last bandage with his scissors, drops his instruments into the boiling water, and rises to his feet, a little unsteady for having knelt so long.

"He thinks it's August 30, 1800," I say.

"He must be crazy then."

"Must be. Does that date mean anything to you?"

"No. Before my time."

"What is your time, Earl?"

"You're the one with the watch, or did you swap it to some other fellow?"

"I don't mean the time of day. What is the date where you came from, Earl?"

"No dates. No names." He looks downstream, and I circle around him so that he must face me, but he will not look me in the eye.

"You already gave me your name."

"I take it back."

"You thought it was 1864, didn't you, Earl—and then everything changed?"

"I don't think anything. I have no opinions, no beliefs."

"It's 1999. Do you know that?"

"So I've been told." He holds his palm as if it supports a sheet of paper, and points at it with his other hand. "Put your name here, your so-so security number here, your date here, your address here, your closest living relative—"

"Were you a prisoner on Belle Isle?"

He wags his head and speaks as some see fit to address children, gesturing at the imaginary piece of paper in his hand as if it were a signed confession. "Only crazy people think things like this, Peter. That terrible prison was long ago and best forgotten. Only a crazy person would even remember it. We call such bad memories *delusions*, Peter. Fortunately, there are effective medications for delusions." He reaches into his doctor's case, brings out an orange vial, and shakes it. It emits the distinctive dull clatter of plastic. "Take your medicine!" he exclaims cheerfully and tosses the vial to me. I examine the label in the firelight. It is worn and hard to read, but it was dispensed by MCV Hospital. The names of the medicine and the physician are both illegible. The instructions remain: *Take one a day with food*. What's left of the date reads *ember 12, 199*.

"How long have you had these?"

"A while."

"How long did you take them?"

"A week."

"Why did you stop?"

He giggles. "I didn't have any food. They told me they could make me sick if I didn't have any food. But by the time I got some, I wanted my delusions back. There was nothing to take their place." He knocks on his head, his mouth in an O, and makes a hollow-sounding cluck. "Empty-headed." He looks over his shoulder as if to see something there, continues to turn in a circle, finding nothing. He throws up his hands. "Nothing there! No Earl." His laugh takes on the high maniacal tone I've heard from fellow prisoners when they are losing their minds.

"That's because you lived in 1864. It's a long time ago, but not for you. You must have been a Union prisoner."

He wags his finger under my nose. "Ha! I told you my daddy was from Tennessee. Me too. How could I be a Union soldier? Tennessee seceded from the Union May of eighteen hundred and sixty-one. I'd have to be a traitor or a deserter. You calling me a traitor?"

He's clearly all bluster, and he still won't look me in the eye. His antics, no doubt, have become second nature, but they are beginning to try my patience. "Nonsense! As far as I'm concerned, you can only be a traitor to your conscience, you can only desert your fellowman. Now, how did you come to be here? You must understand—tell me the truth, and I *will* believe you. I, too, am from another time."

He looks into my eyes. "You're crazy like me, aren't you?"

"Yes."

"Then tell me your story first," he says.

Fair enough. And so I tell him my tale, from deathbed to this moment. You've heard it all already. But this is my first time to tell it, and I find myself warming to it in the telling, getting worked up on several occasions. I had not expected to feel such relief at narrating my two-day-old life, as if confessing to a priest. Like a priest, Earl keeps his opinions behind a screen until I've reached the end, though he has several questions about Anchee's notions of time along the way. He loses much of his antic pose. I suspect it is a means of keeping his fellows at a distance, though even he may have lost sight of the fact that it is feigned.

"You're much crazier than me," he concludes. He says this matter-of-factly without any negative judgment implied, and perhaps with a touch of admiration. We make a fine pair of lunatics. "Now why do you suppose this angel or future man or whatever he is told you what was going on, but he didn't tell me?"

"I have no idea."

"I think I know," he says with a twinkle in his eye: "He wants to drive *me* crazy because I don't know what's going on, and drive *you* crazy, because you do." He grins as if he finds this a splendid state of affairs. He takes out the two bottles of vodka he bartered for this morning and hands me one, proposing a toast, "To our delusions." We hit them together and drink them off, and thus fortified, he tells me his story, losing all traces of gaiety in the process.

"There was nothing magical about how I ended up in Richmond, on Belle Isle. I was a doctor, a country doctor, like my father; saw to farmers mostly, poor folks. I'd treated slaves a few times—broken bones, things like that. I didn't have any strong opinions about slavery one way or another. I liked to stay out of politics. Then one day a runaway was brought in all chewed up by dogs. Three fingers on his right hand, chewed right off. His face . . . It was horrible. Served him right for running, the slave owners said, complained bitterly about their loss. After that, I didn't have any use for slavery, slave owners either. I spoke up about it now and then when I was feeling brave, which wasn't very often; some folks agreed with me; most folks didn't. And that was that.

"Then it got to where you couldn't talk about it without begging for a fight. Everybody said there was going to be war if Lincoln was elected. They said it so often, they didn't think they had any choice. They knew how I felt and mostly left me alone. But when the war broke out, when the slave owners dragged us all into Hell with them, everything changed. Everybody went crazy. It wasn't just a war, it was the Crusades, the Revolutionary War, and the Second Coming all rolled into one. It wasn't just the bands and the flags and all, that riled everyone up. I think it was the guilt. 'Let's turn it over to God, let Him decide if we should have slaves!' You had preachers saying as much from the pulpit. Imagine—a holy war for slavery. But still, I tried to stay out of it and managed to for a while. But soldiers came to my place, said they needed me, said I had to go with them, that it was my patriotic duty.

"I said no thank you, and they said I had no choice. So now I was a slave, too. Served me right I guess for never facing up to things. I got angry—at the slave owners, at the soldiers, at myself for letting this happen, for not doing what I could before things came to such a pass. But mostly I was ashamed. I'd allowed myself to become a prisoner, a slave—because I wouldn't speak my mind. First chance I got, I tried to run to the North. Since I couldn't stay out of it, I thought I should throw in my lot with the side I believed was right. But Rebel soldiers caught me, brought me here, said if I was so set on treating Yankees, I could have a whole islandful."

"How long were you on Belle Isle?"

"Sixteen months. They had us in a camp, hundreds of tents packed into a little stinking space. There was an earth wall around it, about five feet high. Inside the wall was a ditch they called the dead line. I saw more than one man cross that line deliberately so that he'd get out of there the only way he could.

"Men died all the time. There wasn't really much I could do for them. To tell you the truth, I started into envying those who died. Then it got cold, terribly cold, day after day, and everything got worse. One bitterly cold night, I couldn't stand it anymore. I went to sleep hoping and praying I wouldn't wake up at all. When I woke up, the camp was gone. It was just a grassy field with this huge bridge passing over it—though at the time I had no idea what it was—huge stone pillars a hundred feet high. It was warm, and the sun was shining, and people were walking around happy as you please with scarcely any clothes on. I thought I was dead. I started screaming, and that was the first time they took me into town and talked to me, gave me some effective medication. After that, I was Crazy Earl. They know me there in town. I get along with everybody now, but mostly I stay out here. Unless there's a flood or bad ice or something.

"It's nice here. There's plenty of wood. Pawpaws growing everywhere, squirrel, muskrat, rabbit, fish. But listen to me now: You can't have anything to do with anybody. Nobody here will listen to you. Nobody here will believe you. Nobody here wants to hear what you have to say. And if you get mad when they treat you thataway, they lock you up, give you those pills there. And then you sit in a little room and don't argue while they tell you who you are before they'll let you go. *You've got to have a more positive outlook, Earl. We don't want to see you in here again!"*

He starts crying. "I wish I could forget. I really do. But a man needs to have something to remember, doesn't he? Doesn't he— even if it's awful? Otherwise, he might as well be a . . . a stone or a tree."

"Listen to me, Earl: You're not crazy. You don't have any delusions." I open up the vial and dump the contents in the river.

He stares at me dumbfounded. "You shouldn't have done that."

"Why not?"

He wipes at his tears with his hands and smiles. "All those poor fish are going to wonder who the hell they are."

"Maybe they'll be easier to catch that way."

I awake in the morning with the inelegant thought that, *Damn, I have to go to work today!* And a terrific headache. I have one of those as well. I open my eyes with a pained flutter and generally feel a good deal less stable than Brad tilting back and forth in his chair fetching beer after beer. Yesterday flashes through my mind like the frantic airborne movie, and like the movie, I cannot take it all in. So far this life has been a good deal more hectic than my previous one. But I am not complaining, even about the headache—a small sacrifice to make for the pleasure of boisterous company.

When I was young the first time, and I would hear old men say they would live their lives somewhat differently if they had it to do over again, I'd smugly think, *not me—I am doing exactly what I want with my life.* By the time I understood what those men meant—that it's not so much the doing or not doing of this or that, but how one regards it—I was, of course, no longer young. Emma once called me a Puritan, and even Sophie had to laugh at how puffed up I became over such a thoroughly just accusation. The single-minded purity of youthful idealism can some-

times set aside joy as if it were a distraction from the more important business of life. Joy in life, on the contrary, is a willing
ally to most worthwhile endeavors—even being a revolutionist,
even a revolutionist with a hangover.

My patient is sitting before the smoldering fire, watching me
stir to life. He is wearing his pants and the Hawaiian shirt I gave
him. He holds the pocketknife—long blade open—in his right
hand. He's been quite busy, apparently, while I've been dozing.
Earl has gone wherever it is Earl goes; someday, I suppose, I'll
find out where.

"Good morning, I'm Peter Kropotkin," I remind my guest. I
doubt he remembers much of our previous conversation. In my
exhaustion, I bedded down in my clothes. When I stand up, I see
how much of this man's blood I managed to get on them, and so
does he. I look like a butcher just getting off work. "I hope you're
feeling better this morning," I say.

He nods cautiously. "Feeling better, thank you. Where you
come from?"

"You mean my accent? Russia. You wouldn't think I'd lived in
England for over thirty years, would you? An English friend of
mine said I sounded like a music-hall comedian putting on a
Russian accent. Would you like some breakfast?"

He nods with certainty. I take out the bread and divide the remainder between us. He fairly pounces upon his portion.
"Would you like some tuna with that?" I ask. He looks at me
doubtfully. "I'll need the knife to open it." I hold up the tin. "I
don't suppose you had these in 1800, but there's fish inside
here." I point at the label where a picture of the creature bolsters
my case. I point at the knife in his hand. "One of the blades is a
can opener. You cut off one end to get inside. Do you want to do
it?" I offer him the can, and he takes it.

"Just close the knife blade, and open this blade right here."

He does so with remarkable facility. I gather he has spent
some time familiarizing himself with my knife.

"Now hook this part under the lip of the can here, and press
the point of the blade inside the lip here, and lift up like so."

He does, piercing the can. A little oil oozes up out of the hole. He holds it to his nose and sniffs. He is pleasantly surprised, as much, I'm guessing, by the marvel of the can itself as the fish inside. "What do I do now?"

"Set the can on your knee and cut it all the way around the lip like this." I imitate the necessary hand-rocking motion, and he gets it almost immediately. "Watch that edge—it's sharp," I say, as he pries the top open. He closes the opener and opens the knife blade, spears a few pieces of fish, eating them with great pleasure, and hands knife and tin to me. I take a bite and hand them back.

"This be 1999, you say."

"That's right."

He looks around the island. "Springtime?"

"Yes. April."

He thinks on this, nodding his agreement, giving a little laugh. "It sure ain't August."

"I know this must be hard for you," I say. "I have come here to this time from 1921—seventy-eight years, nothing really. But you—a lot has changed since 1800. I'll help you with what I know about—like canned tuna and fancy pocketknives."

"Why do you want to help me?" he asks matter-of-factly.

With a shrug, I name the only bond we seem to share other than our humanity—"We're both strangers here"—and he nods in agreement. Apparently that suits him as motive enough.

He looks intently out over the water, studying the shoreline. "I am no place I know," he admits. "I know this river though—upstream and down, and this here's my river—James River. I know her, even if she done changed in a thousand ways. But she ain't the same river I know. And this ain't August, not even close. *Must* be like you say—same river, different *time*." He has some more tuna. "Men still the same as always?" he asks.

"So far it seems so. I've only been here a couple of days myself."

He nods thoughtfully. He strikes me as a thoughtful fellow all the way around. "Everybody I know—they be gone? Dead."

"Yes. All gone." There's no way to soften this blow, and I let him ponder it in silence without any prattle from me, while I gather up some small wood for the fire. There are enough coals to stir the fire to life with little difficulty, and I put on water for coffee. He sits all the while, still as a statue, staring into the fire pit. I wonder who is back there, across the gulf of time, he would not willingly have left behind. Whoever they are, their loss is writ deep in the lines of his face.

In the light of day he looks somewhat younger than I first took him for, but it is near impossible to judge his age, for he has the weather-beaten look of a man who's spent the better portion of his life out of doors. His life as a slave has no doubt aged him beyond his years.

As if he knows what I'm thinking, he asks, "Am I a slave still?"

"No. Slavery has been illegal for over a hundred years in America. But I cannot lie to you. You have no legal identity. You own nothing. You have many things to learn. It could be very hard. Do you read and write?"

He shakes his head. "No schooling for slaves," he says. "Be a law against it."

"It was the same in Russia," I say. "Masters think slaves who can read and write might learn and plot. When the serfs were freed some of us formed classes to teach them to read and write. We had it down to nine sessions of a few hours each. Good thing too, for they shut us down soon enough when the reaction set in. English may take a little longer, of course. Russian is more phonetical. But I'll be glad to teach you. If your linguistic aptitude is anything like your mechanical, you should be penning novels by summer."

He laughs again. "You be one crazy man . . ."

"Peter."

"Jonah."

I offer my hand again, and this time he takes it. His callused hand squeezes mine and lets it go as if he is afraid he might hurt me, or that I might vanish like the imaginary creature I must seem to be. Or perhaps he is yet wary of my white skin.

We hear laughter behind us and turn to see a flotilla of eight rubber boats heading our way, each one filled with novice paddlers in helmets and life jackets, an adept in the stern giving orders. I am pleased to see that a majority of the captains of these vessels are women. They all wave as they go swirling by, laughing, as if they were riding a merry-go-round. Most of these adventurers are white, but some of them are black. One young couple I would judge to be Japanese. Jonah stares after all of them in amazement. These must be the pleasure boaters Earl spoke of.

A woman calls out to Jonah from the swirl of laughter and voices, "Cool shirt!"

He looks to me in bewilderment. "What she saying?"

"*Cool shirt.* It means she likes the shirt. *Cool* is a word I've heard often since I've been here to mean good or interesting—in addition to its usual meanings." I spell it out in the sand with a stick, C-O-O-L, pointing to the letters as I sound it out.

"Cool." He considers this—the letters more than their meaning. He is thinking, I suspect, that all meanings might be conveyed with marks like these, if one only knew how.

"Let me show you the alphabet," I say. I find my pen, peel the label off the tuna tin, and start printing the letters as neatly as possible on the inside.

He watches my writing with the utmost attention. When I hand him the tuna-label alphabet, he runs his fingertips across it, traces a few of the letters. But his eyes keep returning to the pen in my hand. I twist the barrel, showing him how the point extends and retracts, and hand it over. He carefully lays the tuna scroll aside and takes the pen. He turns it several times, and then several times more; I fear he won't tire of this exercise. And then, in a manner I don't see, he has it apart into two, then three pieces: a silver cartridge that must hold the ink, the top where the clip is attached, and the barrel. He holds the barrel up and looks through it as if it were a tiny telescope. He studies the structure of the ink cartridge, and I fear he will attempt further disassembly. I am reassuring myself that I will no doubt find another pen in the garbage today, though perhaps not as nice as this one, when he puts the pieces back together, holds his pale palm up, and puts the pen to it. "Mister Charles's niece, she teach me my name once, long time ago." He writes JONAH on his palm. The J is backwards, and the H is lopsided, but altogether it is an impressive performance. "Mister Charles have himself a fit over that one, so she don't teach me no more. My mother say English—she call it 'white talk'—eat up your words till you got nothing to say for yourself. She never learned to talk it, except to say, 'Yes, Mister Charles.' Mister Charles, he say that all she need to know, far as he's concerned." He laughs. "He don't know what she be calling him when he ain't around."

He starts to hand the pen back to me, but I suggest he keep it. "You can practice the alphabet," I say. He is clearly pleased and nods his thanks. I don't need to ask who Mister Charles was. Fortunately he's two centuries away and good riddance. "What were you doing when things changed?" I ask—"before you found yourself here."

He hesitates to answer my question. He understands what I mean, I believe, but looks away, his brow furrowed in thought. The water boils, so I leave him to ponder things while I prepare two stout cups of coffee.

His eyes light up at the smell, and he nods his satisfaction at the taste. "Yesterday is long over and done with, you say? Everyone dead and gone?"

I suspect the source of his hesitation. I've been a conspirator often enough to recognize the symptoms. "It is 1999," I reassure him. "There's no one left to betray."

He nods his head decisively. "Then I'll tell you about it. Wasn't just any night. It all started with a slave hereabouts, name of Gabriel, always talking about freedom, talking about things everyone else too scared to talk about, saying if we want freedom, we have to fight for it, saying if we *didn't* want freedom, how could we call ourselves men? Pretty soon every other man say he be with him if the day come. 'Just give us the word,' somebody said to him, 'just blow on your horn, and we *all* go to heaven.' And folks be laughing and afraid.

"That was me. Mostly afraid, I guess. After that first time I hear what he got to say, I don't want to hear him no more, though everybody be talking about him. And sure enough, Gabriel he raised up a secret army. And last night—or whenever it was—I hear the word from a slave say he come from near Prosser's place that Gabriel and his men meeting up round midnight. He don't know, or he don't say, exactly where, except they going to take Richmond. Ever since I first hear Gabriel, it work on me and work on me, scaring me, cause I know he was right. I don't have to be no slave 'less I want to be, but if I fight, I probably end up dead, and I didn't want that. But when I hear the news that it's actually happening, that slaves are rising up, I don't even think twice about it, I just sneak out, and head on into town."

He shakes his head at his own recklessness. I have heard such stories before from those who've taken part in revolutions. They found themselves at the barricades without ever having seriously considered it until the time came.

He drinks from his coffee and continues. "So here I come, down along the river, heading into town, hoping to meet up with Gabriel and them, when a big storm blows up out of nowhere and washes everything out, knocking down trees, the river rising up so fast I thought it might wash away the town before I get there. So I take the high road, thinking nobody be out on a night like that, but then some white men come up on me all of a sudden, asking what I'm up to, asking what *Gabriel* up to, so I figure they know everything already. I say I don't know nothing, but they beat me till I talk. I don't tell them nothing they don't already know from some old fool who done give it all away for nothing. The man beating me tell me that. He say, they hang us all, and I be thinking that fine by me. They leave me chained up in the pouring rain, saying they got more nigger-hunting to do and they be coming back for me in a little while. Last thing I remember is the sound of their horses riding off.

"When I wake up, chains is gone, men's gone. I'm lying by the river round sunset, hurting, but I can still get along. So I head for town like before. But nothing's right. No rain falling, ground almost dry, river low. All manner of strange things everywhere. But still I come down the river to do what I say we do, the word Gabriel give out."

"And what was the plan exactly?"

"That we all coming into Richmond to fight the white people—except Frenchmen, Methodists, and Quakers—who don't keep no slaves. The plan was to take the arsenal and the powder house first—but I didn't tell them white men that part of it."

"Then what happened?"

He shrugs and laughs. "Then I find you."

"So this was a rebellion, a fight for your freedom, an attempt to overthrow your oppressors."

"You talk like him," he says. "Like Gabriel."

"Then I'm sure he was a very fine fellow. Why didn't you kill me, by the way?"

He smiles. "I was pretty sure you wasn't no Frenchman, but I thought you might be a Quaker. Never heard no Quaker. You didn't act like a white man, didn't sound like one, didn't look at me like one." He shakes his head. "I can't explain it. I don't have no taste for killing anyways. This Russia, she be a good place? Better than this here?"

I laugh grimly at the thought. "No, I certainly wouldn't say that. Far from it. Where are you from—before Virginia, I mean?"

"I come out of the ocean—born on a ship. The captain he named me. He told my mother if she can't keep me quiet, he throw me overboard like Jonah. You know that story?"

"Yes."

"My mother she don't know it till later. She say the captain tell it to her. My mother say I don't cry again till she step off that boat with me in her arms, and we be in Virginia—then I *never* be quiet."

"And your father?"

"Captain shot him cause he put up a fight, mother say. Fighting about her, I suspect, but she don't say nothing about that, and I never ask." He takes up the alphabet scroll, spreads it on his knee, and finds the letters of his name with his fingertip, one by one. "Tell me about your own self," he says. "Tell me about Russia." He looks up from the scroll and smiles. "Tell me about 1999."

I realize I've met another fellow who has longed for the future. I hope it doesn't disappoint him. I try to fill him in on what I know of the two centuries he has missed.

I tell him about the American Civil War, Abraham Lincoln, and the Emancipation Proclamation—from a perspective unlikely to have met with Varina Davis's approval. She said the war was a matter of States' Rights. I told her since I didn't believe in States, I wasn't too keen on their rights, especially when they seemed chiefly to consist of depriving men of theirs. For Jonah, however, I leave Varina out of it. Slavery's done, I'm glad to report, here and for the moment at least.

I tell him of the marvelous scientific advances of the nineteenth and twentieth centuries (as far as I know of them), and he is particularly intrigued by machines, especially ones that fly. I explain the airfoil, which he seems to understand, and point out an airplane high overhead, though he is not quite convinced it isn't a bird.

"Are you a schoolmaster?" he asks me during a lull in my discourse, and I plead not guilty to the charge. "You like to teach things," he observes tactfully. "Tell me how *you* got here."

I blush to realize that the responsibility of informing him of two missing centuries has kept me from telling him about myself as he requested, so once again I proceed with my tale.

Unlike Earl, Jonah is full of questions, stopping me often for more information, particularly if I mention anything mechanical. In the midst of a narrative of my poignant arrival, I find myself explaining the internal combustion engine to the best of my ability, so that the limousine can depart the airport; I draw a simplified rendering of Rachel's bicycle in the sand at the same time I'm trying to explain how I feel about her; and I wait patiently while he disappears under the Hawaiian shirt with the flashlight so that he can witness its operation without the competition of sunlight.

But he has questions about Anchee as well, and he takes particular note as I did when Anchee changes from black to white. He mutters a phrase under his breath in a language I'm unfamiliar with. He translates it to me as "spare us from demons."

"Why did Anchee bring you here?" he asks at the end of my tale.

"I don't know."

"Let me see it," he says.

"It?" I say, for I really have no idea what he's talking about.

"The watch," he says. "Let me see the watch."

I hand it to him, and he examines it carefully. I will let him discover for himself that the stem doesn't work, that the back is hinged, and inside is concealed a square of plastic. But when he opens it, the square of plastic has been replaced by a tiny piece of paper. It flutters to the ground between us. A tingle crawls up the back of my neck. "He changed it," I say. "He probably picked my pocket when we were standing there in the street." When was it? I wonder. While I was petting the cat? Watching the television? He stops time and does whatever he likes with me. It's all I can manage to contain my rage.

Jonah picks up the paper, unfolds it, and hands it to me to read. It is a handwritten poem I've never read before, though I know the story from Greek myth. The color of the ink matches my pen; I assume the handwriting to be Anchee's. I read the poem out loud:

LEDA AND THE SWAN

A sudden blow: the great wings beating still
Above the staggering girl, her thighs caressed
By the dark webs, her nape caught in his bill,
He holds her helpless breast upon his breast.

How can those terrified vague fingers push
The feathered glory from her loosening thighs?
And how can body, laid in that white rush,
But feel the strange heart beating where it lies?

A shudder in the loins engenders there
The broken wall, the burning roof and tower
And Agamemnon dead.
                              Being so caught up,
So mastered by the brute blood of the air,
Did she put on his knowledge with his power
Before the indifferent beak could let her drop?

—WILLIAM BUTLER YEATS

"I don't understand," Jonah says.

"The swan is a god, Zeus. He turns into a swan so that he can rape Leda, a beautiful human woman, when she comes down to the river."

Jonah nods as if this makes perfect sense to him.

"After he rapes her, she has several children, including an incredibly beautiful daughter named Helen. She is kidnapped by a man named Paris, causing a long and horrible war and the destruction of a great city. Another daughter, Clytemnestra, murders her husband Agamemnon when he returns from that war. The poet is asking if Leda *knew*, like a god, what would happen as a result of this moment, what would befall the children born of this rape."

"That's a good story," Jonah says.

"The Greeks have many wonderful stories," I agree. "But there's something else. I *met* the man who wrote this poem—William Butler Yeats—at a friend's house. We were talking about history, and who made it, and whether, caught up in the tide of events, one could understand the significance of one's own actions, or even the actions of an entire nation or generation. He used this story to illustrate one of his points. He spoke of it quite passionately. For all I know, he was working on this poem at the time, or perhaps our conversation was its catalyst—I have no idea. But Anchee's message is clear. He's saying that I am like Leda, a plaything of the gods, and to prove it he demonstrates his knowledge of the smallest details of my past life, while I am totally ignorant of him, his powers, and his intentions—exactly like Leda raped by Zeus."

"Oh but Leda must *know*," Jonah objects. "She have—what it say?—*god* knowledge, *god* power. Is *certain*."

"You think so?"

"She have the god *inside* her. She be the mother of the childrens. She *know*." I suspect his judgment has less to do with reason than with his high opinion of mothers, a prejudice I can hardly fault him for. Still, he has a point. Anchee has provided me with a good deal of knowledge when I could have been plunked down here in ignorance like Earl and Jonah. Perhaps I know more than I think.

Jonah has been fiddling with the watch the whole time we are speaking, and I start to tell him to give it up, that he has exhausted its possibilities, when he grasps the open lid, roughly perpendicular to the watch, and turns it as if it were a key in a lock. I fully expect it to break, but instead it turns with a click. The watch emits an audible hum and a bluish glow that expands to fill our island. "What does it say?" Jonah asks, showing me the face of the watch. Gone is the familiar watch face. In its place are letters and numerals in blue light:

8:55 AM
April 10, 1999

I read them aloud. Oddly, I am more unnerved at this turn of events than Jonah, who, apparently so far out of his element that he expects to understand nothing, has wisely resolved to be surprised at nothing.

"What's that light?" he asks, as if I will know.

"I have no idea."

Before I can stop him, he tries the stem again, giving it a twist, and the numerals on the face of the watch count backward. At first, everything beyond the blue glow vanishes as if we are passing through a tunnel, but then it reappears, monstrously transformed—the river running backward, leaves flying up into the trees to be swallowed by the branches in a dizzying progression of seasons, the sun flying breakneck into the east. "Stop!" I shout, and he does.

Snow is piled deep everywhere along the shore and on the other islands, though ours remains unchanged. The world is quiet and still. The face of the watch reads

3:12 PM
February 8, 1988

In the trees along the riverbank, a flock of crows is perched in the snowy boughs. One of them takes flight in a shower of snow and flies toward us, croaking loudly. He circles overhead and perches in a low tree at the other end of the island, where everything appears to be as warm and dry as it is at our end. The crows discuss the matter in muted caws back and forth across the channel.

"Turn it back the other way," I say. "Back to where it was."

"Can't read," Jonah says and hands me the watch. "You do it I turned it this way." He twirls his fingertip over the stem in a clockwise motion. I turn it counterclockwise, and the process is reversed. The speed of time travel is controlled by how far one turns the stem. As we approach the time we left, I slow down and take careful note of the time. The blackout occurs at the precise moment I arrived at the close of the millennium, and ends when the face shows *8:55 AM April 10, 1999*, once again, at which point the counterclockwise turn of the stem has no further effect. So if I want to witness, for example, my arrival on this island, I cannot. A good thing, too—since I have no idea what I would say to myself. And if I want to see the future, I'll just have to be patient and experience it in the usual way.

The crow on our island emits a raucous croak that states his opinion on the matter and springs into flight, circling the shore, calling repeatedly, desperately, wondering where on earth his companions might have gone. Soon, the entire avian population of the vicinity has joined in the tumult. No doubt they are denouncing our accidental crow to be as mad as a hatter.

10 ⑤ Cassandra Pleads for Refugees

> In the course of my conversations with the "savages" during my travels in Siberia and Manchuria, it used to be very difficult for me to explain how it was that in our Christian societies people frequently die from hunger, while side by side with them other people are living in affluence. To a Tungus, an Aleut, and to many others, such a situation is utterly incomprehensible.
>
> —PETER KROPOTKIN, *Ethics*

> "It's a poor sort of memory that only works backwards," the Queen remarked.
>
> —LEWIS CARROLL, *Through the Looking-Glass*

I turn the watch lid back to its normal position, and the watch quits humming, the blue numerals vanish, and the watch looks like an ordinary watch again. More than ever I am tempted to toss it into the river, but I snap it shut and slip it into my pocket instead. "Preserve us from demons," I say, or hope I say, in Jonah's mother tongue. If I have it wrong he does not correct me.

"Everything be going backwards," he says excitedly.

"Is that where you want to go? Into the past? The past hasn't treated you so well."

"Why are you angry?"

"Because this damn Anchee is manipulating my supposedly new life for his own amusement. I hoped I might actually accomplish something with it. Instead I'm kidnapping crows from

1988 and interpreting poems by some young chap I met at a dinner party a century ago!"

Jonah listens calmly to my bluster. "Seem to me," Jonah says, "he be playing tricks with you. My mother say the gods be laughing all the time. As for me, I figure my ownself for a dead slave. But I wake up a *free man*. For me this be . . . how you say? . . . *cool* day. This be *very* cool day."

After such a sincere announcement of good feeling, how can I possibly persist in reciting my paltry woes? I have to laugh at myself. "It was quite a thrill, wasn't it?"

"Never see nothing like it. Snow falling *into* the sky." He enthusiastically throws his hands into the air to evoke the snow, and groans in pain, paying a stiff price for momentarily forgetting his wounds.

He sways a little, and I fear he will pass out again, but he reassures me he is fine. I check his bandages, and they are clean and secure, with no evidence of serious bleeding. I am about to advise rest when, for once, I witness Earl's approach before he arrives—he is near the shore, hopping rock to rock with a string of fish in one hand and his doctor's case in the other. I point him out to Jonah. "Here comes the doctor who treated you." I proceed to tell him a much abridged version of Earl's story. Fortunately, no machines show up in the telling to impede our progress, so that I have concluded it by the time Earl stands on the rock that has become my front gate.

"Earl, I would like you to meet Jonah. Jonah, meet Earl."

I'm not sure what I expected when these two met, but I am surprised nonetheless. Through my eyes, they seem to have little in common, but my vision proves faulty. They are both Southerners on the same side of the slave question—apparently no small matter in itself. Separated in time by a mere sixty-three years, a short time in the history of such a stubborn issue, they share their opinions forcefully. Jonah is eager to hear more about the war and the events leading up to it. Earl is curious about the African slave trade and the plantation system. Their conversation is spiced with phrases like "Ain't that the truth?" and "You can say that again!" and "That's telling 'em." They understand, in all its subtleties, just what that "that" signifies, while I can only guess at it. But I am a contented listener. In addition to their good sense, there is a music to the discourse of these two I find utterly delightful, a music they seem to bring out in each other, like the harmonizing of brothers.

I note how similar are their accents to my foreign ear, which remind me, in many of their vowels particularly, of Edinburgh where I—newly arrived in the English-speaking world—was often reduced to trading notes on scraps of paper to communicate with my landlady, even though I could write a pretty speech in English given sufficient time, paper, and ink. My own spoken vowels, judging by the dazed expressions of my auditors, must have been frightful. Even later in life a friend advised me after a public lecture that perhaps I should endeavor to distinguish more clearly between the words "law" and "low," for as it was when I spoke of the abolition of the *law*, my audience might easily understand me to say the abolition of the *low*!

After Earl confirms my opinion of Jonah's bandages, they rehearse their stories in great detail, each finding in the other the ideal audience for his woes. As Jonah tells his tale, Earl applauds Gabriel's brave call to arms; roundly curses the storm, the vile horsemen, the cruel lash—as well as slavery, slavers, slaveholders, and their kin; and testifies in no uncertain terms that he would incline to be a Methodist, if he ever took to religion, which, unfortunately, he did not. They confess to one another in hushed tones that neither is a Christian, and I loudly proclaim that makes three of us.

Jonah—while absorbed in a meticulous examination of Earl's medical instruments at Earl's invitation—nonetheless attends to every word of his narrative. When Earl narrates the scene of his conscription, Jonah takes up Bonesaw as if it were Excalibur and looks prepared to slay anyone who would misuse his doctor so.

And when Earl speaks of men freezing to death in the night, Jonah hugs the case of instruments as if it were the corpse of a lost comrade, his eyes brimming with tears. And when Earl denounces himself for not having raised his voice and arms against slavery long before, Jonah forcefully disagrees, pointing out that one man could accomplish little but his own enslavement when the law, the soldiers, and the wealth were all lined up against him.

These two I had thought so different understand each other perfectly. They were both victims of the same tyranny, homeless and silenced in their own land, labeled traitors by virtue of having a conscience they dared act upon. Perhaps a measure of their passion comes from the fact that they could not have held this frank discussion in their own times without enduring the lash, imprisonment, or both. My experience in Russia is that slavery enslaves a whole culture—master and slave, proponent and opponent. No one is free; all are enslaved by the notion that one man can own another. The day the serfs were freed it was as if all of Russia were let out of a dungeon.

These two, whatever woes they may have suffered, have miraculously escaped. Jonah is still giddy with his freedom; for now, it eclipses all other emotions. When one has paced a cell for years, then steps outside, it's hard to take one's eyes off the horizon. Earl, who has discovered the hard ground between this river and his aspirations, is decidedly less sanguine. But still, four years ago, he escaped death in prison—an experience, I can testify, that leaves one with an unshakable gratitude for life—but until now he has had no one to share it with, no one who would believe him, no one who would understand what he's been through. So he, too, has a new sense of freedom this morning. Freedom for a social animal, after all, does not consist in solitude but in free association and mutual understanding. Of all the human emotions, loneliness, in my experience, is the worst.

My two companions share an enthusiasm for fish as well, cleaning and dressing and commenting upon them as they continue to talk. I do my part by building up the fire and securing green saplings with which to cook the fish. Begrudgingly, I check my watch-cum-time-machine and see I have to be at work in lit-tle more than an hour. I ready myself by changing into my other trousers—still damp, but free of bloodstains (not usually the best attire for a promenade past the police station)—and sit close to the fire to dry them out and watch Earl cook the fish.

"You seem awful quiet," Jonah says to me. "Something the matter?"

"I was just enjoying listening to the two of you talk."

He nods thoughtfully. "You be missing home?"

"Russia? Yes, I guess I am. I didn't live there much of my life. I escaped from prison in 1876 and fled the country. I couldn't re-turn until 1917 when a revolution overthrew the old aristocracy. I came home an old man, but still, I had such hopes . . . I thought, *This is it! The revolution!*" I shake my head. "Ah well, it doesn't matter now. The bullies and thugs took over, and the chance was lost. I miss Russia, but I've missed her most of my life."

"My mother she was like that. She *all* the time be telling me stories about *home* she call it." He shakes his head and laughs. "I miss a place I never see, and people I never know!"

Earl serves the fish on still-smoldering sticks, and we set about devouring all but the sticks, and I consider chewing mine for whatever juices might linger there. As Jonah and I sing the fisherman-cook's praises, he is touched by our accolades, almost shy in his protestations, and I catch a glimpse of the man he used to be 130-some years ago before war destroyed his life. Maybe *that* man, and not just Crazy Earl, can gain his freedom someday, can have the life the State stole from him fighting for its "rights." Poor State, so misused by traitors and "disloyal" slaves it can hardly manage to conduct its chief business—attending to the many needs and rights of the privileged classes.

"What about you?" Jonah asks Earl. "You be missing Ten-nessee?"

Earl shakes his head. "No, not so much. Me, I miss my wife. If I could see her again, it wouldn't matter where."

I nod my understanding. "Me too," I say quietly.

Jonah says, "Don't have a wife. There was this girl in town, but she was sold and gone to Carolina a few years back. After that I don't get so close again. Slaves ain't allowed to marry anyway."

"You're not a slave anymore," I say.

Earl shakes his head sadly and says to Jonah, "No, now you're a homeless, jobless, crazy person without a nickel in your pocket. Women just *swoon* when they see *me* coming." He does a comic impression of a cocky young swain swaggering down the avenue and has us both laughing, but it's a laugh with a sting to it.

However just Earl's observations may be, I fear they're not the sort of sentiments Jonah needs to hear right now, and I start to speak up, but Jonah, it seems, is undaunted. "I still ain't no slave," he says pointedly.

It's clear that Earl has further ammunition for his argument, but holds his fire. "Just don't be getting your hopes up is all I'm saying."

Jonah laughs. "I ain't dead! I am *free*! I'd say I got enough good news to celebrate."

With regret that I must part from such good company, I rise and wash my face and hands in the river. "I work late tonight," I say. "I won't return till midnight or later."

"You can't stay here," Earl says, pointing at the horizon upstream. "The river will be on the rise soon, be raining here inside an hour." Jonah and I study the same bank of clouds and concur with Earl's opinion.

"You think the water will cover the island?" I ask doubtfully.

"No. Just half them rocks between here and the bank. Y'all are welcome to stay at my place until you can find something else. It's small but dry." He smiles at me with a twinkle in his eye. " 'Less you want to build yourself another boat."

"I think my days as a shipwright are safely concluded," I say, laughing.

I pack up my belongings, and Earl and I help Jonah to shore. He does not complain, but he is still unsteady on his feet, and our jostlings must cause him pain. When we reach the shore he and Earl insist they can manage the rest of the journey to Earl's without me, so that I may proceed to work. Earl draws a map in the sand to show me the best route to his place when I return. One enters the hole in the fence by the stairs and continues along the railroad tracks until there's a second opening in the fence. "Go through the fence, turn left, and it's a dozen yards or so."

"What does it look like?"

"A briar patch. It's a hole, lots of us dug them on Belle Isle since there weren't near enough tents and blankets to go round. Soil's better for digging though up where I am now, got some timbers bracing it. Too sandy on that island for anything more than just burrowing in."

"You've built a dwelling underground large enough for the three of us?"

"Long as no one stands up," he says, adopting a stooped-over posture and passing his hand over his head to conjure up his ceiling.

"Even me?" I ask. We are almost eye level. His hand would easily clear my head no matter how straight I might stand.

"No jumping," he advises with a good-natured smile, quite different from Crazy Earl's maniacal mask.

I regret that I will have to postpone my examination of Earl's lodgings until after work. The prospect of an underground dwelling brings to mind the vast subterranean prairie dog villages I found so fascinating when I visited the American plains. Imagine a vast prairie. As far as the eye can see are heaps of earth, and on each of them a prairie dog stands, engaged in a lively conversation with its neighbors by means of short barkings. As soon as the approach of man is signaled, all plunge in a moment into their dwellings; all have disappeared as by enchantment. But if the danger is over, the little creatures soon reappear. Whole families come out of their galleries and indulge in play. The young ones scratch one another, they worry one another, and display their gracefulness while standing upright, and in the meantime the old ones keep watch. They go visiting one another, and the beaten footpaths which connect all their heaps testify to the frequency of the visitations.

However pleasing this remembered image, I've no desire to turn rodent just yet, not until I've given human another try. And while I might fare well living in a burrow by the river in my new healthy incarnation, Jonah would surely be aided by a warm bed and a roof over his head. In fact, it is a matter of some urgency if he is to recover properly. Unfortunately, while I might, in a week or two, be able to secure a room if I am frugal, these could be crucial weeks for Jonah. Perhaps, the shelter Rachel spoke of . . .

Then I recall Rachel's explanation of her very own agency's mission—*helping refugees*. Surely, by any sensible definition of the term, Jonah is a refugee—fleeing persecution in his homeland, the victim of a barbaric regime to which he cannot return without facing certain death. And no matter how reactionary Richmond may yet be, I doubt if it maintains an extradition treaty with the Confederate States of America.

As I climb the stairs and cross over the bridge, the idea begins to grow in my mind. By the time I reach Meadow Street, I am resolved. I pause to survey the line of dark clouds at the horizon—rain does indeed seem certain—but pay them no mind. I consult my map and the watch. It's practically on the way, and I have plenty of time. I alter course for Rachel's house, intending to persuade her to accept a slave from 1800 Virginia as a refugee.

I wonder where refugees come from these days and if Jonah might plausibly pass for one of them. With all the talk in the press of the *global economy*, I assume—since war and economics have always been close companions—that refugees will be equally global. In truth, I have no idea what I will say to Rachel other than here's a fellow who needs some help.

I pass through a lovely park identified on the map as Byrd Park. There are even more running people here than in the Fan, but a few strolling couples as well. Several fishermen try their luck in attractive stone-lined ponds where shrieking children feed geese and ducks from plastic bags of bread. Despite signs reading NO DOGS ALLOWED, there are several in evidence with their masters in tow (no doubt against their will). It is a scene to warm the heart, this human village—men and women, black and white, young and old—enjoying life on this common green, undaunted by the storm clouds' steady approach. I feel a rush of optimism that perhaps I've come to the right place after all, a feeling aided, I am sure, by the imminent prospect of seeing Rachel again.

I confess that up until the moment I decided to call on her this morning, the day and night ahead seemed a barren desert between me and the oasis of our reunion in the morning. Given the smell of approaching rain and the sogginess of my impending labors, perhaps a less desiccated metaphor is in order, something for my buoyant spirits. I'm swept along by the prospect of seeing her again. It's all I can do to keep my head above water. Reason cautions that I may be chasing the mirage of infatuation, but neither heart nor feet listen, and both step and pulse are as quick and light as a spider on the water.

I round the corner on Rachel's block and survey the neat row of houses—probably new when I died—none shabby, none grand. I locate Chris's house first, with a trim terraced garden. And then I hear her, or what proves to be the sound of her labors, and approach. She is sweeping her front steps, descending them backwards, swishing the broom, her body switching back and forth in a hypnotic counterpoint. Her small feet are bare. Dressed in simple knit clothes—a once-black knit shirt and darker, close-fitting pants—she is a disarming vision indeed. Her clothes are not immodest by current standards, I know, but leave no mystery at all as to the conformation of her body and limbs, and I find her beautiful beyond words. Seeing her so, my heart soars, but when she catches sight of me out of the corner of her eye and turns to find me staring at her posterior, the look on her face is not altogether welcoming, and I am dashed upon a rocky shore.

"Peter. I thought we were getting together tomorrow." She assumes a forced pleasantness which might be a descendant of Varina Davis's manner toward me, a sort of ebullient malice—a Southern social skill I was later informed.

"We were . . . or are . . . or *will* . . ." I say, laughing much too much, as flustered as a schoolboy. "I'm sorry. I was just on my way to work, and I thought it would be all right to call on you. I had a matter I hoped to discuss with you. I didn't intend to be a bother."

Her manner makes it clear I've failed in my intentions, for she gives me a businesslike nod and gestures toward a pair of rockers on the porch, as if we were back in her office the first time we met. No. She was much friendlier then, when I was a stranger. Before I cried in her arms. As she stows her broom by the door she seems to be taking stock, avoiding my eyes, wary of me for some reason I can only imagine. It can't be my attraction to her— as Anchee remarked, she is well aware of that already, pleasantly aware, or so it seemed. No, something has happened since I saw her last to erode her opinion of me.

"Sit, please," she says, for naturally I have waited for her, and I obey. "Are you having second thoughts about the class?" she asks, almost hopefully it sounds to me. The class is our only real connection. If I were to quit the class, she needn't have anything further to do with me.

"No, no. It's nothing to do with that. I've met an unfortunate fellow down by the river. He's in poor health and very much down on his luck, and I'm concerned for him. He's a refugee, and I recalled that your agency helps refugees secure housing and other necessities. So I've taken it upon myself to speak to you on his behalf. I would have consulted him, of course, but I only just thought of it on the way to work, and I was in the neighborhood." I smile at the neighborhood to show what a nice place I think it is.

A young black boy on a bicycle coasts by, regarding me with open curiosity. "Hi, Rachel," he says.

"Hi, Gerald," she calls with a friendly smile, a smile she withdraws when she turns her attention back to me. "Where's he from—this refugee?" she asks as if scarcely believing in his existence, much less what I've said about him.

"He was born at sea," I say, grateful for this honest evasion. "His parents were from somewhere in Africa."

"Somalia? Is he Somali?"

I recall that the British, French, and Italians carved up Somaliland, but that would be on the east coast, and Jonah's roots are more likely in west Africa. But still . . . "I suppose that's possible," I say. "If he were, what kind of aid might be available?"

She sees right through me. *Not so fast*, she seems to say. "Maybe we can figure out where he's from. What's his name?"

"Jonah."

"Biblical. Could be anywhere. Last name?"

"Just Jonah, I believe."

She knits her brows skeptically, leans back in her chair, letting it rock back and forth. "Just Jonah, born at sea. This just keeps getting better. What languages does he speak?"

"We spoke in English. I don't know his mother tongue. He is illiterate, though I've offered to teach him."

"Of course." There's a chill in her voice that breaks my heart. Our eyes meet. She sees my distress, and I see her anger, but while she must know the source of my pain, I have no idea what I have done to anger her so. She continues her interrogation. "Living relatives?"

"None."

"Why am I not surprised? Does he have any identification? Documentation? Anything at all that could be used to establish his identity?"

"Nothing."

"You seem awfully certain. It can be anything—his airplane ticket, for example."

"I know that he possesses nothing at all except a pair of pants and a shirt I gave him. And a pen. I gave him that as well."

"How did he manage to get here without so much as a ticket stub? Did a great fish spit him out?"

"I don't fully understand that myself."

"But you believe he is an African refugee? Why? Even if he is African, how do you know he's a refugee? You don't even know what country he's from, though you seem to know everything else about him. What makes you think he's a refugee?"

Her tone gets my back up, and I answer forcefully. "Because he should be by any sensible definition. He bears the unmistakable marks of torture and subjugation—scars from lash and shackles. They are more eloquent than any 'documentation.'"

"You've seen these scars yourself?"

"Yes."

"Has he been to the INS?"

"INS?"

She cocks her head to one side, clearly finding my ignorance unaccountable. "Immigration and Naturalization Service, Peter. You know—the people you dealt with to enter this country?"

"Oh yes, them." She's certain I'm lying. And I *am* attempting to deceive her with the half-truths I'm telling, but I do not wish to lie to her. I blunder on. "He has spoken with no one other than me and my neighbor I told you of. He only just arrived here."

"Why Richmond? Is he a reader of Dickens as well?"

I blush crimson. "Perhaps you could just talk to him?" I offer without much conviction.

"Tell him to come to the office on Monday. You might also tell him it would be helpful if he recalls what country in Africa he—or his parents—are from, and how he managed to get here from there without talking to anyone or having anything to show for it."

"I . . . I will." My business is done. I've made a big enough fool of myself for one day. I should rise and leave. If I hurry, I can make it to work on time. But I am overcome with a wave of loneliness that pins me to my chair. My chest is leaden as I realize that after this incident, I may very well never see Rachel again. Only this morning I witnessed the joy that speaking the plain truth can bring to a pair of like-minded strangers. And here I am lying—for what else can you call it—to the one person in all this new world I would most like to befriend; and worse still, she *knows* I am lying. "I'm sorry to have bothered you," I say.

"Peter," she says quietly, in an altogether different tone of voice, "is there anything you want to tell me?"

I look over at her, and she regards me with a steady gaze. It seems I am being given a chance to confess, but unfortunately I don't know my crime. "A good many things," I say. "But until I know what has occurred to alter your opinion of me since you saw me last, there's no point in my saying anything—for whatever it is casts a shadow over all. I know that Jonah's story must sound outrageous, but you were upset the moment you laid eyes on me. Have I done something to upset you?"

She considers her response. "'Upset' me? Yes, I guess you could say that. Disillusionment is upsetting, isn't it? Disappointment. I wanted to read something you'd written. You seemed like such a nice, interesting man. I was curious. Okay—I was *interested.* I wanted to know more about you. So after work I took your application to the library to look up some of the things you listed there. I wasn't trying to check up on you. I was *certain* all those articles would be there waiting for me. I didn't have the slightest doubt. I was like an excited little kid.

"I must've been nuts. As you know, they don't exist, Peter. Not a single one of them. Why would you lie about something like that? We don't require our tutors to publish in *Nature* and *Atlantic Monthly*. Were you trying to impress me or something? And now this crazy story . . . I liked you much better before you lied to me."

My heart is breaking. I can't allow her to think so low of me. "I did not lie. I *did* write all those pieces. I merely changed the dates."

"You what? But why? I don't get it."

"Because I had to. I don't know if I can explain, if you can possibly believe . . ." I throw up my hands in exasperation. "Please try to trust me. You are the last person in the world I would want to think ill of me. I hold you in the highest possible regard."

She clasps her hands together as if they are cold or she is praying. "Peter, I know you like me, but you scare me. If we're going to have any kind of relationship at all, I need to know who you really *are*. I know what your papers say, and I've read your application, but none of it—true or false—adds up to somebody who flies to Richmond on the heels of his wife's death to live a homeless life on the river—taking up the cause of mysterious Africans who, like himself, just so *happen* to show up in Richmond, Virginia, as if dropped out of the sky! Jesus, Peter! *Trust* you? How? How do I do that? I know you *have* a green card—I've seen it—but how on earth did you get it? You haven't even *heard* of the INS. Peter, please just tell me what's going on, who you really are. If I check everything on that application—the writing, the teaching—is there *anything* that's, well . . ."

"The truth? All of it. You want the truth? Very well. I will tell you the truth, all of it. I had to change the dates to make them plausible. I wrote most of those articles over a hundred years ago. You see, my actual date of birth is December 9, 1842."

"I . . . I don't understand."

"I hoped to tell you everything after you had the chance to get to know me and know I'm not demented, but that was a foolish, romantic notion. You know my name. I'm known to history, apparently. The young man I met at the airport and used as a reference did his senior thesis on me—one of the reasons I liked him so much, I suppose. You see—I am 'the' Peter Kropotkin, sometimes called the Anarchist Prince—a persistent label I despise. I came to this time day before yesterday from my deathbed in 1921."

She stares at me dumbfounded. Finally, she speaks: "You're saying you're a *time traveler?*" Her voice is almost a whimper.

"Please," I say. "Please hear me out."

It is only because she strives to understand the strange and foreign as a matter of habit and principle that she accedes to my request. She nods for me to proceed, her emotions barely reined in. I don't think I could have upset her more if I had told her I was, in fact, a drug dealer or a thief. There are agencies to which I could be referred in those cases. As it is, she's my one chance.

So although I will likely be late for work as a result, I tell my tale a third time, now something of a ritual in this new life, though I tell it differently each time—recalling new details but inventing none, recounting the same episodes but with different meanings. To Earl I was a fellow madman; to Jonah, a fellow foreigner; to both, a fellow escapee, a former jailbird. The telling of it to Rachel, it seems to me, is its true form, the one closest to my heart. For all I want it to say is that I am Peter Kropotkin, a good man I think, in over my head in a business I don't understand, but with no intentions of drowning—not with a new life to be lived in the offing. I don't know why I'm here, but I intend to do as I've always done—to do what I can, however insignificant, to make the world better.

"In the face of death I was offered a new life in the future, and I took it," I conclude. "And for the most part, I'm glad I did. I feel young again—I *am* young again. I feel purposeful again. I'm even hopeful. To borrow a phrase from my favorite creation of Mr. Dickens, young David Copperfield, I intend to be the hero of my new life." I smile, but she does not smile back. My tale moves her deeply; her eyes are moist with tears whose meaning I cannot interpret. They began as I recounted the Tim Binder affair by which Anchee had arranged our last meeting. I announce myself in any event: "I also wish to say that of all the wonders of this new life, I am most glad to have made *your* acquaintance, Rachel, and I sincerely hope that we may be friends for a very long time to come."

We stare at each other, and I see in her face what she cannot bring herself to say, so I say it for her: "You don't believe me, do you? Not a single word." Now it is I whose eyes flood with tears.

"Oh Peter," she says, reaching out a pitying hand to me.

I stand quickly, setting the rocker careening across the porch like a startled cat. "I'm late for work," I say, and hurry down the steps as fast as I can go. She calls my name, but I don't look back, and she doesn't come after me.

I suppose I should be flattered that she is so upset to discover that I am insane—when I seemed like such a nice, even promising young man—but I am not. Crackpot, devil, foolish dreamer—I've been thought all those and worse, but never dishonest, never insane. It's a bitter pill.

Send me a poem about Cassandra, I say to Anchee in the rage of my thoughts. *Enslaved by Agamemnon and brought home as spoils of war, cursed by Apollo with knowing the truth and being compelled to tell it, but never, ever being believed—now* she *would be a myth more to the point, don't you think? Have Yeats scratch out something along those lines, why don't you!*

As if he hears my thoughts and his powers extend even to the heavens, a hard rain begins to fall. By the time I get to work, I am soaked to the bone.

11 ✿ Mutual Aid

All belongs to all. All things are for all men, since all men have
need of them, since all men have worked in the measure of
their strength to produce them, and since it is not possible to
evaluate every one's part in the production of the world's
wealth.
— PETER KROPOTKIN, *The Conquest of Bread*

Don't compete. . . . That is what Nature teaches us.
— PETER KROPOTKIN, *Mutual Aid*

The rain falls all day in fits and starts. The long
shift I dreaded proves a refuge of sorts—I have a roof over my
head, and the drudgery and monotony of work help numb my
mind and senses. Though my mind, at least, must have already
been numb to have thought Rachel could possibly believe me.
My senses, I suppose, were anything but numb. I recall an arti-
cle I read on the airplane on *pheromones* and understand most
clearly what the author was driving at. When I was a cadet, there
was a crude term for that sort of thinking. I assume you have the
equivalent in English, so I'll spare you.

After lunch, I take a break in the kitchen where Ahmed, an
Iraqi who tends to salads and breads, keeps a TV going constantly. "Help English," he explains, but the noise of the thing
makes any sustained conversation impossible, so I don't know
how effective an English instructor it is.

I try to watch it, but it exhausts me. The quick, evocative images coax all manner of emotions—fear, lust, nostalgia, devotion—that are promptly and shamelessly conscripted into the

service of consumption. *Joy?* Consume. *Lust?* Consume. *Embarrassed?* Consume. *Lonely?* Consume. *Love?* Consume. In no time I'm emotionally drained, funneled, bottled for shipment like a Coca-Cola. I've flown over mountains, fallen in love, cradled a baby, lost my husband, rescued a cat from a high tree—all to empty my wallet. Perhaps that's what I need to learn to survive here—how to watch television—or rather, how to steel myself to its insidious sway.

But not today. I take advantage of the lull between lunch and dinner, to scrub out pots and pans too large for the dishwasher, a welcome break from the routine of feeding the mechanical maw of that damn machine. For a brief time, there is not a soiled dish in the place. I enjoy the small pleasure of a job well-done and go out front to watch the rain fall. It thrashes against the windows with a terrible racket, blurring and twisting the world outside. I hope Earl's burrow is as dry as he claims. With a grim smile, I note the irony of bedding down in a hole in the ground, when by all rights I should be residing there long since.

There are only four tables of customers, all in a proper torpor, waiting out the rain with chocolate desserts, cups of coffee, and cigarettes. I consider smoking a cigarette myself, but reject the idea immediately. My rejuvenated body doesn't crave tobacco as the old one did. After a lifetime of smoking, I have had my fill, had it, in fact, a few decades before I died. I should be quite the miserable fool if I were to take it up again, so I sit, smokeless and miserable at the bar.

A bartender and two waitresses, all unknown to me since they didn't work yesterday, play cards at the other end of the bar. They ignore me as if I were invisible. They have assumed I speak no more English than the three-word sentences I speak to management, and I have let them. Just now, I prefer invisibility, for to reveal my true identity—my experience with Rachel has forcefully brought home to me—is to banish myself from human society, and the alternative—lying—kills the soul.

Once again I take stock of the Peter in the mirror behind the bar. I no longer see Old Peter, or Young Peter either; now I see

Crazy Peter—soon to be known about town like Crazy Earl: *Thinks he's a time traveler. Imagine. Quite mad. Such a shame. Seems a nice fellow otherwise.* For the hundredth time I see Rachel's comforting hand, her pitying voice, and I clamp my eyes shut. *Nobody here will listen to you. Nobody here will believe you. Nobody here wants to hear what you have to say.*

"Gin," one of the waitresses says, and lays down her cards.

I try to make my mind a blank, but recall instead the first time I saw Rachel, a sheaf of forms in her hand, each one dubbed with a meaningless string of letters and numbers, but in her careful Spanish the jumble of numbers gradually turned to hope. The forms *would* make life better once one found the answers and set them down, paid the bribes or fees or taxes or whatever they're called this time round, engaged a lawyer, of course. But it would all, by this torturous route, she promised, work out, don't you see? And the family was heartened and convinced. The needy and the well intentioned, if they were only patient, could eventually help one another by way of the proper forms.

For me, for Jonah, for Earl, there are no forms, no procedures, no one who will even accept our bribe. We've escaped death, war, and slavery, only to end up ghosts, impossible and inconvenient phantoms from the past.

My father was fond of ghost stories and liked to frighten himself with the telling of them to my brother and me. We would gasp at all the right parts, but we never actually believed in them in the way our father—who narrated them with passionate conviction—clearly did. I first learned my skepticism by observing my father's credulity.

My favorite of his ghost stories has no ghosts:

On her deathbed, in her final hours, my mother extracted a sworn oath from my father that he would set her maid Másha free, but after Mother died, he predictably "forgot" his promise. Másha, who had heard him swear, dared not speak up to remind my father, for he might easily take it upon himself to marry her to a drunken soldier for such impudence. She was forced to employ more subtle means. A year after my father's oath, she dressed in one of Mother's white gowns and appeared before my father as the ghost of his wife. Imitating her manner of speaking and addressing him with pet names she had overheard over the years, this apparition chastened him for not yet honoring his promise. My father was completely taken in, and the resourceful woman was set free at once. I had the story first from my gullible father when I was a child; from the "ghost" herself much later, when she had lived some years as a free woman and my father was in his grave. It often happens that a ghost, or at least a belief in one, proves more persuasive than a living soul. Saints to the man—and woman—are all dead.

But I am not my superstitious father, and neither, I'm certain, is Rachel. She's no believer in ghosts. If she were, I wouldn't be so desirous that she believe in *me*. It's precisely in her strong, clear, intelligent eyes I want to see myself reflected as *who I am*. *Wanted*, I correct myself. There's no chance of that now. *Nobody here will listen to you. Nobody here will believe you. Nobody here wants to hear what you have to say.*

I'm stirred from my melancholy reverie by Brad, who takes the stool beside me and eyes me with concern. "You okay, Peter?"

Outside, the rain has slackened to a drizzle. The card players are nowhere to be seen. I had noticed neither change. I put on a cheerful face. "I'm fine, just fine. I didn't know you were working today."

"I'm not. I just came by to pick up my pay." He waggles a white envelope in his shirt pocket, identical to the one that contained Tim Binder's bounty. "You sure you're okay? You look really wasted."

"I didn't get much sleep, I'm afraid—still adjusting to things here; it's all a bit overwhelming. Though I must say I had a wonderful time at your kitchen table yesterday evening. I thank all of you again for your splendid hospitality."

Brad laughs. "I wish my mother could hear you say that— 'splendid hospitality.' She's always on me about being rude." He pauses a moment, tugging pensively on his nose ring. "Everybody liked you a lot, too."

Angel, the Dominican busboy, passes us with a full tub of dishes. The customers apparently all left with the rain. The dishes are smeared with ashes and chocolate; the napkins have been shredded into drain-clogging confetti; the plastic straws twisted into knots. There was someone yesterday who fashioned them into tiny animals. When he brought back that tub, Angel said, "*Mira, Pedro, el arca de Noé.*" (*Look, Peter, Noah's Ark!*)

Fresh customers, six by my count, come in the door and shake their umbrellas on the tile floor.

"We must talk again when I'm not chained to my post." I start to go back to work when I am struck by a sudden inspiration. "Do you ever take in new residents in your commune?"

"Sure. TJ says there's been as many as a dozen in the past, but that was before I lived there. You interested?"

"Yes, I certainly am."

Brad is overcome with enthusiasm. "*Really?* That'd be so awesome. All the really good rooms are taken, but the basement could be pretty cool with some fixing up. TJ's uncle Chaney used to live and work down there. He's a sculptor, and there's still some of his shit down there, too heavy to move—a torch and an anvil and some of his pieces—but it's not in the way or anything. There's plenty of room. There's even a little bathroom. You can always throw a blanket over the art."

"I take it you don't care for the uncle's work?"

"I think it totally sucks, but at least he was doing shit, you know? If you're not making art, you're not an artist, know what I mean?"

"Indeed. Is this room large enough for two by any chance? I have a friend who is also in need of a place to stay."

"Oh it's huge; it's like a whole apartment. It's already sort of divided into two rooms. TJ and Chaney put all the old furniture down there in a line down the middle making two rooms out of it. If you need any furniture, by the way, just take it off the stack."

"We haven't moved in yet."

"You will. You're going to love it. Your friend—is he Russian, too?"

"No. He's an African."

Brad rocks back and forth on his bar stool, grinning. "Cool. That is *so* cool. I've never met a real African. What is he, South African?"

"West African, I believe."

I'm not sure what constitutes a "real African" as opposed to some other sort, but don't pursue it. Brad and his friends possess a hunger for the exotic, it seems, as intense as others' need for the familiar. If Jonah and I were Americans with scolding mothers and nose rings and tattooed heads, I don't imagine we would be nearly so cool, so awesome. "When might we move in?" I ask. "Is there some procedure for joining the commune?"

"Sort of. We do everything by consensus, so everybody has to agree on new people. But I don't see a problem with it. Like I said, everybody liked you, and the room's just down there, not being used for anything except to stow Chaney's bad art. When do you get off work?"

"Eleven."

"Come on over to the club after. The whole house will be there then if you want to talk about moving in. You said you wanted to hear us play anyways. We go on a little after midnight."

Since my morning plans with Rachel are no more, a rainy night on the town with Hemlock Cocktail sounds like just the thing. I'm sure Jonah and Earl won't lose any sleep over my absence, and the rain has persuaded me that we'll all sleep a good deal easier if I can secure proper lodgings. Brad draws a map to the club on a napkin, and I go back to work.

The evening crew includes most of the people I met yesterday, including Deidre, who cheers me considerably with the gift of a picture of her dog Buster. He's a handsome fellow indeed, and I tack his image on the wall above the pond to provide the frog and myself with an ever-cheerful companion.

The rain returns off and on from light drizzle to gusty showers. But rain or not, Saturday night proves to be very busy, and I am glad to be steadily occupied, for though I fight it, my idle thoughts tend to self-pity and self-doubt, and I find myself miserable company. But I continue my food-conservation efforts on Buster's behalf, expanding my dependents to include another dog, a cat, and an iguana. And while I'm at it, I include Earl, Jonah, and myself. For the dogs, I salvage beef and bones; for the cat, chicken and fish; the iguana claims discarded lettuce and parsley; while my accidental friends and I inherit several plastic bags of bread and corn muffins, with an ample supply of butter, as well as several bags of sliced oranges (a mere garnish here where no one dreams of scurvy).

But that is but a small portion, a tiny drop spared from a huge bucket. And once I've started saving food from being thrown away, I find it hard to stop, reasoning that if I or my neighbors can't use it, there must be others who can. The busboys take an interest, and with a minimum of cooperation from them, the harvest increases substantially.

Once word spreads of what I'm doing, something of a competition springs up among the waitresses and busboys to see who can bring me the tastiest morsels, and soon dozens of pets and unfortunates have been enrolled to take advantage of the resulting bounty. Ahmed—who fills the baskets of bread in the first place—supplies me with empty plastic bread bags and plastic-coated wires with which to secure them. Bread is our leading crop, for a bread basket typically reaches me, by way of a customer's table, a little more than half-full. The bread bags prove an excellent means of storing not only the salvaged bread, but most anything at all. I soon run out of storage space for the harvest, and Ahmed comes to my rescue with an empty bread rack I can wheel about wherever it's needed. For perishable items, Pierce clears part of a shelf in the walk-in refrigerator for my use. After a brief consultation, the busboys alter their route to include a stop at the walk-in. They suffer no loss of efficiency, however, since the garbage container now takes twice as long to fill, and fewer trips to the bin in the alley they call the *Dumpster* are necessary.

When the dinner dishes are at their peak, and I am working

on a literal peak of stacked bus tubs, Doris comes into the dish-room, as my territory is called, and watches me work. This is a singular occurrence. Not since my five minutes of "training" has management—even the various assistant managers whose job seems to consist of maintaining a certain level of anxiety—set foot in the steamy domain of the dishroom, and here is the one, like Frol, generally acknowledged to be responsible for the smooth operation of practically everything.

I do not alter my food-salvaging routine in the least, but like a cadet performing a long-practiced drill on parade before a visit-ing general, I muster all my skill and showmanship, and play to the grandstand. Buster, as always, looks wildly enthusiastic; the frog jumps for inexhaustible joy; but Doris stands at the edge of my vision smoking and watching, smoking and watching, her opinion shrouded in a cloud of smoke and steam. As for me, I am quite proud of our efforts. Several of the waitresses—organized by Wendy of the commune, I believe—have sensibly decentral-ized the process by keeping their own stash of bread bags at each wait station, so that easily half the food has been bagged before it reaches me. Someone else has distributed markers, and another has developed a simple code so that each bag is marked with its contents. All I have to do for a good many of the tubs is to sort the bags using the bread rack as a holding area. Fearing manage-ment's wrath, some of the busboys and waitresses are not partic-ipating so that there are still tubs coming back with food and dishes all a-jumble, but their number is steadily shrinking.

When I stop to change the gross water, Doris steps up to the bread rack and examines the bags, apparently figuring out the system. From the vegetable shelf, she holds up a bag of French fries, a favorite wasted item. From the perishables shelf she ex-amines a T-bone steak with scarcely a mouthful cut from it that would easily provide dinner for a small family. It would have been in the walk-in by now but the busboys are staying clear of the dishroom as long as Doris is around. She carefully returns each bag to its proper place. The top shelves are filled with bags of bread that look remarkably in the same condition as they began the evening. Modern American bread is so soft, in my opinion, that it is actually the better for having a bracing turn in the fresh air before it is eaten.

She counts the number of bags of bread, and smiles ever so slightly, then turns her calculating look on me. "This is about half the bread we sent out tonight."

"Is okay save?" I ask.

She laughs. It's an odd sound, almost mournful. "Don't try to shit me with this speaka no English stuff," she says. "Okay?"

"Okay. I apologize for the deception. Your husband . . ."

"Apology accepted. Tell me about the bread."

"It's all bread that would have been thrown away, I assure you."

"Oh, I know that. But you *didn't* throw it away. Why not?"

"It is food. I only need three words to say why: *It is food*. How can I throw it away if even a dog might eat it? Why doesn't the restaurant give the customers less instead of wasting so much?"

If my question angers her, she makes no sign of it. In fact, she doesn't seem to be angry at all, more curious, I should say. "They expect a full basket. In a way that's what people are paying for. They want to feel pampered, waited on, special. If we served smaller portions, a lot of customers would think we were cheap and go somewhere else."

"What if you charged less?"

"Then the quality of the food would be questioned."

"So the customers pay so much and waste so much so that they might believe they are special, and be assured that the food, half of which they pitch into the garbage, is of the highest quality?"

She purses her lips and nods. "You might say that." She considers the matter further. "You could definitely say that." Her weariness seems to descend upon her again out of the steamy air. "Yes, that's *exactly* what they're doing." She gives me a wry smile, shakes her head, and starts to walk off.

"It is okay then? What we've been doing?"

"Oh yes. It's fine. Better than fine. If I had any sense, I'd tell you to stop it at once. But if I had any sense, I wouldn't have spent half my life in this place. Now, would I?" She exits quickly. She's had enough of talking to me for one evening.

Our entire conversation in the noisy dishroom has been shouted so that we might hear one another, with the result that anyone close by could hear as well. Two busboys appear moments after Doris's departure to convey food to the walk-in. From the smiles on their faces, I gather that they heard every word. Soon the entire crew knows, and every single one of them helps rescue quality food from the pampered plates of those who've been brought up good capitalists since infancy to measure their worth by consumption, and since even a glutton can only consume so much, they end up measuring their worth by how much they can waste. They are not evil, nor do they make any truly evil decisions. It's how the economy is structured. Modern America is the plumpest place I've ever seen. But even so, with a consumption ethic and prosperous times, it's a wonder the whole place isn't a-waddle. It's a miracle that anyone at all is thin. Perhaps that explains all that running.

Toward closing time, Wendy stops by the dishroom and shouts over the machine, "Brad told me you need a ride to the club?" I enthusiastically accept this invitation. She further suggests we might find people in need of our salvaged food in Monroe Park across from the cathedral, and we can stop there on the way to the club.

At the end of the evening, the remaining crew loads the bread into the back of Wendy's car, which they all refer to as a boat. "It's my dad's old car," she guiltily explains to me, though I don't know exactly what she's explaining. After a rather spirited debate, the vegetarian minority prevails in the opinion that the meat should be given to dogs and cats, undeniably carnivores, rather than to humans about whom there is clearly some disagreement. Pierce, claiming a contact at the Humane Society, agrees to take charge of the meat—first stop, his aunt's freezer. The rest of us head for the park.

Although I met Wendy last night at the commune, I didn't have a chance to talk to her directly—since she was sitting at the other end of the table—though, as I recall, by the end of the evening she was sitting in Brad's lap. I like her a great deal, her resourcefulness and spirit, but I find her somewhat disquieting as well, though I'm not sure why.

At first I find her *buzzed* head (a term she teaches me) distracting. But she is such a sweet, sensible girl, no more than twenty-one or -two, I soon forget her appearance. Actually, that is not quite true, for she is quite the beauty, a fact rendered more forcefully somehow by the dramatic setting of her shaved head. Her shift done, she has changed into farmer's overalls and a scant knit shirt. The effect is rather endearing—Venus as a tomboy.

She invites me to *ride shotgun* (another term she teaches me when I inquire) explaining its Wild West origins, as four of our fellow workers pack themselves into the rear seat of her car with little room to spare, Deidre in Ahmed's lap and two others whose names I don't recall. Wendy has worked at the restaurant as a *waitron* (another term she teaches me) for two years, and until tonight, never thought there'd be a single good thing about the job except the money.

"What you did was so totally cool," she says.

"We did."

She beams at me. "We did."

As I watch the houses sliding by, I see we're driving past the very spot where Tim Binder picked me up, and I recall my previous journey. Anchee's vision of the future has proven somewhat defective. I met Rachel, just as he wished. I can't say I'm happier for it. At the moment, I should say, I'm rather miserable for it.

I mention to Wendy the possibility of Jonah and me moving into the commune, and she proclaims it an awesome idea and agrees with Brad that there should be no objection from anyone.

"You look like someone who'll do his share of the weeding," she says.

"Indeed I am."

"Mike will be in heaven, living in the same house with Kropotkin himself."

"But I'm not *that* Kropotkin," I say, which is true enough. That fellow's dead and buried. Whoever I am, I've decided, I'm not he.

"You're close enough," Wendy says. "Mike's into Concept. Reality's boring. After all, he didn't write it."

"Mike seems to occupy a special status in the group."

"Yeah. The philosopher king, the alpha male, the Boy Wonder, though Batman split some time back. Here we are."

We come to a stop, and she kills the engine. My brimming questions can wait. I peer into the shadows in and around the rainy park. At first, I see no one. Then the shadows begin to shift and move. Gradually I make them out for what they are: Under every available shelter from the rain—doorways, trees, battered umbrellas, cardboard cartons—dozens of people, mostly black, mostly men, huddle together. There are several children and women in among them, a few dogs looking out from behind a forest of legs. All eye us with curiosity as we inexplicably emerge from Wendy's car into the rain.

We each take an armload of bread. Wendy holds up a pair of loaves and hollers, "Free food!" and we walk among the crowd, each of us immediately surrounded by the hungry. If we possessed Christ's skill at multiplying the loaves, still we would not have had enough for everyone to eat his fill, though I'm not surprised to see that many who reach us first and secure a loaf don't hesitate to share it with comrades less fleet of foot, just as they have no doubt been sharing the scant shelter from the rain all day long.

I had hoped by now that those with true abundance might be as willing to share their excess as these folk huddled under dripping eaves are to share their pittance, but the rich typically possess a superfluity of greed—which helps explain, I suppose, why they are rich in the first place.

Sometimes, however, the young provide the conscience for several generations. So it happened in Russia that the "to the people" movement sprang up in which the best of a generation turned its back on privilege bought by slavery and no virtue of their own, and sought instead to teach the common people to read and write, a "privilege" the State had denied them. By this simple act of justice the seeds of revolution were sown. They had no thought of revolution, any more than these young people have—all strangers to starvation themselves—when they snatch food from the garbage and give it to the hungry.

No one, it seems, in this time and place, can sensibly plead scarcity as an excuse for hunger anymore. Enough food is thrown away every night to feed all these people and more. Those with faith in the State and so-called representative democracy can wring their hands and wonder aloud why the State is allowing such an inexcusable outrage as these homeless, hungry people. The more determined will demand that their elected officials *do* something. Who knows? A committee might investigate the matter, write a report, make recommendations. In the meantime, the police will likely get these poor people out of sight so they don't cause so much concern among the populace.

Or, as we have done this evening, one can simply take the bread from where it is not needed or appreciated and deliver it to where it is. No doubt we've broken several laws in the process. Fortunately, the evidence of our crimes has all been consumed within moments.

As we are returning to the car, a man reaches out and seizes my forearm and spins me about. He is black, grizzled, and angry. "Hey, Red, what the *fuck* do you think you're doing?"

"Well, Gray, what the fuck does it look like I'm doing?"

"Cute. Giving handouts to the po' folks is what it looks like. The people don't need more handouts. It's the system that's fucked."

"I absolutely agree."

He narrows his eyes and takes stock of me. "Then what are you doing this shit for?"

"Waste kills the spirit. We wanted to remind *ourselves* of the difference between food and garbage."

He smiles. "Where are you *from*, man?"

"Russia."

"No shit? Communist?"

"If you mean that state capitalism of Marx and Lenin, no. I'm an anarchist."

"I can relate. Let me tell you though—don't be saying that shit. Watch your back."

Forgetting this is a figure of speech, I turn for a moment and see my companions waiting for me in Wendy's car. I turn back to learn Gray's proper name and wish him farewell, but he is gone.

As we drive away, I catch a glimpse of him moving through the crowd talking to this one and that. Organizing, I would say. Takes one to know one.

"What did that man want?" Deidre asks me.

"Justice," I say.

12 ✿ A Theatrical Evening and the Morning Review

> The Italian opera, in those years, was in some strange way intimately connected with the radical movement, and the revolutionary recitatives in "Wilhelm Tell" and "The Puritans" were always met with stormy applause and vociferations which went straight to the heart of Alexander II.; while in the sixth-story galleries, and in the smoking-room of the opera, and at the stage door the best part of the St. Petersburg youth came together in a common idealist worship of a noble art. All this may seem childish; but many higher ideas and pure inspirations were kindled in us by this worship of our favorite artists.
>
> —PETER KROPOTKIN, *Memoirs of a Revolutionist*

> Spies can imitate anything else but ethics.
>
> —PETER KROPOTKIN, *Memoirs of a Revolutionist*

I'm not sure what I expect to find at the club (if the club has a name, no one bothers using it)—something a good deal more "modern" certainly, filled to bursting with drum machines, synthesizers, and electric guitars. What I find is a play in progress on a homely wooden stage surrounded by an audience that mostly stands in a theater made entirely for groundlings. A bar runs the length of the wall opposite the stage providing seating for the shorter rather than the wealthier on its somewhat damp surface. Wendy and I find snug places there beside Dave, who stands, and Caitlin, who sits behind him with her legs wrapped around his waist, her elbows resting on his shoulders.

Just as I am settling onto the plastic surface, the crowd gives out a tremendous yell, and I jump into the air. No one seems particularly startled but me. Caitlin and Dave explain what is going on: The audience has been given the line "Free Trade!" to be shouted in full voice when any character gives the cue, "We call this . . ." The one exception is the heroine, to whom we respond, "Revolution!" This participatory element keeps everyone in boisterous spirits awaiting the next opportunity to shake the rafters, or in this case, pipes, for the ceiling is a maze of them. The club is in the basement of a large building I take to have been a church at one time, though I didn't get a proper look at it before I descended the winding metal stairs.

The plot of the play is pure melodrama: A virtuous maiden, Tercera, and her sickly, aged father, Antiguo, are set upon by various vile thieves and seducers, while Tercera maintains her virtue and pluck throughout. Antiguo, since the play was undoubtedly penned by a young playwright, has very little to do but dodder. Despite the grim subject matter, the episodes are rendered outrageously with flamboyant good humor. I'm reassured the play has only just begun and settle in, eager to be enchanted.

In the present scene, Supermarket Man to the World is refusing to buy Tercera and Antiguo's crops unless they use his outrageously priced patented seeds (stolen from the old man years before). Supermarket Man wears bright blue tights, red hose, and a cape, with the letters SM on his chest, a costume, my companions explain to me, which brings to mind a hero famous for upholding "Truth, Justice, and the American Way"—a trio who appear in the play in the guise of the Three Blind Mice following Supermarket Man about with tin beggars' cups and cardboard signs around their necks identifying them. Now and again, after some underhanded dealing or other, the trio will rattle their cups furiously, and Supermarket Man will drop a few coins into each one, inquiring of the grateful rodent, "What do we call this?"

Free Trade!

". . . and this?"

Free Trade!

"... and this?"

Free Trade!

He sports an outrageous stuffed phallus he calls the Little Man of Steal, waving it about to great comic effect until Tercera, in a forceful renunciation of his unwelcome advances, lops it off with a machete. "My seed! My seed!" he cries, as Tercera sprinkles the crowd with its confetti stuffing. Tercera, holding machete and her now-limp prize aloft, asks the crowd, "What do we call this?"

Revolution!

"I didn't hear you!"

Revolution!

Her victory is short-lived, however, for she must fly from the World Trade Police, who have been alerted by Supermarket Man's cries. They wear helmets reminiscent of welders' masks (plastic, of course) and carry very nasty-looking nightsticks, but their badges (emblazoned with dollar signs) are pinned to the lapels of spruce business suits. Their prim care to avoid soiling these suits impedes their progress to such an extent that Tercera and Antiguo manage to escape by running through their cornfield.

But the hapless pair runs right into Enormous Mack. He is dressed in a music-hall cow suit with the addition of a curly red wig and a clown's bulbous nose. Teetering atop his head is an extra pair of horns, Texas longhorns by the look of them, with which he manages to gouge, tangle, upset, or break everything that crosses his path—trees, crops, members of the audience. He's very jolly with a wild-eyed look, all the wilder for his having three eyes.

He offers Tercera a sandwich he calls The Mirthful Mouthful, but when she cautiously accepts, he produces a syringe of bright green fluid with which he injects the sandwich. "What's that stuff?" Tercera demands.

"This? We call this . . ."

Free Trade!

"Would you like me to supersize that for you?" he asks, producing a syringe the size of a salami. When she refuses, he tries to force it on her. In the ensuing slapstick struggle, Tercera and Mack freeze repeatedly in tableau—his foot upon her neck, sitting on her back, twisting her leg—and he will shout each time in his jolly voice, "We call this . . ."

Free Trade!

But the tide turns, and she manages to inject him with his own syringe. Whereupon he undertakes a hilarious aria of gags and retches culminating in his dropping dead, managing somehow, with his dying breath, to call for the cops.

Tercera throws horns and syringe in the path of the pursuing World Trade Police, and they fall all over one another in a hilarious heap, as Tercera extols the crowd for cry after cry of *Revolution!*

Tercera and her father flee to the forest (by means of hinged tree flats springing upright all around them) hoping for a new life there and singing a song to its virtues. (A bit sappy and tedious, that, so I'll spare you). When all of a sudden, the chorus is cut short by a loud motor firing up, and Kimberly Clark Kent steps onto the stage. He is the very soul of a proper butler—except for the roaring motorized saw he uses to slice his way across the stage toward our heroes, the hinged tree flats falling to the boards with a resounding slap. As each tree falls, Kimberly Clark Kent shouts out, "We call this!"

Free Trade!

"We call this!"

Free Trade!

"We call this!"

Free Trade!

I'm laughing, shouting with the best of them, even though I don't get a good many of the jokes—and would probably not find them quite so funny if I did—when I feel a tapping on my shoulder. It's Mike, standing behind the bar. He motions for me to meet him at the end. I jump down and follow him into what turns out to be the green room, and he closes the door behind us.

It's a narrow low-ceilinged affair, more like a hallway than a room, packed with people, and pungent with several varieties of smoke burning at once—cigarette, cannabis, candles, incense, a cigar sometime in the recent past. Along the wall beside the door are several TVs and computers. On the TV screens is the ongoing play from three different perspectives. Three other screens are dark. Brad is at one of the computers—completely engrossed in his labors and not to be interrupted, I'm told, for he is making last-minute adjustments to their impending performance. Interestingly enough, neither TVs nor computers seem to be making a sound.

The room, however, buzzes with a dozen muted conversations. Mike steers me through the crowd too quickly for me to follow the thread of any one of them, but the play's the thing, it seems, that's on everyone's tongue—the line, the cue, the laugh, the applause—when all of a sudden the crowd out front shouts *Revolution!* rattling the walls, suspending conversation, as cast and their satellites smile with satisfaction and wait out the deafening roar. They have every reason to be pleased: They're bringing down the house, perhaps a good deal more.

Enormous Mack, his cow head under his arm, proves to be TJ, and I compliment him on his comic performance. Truth, Justice, and American Way are passing a cannabis cigarette which I decline. Zipper (American Way), still in dark glasses and mouse whiskers, welcomes me into the household, and TJ adds his voice to this sentiment.

That was fast, I think. But before I have a chance to say much more than "thank you," Mike takes my arm and maneuvers me through the rest of the crowd to the other end of the room. "We all discussed it," he says. "You and your friend are welcome to move in anytime."

"That's wonderful news, but don't you think you should at least meet Jonah first?"

"Your vouching for him is good enough."

"Is this your usual procedure? We don't want special treatment."

Mike snickers as if I've made a joke. This is the first time I notice that his eyes are no longer violet but a jade green with catlike irises. "I want you to meet someone," he says. A fortyish fellow in a rumpled linen jacket steps forward out of the general press aiming his hand at me, and I'm rather obliged to take it.

Mike says, "Peter Kropotkin, this is my advisor, Dr. Richard Sapworth."

"A pleasure," he says, tilting his head back in order to assess me, I gather, through the proper portion of his spectacles. His hand retreats upon arrival without ever actually grasping mine. "Cole tells me you're an anarchist."

"Yes."

"Bookchin? Chomsky? Or what's that fellow in Oregon's name?"

"Don't know. I'm a Kropotkin man through and through."

"Oh *really?* That's unusual. Relation?"

"No. I just like the way the man thinks."

He waits for me to elaborate, but I don't. "Interesting. Where is it you teach?"

"I don't."

I smile pleasantly, and he decides I'm a wit. "I know how you feel. They get stupider every year, don't they?"

"The faculty?"

He smirks at my irony. "Them too."

"What's *your* field?" I ask, for I know the etiquette.

"Consciousness Enactment," he says, squaring his shoulders.

"What's that?" I ask.

"Well," he says, rising up on his toes and chuckling, "that *is* The Question, isn't it?"

I would have thought there were several others more pressing, but he considers the matter settled. "Let's start with *The Republic*," he says, and does, and continues on from there without pausing for my *Let's not.* I try to listen, but it all sounds to me like it's just another lemming trek down the it-doesn't-matter-*what*-you-think, only-*how*-you-think road over the it-doesn't-matter-what-you-*do* precipice to drown in a sea of precious pointlessness. I distract myself by observing Sapworth's glasses, which refuse to maintain a purchase on his face, and start a slow, steady slide toward the tip of his long, tapered nose, prompting him to compensate by tilting his head farther and farther back so that he might see me through the lenses, until both he and I are staring at the very tip of his nose—where the glasses teeter, their imminent fall a near certainty—when, with a surprisingly forceful gesture that makes me jump every time, he jams the wayward spectacles back against his face with right index and middle fingertips, blinks a recovery, and the process begins all over again. Both glasses and nose look fairly battered from such treatment, so I gather this is an avocation of some standing.

"No doubt I'm boring you," he says without a great deal of concern. "The work, the work," he says. "I'm sure you understand."

"It sounds quite interesting. I've never thought of Kant in quite those terms before."

"I can e-mail you the paper, if you like."

"Peter's not settled in yet," Mike says. "I'll loan him my copy from the seminar."

Sapworth nods approvingly. "Peter," he says. "I wonder if I could ask you a favor."

"Why certainly." As long as I don't have to listen to you utter another word about consciousness.

"The department does this lecture series for the *honors* program—one of those 'serve the larger university community' things—and you know how undergraduates are, they're always requesting *social* theory, and we don't really have anybody since Ditameyer took early retirement last year. Mike suggested you might be willing to do the next lecture. He passed on your *vita*. Your list of publications is really quite impressive. I know you're on sabbatical, but we've had a last-minute cancellation, and this would get me out of a jam. There's a small honorarium. Nothing much. You can tell them about Kropotkin and *anarchism*."

He says the word with the same tone a chemist might use when speaking of *phlogiston* or the *philosopher's stone*. I should say no, I suppose, especially since Mike has obviously lied to the man, even forged credentials, but someone should pick up Dita-meyer's fallen banner and set this sneering fellow straight. "Certainly," I say. "I'd be delighted. What sort of audience might I expect?"

"Oh, twenty or thirty, juniors and seniors mostly. They're supposedly the best and brightest, but they just fall asleep like the rest of them. Except Cole here." He tilts his head to take in Mike at the proper angle. "Bright lad."

The bright lad says he needs to be getting onstage pretty soon, and we retreat from Sapworth. "I'll call," the doctor says by way of farewell.

"What did you tell him about me?" I ask Mike when we're out of earshot.

"That you're an anarchist like he said. An expert, in fact. I thought you'd welcome the opportunity to address a group of bright young people on the subject of anarchism."

"Yes, I suppose I would." *How is it you know that?* I think to ask but don't bother. After many years experience with the profession, Sophie and I eventually came to the conclusion that if one can bear the fellow, it's best not to smoke out a suspected spy, for his place will only be taken by someone more disagreeable or subtle.

Free Trade! the crowd shouts, and Mike, pleading his imminent performance, quickens our pace. "How do you like the play so far?" he asks at the door.

"I like it very much," I say.

"It's mine," he says proudly. "I wrote it."

I return to the audience, and the door closes behind me.

In the play, meanwhile, matters have taken a dark turn. Tercera's father lies center stage, dead of causes unknown to me. The General—his chest so festooned with medals that he lists under their weight—pursues Tercera down a lonely road. Tercera, Caitlin fills me in, has been laboring long hours at low wages in the General's factory making Senseless Useless Vehicles. Her father has just died from a heart attack brought on

when he hears of a girl murdered on the road and becomes convinced it's Tercera.

The General is truly obese and wheezes along with little
chance of catching her, but Tercera, who has grown exhausted
and sickly, discovers her father's corpse and gives way to despair, falling to her knees. The General seizes her, shrugs off his
clanking coat, and pins her to the ground with its weight.

"I may be old and fat, but I always get my way!" he says,
dropping his pants, and then proceeds to rape her, cupping one
hand to his ear as he calls out his line, thrusting precisely when
the crowd answers its cue, so that we are all made complicitous
in her violation:

"We call this . . ."

Free Trade!

"We call this . . ."

Free Trade!

"We call this . . ."

Free Trade!

On this horrifying image, the lights dim, a chord strikes on an
electric guitar, and the lights come up on Hemlock Cocktail.
Mike steps forward, fist raised, and shouts: "We call this *Revolution!*"

The noise of the crowd and the music is like a terrific explosion, reverberating through every atom in my body, and without
quite knowing how I got here, I find myself bobbing up and
down in a turbulent sea of youth shouting—*Revolution!*

After several hours at the club, a dozen of us go for an early
breakfast in a diner, a modern eating establishment filled with all
manner of persons—students, workers, carousers, lovers—all attempting to prolong Saturday night.

The place, my companions explain to me, is decorated in the
manner of a vision of the future common in the 1950s. They call
it *retro*—a future old before its time—a concept I would find

more amusing, I'm sure, if I were entirely certain it doesn't apply to me. There is chrome on everything from napkin dispensers to barstools. Plastic replicas of cigar- and saucer- and donut-shaped spaceships dangle everywhere from fishing line. They figure as well in a garish mural that covers one wall—along with mechanical men resembling napkin dispensers and barstools, and people from other planets who are as bald as Wendy, their eyes even larger, their skin the color of moonglow. I can't say there is *more* plastic than usual, though it is less discreet, rather proud of itself you might say, in bright shiny colors emblazoned with patterns no tree or stone would ever come up with, like the table-top—turquoise covered with tiny gold boomerangs the size of peanuts. Nowadays, it seems, plastic is more likely to look like wood or marble or leather or some such. My guess is that plastic used to mean the future, and now it means phony or cheap, even though it's everywhere.

The noise in the diner rivals the racket in my dishroom, and I am already hoarse from shouting to be heard in the club. All night long, however, I've asked endless questions, and my young friends have answered tirelessly. *What is withholding? What sort of company is Microsoft? There is another Madonna? What is a Munchkin? What does "hard-core" mean?* Remedying my ignorance becomes something of a game, and I get caught up in the spirit of it and am not as circumspect as I should be. Although my foreignness forgives my ignorance of practically every-thing—as does the youth of my informants (the young easily accept, even expect, ignorance on the part of someone even a decade older than themselves when it comes to matters of any real importance)—my unbridled excitement at being informed that men and women have, in fact, traveled into space, even to the moon and back, stretches their credulity to the breaking point.

"How could you not know?" a drunk fellow, whose name I don't recall, demands, clearly voicing the unspoken opinion of the majority. "Have you been living in a fucking cave or what? There's like cosmonauts and shit, right?" He turns to his companions. "How could he *not* know? *One small step for man* and all that shit?"

Just then, there are approximately two dozen loud conversations going on at the same time as our own, some accented with bursts of laughter, table banging, and swearing. Roughly a half dozen whirring, chugging, churning machines are in operation. The clatter of dishes provides percussion for the music, a lively tune I would guess is called "Jailhouse Rock," resounding over all. Perhaps it's the prison theme that brings an answer to mind. Recalling the effect the place had on Alicia, I shout full voice into the din, "I lived in *Siberia*," and vanquish my drunken critic in an instant. Judging from the reaction of everyone, the Bolsheviks must have outdone even the czars in turning that vast and beautiful region into an infamous prison whose borders are impregnable to any news that might resemble hope.

At this moment, the din lulls, seemingly of its own accord—conversations pause, machines stop, the last chord of the song sounds, not a dish touches a dish—and Mike languidly addresses the assembly in a normal tone of voice: "If you want to know what people *everywhere* know about America, it's not NASA. Guess what's the second most widely recognized English word in the world after 'okay.' " He doesn't wait for our guesses but smiles knowingly and announces the answer himself: "Coke!"

No one in his audience is surprised by this fact but me, and even though most of them are drinking that very beverage as they denounce it—as am I—they find this information wretched in the extreme. Fortunately, when asked, I can honestly claim a long-standing familiarity with Coca-Cola (having drunk it several times in New York in 1901). My knowledge of Coke, in spite of my sojourn in Siberia, wins Mike a toast to his cleverness largely consisting of this same beverage, an irony he makes much of. Mike is, perhaps, a performer who never leaves off performing.

I drink several bottles of Coke during the course of the evening and find the quality much eroded, though I keep this opinion to myself. It used to be quite a frisky concoction as I recall. The modern stuff seems paltry by comparison. I suspect the quantity of cocaine has been greatly reduced or else eliminated altogether.

Outside the diner, Wendy volunteers to take me to get Jonah, and I readily accept. Mike and Brad say they'll proceed to the house and ready the basement for occupancy. I object to any special efforts being made, but they assure me they only mean to straighten up a bit.

Everyone is being so kind to me, I feel terrible when Mike takes me aside as we're walking to the cars, and asks my opinion of his play now that I've seen the whole thing, and I have to tell him the truth. "I liked a great deal about it"—I enumerate several favorite moments—"but I didn't care for the ending at all."

"Why not? Did you want some kind of *happy ending?*"

I recall Sapworth's snide *anarchism* and imagine Mike's advisor is advising him on manners and humility as well as academics. "The woman is raped, Mike."

"Yes? Did that *shock you?*"

"I should hope so. But that's not my objection. It communicates despair. We follow this woman through all sorts of trials and tribulations. For things to end that way—it's awful. It is hope, not despair, which makes successful revolutions."

"There's hope only if people rise up."

"Perhaps. But Tercera is still lying there raped. She rose up, and look what happened to her. What's worse, we were all made to watch—almost to participate. How will that inspire your audience to act?"

"I don't want to *inspire* them. I want to piss them off. I want them to turn their anger into action. There's hope in action."

"I agree. But hope for whom? What is *her* hope—to provide the motivation for young nightclubbers to revolt? She's raped by the villains, but she's abandoned by the playwright."

"You're being too literal. It's just a play. She's just a symbol."

Just a symbol. I try to imagine Turgenev saying such a thing—he who used to keep personal diaries for his characters—and I'm not quite sure what to say. "Symbols are never *just* symbols, are they? People's lives are changed by symbols—by Hamlet talking to ghosts, Quixote charging windmills, William Tell fighting oppression. More than one fellow—Kropotkin included—has been willing to fight to carry a flag that *stands* for something. But a symbol that's just a symbol isn't worth bothering about."

His face is a pleasant mask. I didn't like his play. He heard that much (and that much only) of what I've said. "I'll see you at the house," he says, and gives me an indifferent smile.

13 ❀ Losers' Lane

Our new government is founded upon exactly the opposite idea [from the U.S. Constitution]; its foundations are laid, its corner-stone rests upon the great truth, that the negro is not equal to the white man; that slavery—subordination to the superior race—is his natural and normal condition. This, our new government, is the first, in the history of the world, based upon this great physical, philosophical, and moral truth.
> —ALEXANDER STEPHENS, Vice President of the
> Confederacy, March 21, 1861

Our particular legacy causes us some real problems—additional difficulties that other communities do not have. In a lot of ways, the Civil War has been an albatross around our neck.
> —TIMOTHY KAINE, Mayor of Richmond, 2000

At the first light of day, Wendy drives me down to the river to get Jonah. "What were you and Mike talking about?" she asks.

"His play. I told him I didn't like the ending."

"Ooh, I bet that went over well."

"I felt bad, but—"

"Don't worry about it. The damage'll do him good."

Fog shrouds everything, and the rain threatens to begin anew. The feeling of unreality is increased by our being the only persons stirring except police cars and men delivering newspapers. "Richmond's dead on Sunday morning," Wendy observes. "When I first moved here as a kid, I got up on Sunday, went outside, and thought the world had like totally ended or something."

I know from our evening's conversations that her relations

("my people," as she puts it) are all from Richmond, but she spent her early years in Houston, where her father had had some business dealings at the time. She considers herself a Richmonder, she says, even if her aunts don't quite agree, having missed some key component of her education by failing to attend the right schools until she was almost twelve and it was too late. She squints at the street sign. "Turn here, right?"

"Right."

She has been half following my directions, and half her instincts up to this point. She's asked me to let her find the place on her own if she can, shunning any glimpse of the map, a test of her memory I gather. "I think I know where it is," she says repeatedly, as if I were expressing some doubt. "I'm pretty sure." From here on, the brown James River Park signs guide her, and she smiles at her triumph as we pull into the parking lot, a sizable slab of tarmacadam. The city is littered with them, the majority of the time, like this one, entirely empty—and although I find the longing for order evident in their precisely drawn parallel stripes (like primitive taboo lines) childishly touching, I can't help remarking that a quarter of this acreage under cultivation could easily feed the entire city.

Wendy stops the car where there are no stripes, in front of the NO CAMPING ALLOWED sign, and shuts off the engine. "Here we are," she says.

We're slow to move. Neither of us has slept a wink. It's tempting to just sit here. Finally, Wendy pulls the keys out of the ignition, and we get out of the car. The echo of the closing doors fades into a deep silence. I breathe in the lush damp air and feel immediately refreshed. It's hard to imagine that all the long and noisy night this peaceful stillness waited here. Maybe Earl's right, and there's no place in the city for the likes of me. But Man—or as my young friends have corrected me when I speak in this sexist fashion, *humans*—are a social species: we want to be with others of our kind. The river will always be here waiting should I need its refuge, or should I wish to sail away to wherever it is one goes these days to start all over again. The moon, perhaps. I shall become—what is the term my drunk accuser used? a *cosmonaut.* I chuckle at the thought.

In the distance some geese call to one another, and, closer by, crows comment on our arrival in low, confidential croaks. I wonder if one of them might be my kidnapped friend. It's nice to think he's enjoyed the same success as I in finding a compatible rookery, though perhaps, like Earl, he's decided—or been forced—to go it alone.

Wendy looks around with a drowsy feline smile. "I knew I knew this place. I've never been here in the daylight before. There's like a little bridge and a ton of stairs and a muddy trail, right? I came here skinny-dipping a few times. I *thought* this was where we came, but I didn't know for sure. I never was driving, thank God." She rolls her eyes and head in a comic rendition of blissful inebriation, which turns into a stretch, her hands up high, standing on tiptoe, then settling back down.

"'Skinny-dipping'?" I ask.

"Swimming. You know—without a suit. *Nekkid!* In the summer, after work, on a hot night—it's the best. A bunch of us used to come down here late when there was a moon, get high and swim."

"The . . . uh . . . waitresses?"

"Oh everybody. This is when Chaney was still around, and we'd all pile in the back of his pickup."

I imagine, somewhat too vividly, all my coworkers naked, cavorting in the moonlit river like a family of otters. "This is a common recreation?" I ask, my voice an unintentional croak, appropriate, I suppose, for a cold-blooded observer of this warm mammalian party.

"You're embarrassed!" she accurately accuses, and there's no point in my denying it. She finds this amusing, and, if possible, my embarrassment deepens. "It's a pretty 'common recreation,' " she reassures me. "My *parents* wouldn't do it—though who knows—when they were young in the sixties. It wasn't like an *orgy* or anything; we were just swimming, hanging out, enjoying life, you know?"

"Yes," I say, my voice still perilously shrill. "I imagine it is a good deal warmer in Richmond than it is in Russia." I say this with some conviction to underscore my broad-minded view of the matter, and to provide some scientific basis and direction for the discussion.

"You know what Tom Robbins says about Richmond summers?"

"I can't imagine."

"'Hotter than the inside of a napalmed watermelon!'" she quotes cheerfully. "He's from Richmond, you know. Have you read his stuff? It's pretty cool."

"No, no I haven't."

"Anyway, I think nudity's cool," she says. "Least it's not about shopping and posing and all that shit. You don't have to *buy* anything to get naked."

She's right, of course, and I tell her so, but have no desire to linger on the subject. Actually, I have precisely that desire, but am not sure how I feel about having it. I am obviously not so cold-blooded as I thought. I'm not seventy-eight anymore, I remind myself, or rather, I am seventy-eight. It's only my body that's young again. Now, however, doesn't strike me as the most opportune moment to explore this discrepancy.

I've given Wendy the sketchiest narrative of Jonah's situation—telling her that he's a refugee in ill health, having been abused by his oppressors—and unlike Rachel, she has accepted the story at face value. Sooner or later, however, the deception will have to be tested. It may as well be now. It's possible, of course, that Jonah may prefer to remain here on the river—I have had no opportunity to consult him in the matter—but at least he should meet someone from the present-day city before he makes up his mind. I can think of no better representative than the forthright Wendy.

We come bearing shoes, for in the process of narrating Jonah's tale I recalled that he was shoeless, and I could not imagine his faring well in the city for long without shoes. As I'd hoped, the offer of shoes was forthcoming from all quarters—in a range of

sizes excavated from various cars. The drunk fellow donated the
size nines I predict to be the most likely to fit, though we also
have eights, tens, and a largish sandal called flip-flops. Plastic, of
course.

As we descend into the foggy woods and across the bridge, I
spot a V-shaped ripple in the canal and point out a beaver swimming just below us, a stick in its mouth.

"Awesome," she whispers so quietly I wouldn't have known
what she said if I hadn't heard the word so many times last night
I expect it. I can't decide whether the word has been emptied of
all meaning in modern times or whether these young people
react with awe to a wider range of phenomena than was common in my day. In the case of beavers, however, a highly evolved
and industrious social species whose engineering skills are unri-
valed, I must agree that they are indeed truly awesome. Her eyes
shine as she watches it disappear into the fog; the transforming
look on her face is most definitely awe.

At the bottom of the stairs, following Earl's directions, we
pass through the fence and walk along the railroad tracks.
"These are the tracks where the damn coal trains go," she says.
There's a coal-fueled electric-generating plant east of here, she
tells me, pointing downstream with a black loafer; there's also a
seaport from which coal is exported in prodigious quantities for
combustion in similar facilities throughout the world.

I would think this good news—for isn't the labor of electri-
cally powered machines to be preferred over the backbreaking
efforts of fellows like Jonah? But I catch her tone, and ask cautiously, "Is there something wrong with that?"

As we walk along, she explains to me, with remarkable clarity
and concision, the greenhouse effect, acid rain, and global warming (with side trips into the evils of strip-mining and the virtues
of sustainable resource management), and for the first time I
learn that, like myself, she is a serious student of the geographical and biological sciences, and a dabbler in several others.

"My wife," I tell her, "was a scientist also." All evening, for
some reason, Wendy has been the one I say such things to. *My*

wife loved the mountains. My wife was very brave. Recalling the look on Wendy's face as she watched the beaver swim away, I realize why that is: She reminds me of Sophie.

"So y'all must've talked science all the time."

"Indeed we did. And politics."

"You must miss her a lot," she says.

"Yes, I do. You . . . remind me of her—when . . . when she was your age."

"Really?" She smiles, looking more pleased with this information than I hope I intended when I blurted it out. But it's true nonetheless. True also that she reminds me of my daughter, though I can't very well say *that.*

When she was your age, I said—which is to say, about twenty-two, Sophie's age when I married her. I was thirty-six at the time, four years older, in a sense, than I am now. Forty-two years ago.

"Do you possibly know anything about time travel?" I inquire, changing the subject, or at least the perspective.

"Just the stuff everybody knows," she says. "Einstein and relativity and all of that. I'm not into physics so much. It's so male, you know? The Big Bang! I mean, what's that about?"

I would confess my total incomprehension of everything she has just said and request she explain it all to me beginning with "the stuff everybody knows," but we have reached our destination, the second hole in the fence, and before we proceed any farther, I see fit to inform her casually, so that she won't be unduly surprised or alarmed, what to expect: "Jonah is still somewhat disoriented from his experiences before coming here, so he might seem a bit confused. He's been staying with another fellow who lives down here—rather eccentric, as you'll see, but no harm to anyone, I assure you."

But she doesn't need my assurances, not for herself at any rate. "Another homeless man?"

"Homeless? I guess you would say that."

"Does he need a place, too?"

She seems perfectly prepared to take in another unfortunate at the drop of a hat, and although I'm touched by her generosity, I feel confident in stating Earl's opinion on the matter: "No. He'd prefer to stay here, I believe. He holds some rather strong opinions of the city. It hasn't served him well."

She steps through the hole in the fence as if passing through the gates of a country estate. "Awesome," she says, for there is a grand view of the river and Belle Isle, looming in the fog. Sweeping over the far end of the island is the enormous automobile bridge that terrified Earl when he first awoke. Wendy calls it the Lee Bridge. Below it is the footbridge where I was to meet Rachel in a few hours. I fleetingly imagine this meeting as I first fancied it—filled with joy and passion. What is it Jonah says? *I miss a place I never see and people I never know.*

"Peter," Wendy asks softly. "Are you okay?"

"Yes, I'm fine. Just a bit ragged at the edges. Exhaustion makes me wax philosophical."

"Is that what does it?" she teases.

"Maybe I should try to rouse our hosts," I say. I had expected the watchful Earl to have welcomed us by now, but there's not a sign of anyone. "Hello!" I holler cheerily. "It's Peter. I've brought a friend."

The only sound is the roar of the rapids at some distance below. The narrow trail only goes one way, and we follow it for a dozen paces but can go no farther. It reaches a promontory that drops off steeply, a lone oak leans precariously over the water. Greenbriers block our passage in any direction other than the one we've come. After being snared by thorns repeatedly, my patience snags and tears. "Jonah! Earl! Where are you?" I shout at the top of my lungs.

There is no reply.

"Are you sure this is the right place?" Wendy asks. "Maybe we should go back."

At the sound of Wendy's voice, fierce whispers start up beneath our feet as if we have stumbled upon a congress of snakes in session. The whispering rises in sputtering intensity until Jonah's baritone breaks free in full voice: "We're down here, Peter. Earl's scared of the woman."

"I am not *scared*," Earl protests—and to prove his point flings open a trapdoor at my feet with a resounding bang against my shin—then sticks his head out of the ground like a prairie dog. I howl in pain and momentarily imagine myself a large raptor drawing a bead on Earl's prairie dog brains. I advise him rather forcefully to be more careful in future. But neither Jonah nor Earl attends my bellowing. They are completely befuddled by Wendy. Both of them gape at her with expressions of blissful anguish or anguished bliss; it's difficult to settle on the precise proportions. The unexpected sight of a pretty young woman accounts for their pleasure, but what they find so unsettling I can't imagine. Perhaps it's her buzzed head, though I would've thought Earl inured to such sights of the modern world by now. I've only been here a few days, and as Wendy would say, the hair's no big deal.

But whatever has struck them dumb, it's long past time to move beyond staring, however smilingly. I signal for my comrades to show some manners and climb up out of the ground, and they immediately comply.

"I know you," Wendy says to Earl before I have a chance to introduce them. "You're Earl, aren't you? I'm Wendy. Remember me?"

"Crazy Earl," he says with a halfhearted antic face and a shuffling dance step. He's wild-eyed, his smile a pained grimace. It's as if he's been seized with a terrible case of stage fright. "This gentleman here is . . . is . . . Jonah," he says. The hand he sweeps Jonah's way trembles like a leaf in a gust.

There are many sources of Earl's discomfort, I'm sure. But mostly, I believe, the man's embarrassed, deeply embarrassed, and my heart goes out to him. I should've realized. I imagine him on his front porch over a century ago, offering his hospitality in good Southern fashion, his wife at his side. Now he lives in an oversize grave. He bends at the waist, impaling himself on a greenbrier.

Meanwhile, Jonah, equally jittery, ducks his head in an obsequious gesture befitting a cautious slave introduced to an outrageous-looking white woman, and will not look her in the eye for fear of giving offense. Just as I despair of being responsible for arranging this disastrous meeting, Wendy grabs each of them by the hand and gives them both such a good shake that they're yanked into standing upright like the men that they are. Wendy, whose blessing is the true measure of this ritual after all, smiles like a young goddess, and we all feel as if we're clever fellows indeed to have pleased her so.

She knows Earl, she tells me and Jonah, from a volunteer organization that provides a free meal every Sunday in the park, an event where Earl was once a regular, an event to which she invites us all. "No animal products of any kind," Wendy says proudly of the healthy fare.

"No meat," Earl agrees forlornly, but hastily adds, "Good though. Real good." He looks around apologetically, suffering a fresh attack of the troubled host. "I don't have but two chairs," he says in a panic, looking prepared to thrash himself for this lapse in etiquette.

"Who needs chairs?" Wendy says. To make her case she sits on the ground, and we all express our solidarity with her by planting our bottoms on the damp earth in a semicircle before her.

"How long have you been in America?" Wendy asks Jonah, who has been observing her with the same care an angel come to announce the Second Coming might afford from a devout Christian.

"Last night," he says. "I come to America just yesterday."

"You're kidding!" Wendy exclaims. "That's *so* awesome!"

And once again I must agree to the aptness of the term. And she doesn't even know the half of it.

As I would've predicted, Jonah welcomes the offer of a residence in town, and Earl cringes at the mere suggestion. While Wendy explains the workings of the commune to an intent Jonah, as he tries on shoes, I take Earl aside and thank him for everything he's done and apologize for invading his privacy.

"Woman gave me a turn is all," he says in his defense. "I . . . I . . . wasn't expecting her. I'm all right now. She's a good one. I remember her. Jonah should be okay with a few days' bed rest if he doesn't do anything foolish. I changed the dressing, and the bleeding looks to be under control." He slips me a roll of white cotton gauze wrapped in plastic and a tube of ointment. "This stuff here is real good."

"Where did you get these things?"

"They always stick you in a little room with swabs and bandages and such. You'll see. *The doctor will be right with you.* You sit there for days, weeks. Anymore, I just get what I need and take care of myself."

Wendy, spotting the roll of gauze, thinks to ask Jonah how he's doing. "Are you still in a lot of pain?" she asks sympathetically.

"It hurts a bit," he admits. "But I'm feeling much better, thank you."

"Are you taking anything for it?"

"It?"

"The pain." She searches in her handbag and pulls out an orange vial much like the one that previously housed Earl's medicine turned catfish food. "They gave me these when I was in a wreck last year," Wendy says. "Rolled three times. Totaled it. Nasty bruises. Trust me. These will make you feel *lots* better." She shakes one capsule into her hand, shrugs, then a second, and places them on Jonah's upturned palm. "Try these out."

He pops them into his mouth and swallows.

"It takes a while," Wendy says. "Twenty–thirty minutes."

As I predicted, Jonah has selected the drunk fellow's shoes. Wendy says they are running shoes, and they look indeed as if they have traversed a good deal of pavement. Jonah is quite pleased with them.

Earl advises that we best be on our way sooner than later, for a train will be coming through directly. I suspect he's trying to rid himself of us, for try as he might, he can't seem to relax completely in the presence of such a large company. He fetches my things, neatly stowed in a plastic bag, and puts them in my knapsack for me. I ask him to look after my fishing pole, and he solemnly accepts that responsibility.

He holds stray bits of briar and low-hanging branches out of our way as he accompanies us to the hole in the fence which serves as the threshold of his domain, and there he wishes us a fond farewell. The loneliness of his life on this accidental strip of real estate between railroad and river seems embodied in his forlorn wave, and it occurs to me as we round the bend and he disappears into the briars, that he is not one who doesn't care about his fellows so much as one who fears caring about them altogether too much. I resolve to call on him again and make some use of my fishing pole.

Realizing I never got to see his underground dwelling, I ask Jonah about it.

"It's a hole in the ground," he says, shaking his head. "Don't care much for it."

"He must think it suits him though."

Jonah's not so sure. He shakes his head. "Earl, he got some troubles in his mind. It's hard to say what suits him anymore."

"Do you know his story?" Wendy asks. "When he used to come to the park, he always seemed like a really nice man, but he didn't like to talk about himself."

"He told his story to me," Jonah says. "He got put in a terrible prison. He said he watched too many people die there. I think he said right. Broke his heart, seems like."

"What was he in prison for?"

"Not sure what you call it," Jonah says. "He got put in jail for lifting up his hand against slavery."

"A prisoner of conscience."

Jonah chuckles at the phrase. "I like that," he says. "Prisoner of conscience. But his conscience be free—elsewise they wouldn't be locking him up. I think he was the prisoner of men with guns and chains, what you think?"

Wendy is more than happy to agree, and I'm delighted to see these two getting along so well.

When we get to the stairs, Jonah is brought up short. He stands in the trail and looks the structure up and down. He's never seen anything quite like it before, a boxy hulking thing of concrete and rusting metal. "What's the other side of the bridge?" he asks.

"Another hill. Do you need a hand?" I ask, only out of politeness, for it's clear he does.

"No. I be fine," he says, though exhaustion is written all over his face.

Wendy sticks out her arm and insists he take it, and he readily complies. I can see that she has a most persuasive effect upon him, as perhaps the medicine he swallowed does as well, for his smile, though weary, is positively beatific, and he has ceased wincing from the pain of his wounds. She has indeed proved an angel of mercy. She helps him mount the several flights of stairs, and supports his weight as we rest on the bridge. Just then, a coal train shows up as Earl predicted, and Jonah does not tire of watching it slide by in an endless clanking slither, dozens and dozens of cars, each with a mounded black loaf of coal weighing a hundred tons or more. We watch until it's out of sight, on its way to enshroud the world in soot.

When we are settled in the car—Jonah in the honored shotgun position—Wendy asks him if he would be up for seeing some of the city before going to the house, and naturally he agrees. Regardless of the destination, he can scarcely contain himself at the prospect of riding in an automobile, the general principles of which I explained to him previously. He examines everything, opening and closing a compartment in front of him, raising and lowering a flap above the window, cranking the window up and down. He asks Wendy about the operation of the gear-shifting lever, and I fear she will wonder at his ignorance, but she takes it in stride. Apparently not everyone drives so many automobiles as Americans do. She calls it a stick shift and confesses that she only recently learned its operation herself. I gather from this it must be the latest technology. Jonah is so intent upon learning about it, the steering wheel, the pedals, the radio, the door lock, the gauges, and so forth . . . that he scarcely seems to notice the city all around him, except the traffic signals. He is particularly taken with the pedestrian signal lights—a raised orange hand and a walking white man for stop and go respectively.

But when we pass a black man in a business suit getting into an automobile, Jonah swivels about and watches with rapt attention as the man gets in his car and drives away. Jonah looks to me and mouths his question—*free?*

I nod yes, though I suspect from my observations thus far, matters are a good deal more complex than a simple yes or no. But he'll learn such subtleties soon enough.

Wendy notices none of this. Her spirits are high, and she is eager to show us the sights, an enthusiasm which translates into a livelier style of driving than heretofore. She speaks of getting "a second wind" and is, perhaps, still under the influence of the cannabis, alcohol, and Coca-Cola I saw her consuming during the course of the evening, and perhaps a good deal else I didn't see. We have the streets practically to ourselves, it seems, so I am not overly concerned. And to my surprise, Jonah delights in our speed, inquiring more than once how fast we are going and responding with a measure of glee proportionate to the rate of speed he is told. From where I sit, I have a clear view of the gauge indicating velocity. When the dial exceeds fifty miles per hour, I can bear to look no more.

"Okay," Wendy announces in a commanding voice, "the first thing you got to see is Monument Avenue—or as I like to call it, Losers' Lane. I did a report on it in high school that almost got me kicked out," she adds proudly. "Do you know about the American Civil War?" she asks Jonah.

"Peter told me about it," he says.

"So you know the South lost."

"Yes," Jonah replies.

"Then that puts you way ahead of some Richmonders," she says, laughing. "I mean, like where else do you have statues for the losing side, much less a whole avenue? You see any British generals around here? You think they have statues of Rommel and Goebbels in Germany? Do you think they have *Hitler* Day? The thing about Richmond is for a few years there it was the capital of the Confederacy—a whole other country—and never got over it. It's like they don't know they lost.

"These monuments you're about to see are protected by a state law passed in the seventies when the city was about to become majority black because of white flight, empowering the governor to call out the state *militia* if the city ever tries to get rid of these losers. I say, *bring 'em on!*"

I understand only a little of this, and Jonah must understand less. But I add Rommel and Goebels and Hitler to Einstein as Germans I must investigate. Before I can inquire what *white flight* means—I picture a huge flock of egrets—we reach our destination.

"Here we are!" Wendy sings out. A bronze statue of a man on horseback lies dead ahead, and we are on a collision course with the horse's hindquarters.

"This is Jeb Stuart," Wendy says, putting the automobile in a tight circle around the statue so that we swirl about it as if in a whirlpool. It is one of the most dramatic soldier-on-horseback statues I have ever seen. The subject is turned in his saddle, looking back, blade drawn, about to order a charge, no doubt. The horse is stopped, but its mane and tail fly wildly, every muscle is tensed like a coiled spring, so that one expects it to leap into action at any moment. Our orbiting vehicle completes the illusion that we are flying along breakneck with this literally dashing character. All is rendered in naturalistic detail—his cloak, his spurs, the horse's sex and bulging veins. Despite this seeming vitality, horse and rider are tightly penned inside a black-iron fence decorated with crossed sabers.

"He commanded the Confederate cavalry," Wendy says. "They call him 'The Last Cavalier.' Can you believe that shit? The whole thing is so feudal—like *Monty Python and the Holy Grail*. He used to wear a lover's knot in his lapel and a peacock feather in his hat. Is that like seriously arrested, or what?" She reads the inscription aloud: " 'HE GAVE HIS LIFE FOR HIS COUNTRY

AND SAVED THIS CITY FROM CAPTURE.' More like he revolted against his country, and the city was captured anyway. Supposedly he said, when he got The Fatal Wound, 'I had rather die than be whipped!' My history teacher loved that line. (Course, he loved *Gone With the Wind*, too.) Lucky Jeb, he got both—dead *and* whipped. Moving right along."

Wendy abruptly turns the wheel, and we quit our orbit of Stuart and hurtle west on Monument Avenue at high speed. The road surface, asphalt blocks apparently, is a good deal rougher than the other streets I have traveled thus far. The world, everywhere I look, vibrates like a struck tuning fork. Even so, the grand houses and trees of this broad thoroughfare are lovely as they go jiggling by. It's a fine setting for old splendor.

Wendy continues: "Next up is The Boss—Bob E. Lee—God of Richmond—even though he never actually lived here."

I spot him up ahead through the treetops, he and his horse astride the road it seems, as large and monumental as Stuart was small and quick, a man on horseback as leisurely as Stuart was frenetic. The monument is remarkable for its lack of inscription. LEE, it says, and little else I can see except a couple of lions' heads for decoration. Wendy's speed precludes attention to detail. Lee commands a good deal more real estate than Stuart, with an apron of grass around him, allowing Wendy's orbit to be larger and even faster, propelling me sideways by centrifugal force until my thigh comes to rest against the door, which I make sure is locked. The automobile's tires emit a steady squeal as Wendy resumes her narration, her speed and volume mounting as she goes:

"There he is folks, the paragon of Southern virtue: He bought and sold slaves but thought slavery was evil. He believed in and swore allegiance to the Union but commanded the Rebel forces. He was the smartest military man in the country and *had* to know the South was going to get its butt kicked but didn't have the balls to say so and save thousands and thousands of lives. Let's just say the big guy was confused, and be done with him. But no, it's an obsession. Besides the big bronze boy here, there's schools, bridges, highways named after him. His picture is everywhere, like Jesus or Joe Camel. Sometimes I think if I see his constipated stoic mug one more time, I'll like totally lose it. What did he *do*? That's what I want to know. What did he *do*? I couldn't even escape him by being born a girl! My middle name, like many an unfortunate Southern lass, including my two sisters, my mother, most of my aunts, my grandmother, all my great aunts, is *Lee*. Just in case you're thinking this isn't totally insane, there used to be a porno movie theater called the *Lee Art Theater*, and there was even a restaurant in town named after his fucking *horse!* God spelled backwards is dog; Lee spelled backwards is eel. Enough *Lee!*"

We veer away from Lee at an incredible speed. I'm afraid that if our tour reaches any greater velocity, I will be ill. I'm greatly relieved when after a few blocks she pulls the vehicle over to the side of the road and stops across from the altogether different monument to Varina Davis's husband Jefferson Davis, the President of the Confederate States of America. No horses here, but architecture—symbolically, the house of State with its leader posed before it. Naturally, I hate it.

"This one," she says, "you got to walk around and have a look-see to realize what an obscenity it is."

Wendy helps Jonah out of the car, though at this point he may be steadier on his feet than I. He straightens up slowly, cautious of his wounds, and looks back at Lee. "I know men like him," he says.

"In Africa?" Wendy asks.

Jonah looks at me, and I recognize the look of a man struggling not to lie. "Till yesterday, I be like him," he says. "Too scared to do the right thing."

Wendy is clearly impressed by this remark and gives him a look of undisguised admiration, as we cross the road to Davis. "The president here didn't have that problem," she says. "He was a true believer. Died one. Champion of the Lost Cause. The right thing never crossed his mind. He *believed* in slavery."

Davis stands before a row of columns, each one representing

a slave state, in an oratorical posture. Directly behind him a woman perched high atop a towering pillar at least fifty feet high points up to heaven. The inscription below her reads DEO VINDICE.

"That's Vindicatrix," Wendy says. "She's supposed to be the spirit of the South. White, of course." Wendy notices me reading one of the several inscriptions, and says, "If you like to read your statues, Jeff Davis is the man for you. There's like a whole essay on this thing."

I see what she means. There is writing everywhere—the army, the navy, the citizenry—all have a paragraph somewhere. In one of the more prominent discourses, a shrill reactionary defense of the man and his cause, I see the phrase Varina used, "the rights of the states," and ask Wendy what it means exactly.

"The right to own slaves," she says. "The right to be a bigot. Whenever they talk about *rights*, they mean slavery."

I had begun to wonder if Jonah could follow the proceedings fully, for he cannot read, and the events to which we allude are unknown to him, but he laughs appreciatively at what Wendy has just said. "That be it *exactly!*" he exclaims, and gives her the same admiring look that only moments ago she gave him. He looks around at the words upon words, and he can't read a one of them, but he knows *exactly* what they say, knows with a precision that surpasses the understanding of the men who wrote them, for their meaning is inscribed in code across his back, across his soul. He glares at them in triumph, having seen through them once and for all.

Although I originally doubted the wisdom of Wendy's tour of this reactionary boulevard, I can't imagine a better way to welcome a newly freed slave to the city than to mock those who would have kept him in chains as a "right." Maybe someday this thing can be melted down and the metal put to some useful purpose. At least it's not cannonballs, and I suppose it's some comfort to the descendants of those poor unfortunates who lost their precious human property to have this popinjay in bronze preach to the pigeons the justice of slavery.

Overcome with emotion or exhaustion, Jonah wobbles a bit on his feet and must steady himself on Wendy's shoulder. "I think I need to sit down," he says, and she reaches up and squeezes his hand.

We return to the car, where Wendy insists we cut our tour short so that Jonah might get to bed as soon as possible. With only half an orbit around Davis, we head east on Monument Avenue at a more sober pace than before. Worried that she has jeopardized Jonah's health, she asks for frequent reassurances that he is all right. The smiles he gives in response to her concern should lay any fears to rest.

"You told us how you got your middle name," I say, as if that had been the entire purpose of our recent expedition. "But how did you get the name Wendy?"

The question seems to please her. "My father, bless his heart, was a *Peter Pan* fan." She laughs. "As you might guess, he had one truly awful midlife crisis about the time I was getting kicked out of school. Do you know *Peter Pan?*"

"Oh yes. I saw that play in London. I quite enjoyed it. What was that last part—some sort of crisis that befell your father?"

For a moment she can't seem to recall her own words, then it comes to her. "A *midlife* crisis?" She laughs. "You don't need to know that one. Trust me."

If Jonah cares to know about Peter Pan or midlife crises, he makes no sign of it, for he is intent upon his own thoughts. The next time Wendy asks if he is all right, he replies, "I would like to see a play someday."

"I can't afford a play, but how about a movie sometime?" she suggests.

And though he can't possibly know what she's talking about, he wholeheartedly accepts her invitation. Before we turn off Monument Avenue, she points to a particularly fine and imposing mansion with impeccably manicured grounds— a mansion among mansions. "That's my parents' house," she says. "That's where I grew up." She turns at the next corner and allows herself another burst of speed to put some distance between herself and this edifice, and neither Jonah nor I have any objections.

When we arrive at the commune, Mike and the slumbering cats await us on the front porch. He greets us enthusiastically sotto voce and shows us inside. Without a can-opener reveille the cats do not stir. Brad bustles about barefoot, getting ready for work, hunting for a second sock it seems, but he pauses in his quest long enough to meet Jonah, his real African. He doesn't seem disappointed and shakes Jonah's hand with vigor, waving the sock in his free hand by way of apology, as he resumes his search, and we file into the hallway.

Everyone else has crawled into a warm bed to embrace blessed sleep—or at least that's the way I imagine them all. There are muted snores enough from various quarters of the house to justify my hypothesis. It's a chorus I long to join, for I'm dead on my feet. Jonah, too, is exhausted from his wounds and his excitement, and grows bleary-eyed and stumble-footed. The capsules Wendy gave him may have contributed somewhat to this condition.

"I expected you sooner," Mike says over his shoulder.

"I gave them my famous tour of Monument Avenue," Wendy says.

"And you've lived to tell the tale?" Mike asks me and Jonah as we reach the kitchen.

"We didn't even get to Stonewall Jackson and Matthew Fontaine Maury," Wendy says.

"How unfortunate," Mike says.

"Is that Maury, the oceanographer?" I ask.

"You've heard of him?" Wendy asks.

"I read his book, *The Physical Geography of the Sea*. His politics were dreadful, but he was a brilliant scientist."

"My favorite combination," Wendy says.

"Did you drop in to visit Mom and Dad?" Mike asks with a significant glance in Jonah's direction.

"Yeah, right," says Wendy.

She turns her back on Mike and gives Jonah and me each a big hug, mindful of Jonah's bandages. "Welcome to the nuthouse," she says. "I'm so glad you guys are moving in."

"Thank you for the tour," Jonah says. "It was very, very good."

She basks in Jonah's praise and makes a face at Mike. "See there, smart guy? I'm off today," she says to Jonah. "Maybe later we could finish the tour—or go to a movie—or just hang out around here if you want. Whatever you're up for."

"I would like all of that very much," he says with conviction.

"And you too, Peter," she thinks to add.

"I'll take a rain check," I say. "I want to get to the library today. I'm speaking to an honors seminar, it seems, and I need to prepare. I've been out of touch for a while."

The basement stairs are behind a door in the kitchen. Fortunately, Mike and Brad have assumed quite rightly that our first order of business would be sleep, and two freshly made beds await us.

Brad has not misrepresented the place. It is spacious, with a water closet under the stairs and two rooms created out of one by an assortment of furniture—wardrobes, bookcases, and chests of drawers—being shoved into the middle. Miscellaneous bric-a-brac is everywhere, including a good number of bronze figures, both human and animal, I take to be Uncle Chaney's work. Beside the entrance to the bath under a musty chenille bedspread lurks something roughly the size and shape of a person. "What's this?"

Brad, descending the stairs in his heavy boots, says, "that's one of the sculptures I told you about. I thought you'd want it covered up. It weighs a ton."

I lift the nubby cloth, and a familiar face smiles back at me— black, white, now bronze with a rich patina that would appear to be older than the thing itself. It is Anchee—Chaney—I should've seen the similarity in the names. He stands in the identical pose as Jefferson Davis, his left eye drooping in a permanent wink. "I take it this is a self-portrait of TJ's uncle."

"Yes, how did you know?" Mike says.

"A lucky guess," I say. "A nose for pretension."

I'm not sure what I suspect Mike of, but I suspect him nonetheless. And the look he gives the thing—as if it isn't just a hunk of bad art, but an *idol*, with him its chief idolater—confirms my suspicions. But my only purpose remains to sleep, and it will take a good deal more than Anchee's pranks to dissuade me of it. I let the veil drop over Anchee's unwelcome monument to himself. It could be worse, I reason, Davis himself could be down here to trouble our sleep.

"I'm taking off now," Brad says. "Welcome to the commune."

Mike follows him up the stairs. "See you later," he says. "Dinner's at six-thirty."

When Mike closes the door at the top of the stairs behind him, Jonah lifts the veil to have another look at our friend. "This here is Anchee?"

"That's right."

"I see what you mean about him messing with your life. Remember the fellow I told you about, the one told me Gabriel was headed into town?"

"Yes."

"This be the man right here."

14 ⑨ Dreams Within Dreams

And all should cry, Beware! Beware!
His flashing eyes, his floating hair!
Weave a circle round him thrice,
And close your eyes with holy dread,
For he on honey-dew hath fed
And drunk the milk of Paradise.
> —SAMUEL TAYLOR COLERIDGE, *"Kubla Khan"*

Is *all* that we see or seem
But a dream within a dream?
> —EDGAR ALLAN POE, *"A Dream Within a Dream"*

I know I'm dreaming, but I don't care to admit it to myself just yet, for then the dream might end, I might awaken, and how would I ever find my way back here again? I'm dressed in a costume I know well, for it has figured in my dreams before. It's an outfit—that of a young Persian prince—I wore in reality only once at eight years of age to a costume ball in honor of Nicholas I. The lad who was supposed to have impersonated the prince in the company of his equally authentic Persian princess mother—a friend of the family—had fallen ill, and as it happens, I fit the clothes. The czar was so charmed by evening's end, I was inscribed as a candidate to the corps of pages, thus ensuring my future education and military career, a blessing completely lost on me, for I had fallen asleep with my head in the lap of the good-hearted Marie Alexándrovna, the wife of the heir to the throne.

The ironies of that episode were numerous and delicious, but

I'm not concerned with them now, for in this dream I'm not a lad, but a man, and the costume has expanded to suit me, so that I feel like some rogue out of Byron, as I ride a dark stallion—Stuart's horse, I realize—full gallop through the woods, my silk trousers snapping like flags in a high wind, the reins in one hand, the other occupied with keeping my high Astrakhan fur bonnet atop my head, pursuing . . .

There's the rub. I don't know. I haven't a clue. A person, I believe. Or persons . . .

As I pause to consider what emotions fuel my sense of urgency, a low limb knocks the silly hat off my head, and it's no sooner gone than forgotten, and I turn my attention, not to my mad charge through these woods at speeds rivaling Wendy's car, but to my belt—thickly encrusted with jewels—for this was, of course, an exceedingly *rich* prince I portrayed. My dream belt sports fresh embellishments: Dangling from it is a saber I've apparently stolen from Stuart, and tucked inside it is his dagger. I would seem to be armed for battle, circa 1860.

I had rather die than be whipped! I think, or my dream self thinks, but it's not Stuart's sentiments I'm echoing, despite my princely attire and martial mount, but Jonah's.

The steed and I burst out of the woods in a shower of sand and gravel to arrive at the river—the James in flood, swollen to a torrent. Uprooted trees swirl by in the brown current, brown people in the limbs clutch small bundles of belongings and peer anxiously downstream, where the churning water smashes the trees to twigs, and thousands are swept away. A trio of peasants are here on the shore, sitting on their overturned boat, watching the spectacle. I recognize them from the family estate in Nikólskoye, but I can't recall their names. They speak to me in Russian:

"Prince! Prince! Come see the flood! The serfs are freed!"

Stuart's horse is a skittish beast and shies from the rushing waters and the shouting men, and there's little I can do to control him. One of the peasants jumps up, catches the horse by its flying mane, and the beast promptly turns to bronze in the pose of his Losers' Lane likeness. I turn round in the saddle, slide off rump and tail to the ground, and step over the low black fence that surrounds us. "I wish to hire your boat," I tell the helpful peasant. "I must reach the island immediately." I point to Belle Isle, still shrouded in fog, where business awaits so undercover that my dream self reveals it not even to me.

The peasant shakes his head. "The current is much too strong," he says. "You might drown, and your death would be on my soul."

"I will pay," I say, taking off the belt and showing him the incredible wealth it represents.

He turns to his companions. "He wants us to take him to the island."

"His death would be on our souls," they say, shaking their heads.

With the dagger I pry an enormous ruby from its setting and give it to the first peasant. He takes a bite from it as if it were an apple and tosses it to his friends who, following his example, share it between themselves.

"Perhaps, if you gave us a receipt," he suggests thoughtfully.

"A receipt?"

He points at my saber and gestures to the sand at our feet. "I will tell you what to write, and you sign it."

"Very well," I say, and as he recites, I inscribe the following in the sand, smiling at the memory of just such a "receipt" requested by real peasants long, long ago before they would conduct me across the frozen river Tom:

I, the undersigned, hereby testify that I was drowned by the will of God, and by no fault of the peasants.

I sign it, *P. Kropotkin.*

No sooner have I done so than a wave washes it all away. "Do you want me to write it again?" I ask, wanting to uphold my end of the bargain, even though I don't believe in God, and know I will not drown, because, after all, this is just a dream.

"No," he says. "That won't be necessary. God had more than enough time to read it."

There is a great clap of thunder, and a reverberating voice booms down on us from above: "I have just one question." My head snaps back, and there's an Anchee of enormous proportions enthroned on a cloud, smiling down on me. "What does the P stand for"—he asks—"Prince or Peter?"

I come awake, his laughter echoing in my brain. The only other remnant of my dream is my fist shaking at the low ceiling, sans saber. I fall back with a sigh. "Peter," I whisper angrily, and immediately feel like an imbecile. It's just a dream. And though it occurs to me that it may be more of Anchee's magic, I don't want to know about it if it is. If the scoundrel wants my dreams, he can have them—as meaningless and chaotic and worthy of indifference as I've always found them to be. If Pharaoh had had my dreams, Joseph would have died in prison long before he could have spun a plausible prophecy out of them.

In any event, whatever this one may signify is entirely lost on me, for to think about it at all leads inevitably to the intense, visceral desire to wipe that smug smile off Anchee's celestial face and stuff it in his back pocket. So whether this dream is another message from my tormentor or just my usual nonsense, it would seem to further Anchee's cause in any event, namely, to keep me off-balance, boxing with shadows, in a constant state of agitation—more *interesting* that way, I'm sure, more *entertaining*. A cat, after all, soon bores of a dead mouse. If I thought the future would be less barbaric in its entertainments, I've been disabused of that notion.

In the back of the diner last night were three games—at least that's what my companions called them. The least gruesome gave the player the illusion of driving a car at incredibly high speeds, occasionally running over some hapless pedestrian, nun, or baby carriage; or crashing into other vehicles, buildings, or trees with a good deal of boom and flame. There were points earned and deducted for this and that, but they scarcely seemed to matter—speed and noise were the heart and soul of the thing. In the second game, one assumed the role of any number of exotic gladiators fighting an equally strange opponent to the death in the most brutal manner imaginable; the style of fighting, almost balletlike, made it seem strangely attractive, even erotic, to kill another. The third, the most straightforward, was the old shooting gallery updated: The shooter cradled a huge machine gun in his arms, tethered to the apparatus by an umbilical of wires, firing at dozens and dozens of life-size human assailants, who didn't merely fall over when shot like vanquished tin bears, but suffered grisly wounds, severed limbs, exploding heads. In the midst of this carnage, their cries were made to sound almost comical. The player I watched, at least, laughed hysterically throughout.

"It's just a game," my guides assured me, but, I had to ask, if *these* are games, what horrors constitute reality?

I sit up in bed and rub my eyes. Enough morbidity, enough fear. What was the phrase that flashed on the screen? *Game Over. Game over, Anchee: I refuse to play.*

A diffuse light makes its way into the basement through two small windows opening onto a narrow walkway between this house and the next. Rain falls there, but not too heavily at the moment. In here, Jonah's deep, slumbrous breathing fills the room. He will sleep, it seems, for a good long while, waking to whatever afternoon the beautiful Wendy has planned for him. I trust he won't miss me overly. I fish the watch out of my pants pocket, and hold it up to the light—ten-fifteen, still time to make something of my Sunday. I slip into my clothes and pad up the stairs in sock feet, knapsack and shoes in hand. The whole house, like Jonah, sighs with sleep, and I strive to make as little noise as possible, for I desire no company. It's not that I'm unsociable exactly. I just don't wish to be detained in my purpose.

Ahmed showed me how to operate the microwave at the restaurant, and this one is similar enough so that after a few tries—and many loud bleats issuing from it at the slightest touch—I've heated a cup of water and made myself a strong coffee. I suppose if I knew more about the machine, there would be a way to silence all these superfluous noises, though gratuitous electronic racket seems to be the order of the day. I breakfast from my own provisions for now, not certain what food in the kitchen is part of the common larder. I select crackers and peanut butter and discover that my closely trimmed moustache makes it a more enjoyable meal than I recall from my previous experiences with it. I wash my face and hands in the sink and promise myself a proper bath when I have a clean change of clothes. But first, there is something I need more than yet another shirt on my back. I need to lose myself in *studies*.

It was Sophie who first characterized my studies as an addiction, teasing me that I outdid even Coleridge and Poe, for I needed no opium to transport me to other realms, my curiosity alone being sufficient; and I confess it's true. It doesn't matter what the object of inquiry. Just to pursue the thing—weather balloons or chimpanzees or Keats's "Ode to a Nightingale"—each one opening up new, unsuspected horizons, beckoning to be explored and understood, enticing me further and further into the wilderness of *studies*—discovering those places, deep in the heart, where all paths seem to converge, and we discover who it is we really are and what we truly care about. I love it. And now I have fresh eyes to exhaust on new texts, new maps, new mysteries. And though I'm a lifetime behind in one sense; I'm a lifetime ahead just there, deep in the heart of that wilderness.

By the back door in a small vestibule off the kitchen, there are roughly a dozen pegs jutting out of the wall, several layers of coats and slickers and scarves and hats packed into place around them so tightly that to remove one garment is to be showered with several. There are enough here to protect the entire household, perhaps the house itself, from the harshest elements for several days on end. I choose a couple of items from the older strata, assuming they won't be missed for the day. Wearing a long black raincoat, I head off to the library beneath a broad, black umbrella that volunteered by springing open of its own accord, demanding I defend myself, swatting the last cobwebs of drowsiness from my brain.

If I look like an undertaker, I'm not out of place, for no matter how many cars snicker by with people in their bellies, the city is still dead. Where I walk there's no one, not even the runners and the dogs. I know it's raining, but the umbrella is still an effective technology, and even if it were a lovely day, I suspect, there would be precious few neighbors out strolling, and the friendliest of those would be on the canine end of a leash. It's not that people are unfriendly in general, quite the contrary. But the street isn't where that friendliness takes place. The streets belong almost entirely to the cars. There's something precious lost in that surrender, it seems to me, but perhaps I'm being old-fashioned, perhaps even—I shudder to say it—reactionary.

Still, I'm beginning to detest what Anchee so rightly termed an infestation, this profligate squandering of resources, and amuse myself with mentally melting down these endless autos and fashioning them into ocean liners I moor along my route, two or three per block, as if a fleet of *Titanic*s had steamed into town unnoticed and beached themselves on the slick streets.

Standing in the foyer of the library, shaking the rain from my umbrella, I forget my small troubles. Here are riches finer than rubies, an inexhaustible storehouse of dreams. The library offers a temporary refuge in an ocean of flux, for here all times are present, on one page or another, and everywhere is here, if you know where to look. The inner doors whisper open at my approach, and I pass through, seeking sanctuary, smiling at the blessed scent of books, unchanged I'm pleased to report, since my passing (and not entirely obscured by the plastic aroma of a lobby full of computers).

In a strange library, I find, it's best to head directly to the reference librarian, for he or she knows the quirks and peculiarities of the place and can save hours of frustration. Since this library on Sunday is only slightly more populated than the streets, it's no surprise when I find this reference librarian waiting anxiously behind his high desk like a dog in his yard vigilant for something, anything, to sniff out, chase, or fetch. He's tall and thin with exotic dark features, Lebanese perhaps; and quick, darting eyes that see me coming long before I arrive. I return his friendly smile and announce myself in search of materials on a wide range of subjects.

"What subjects?" he asks eagerly, awaiting my command, his fingers poised over a keyboard always at the ready. His eyes flit back and forth between me and a computer screen sitting on the desk like a child beside us.

"Several," I say. "First, I suppose, would be the events of August 30, 1800. In Richmond. A slave insurrection . . ."

"Gabriel's Rebellion," he says, his fingers flying, the flickering screen reflected in his large eyes. They widen with satisfaction at what the machine reveals. The corners of his mouth turn up in a smile. I know the look: question posed and questioned answered—not *Eureka!* exactly, but its soft-spoken cousin; not curiosity satisfied, for clearly such curiosity is dead; but curiosity encouraged, curiosity embraced, curiosity ready for the next question. Not surprisingly, the reference librarian is a fellow addict of *studies.*

I lean around the desk to have a closer look at the precocious electronic child in action, the ally of his curiosity, the cause of all this fuss. Whenever last night's conversation most thoroughly confused me, the topic of discussion was inevitably computers. As I look at it now, it's a television with a fondness for words—or so it appears to me. I recall the enormous automobile churning across the television countryside in quick, fractured images, and this glowing text seems positively benign by comparison. But like the television, the computer, I suppose, must have many faces.

"We have several things on that," my Virgil informs me. "Let me print that up for you." He types a few more strokes. "Anything else?" Beside the computer screen, a machine begins printing lines of text—authors and titles of books about a two-hundred-year-old revolution I had frankly never heard of until yesterday. Perhaps computers aren't so vile as Rachel seems to think they are.

"Could you show me how to operate one of these?" I ask, pointing at the computer.

"Certainly," he says with such heartfelt conviction that I feel as if I'm being inducted into some proselytistic brotherhood. He escorts me to one of the several other computers perched on high desks, pulls up a high chair, and bids me mount the throne.

When I'm properly situated, he turns the computer on and drums his fingers, waiting, and I wait as well—or at least adopt the pose—for I have no idea what I'm waiting for. Images and words appear and disappear on the screen, but nothing makes any sense. He stops drumming his fingers. The image is now stable, if still indecipherable. "This is the start-up menu," he begins, and I stare at the screen, covered with words and symbols, and attempt to penetrate its mysteries.

"Why is there a picture of a house?" I ask, for I must start somewhere, and I'm quite certain that that is indeed a depiction of a small gray house, and there's not much else on the screen I'm sure of.

"That's Home," he says.

"Whose home?"

He looks at me; his eyes blink. He determines, I gather, that I'm not feigning my ignorance. I'm getting used to this look. "No one's. It's where you start out. This screen here is Home. That's why the icon is grayed out."

"The icon is grayed out?"

"The icon is gray."

I nod as if I understand the profound significance of this because I want to move on, to escape the confines of this house, this gray home. "So it's like baseball, correct? You start at Home?" He likes this analogy. As with most willing teachers, any sign of understanding from a student, however infinitesimal, is a cause for joy. Unfortunately, I'm still confused. "I thought this was the—what did you call it?—'the start-up menu.' "

"It is. They are the same. Home is where you start out. In this program it's a menu."

"Menu like a restaurant?"

"Exactly. Only you order *information*."

He's pleased with his own analogy, I can tell, though I don't care much for it. Order information, then gobble it down I suppose, or given my recent experience in such matters, toss it in the garbage. But I don't say any of this, for I want to know how the thing works, not beleaguer this helpful man with some rant about consumption. "What is a *program*?" I ask, which proves to be a good question, leading as it does, to some general principles. And eventually, through his patience and my persistence, it starts to come clearer, bit by bit.

". . . and to get the bibliographical information on the entry, you just click on the title."

"I beg your pardon? Click?"

"I'm sorry. This is a mouse."

"A mouse?"

"That's right. It makes the pointer move like this, see? You try it."

"The mouse makes the pointer move." I indulge myself in this simple pleasure.

"That's right. The left button . . ."

And so on. But you likely know a good deal more about it than I do. Soon, however, if I may boast, I am piloting the thing on my own, embarrassed to confess that my test inquiry is *Peter Kropotkin, 1842–1921*. I flush with pride that the library has all my books and that quite a number of them are checked out at the moment. There are also a few about me written by strangers—critical biographies I believe they're called—but I resist the temptation to discover just how critical they are. It seems a terrible waste of time to read about myself, or rather, about Dead Peter as I've come to think of him. Since he was clearly wrong about so many things, I imagine my time would be better spent pursuing other lights.

"What is that?" I ask. At the bottom of the list of library holdings are several lines of blue text.

"Those are Internet links. Are you student or faculty?"

"Neither," I confess, "I'm not associated with the university—just a curious soul with a day off from work." I've heard of the Internet from my young friends, and though I can't quite wrap my mind around the concept—some sort of vast electronic Never-Never Land—it is high on my list of subjects of inquiry.

"That's too bad; you need a student or faculty number to access the Internet from these computers. It used to be open access, but we were having a problem with homeless people, or at least *some* people thought it was a problem. If you ask me, they were making better use of the machines than most of the students do."

I decide I like this fellow for not siding with *some* people. "That *is* too bad," I agree. "I was rather keen to learn about it—though I'm sure there's plenty to keep me busy on the bookshelves." A more disappointed acolyte at the fount of knowledge, you can't imagine, than the one I heavy-handedly portray—my curiosity quashed on his watch, all because of the prejudices of *some* people. Such an unjust state of affairs contradicts his very nature.

"Screw it," he says, reaching for the keyboard. He types and clicks with an occasional furtive glance over his shoulder, ushering me past a couple of solemn, official-looking screens. There's a certain boyish appeal to codes and passwords, I can testify, having sent more than my fair share of coded missives; and the computer seems to take on a bit of that cloak-and-dagger atmosphere. Perhaps instead of Home it should be called The Hideout.

"Okay, you're in," the reference librarian says. "I just used my number and password." He returns the controls to me. "Now, let me show you some of the better reference sites and walk you through a few simple searches . . ."

At first, by sheer force of will and technological timidity, I manage to stick to the mental laundry list of topics that brought me to the library in the first place.

Gabriel's rebellion, I discover, was a full-fledged revolutionary plot with a high chance of success—if a terrible storm hadn't forced postponement and given the game away. The impressive Gabriel had raised an army of some five or six hundred conspirators with a network of communications stretching over enormous distances for the time. The very fact that the slaves did all the labor—including pilot the boats and drive the wagons—made this possible.

By the end of the affair, twenty-seven brave men had been hanged for plotting to be free in a land that prided itself on being the Land of Liberty. In fact, it was that sort of talk, so much in the air during the constitutional debate, that had inspired the young Gabriel to action. The banner the conspirators were to bear into battle read "Death or Liberty."

Thomas Jefferson, vice president at the time, who talked rather grandly of freedom, did nothing to bring it about for African slaves—even though modern science has confirmed the rumors making the rounds in my day of a slave mistress and slave children. Perhaps, sadly, there's no contradiction there. To free one's slaves is invariably to lose more than one intends, and Jefferson, unquestionably a brilliant man, would have known that. Squeamish about the hangings, however, he suggested "exportation" to the fields of the Deep South as a means of dealing with the rest of the conspirators. The noose would have been more humane. Jefferson thus anticipated the modern expedient of exporting suffering so that it might not cloud the pursuit of one's own life, one's own liberty, one's own happiness. As for Jefferson's happiness, the unwanted spectacle of hanging dozens more freedom fighters—which would have proved ruinous in the upcoming elections—was avoided, and he became the third president of the United States.

A truer champion of freedom it seems to me was Richardson Taylor, a white boat captain who took Gabriel—a much publicized fugitive since the abortive revolt—on board his vessel, and, at great risk to himself, attempted to spirit Gabriel to Norfolk and possibly to freedom beyond. But they were betrayed by a slave named Billy, who was tempted by the bounty on

Gabriel's head, a sum sufficient to buy Billy his own freedom. As a slave, however, this Judas was denied the full measure of his reward because, his betters reasoned, he was just a slave—and so he remained—and so they *all* remained for decades to come. I can't help reflecting what effect Gabriel's rebellion might have had on the young nation if it had succeeded in its goal of liberty and justice for all. Perhaps Anchee could tell me—if one of his realities has it so.

It was, however, by all accounts in *this* reality, a largely urban affair, the conspirators mostly artisans, city laborers, and watermen—including some whites. And though the hope had been that plantation workers such as Jonah would join the effort once the die was cast, he would have been on the periphery of the conspiracy at best, and certainly wouldn't have been summoned to arms the night of the abortive attempt. The slaveholders had gotten wind of the plot. Riders rode that night, it seems, scouring the countryside for revolutionists, but there were none to find since the terrible storm had canceled the attempt. It wasn't until later that the conspirators were betrayed and rounded up. Anchee would have known all this, I'm sure. He deliberately lured Jonah into the path of danger, and, most likely, into my path as well. But to be fair, the result is that Jonah is no longer a slave, and wouldn't likely, of his own free will, return to 1800 even if he could. Thus far, at least, Anchee has proven himself a fortunate deity in Jonah's universe—if one ignores the stripes laid on by his captors.

Mulling over this conundrum, I move on to my next topic, time travel itself, which proves a more elusive field of study. Once I've learned "what everybody knows" from a few encyclopedia articles, most of what I can discover about the subject in this time—a time when time travel is scarcely thought possible— is fiction or discussions of twins traveling at the speed of light that, except for their dullness, read like fiction. As for the many novels and stories that treat the subject, the synopses I read make them sound varied and clever, a mental playground for the lover of paradox, but they don't quite suit my purposes, for my key questions regarding Anchee are not about his science or his paradoxes or even his magic—but his motives. In that sense, perhaps, the fictions shed some light, if only by analogy: If in Anchee's view there is no one reality, as there is no one story, then each one he creates becomes like a fiction, a single novel on an endless shelf of novels. That's not necessarily a bad thing. My brother used to say that poetry makes men better, and I believe that's true, or can be, depending on the poetry, of course. And it's the same with novels: I have read novels that have made me a better man; I have also read novels that made me wish the *author* were a better man. It remains to be seen which sort of fiction Anchee has in mind for me. Or, for that matter, what sort of person takes such a novel from the shelf and reads it by the fireside!

I can't imagine, and when it comes down to it, *I can't be bothered*. I don't care to fritter away my time grappling with Anchee's methods and intentions, wringing my hands wondering how on earth I got here like hapless Adam—when what I really need to know is what all *here* encompasses, what I really need to do is explore the new territory of my life so that I may make the most of it. Anchee may have his intentions for me, but my best defense against them is to know my own. Mentally, I wad up my list of questions, toss it aside, and begin, as my Internet mentor termed it, "to just surf."

I read about the moon landing, automobiles, the INS, JFK, and TV. At every turn, there are new discoveries: Martin Luther King Jr., fossil evidence from Mars, Fidel Castro, Vietnam, Jerry Seinfeld—a nihilist comedian!—and of course the Internet itself (for it seems to be about itself as much as anything else). I finally understand the suffix "dot com," which has been sailing past me with remarkable frequency since my arrival and envision with a shudder the ultimate apotheosis of capitalism in the trinity of Internet, credit card, and global sweatshops. I find several sites dedicated to plastics where I linger entirely too long, escaping to petroleum, and from there, OPEC, the Gulf War, the IMF, and Amnesty International. I find out more than I care to about prisons, but as an old jailbird, I'm compulsively drawn to the subject. Largely because of a draconian crackdown on the black market in drugs, the United States, with 5 percent of the world's population, boasts 25 percent of the world's prisoners, with a higher proportion of its citizens in jail than *any other country in history!* The racism of the demographics are truly staggering, and yet there's some pretense that racism is a thing of the past. I laugh out loud when I realize that one of the reasons for the current low unemployment rate is the surge in the number of men—especially young black men—in jail!

I retreat to Einstein, such a pleasant, brilliant fellow, whose importance I didn't begin to appreciate in my previous life. But then I stumble upon Adolf Hitler, and only find my way out of that horrific narrative by exploring the Spanish Civil War, where, however badly things ended, anarchism showed it *could* work, even under the most adverse conditions. I note several links to anarchism here that tempt me, but my ignorance pleads the greater need, and I click back to World War II, and from there to Hiroshima, Nuclear Winter, Mutual Assured Destruction, Ronald Reagan, Star Wars, The Evil Empire, Luke Skywalker and Darth Vader. I find them on sale and understand the fellow on the airplane—*I have a Skywalker at my mother's place must be worth a couple hundred by now—still in the original packaging*—I see him there behind a plastic window, slowly appreciating, worth a good deal more, it seems, than his owner realizes. I push myself back from the computer and almost fall from my high chair.

That's when I decide to take a break, for I'm losing the distinction between real and imagined, or perhaps the modern world has dispensed with it altogether. In any event, I should eat something, for it's the middle of the afternoon. My head is swimming. Or clicking. I'm not sure whether the Internet is a marvelous aid to inquiry or the most distracting and demented pastime yet devised—rather like a public lecture where the identity of the speaker remains anonymous and one is constantly besieged by all manner of persons, delivering an erratic series of discourses on almost everything from the trivial to the profound, interrupting each other, prompting one another, finishing each other's thoughts. Alice's tea party was a sensible affair by comparison, but not nearly so informative.

My mind is a crowd set loose, as much as I might appear a single fellow beneath a black umbrella, my thoughts racing in all directions, promptly getting lost down one blind alley or another. I have only explored the tiniest corner of my ignorance and am already overwhelmed. Not only has everything changed, but the *rate* of change seems to be constantly accelerating as well, so that what I think I know today will likely prove out-of-date next week.

I try to imagine lecturing to bright young university students—all of whom will know the horrors I learned today and more. Will young people raised on Auschwitz and atomic bombs find me laughably naive?

I look for hope, but find little in evidence. What's needed most, it seemed to me in my day, was a greater sense of community, commonality, the sense of belonging to a *single species* for goodness sake! I deceived myself in my old life that there were forces at work that would soon bring it about, but things seem even worse now. I come across vague claims that somehow the Internet will provide that community, but I am skeptical. In prison, we tapped out messages to one another in our separate cells—a pathetic substitute for human contact, but one which saved many a one of us from going insane. Such, perhaps, is the Internet. But how much comfort is it to trade missives with someone in Sweden or Kamchatka but live surrounded by strangers you fear and mistrust?

Meanwhile, the city in which Anchee has plunked me down is still celebrating the *Confederacy,* a regime which would gleefully enslave over half the city's population as a *right*! No wonder Wendy—Wendy *Lee*—is driven near to distraction by the place: *Reaction, full speed backwards!*

Once again, I consider leaving town, heading west perhaps. I would like to see the Shenandoah, the Great Plains, the Rockies. I could hitchhike (a word I learned while puzzling out an excerpt from something called *The Hitchhiker's Guide to the Galaxy*).

But no, I'm not a tourist here. This is my world now, like it or not. I can't simply abandon Jonah. And no matter how scattered my thoughts may be, I've promised to deliver a lecture on Dead Peter, who would remind me that revolutions often don't arise in the most enlightened jurisdictions but in the most reactionary. It wasn't Alexander II's freeing the serfs that brought about the Russian revolution, but the reaction which followed, leaving bitterness and injustice in its wake. Not unlike the events here not so long ago. Jim Crow is another term I've learned today.

Many years ago, I wrote an essay called "An Appeal to the Young," a stirring call to action long on inspiration but short on analysis. Among my essays, it was something of a favorite son, popular for its earnest good heart, a sweet tenor in the choir, but certainly no philosopher. Yet it seemed to strike a chord. In my lifetime I saw it translated into dozens of languages. When I wrote it, Sophie and I, not long married, had settled in Clarens in a small cottage overlooking the blue waters of Lake Geneva, with the pure snow of the Dent du Midi in the background. A streamlet that thundered like a mighty torrent after rains, ran under our windows, and on the slope of the hill opposite rose the old castle of Chatelard. We were very much in love, and as Wendy would say, the sex was great. We were so damn happy we could scarcely contain our joy. That's where I'd like to be, in that beautiful time and place with my beautiful wife, writing with the help of her excellent criticism, prolifically, confidently, with the sense that I had something to say, and there were those in the world who wanted to listen. Not here. Not now.

But even then, I remind myself, things change; a few short years after Clarens, I was back in jail and Sophie was wrecking her health living close to the prison so that she could visit me. Her daily, if sexless, visits saved my life. If you don't like the world, I've always advised myself, then change it, one mind at a time. Many a young person joined in the Free Peter Kropotkin movement that sprang up around the globe—a movement that eventually sprang me from jail—after having read "An Appeal to the Young." Like a good son—or daughter—this child of better times worked to free her father when his voice was silenced.

I'm ignorant of a lifetime of change, but it's my sense that, despite surface differences, humans are the same animals they've always been, with the same virtues and limitations, the same needs and emotions. In spite of my ignorance, I'll just have to find a way to speak to that animal. Perhaps that earnest address to youth, an appeal to every young man and woman who ever hoped to make something worthwhile of their lives, isn't a bad place to start. It's an appeal, in a sense, to life itself, for if the youth have no hope or ideals, there's none to be had, and we might as well pack it in like the dinosaurs.

An asteroid. Imagine . . .

I peek out from under my umbrella. No asteroids, only this tedious rain. I've been wandering around the almost deserted campus, lost in my thoughts, mulling over my studies, turning over old memories, sounding the present, trying to get a fix on the future. We all do a bit of time traveling, truth be told. I've described a circle, apparently, for the great white box of a library looms up ahead of me.

Now that I'm back from what Sophie used to call my studious voyage to Xanadu, I'm ravenously hungry. I immediately find what I'm looking for—protection from the rain so that I might have both hands free to eat—in the form of a bus shelter fashioned from transparent plastic of the variety I believe is called Plexiglas. I step under it, park my umbrella in the corner, sit on the end of one of the plastic benches (polycarbonate?), and sup with gusto on more peanut butter and crackers.

I chat with the bus riders who come and go, at least those who don't find me too shabby for conversation. I find that the offer of a peanut butter cracker is well-nigh irresistible to all but the most unsociable and wish I'd brought more. It turns out the bus shuttles medical students back and forth to the medical college—the MCV of Earl's effective medication—and these are, for the most part, aspiring physicians—no wonder they have such bad nutrition. I ask them how their studies are progressing, and like exhausted students in any strenuous discipline, they unload their burdens, speak their minds, and if coaxed, confide their dreams, already bruised from their education before they've even had a chance to try them in the world.

I listen sympathetically and ask them their concerns for the future, and this leads to a discussion, to my horror, of *insurance*! Another triune acronym crops up as usual—HMO—and it takes the whole shelterful to explain the intricacies of this insane notion to me. (No surprise there—the insurance people *are* the ones who came up with the term "life insurance" for what clearly should be called "death insurance," "health insurance" for what should be called "sick insurance"). One fellow asks me what I think of "single payer," and after he explains that notion, I cautiously suggest that perhaps the whole problem is the notion of *payment*, that perhaps we should be thinking in terms of people's *needs*—doctors and patients both (leaving the insurance companies out of it altogether)—that perhaps things could be organized somewhat differently based on the principles of cooperation and mutual aid . . .

He misses his bus to hear me out and gives me a firm handshake before boarding the next one, saying I've given him a lot to think about. He's off to work on Otis Washington—as he calls his cadaver—insisting on referring to the dead man by name and personal pronouns, he says, so he'll never forget that Otis was once a man like himself.

Not all the young are idealists—neither in my former time or now—though the minion of materialism who explains the term "lifestyle specialty" to me, gives me something of a chill with the candor, even pride, with which he announces he's "in it for the money, *like everyone else*"!

His companions—two young women who are in a study group with him—shake their heads. "Not me," one says. "Me either," says the other. Dr. Dollars smirks. "Yeah right. Medicine is a business *like everything else*."

His fellow students don't think these sweeping claims worth debating and fall into a discussion of an upcoming examination.

But I can't leave it alone. It's disquieting, is it not, to be left out of "everyone" and "everything," for where's one to go from there? "You're saying *everything* is a business?"

I've slathered up a peanut butter cracker, and I hand it to him. "Thanks. Yeah. Exactly. Everything's a business. Mmmm. Tha's good."

"And who owns this business?"

"Hmmmm?"

"This Everything Business—who owns it? You say everything is a business. Very well. Businesses have owners, do they not? Who owns the Everything Business?"

"Mmmm. I see what you're driving at. God, I guess."

"Do you believe in God?"

"Well, no, not really."

"Ah, there's the problem, isn't it? It's a bit hard for a man of science to imagine some Grand Puppetmaster. Seems like the Everything Business goes begging for an owner. Let's put it up for auction, shall we? I bid a peanut butter cracker. What do you bid?"

He's been smiling at me, indulging my prattle, but as he looks into the perfectly serious eyes of Crazy Peter, he finds himself a bit unnerved.

"Medicine, I guess."

I laugh out loud. "*Good* guess. I'll remember that when I get sick. You fancy ophthalmology, don't you? I suspect I'll need spectacles soon enough now that I've met the Internet. Another cracker?"

As we continue to talk, I find his cynicism, like many young people's, only fashion deep, and though I make no anarchist of him, his "everyone" and "everything," I hope, are not quite so heartless by the time the next bus roars around the cathedral and squeals to a stop in front of us.

Soon enough I'm sitting in an empty shelter eating the last cracker, the damn watch in my lap. I pop it open. A quarter to three. I snap it closed.

The ESL class is scheduled to convene at three. Perhaps Rachel has canceled the class—she seemed none too eager to take it on herself—but no, I decide, if she could just let it go, she wouldn't have gotten so upset when her volunteer quit. She might already be in the building. I look over my shoulder through the rain-streaked Plexiglas at the library looming over me, as if I could somehow see her through the walls.

People have often complained to me, "Kropotkin, you think men are so reasonable and behave so sensibly all the time. You are sadly mistaken, my friend." But it isn't true. I know how irrational men are, how irrational I can be. It's as clear as day that the only "reason" I now return to the library as if I were punching a time clock is the hope of seeing Rachel again, a woman who thinks me a loony and a liar. How is that *reasonable*? But it is human nonetheless, and not such a bad trait for the survival of the species.

I have seen the future, Anchee whispers in my memory as I pass once again through the inner doors, my heart quickening, and in spite of myself, I hope he has, and that I'm happy there, Rachel in my arms. I want a glimpse of that future as well. I want it terribly.

15 ✺ I Am Believed

Kropotkin's emphasis on the objective forces leading the world toward anarchy led him to minimize the role of personal relations. In some ways he was too much the scientist and benign sage to fully appreciate the emotional appeal of the anarchist call for personal liberation.

—RICHARD D. SONN, *Anarchism*

Analogies, it is true, decide nothing, but they can make one feel more at home.

—SIGMUND FREUD

At the front desk of the library, I inquire after the location of the English class, letting my accent testify to my need for instruction, and a friendly black woman writes down the room number and even draws me a map of the top floor. "It's like a maze up there," she warns.

She's not exaggerating. The room is tucked away in a corner at the end of a warren of corridors. After a few turns, I see two fellows coming toward me. One is tall and lumbering, a pleasant bear of a man; the other is small and prim, older and precise. We size each other up and correctly conclude we're three foreigners brought here for the same reason.

"Is the ESL class this way?" I ask.

"Class killed," the big fellow—Turkish I think—says pleasantly, slicing his throat with his fingers.

"*The* class is *canceled*," the small fellow corrects his companion without looking at me. His accent is strange to me. One of the Latin American nations perhaps? He's a gentleman there, I suspect, wherever it is.

"Is the teacher still there?" I ask the friendly one.

"Still teacher there," he says, nodding vigorously and pointing the way I'm headed.

"*The* teacher *is still there*," the little fellow says testily, and the big man shrugs apologetically for his poor English.

"Thank you very much," I say, and make my way past them before I can spawn any more corrections. I listen to their exchange as they recede behind me.

"Want drive home?" the big fellow asks.

"*Do you* want *a ride* home," the little fellow intones.

"You want?"

"Yes. Thank you."

"You welcome."

"*You're* welcome."

I smile at this symbiosis as I round the last turn in the maze. There's only one door. Through a window in the door, I can see the corner of a large table with chairs around it, a chalkboard on the wall. I step up to the door to have a closer look. In front of a tall vertical window looking down upon the cathedral dome stands a lone individual. I almost cry out, but I don't. I just stand there, fists clenched, filled with impotent rage.

It is Anchee.

He turns and sees me, and hangs his head in mock penitence that, alas, he has "interfered" again.

"I thought I owed you an explanation," he says, as I enter. On the chalkboard, in large block letters, is written CLASS KILLED. Anchee's dark fingers are powdered with chalk. He dusts them off.

"I take it this is your doing?" I catch a glimpse of my reflection in the window—stiff-legged, wild-eyed, a bit red in the face. *Beware the enraged dwarf!* I take a deep breath.

Anchee pretends not to notice. "Afraid so. They were a silly idea anyway. I tinkered with them, but in the end I let them go. They served their purpose."

"Which was?" I ask coldly.

He smiles, a sparkle in his eye. He's in a tell-all mood. "Why, to be spurned in front of you so that you would have the opportunity to rise to the chivalrous occasion." His hand swoops down as if he's caught a fallen standard and holds it aloft. But promptly lowers it, splaying thumb and pinkie to portray a telephone into which he gushes in falsetto: "I just wouldn't feel safe down there, Miss Pederson. Wherever would I park?" The r's in *wherever*, *there* and *park* are silent, and the entire utterance is awash in diphthongs, revealing him to be—based on Wendy's parodies of the local dialects—an aristocratic phony.

"It was you on the phone."

"Mrs. Charles (*Chah-uhlz*)," he says. "Pleased to make your (*yo-uh*) acquaintance." He raises his right hand in a gesture reminiscent of a swaying cobra, but doesn't risk actually offering it to me, knowing, I suppose, that I would gladly wrench his arm from its socket and beat him over the head with it like one of those gruesome characters in the games at the diner. Rather, he ends the performance with a no-harm-intended shrug, as if all that's required to think the whole business delightfully funny is a livelier sense of humor. Once again, I'm certain the man's an actor, whatever else he might be. I don't hold this against him. I once entertained the idea of a life on the boards myself. It's the role he's written for himself I despise. Though it's possible he didn't write this script; I only have his word for that. Rather like the Bible announcing itself the Word of God. One wants corroboration.

"I see what your promises are worth," I say.

His mask turns apologetic: "This business was already arranged before we spoke, I'm afraid—from my perspective at least." He gives a smile condescending enough to register with the upper balcony to convey the huge discrepancy between his grand perspective and my narrow one. "I couldn't get the class back into it without breaking my promise *not* to interfere anymore." His upturned palms seem to say, *What's a god to do?* I recall a question my brother and I pondered when I was twelve—*Can God make a stone so big he can't move it?* I didn't care then, and I don't care now.

"You sent Jonah into a trap."

"I freed him from slavery."

"And Earl?"

"He was moments from death. I saved his life."

"And drove him mad."

"He may yet regain his senses. Meeting you has done him a world of good."

"You said they were 'accidental.' And yet you've deliberately tampered with their lives."

"I said that's what we *call* them. It's derived more from the *musical* sense, actually."

I imagine us all like notes strung out on a staff, and the image gives me a discordant chill.

"I insist you tell me what it is you have in mind for us."

"I will, but not yet."

"Now."

"But you wouldn't understand, *now*."

"To Hell with you, Anchee."

My anger pleases him, and a grin flashes across his face. "My, how the modern world has changed you."

"It hasn't changed me a jot. You want to engage me in your game, part of which consists for you, I believe, in holding forth on what a clever paradoxical fellow you are, explaining the intricacies of your trickery to my drooling self while I rattle the bars of my cage. No thank you. Let me arrange a bit of the plot myself, here and now: The next time I see you, I will, without hesitation, do my best to break your neck!"

"But Peter, I thought you believed in *do unto others*."

"And so I most certainly do. Which is why I dearly hope—if I should *ever* attempt to make someone my puppet, to deceive and manipulate, as you have done with me—that my victim would rise up and strangle me with whatever wires I've fashioned to make him dance!" I'm fairly shouting by this time. I credit the maze with muffling my tirade sufficiently so that we're not descended upon by an army of silencing librarians.

Anchee remains maddeningly placid, unruffled, though he

does take a prudent step backward. "Him? What if the *someone* was a *her?*"

"*Then ten times over would I wish it!*"

"So I suspected, my chivalrous one. So I suspected." He gives a there's-a-good-lad pat on the head to the air in front of him to signify my dim-witted pate, and vanishes in an instant. I find myself on tiptoe poised to lunge at thin air. I must appear quite ludicrous, quite like a puppeteer I realize, my arms aloft, akimbo, as I turn, and see Rachel on the other side of the glass, staring at me, eyes wide.

She steps into the room, looks quickly around. "That was him, wasn't it? The man from the future."

"You saw him?"

"I saw *something*. For a split second."

"But not enough to be certain."

"Certain," she repeats ambiguously, as if she's not quite certain of the word's meaning, surveying the empty room again beneath a furrowed brow. Her face is wet and the hair framing it, her shirt cuffs, the bottoms of her trousers, her shoes. Her knapsack is beaded with rain. She must have ridden here on her bicycle under a hooded wrap. This mental image, which I create in an instant, extrapolating from a few drops of water, touches me, and I catch a glimpse of why I'm so taken with her—a glimpse only, for it remains, in its intensity at least, quite mysterious to me. "I heard you shouting—" She's noticed the writing on the chalkboard. "Where's the class?"

"There never was a class. It was something Anchee arranged. I'm not sure why. . . ." I stop myself. "No that's not true. I'm trying to spare myself some embarrassment." I can't help but laugh. There's no sense worrying about that, I suppose! "Since I've dragged you into this mad drama by finding you so very attractive, the least I can do is let you know everything I know—even if it is crazy. He told me he used the class as a device to draw us together. He's rather keen on drawing us together. I don't know why. I mean, I know why *I* am. I don't know why *he* is. Anyway, he impersonated Mrs. Charles, as it turns out, timing the phone call so that I might—how did he put it?—'rise to the chivalrous occasion.' "

She nods thoughtfully, almost dreamily, a faint smile at the corners of her mouth. "And so you did," she says, sounding oddly pleased. Her fear and anger toward me seem to have vanished altogether.

"You know?" she says, "I never actually *met* that obnoxious woman or anyone in the class either. They were voices on the telephone, a list of names in an e-mail, referrals from other agencies—all strangers. I don't usually work that way. I can't stand to work that way." She stares at me intently, as if, like Anchee, I might vanish. "You didn't drag me anywhere," she says. "To be honest, I was hoping you would be here." Once again her opinion of me has undergone a sea change quite independently of anything I've knowingly done, and I hope it doesn't get to be a habit.

"I was hoping the same," I say.

She considers this, nodding to herself, forming some resolve it seems. "I want to show you something," she says. She unhooks her knapsack from her shoulder and sets it on the table, showering it with water.

She unclasps the knapsack with a click, and opens it. There are a half dozen books inside, a portfolio stuffed with papers. She wipes her face dry with her shirtsleeves, dries her hands on the thighs of her trousers. Out of the portfolio, she pulls a sheet of parchment, gives it a kindly but critical appraisal, and hands it to me. "I did this about three o'clock this morning."

It's a detailed pencil sketch of me, really quite good, expertly shaded, especially around the eyes. I'm quite flattered she remembered my face so vividly. "It's me," I say stupidly.

"So it is," she says. "I copied it from this." She pulls a book from the knapsack. She takes the drawing from my hands and replaces it with the book—open to a photograph of Dead Peter taken in his early forties as I recall. She swipes at the tabletop with her shirtsleeves and lays the drawing down, invites me to place the open book beside it. Her hands hover over one and then the other as she speaks. "I slimmed you a few pounds, trimmed the beard, removed the glasses, gave you more hair on top, smoothed the wrinkles around the eyes." She touches the eyes on the drawing with her fingertips and looks into my eyes, raising her hand as if she means to touch my face, but pulls back before she does. "It's you," she says, taking a step back and crossing her arms, eyeing me as if I've attempted to deny it.

"So you *believe* me?" I try not to sound as astonished as I am, but succeed only to the extent that I'm capable of speech at all. I confess I had quietly adopted Earl's wisdom that no one in this time would ever believe me, and I should put that vain hope behind me.

She heaves a sigh. "I don't know. I don't . . . *dis*believe you. When I saw you just now, in that *first* moment"—she gestures to the glass as if she's still standing out in the hall looking in—"I *knew* in my gut who you are. Not just because I saw . . . *him*, or whatever the hell I saw, or thought I saw . . ." She shakes her head, doubting that earlier self. "But my head's having trouble catching up with my gut."

She looks back and forth from me to the two Peters on the table, speaking as much to them as to me. "I've been reading your books—*Conquest of Bread, Mutual Aid, Memoirs of a Revolutionist*, the *Ethics*. That's just about *all* I've been doing since yesterday. I've had maybe two hours sleep at the most. I can't stop reading." She studies me again, and it's clear she wants to believe me as much as I want her to. "Your books," she says cautiously, testing the thin ice of that phrase, then putting her full weight upon it: "They're so true, so wise and . . . beautiful." She touches the open book and smiles at Dead Peter. "The *Memoirs* especially."

"Thank you," I say.

She shakes her head, looking me full in the face. "No. I want to thank *you*. People talk about books changing their lives, and when I was younger it seemed like it happened all the time, but never like *this* before, certainly not lately. To tell you the truth, I thought I'd outgrown feeling that way—one more misconception of youth chucked overboard. But I started reading these books, and it's like I've been waiting for somebody to say these things my whole life. Do you know what I mean?"

"Yes, I do." Exactly. I remember such a moment in my former life. It's still with me, will always be with me.

"Your books are like you, they sound like you, they . . . *act* like you. *They're* what made me think that maybe, just maybe, you were telling the truth, no matter how crazy it might sound. That's why I did the drawing. That's why I'm telling you all this, I guess. It *is* you, isn't it? It's really you."

"Yes."

"Damn!" She laughs, shaking her head, coming up on her toes, brushing tears from her eyes. "I don't know why I should be *crying!"* she exclaims, bringing a fresh burst of laughter. She grabs hold of her knapsack and gives it a fierce shake, showering photograph and drawing with raindrops, so that all our eyes blear at once. "Damn! This is truly insane. I feel like Natalie Wood in *Miracle on 34th Street*—some jaded kid trying to believe in Santa." She laughs again and plops down in one of the chairs, pulling the knapsack into her lap, hugging it to her chest. "And look what happened to Natalie Wood—she falls off a boat and drowns!" She looks up at me wild-eyed, but at the sight of my perplexity transforms into the soul of sympathy. "You poor thing, you don't have the *faintest* idea what I'm talking about, do you?"

My thoughts are a single chorus: *She believes me, she believes me, she actually believes me.* In light of this revelation, Natalie Wood, miracles, and Santa are as nothing to me on Thirty-fourth Street or any other. "That's quite all right, I assure you. I've had a good deal of experience in the clueless line lately."

"I'll bet you have. *Miracle on 34th Street* is an old movie about Santa Claus, a favorite of mine when I was a kid. I don't know if you'd like it—he's sort of a capitalist character, isn't he, old Santa? At least *now* he is. Then too, I guess: The Natalie Wood character ends up believing in Santa because he gives her a big house in the 'burbs. She dies later. Natalie Wood, not the character." She laughs again, and takes a deep breath to calm herself. "Peter?"

"Yes?"

She looks into my eyes. "Would you like to go somewhere and talk?"

"Yes, very much."

"Is my place okay?"

"Okay? It would be splendid." I feel quite as jolly as Santa. "I can't begin to tell you how glad I am. I was beginning to think . . . Well, never mind what I was beginning to think. What I think now is that Anchee has proven himself prophetic. He said I would be happier if I kept my appointment with you. What-ever else may befall me in this lifetime, that much is certainly true."

She seems a bit overwhelmed by this proclamation, and says quietly, "Let's get out of here," and so we do, walking home in a driving rain, as she pushes her bicycle along beside us.

I can't shut up. Her belief, however tentative, has me babbling on with questions, reminiscences, musings, and everything I've done since I saw her last. And the more we both act as if she believes me in earnest, the more it seems to be true, like Coleridge's *willing sus-pension of disbelief*. She makes me, in fact, tell my whole tale again from beginning to end for the benefit of her believing self. The doubter didn't even bother to follow the narrative thread.

"To be honest, I didn't hear a lot of it the first time," she says. "I had this voice in my head screaming, *get this man a shrink!*"

"A *shrink* is . . . ?"

"A psychiatrist. An alienist."

"Of course."

"I'm sorry."

"Don't be. I understand perfectly. I would've thought myself completely mad. *Shrink*. I like that. Do you know the origin of the term?"

"Short for headshrinker, I think."

"Sounds gruesome."

"It's not so bad. I've had mine shrunk. It grows back after a while."

"And very nicely, too."

The rain is still coming down hard; the sky is low and gray. We're sitting in what would be a sunroom if there were any sun. It's filled with palms and a rangy ficus left for dead in the alley, but resurrected by Rachel. From here, side by side on a love seat inherited from her parents, we watch the rain come down in the park and drink good black tea.

The gusty rain rendered my umbrella useless, and I was fairly soaked by the time we got here. At her insistence, I took a hot shower and changed into some old clothes of her father's. Tea and biscuits awaited me when I emerged, clean and well dressed and much refreshed.

"Tell me about yourself," I say. "Where are you from?"

"Here. Born and raised and left as soon as I could. But I came back. I have a friend who says everyone comes back here. But maybe that's just because he did."

"And what brought you back?"

"The job. My dad. My dad sent me the ad from the *Times-Dispatch*. It gave me the chance to use my Spanish, and do my bit for diversity in Richmond. It seemed like a good idea. I was hating Seattle. Don't believe them: It *does* rain all the time. Dad denied he knew he was dying when he sent me that ad, but I suspect he did. I was glad I was here for him. He died three years ago."

"And you've stayed on."

"The place grows on you. I like Richmond when it's not embarrassing itself fighting the Civil War again—or as they like to call it around here, The War Between the States. But that's not really *Richmond*. Most of those folks don't live in the city anymore—too many black people here—they're all out in the counties."

"Is that what they call white flight?"

We talk about race issues in Richmond, and she agrees with Anchee's assessment that all issues are race issues here.

"But Peter, what I'm curious about is why *you're* here? Why do you think that is?"

"I guess the most honest answer is that I'm here because I was afraid to die, or to put it a bit more charitably, I wasn't ready to die *yet*."

"Oh Peter, don't be so hard on yourself. I meant—"

"You meant, what plans does *Anchee* have for me here—what he means by all that talk about freedom and slavery. And I have no idea. To my shame or not, I didn't inquire as to the where-abouts of my resurrection; I just signed on to *live*. I'll try to do my best at it, but beyond that I make no promises except that I'll make my own decisions—whatever they might be—I've hardly had time to make plans." I have to laugh. "I'm only three days old, after all."

"And awfully defensive even so. It's your wife, isn't it? You feel guilty for leaving her."

I'm stunned by the justice of her accusation. "I didn't even think to ask whether she could come with me or not."

"What would she say if she were here right now?"

I laugh. "Something like, 'Petya, don't be so hard on yourself. You were *dying*!' "

Rachel looks into my eyes. "You can't go back, can you?"

"No. Anchee made that much clear."

"I hope you don't hate me for saying this, Peter. But I'm glad she didn't come with you. Otherwise, we wouldn't be sitting here like this, would we?"

"I . . . I suppose not." For a moment, her face comprises the en-tire universe, but I look away, overcome, as if with vertigo.

She pours me another cup of tea. "You were something of a celebrity in your lifetime, weren't you?"

I'm grateful for the change of subject, the tea to fuss over. "After a fashion. Nothing like an actor or a prime minister. But I was well-known."

"Did you have fans?"

"Oh yes, I suppose you would say that. People had rather romantic notions about me."

"What about Sophie, was she a fan?"

"Most of that sort of thing was later on, but yes, in a sense, when we first met. She was new to the movement. She looked up to me as an old hand."

"What was the difference in your ages?"

"Fourteen years."

"You know what Sigmund Freud would say, don't you?"

I've grown increasingly uncomfortable with the direction of the conversation. "I'm . . . I'm afraid I don't. Others have mentioned him to me. Austrian, wasn't he? But I don't know his work."

A guilty look crosses her face, and she stares out the window for a moment. She takes my hand. "I'm sorry, Peter. I *knew* you didn't. I was testing you. I read that you didn't know Freud's work even though you were contemporaries, and when he popped into my head I . . ."

"Took the opportunity to test my veracity."

"Yes. I'm terribly sorry."

"For putting your doubts to rest? Don't be ridiculous. It makes perfect sense. If I were you, I would do the same. Very clever, too. You could have a future in espionage."

"Since I met you, I've felt like a character in a spy story."

"It's not so glamorous in real life. But you have me curious. What *would* Freud say?"

She shakes her head. "Peter, it doesn't matter. I'm no Freudian. I don't care what he says."

"Perhaps I might be. I won't know until I hear what the man's got to say. How bad can it be?"

"Okay then. I suppose he'd say that because your mother died so young and you blamed your father for her death, you were slow to develop sexually, and that when you did, you were drawn to a much younger woman—like her—a woman you wanted to mother you, even though you must've been something of a father figure to her. Your hatred of your authoritarian father would come in there somewhere, too—in your anti-authoritarian views certainly—and maybe your chivalrous, protective attitude toward women, but I don't really know enough about it to say."

For a moment I'm speechless. "He would've said all that, would he?"

"I'm sorry, Peter. You asked. No one takes Freud seriously anymore. Not me, certainly."

I consider the Freudian analysis. "It all makes sense to me," I say. "Especially the part about my father and mother. But I loved Sophie nonetheless. Would Freud understand that?"

"I don't know. I think he thought everything comes down to sex in one way or another."

"I suppose that's preferable to everything being business. And what do you think?"

"Sex is definitely preferable to business."

"No, I mean, do you think I loved my wife?"

She lays her hand on the side of my face. "I *know* you loved her. And I know that was a very long time ago *and* only yesterday."

She withdraws her hand, and stands, taking up the tea tray to replenish our supplies. "Can you stay for dinner?"

"I would be delighted."

"We can watch a movie I want you to see—it's my favorite spy story. It's called *Three Days of the Condor*. It's based on a novel called *Six Days of the Condor*, but I like the movie better. It's more intense and has a better ending."

16 ✿ Delphian Dialogues

The state is a condition, a certain relationship between human beings, a mode of human behavior; we destroy it by contracting other relationships, by behaving differently.

—GUSTAV LANDAUER

A spy must report. If he should merely say that he has stood for a week in the street without noticing anything mysterious, he would soon be put on the half-pay list or dismissed.

—PETER KROPOTKIN, *Memoirs of a Revolutionist*

One of my favorite scenes in all of literature is the bittersweet morning in *Romeo and Juliet* when the lovers awake in their marriage bed, and Romeo must flee the city in banishment. But allow me to indulge in the narrator's prerogative and do a bit of time travel here, hurrying past a short span of time, the interval during which Rachel and I fell in love. While it is of great interest to us, I choose to omit the details here. For one thing, Rachel and I lack Romeo and Juliet's dramatic interest. We're older by any measure relevant to the matter, and not as prone (as Wendy might phrase it) to nut out. We have lowly jobs to dictate our schedules, no need for the high-handed meddling of tyrannical parents or the conspiracy of comic servants to circumvent them. No lurking danger threatens our evening rambles by the riverside save to lose track of the time and stumble home in the dark. Bloodthirsty feuds don't spring from our spirited discussions and amorous play, and no well-intentioned friar urges us to marry or to swallow poison. But, truth be told, the principal reason I omit such scenes is that I'm still too modest to

dramatize passion, a sentiment Shakespeare would have understood, I trust, if the subject had been his own passions instead of
Romeo and Juliet's.

Besides, people often, when they encounter a couple in love,
invent their own romantic scenes for them and stage them fleetingly in their imaginations—scenes, I'll wager, more pleasant for
everyone than those imagined for the constantly bickering or the
grimly resigned. Everyone we meet—my housemates and her
neighbors, my coworkers and hers, the clerks at the thrift store
and the lad named Gerald, the reference librarian and the widower next door to Rachel who laughs every time he sees us—*all*
seem happy for us. Sophie herself, I'm convinced, if she could
see us, would wish us well.

Both rationalists, Rachel and I try to muster some sober
doubts, but don't have much luck at it. In subsequent discussions of Freud's theories, for example, Rachel suggests that our
sudden attachment and strong feelings for one another may
have been prompted by the extraordinary circumstances of our
meeting—my "birth trauma," as it were—but try as we might,
we fail to find this possibility a matter for concern, since we're
both so pleased with the outcome. We divide our time between
my home and hers, and every day is full to overflowing.

My housemates have dubbed us "cute," and I suppose we are.
Wendy still finds it easy sport to make me blush, and on occasion
Rachel is her accomplice in this entertainment. The Kitchen
Table—that traitorous pile of planks—is the favorite site for this
diversion. Caitlin is Chorus, crying out at the climactic moment,
"Look! He's blushing!" squealing with particular glee when my
scalp peeks crimson through the sparse canopy of my hair. Dave
and Zipper make animal noises and lewd remarks to put the
bawdiest possible construction on the matter. TJ, with his
painter's eye, announces that my face and beard are very nearly
the same shade of red. The others laugh along, though Brad will
occasionally say, "Come on, y'all, lay off him." Only Sondra,
when she is present at the table at all, declines to take part in this
good-hearted teasing.

But she is an odd and moody one, and I don't know what to make of her. For some reason, she seems troubled by my entrance into the household and avoids me at all costs. When our paths cross in the kitchen, porch, or hallways, she immediately finds somewhere else she must be, averting her eyes and ducking her head behind her straight white hair. Rachel's theory is that the girl—pardon me, woman—is smitten with me, but Rachel admits her bias in this judgment. Besides, Sondra avoids most everyone as far as I can tell, except for Brad, and on rare nights when her spirits are high, Mike.

After his initial enthusiasm for me, Mike has cooled considerably ever since I criticized his play. He's quite civil, even friendly in his way, but he has no desire to get to know me or sound my thoughts, though I still catch him watching me or eavesdropping on my conversations with others. He seems to be biding his time, as if we were all here waiting for a train. I would ask him what he's up to, but assume he would only lie to me, so I bide my own time and ride my own train.

I spend most of my "free" time engaged in studies, working *toward* my lecture if not *on* it, for I'm having some difficulty setting pen to paper or fingers to keys. Who am I to speak now, dead for almost eighty years? Rachel reassures me that I have plenty to say that needs saying now more than ever, and I try to believe she's right.

One morning I am returning home from Rachel's by way of the alleys, still basking in the memory of a pleasant farewell we took before setting out to labor in our separate vineyards, when I come upon a garbage truck and its crew and tag along behind.

Since I have been in this city, I have noticed two things done admirably well, I begrudgingly admit, by government; they are mail delivery and trash collection. One afternoon previously I accompanied Penny our *letter carrier*, for such she prefers to call herself over *postman* since she is not a man and finds the alliteration of Penny the postperson insufferable. I picked her brain about the post office, an effective but oddly despised institution, and find her insights fascinating. Often, it seems, one is respected in inverse proportion to one's contribution to society. The letter carrier is said to bring *junk mail*, but the corporations who are ultimately the source of all this postal refuse, rule the roost. The creation of junk mail—advertising—is a prestigious enterprise for a bright young person, while Penny's peers consider her occupation somewhat "loserly" even though it's she who still occasionally brings that most treasured gift, a handwritten letter from a friend. So it's with curiosity and the desire to learn that I introduce myself to the trash collectors and attempt to engage them in conversation.

The younger one, Daniel Seven, maintains a guarded reticence, but the older, Clement Arthur, who says he's been working for the city for twenty-five years, is friendlier, and perhaps as curious about me as I am about him.

The truck itself is a marvel to behold in action. Nothing can resist its mechanical maw, devouring everything from tree limbs to divans with a single bite. Someone has set out a television even I can tell is an old one. Clement grabs one end, waiting for Daniel to finish what he's doing so that he can grab the other end, but I step in and take ahold, and we give it a satisfying heave-ho into the back of the truck.

"Listen up," he says, and in a moment there's a loud pop as if a gun had gone off inside the truck. "Picture tube," he explains.

I tell him how I've admired the efficiency of the city's trash collection and wonder how he thinks it might be improved, but I have difficulty drawing him out.

Finally, he says, "Things would be improved if it wasn't always me picking up the trash. It's a job to me, best I can do with the education I got, but that's all it is. What about you, Daniel? You want to be a garbageman for twenty-five years?"

"Fuck you, old man."

"See there? And I ain't even old yet. I'll just be old before I see anything changing much here in the alleys. Times are good, people be tossing out good stuff. Look at this bicycle here." He has a place behind the truck cab where he lashes salvageable items. The bicycle does appear to be in perfect condition.

"How would you manage the whole business of picking up the trash, if it were up to you?"

"But it ain't up to me. The city makes the rules."

"But what if," I say, trying a different tack, "one morning you woke up and there *was* no city. The people were still here; every-thing was still here, but no city, no government. You came to work, and there were no bosses there, and they weren't coming back. All the trucks are sitting there and trash is piling up all over town. What would you do?"

He laughs gleefully at this vision. "I see where you're going with this. No city at all, just folks and garbage. The truck here's the thing. City left all the trucks just sitting there in the yard?"

"That's right."

He ponders the question in silence while we wrestle a pile of brush into the truck. "I'd pick it up for nothing a couple times, give folks a chance to get their wits about them. Then I'd take a truck round to every neighborhood and leave it there with the keys in it. Every neighborhood would have one, like the routes we got now, but the people in the neighborhood—except kids and old people and like that—would take turns cleaning up after each other." He smiles at the thought. "Might have an effect on how folks act."

"Folks in Windsor Farms working a *garbage* truck!" Daniel ex-claims, though I was unaware he was even listening. "What you been smoking, old man?"

"Who you calling old? I don't need drugs to feel good. Just my dreams and the good clean air." He laughs. "We just talking any-way."

My conversation with Clement Arthur keeps me going on my studies with renewed hope and vigor, and I am always delighted when I can time my walk from Rachel's house to mine to coin-cide with the trash-collection crew. And even Daniel eventually warms to me. He's interested in making videos, he says, but has no equipment. I introduce him to Brad and his computers and they have been collaborating on something for some time now, I believe. I seem to have lost track of time.

I try to meet new people every day and converse with them. I find the city buses a marvelous means to indulge this pastime and a pleasant place to read and think and write should my sociability prove unrequited or wear thin. But that is rare, for I find Richmonders a very friendly people indeed. The thrum of the engines provides a sort of intimacy for conversation or composition—the latter an acquired dexterity skill. If my sentences now are a bumpy ride, perhaps my mind is assuming that familiar rhythm.

I'm aware that those who ride the buses skew my sample of humanity a good deal. The advertising in evidence (always a good litmus in this world) knows its audience: $7/hour chicken factory jobs, the lottery, drug problems, the lottery, the army, loan sharks, the lottery. To meet *everyone* I would have to come out from the dishroom and sit at someone's table or scale a wall on River Road or stroll onto a golf course—all gestures unlikely to be welcomed. So the Richmonders I know are mostly young (if white), foreign (from an impressive range of countries), or black—and not a Confederate in the bunch!

During this time, there's no sign of Anchee. Either my threat has frightened him off, or I'm doing exactly what he wants me to do, so there's no need for his meddling. Before I know it, days and days have passed, and my lecture—such I call it even though it doesn't yet exist!—is only a few days away. This morning, my notes spread before me like a treacherous bog, I recall a vow I made to myself, and promptly quit my burrow, setting out for the river at a brisk pace, crossing over the bridge, and descending to the forest floor, a place which has changed considerably in my absence, for spring in these parts is no aimless idler and chokes the trail with vines and a half dozen new species of plants. A fallen tree, a faint detour around it, gives the trail a new twist, like the sunning snake upon it. A red-crested woodpecker swoops through the treetops with a laughing cry like a child on a rope, and I know I've come to the right place.

I don't head directly for Earl's home, but out to the rocks where first I saw him, and take his perch, looking out across the river, listening to its gurgling motion. In the middle, a flock of cormorants huddles on a rock that seems to have been chosen for its small size, so that dozens of birds stand shoulder to shoulder without an inch to spare, while only a few yards away a rock of twice the size sits perfectly empty. I'm reminded of spontaneous gatherings Sophie and I used to have in our several little houses over the years with so many friends packed inside that they literally spilled out the windows and off the porches into the gardens. Wherever we were, we grew onions and herbs so that when we added water to the soup for newcomers, we might add some flavor as well! I recall those wonderful times; I recall their fading away, our lives withdrawing to a bleaker and lonelier promontory; but still, I'm warmed, as we were even then, by those memories.

I am pondering them still when Earl sits down beside me. "Hey, Pete," he says. "How's things in town?"

"Splendid," I say. "How's the river?"

"As you can see," he says with a proprietary flourish of his hand, "it's doing quite nicely. It's still flowing that way and hasn't risen higher than my hole. Saw the first hummingbird yesterday evening. Osprey're nesting. But they were expected. You'd be the one with *news*."

So I tell him all my news—my new digs and Rachel, my new studies and Rachel, my new rambles about town with Rachel. He listens with a pleasant smile, nodding his head up and down. "So the man from the future—Anchan, or whatever you call him—fixed you up with a girl?"

"Her name's Rachel. I wouldn't put it that way exactly. He introduced us." This is the first time I've shared this euphemism with anyone but Rachel.

"He *introduced* you here in the first place, like plunking down a tree in the middle of a cornfield or throwing a catfish into a stock tank. Me too, you say. Nice to finally know where I come from, so I can tell people: 'Allow me to *introduce* myself. I'm Dr. Impossible from Anchan County. Never hear of it? Well, it's right outside Time, just this side of Afterlife, a little detour around Death. It's where all the loonies live.' Did you tell Rachel where you were from, Pete? What time it was, and how you got here?"

"I certainly did, and she seems to believe me."

"Then she 'seems' to be crazy, too. It's like a disease. It spreads. Since you're crazy, everyone who believes you must be crazy, too. The more people you get to believe you, the crazier everything gets until there's nothing for it but to *lock* you up somewhere until you come to your senses and leave innocent folks alone. And you want to know the worst part?" His voice has risen, and his eyes are ablaze.

"What's that, Earl?"

"They never lock up old Anchoo. They never even *see* him, or they see him everywhere. Like wallpaper. So they don't *care* that he's there, cause he's *always* there, isn't he?" He gives his head a shake. "It. They call him *It*. *It's just the way things are,* they say. *You better get used to It.* You should've stayed down here on the river, Pete. No wallpaper." He laughs. "No walls!" He takes a deep breath, rocking from side to side, steadying himself. "How's Jonah doing? Chinny-Chin get him a girl too?"

"He's doing splendidly. He and Wendy are constant companions, but I trust they've managed that on their own initiative."

"How do you know they did?"

"I guess I don't. But you saw them—they took to each other immediately."

"I'm not doubting that, but two hundred years is a pretty long ways for a fellow to come calling on foot—especially when he ain't got no shoes, and he's been beat half to death. I'm happy for him. Chin-Chan got him a girl. Has he told her where he comes from?"

"I don't think so."

"There you go. When he does, either she gets crazy or figures he is. Awful chance to take. Hard on everybody. Down here, I don't have those sorts of problems." He points to a flock of geese, floating in the current. "These Canadian honkers now, I do wonder about them. When I was in prison over yonder on the island, eating wormy corn dodger and paying the price, you'd see these fat birds coming and going, some staying on as some Reb officer's dinner. I'd dream about them so much I was glad to see them fly away. Now they're here *all* the time, never leave. Cooked one last Christmas and ate off it for five days. You think Chan-Man had something to do with all these crazy geese? I don't think so. And you may be right about Wendy, too. She was already crazy before y'all came along, giving toe-food to all the homeless people. Or do you think Chain Gang put her up to that one?"

"I don't *know*, Earl. I just don't know."

"Hey, Pete, don't be sad. I was just having my fun. I'm sure he didn't have nothing to do with it. To hell with him. Down with tyrants, right?"

That forces a smile out of me. "Right. To hell with him. My real problem is that I'm giving a speech in a few days and haven't the faintest idea what I'm going to say."

"Leastways it'll be short then. That's always a good thing in a speech."

I laugh, and I have to confess to myself what's really bothering me, and I tell Earl: "I'm afraid. I'm terrified. It's not the speech itself. The worst that can happen is I make a fool of myself. But it feels too much like a time in my old life. The first time I was arrested—the first time I was thirty-two, you might say— I *knew* the police were after me. Several friends had already been arrested. A weak-willed fellow who could identify me had recently been taken into custody. It was only a matter of time before he gave me up to the authorities. I should've fled the city, but I stayed on another week so that I might deliver a lecture to the Geographical Society. I spent over two years of my life in jail because I thought I had to make a speech, even though I was filled with premonitions of danger. I feel exactly the same now, yet I must speak."

"Perhaps you should listen to your premonitions."

"I don't believe in premonitions."

"Betcha your friend Inchy does. He's got it all measured out. Just how did you come to be giving this speech anyway?"

"Mike, the bright young fellow who offered me a ride at the airport, arranged it. I strongly suspect he is one of Anchee's pawns."

"Then it's not just a premonition."

"What am I supposed to do? Spend my life doing the opposite of my natural inclinations? Or perhaps *that's* his intention. In which case, to foil him, I should do exactly as I please. Who's to say? Not even he—for why should I believe a word he says?"

"It's a fine pickle," Earl agrees. "What was the speech about you made back then?"

"Glaciation."

Earl nods thoughtfully. "That ain't what they arrested you for, is it?"

"No, they arrested me for spreading anarchist propaganda among the workers."

"Was it a good speech?"

"Yes, I suppose it was. I succeeded in toppling old mistaken notions and was nominated to be president of the physical geography section."

"See there? It all works out. "What are you supposed to talk about this time?"

"Anarchy."

"Maybe you should stick with the glaciation."

I proceed to work. I've traded shifts with one of the other dishwashers so I can get off for my address on Thursday, and I work well into the night. Near the end of my shift, Doris summons me into her office, or *the* office as it is universally identified, even though nobody else ever seems to set foot in it. There would scarcely be room for them if they did. The furniture consists of her desk and her chair and a calendar with a lovely photographic landscape I would guess to be Tuscany thumb-tacked on the back

of the door. I sit in a chair I dragged from the kitchen for the purpose, and there's scarcely room for me and it to sit together. The
small office has been reduced to closet size by ceiling-high stacks
of boxes around its perimeter, interrupted only for door and
desk. The boxes appear to have originally contained foodstuffs or
other supplies but have been conscripted into more abstract service. A few inches to the left of where I sit, for example, a former
box of stuffed olives with *GUEST CHECKS 1996* scrawled in
black across its side resides at eye level. Two boxes sit atop it, but
I'm too close to read their markings without leaning away from
them. Below it, *BANK 1992* nests inside a box of ketchup. The
bottom box in the stack used to house Jack Daniels' but evicted
him in favor of *SALES TAX 198?*, the last digit forever lost in the
box's original, largely black, design. To my right is a similar stack,
and the back of my head rests against another, and so it goes all
around the room two and three stacks deep in the corners so that
the room is effectively an oval. In these boxes, I recognize the
droppings of commerce, always abundant and slow to decom-
pose, and wonder what on earth Doris might want with me here.
I imagine myself stuffed into a box of hamburger dills and set
atop a corner stack to molder—*ANARCHIST 1999.*

Doris's desk is a smaller version of the room: Stacks and
stacks of loitering papers occupy most of the available space as
they await deportation into one of their properly labeled cardboard cousins; a telephone, an ashtray, and a coffee cup make up
the sole desktop furniture, with little room to spare. The ashtray
is particularly hard-pressed. Near full and smoldering under an
unstable outcropping of bills, it appears at risk of avalanche or
conflagration at any moment. In the midst of this tinderbox of
peril, Doris bravely smokes.

"Cigarette?" she asks me, shaking one halfway out of the pack
and pointing it at me.

She always forgets I don't smoke, or perhaps accurately reads
the desire in my eye and enjoys tempting me. "No thanks. I quit
some years ago."

She smiles faintly, an extravagance for her. "Good for you."

She takes a deep drag just to remind me of what I'm missing, and aims the smoke up to the ceiling. "Things have certainly changed since you've been here," she says. Her tone leaves it entirely mysterious whether this is a compliment or an accusation. "I got a call the other day from a fellow restaurant owner in the Fan asking me if it was true we were feeding the homeless over here. He said he caught some of his waitresses squirreling away food, and they said they got the idea from my people." She pauses for a heavy-lidded drag. "I laughed at him and told him he must be drinking up his profits if he believed a story like that. 'I told them it was crazy,' he said. '*Doris?*' Like that, '*Doris?*' I reassured him that nobody was getting any free food from me without Dumpster diving for it like they've always done. I may have gone too far with that crack—too cold even for a bitch like me. I don't think he believed me, started telling me how many laws we'd be breaking if it was true—as if I didn't know that myself. Did you know your little soldiers were recruiting?"

"I had no idea."

"I didn't think so. I want to show you something," she says. She opens what I'd thought to be a cabinet door over her desk, covered with postcards and photos, and we are looking into the restaurant through the mirror behind the bar. A row of bottles fills the foreground, liqueurs by the colorful look of them, their sweetness crusted on the spouts. In the background, on the bar, sits the cash register. The gin-playing bartender (whose unlikely name, I've since learned, is Storm) has his back to us ringing up a sale, making drinks, trying his charm on the new waitress. Shannon, I believe her name is.

"I used to sit here for hours," Doris says, "just waiting for somebody to steal from me some way or other—slipping drinks to their friends, 'forgetting' to ring up a few sales, eating up the oranges, getting high on the nitrous oxide in the whipped cream cans. They think of new ways all the time. I caught a girl one time walking out the back door with a thousand count of to-go cups she planned to make *art* out of. 'We never use them,' she said in her defense. Who cares? You know what I mean? Who cares anymore? I'm sitting here on my ass smoking three packs a day while those kids are working, pretty hard most of them, but *I'm* the one making seventy-five cents on the dollar, *including* all they steal, and they're the ones who can't make rent or buy a car that runs good enough to get them to work on time."

Storm's charm appears to be working, and the waitress is still standing at the bar with a tray full of drinks, conducting the friendliest of conversations with him as the ice melts. Doris shakes her head, and mutters to Shannon, "Just deliver the drinks, and fuck him on your own time." She points them out to me. "Of course, as you can see, there's certain advantages to the life they lead. She gets Tom Cruise there, and I get . . ." She shrugs. "I get seventy-five cents on the dollar. You want to know what I decided a few years back? Let them steal. We'll all be happier. It doesn't matter whether I'm watching or not. Sometimes I think they even steal *less* because I'm not pissed off at them all the time for stealing, you know what I mean?" She takes a thoughtful drag. "But that's not what I want to show you. I worked through that one already." She points to one of the customers seated at the bar. He is staring right at us, at the mirror I realize. His eyes have the vacant sparkle of a drunk's, and he looks quite pleased with himself. He is drinking a glass of whiskey neat, easily a triple. He grazes on a saucerful of maraschino cherries, a treat the bartenders often serve to pacify restless children. His lips have a red patina.

"See that guy? His name is Fred Spurlow. He works for the health department. The rumor got to him, too—probably the same way it got to me—and he dropped in on us a little while ago to watch the whole operation for himself. He was quite impressed with how well organized it all was, wanted to know who the 'ringleader' was. Fred's like that. He uses words like 'ringleader.' " She jams out a cigarette and lights another, pausing to relish the first prolonged exhalation. "Fred and I went to high school together." She winces to convey the distaste this memory brings her "For the sake of our old friendship and a case of Bushmills, he's agreed to forget the whole thing as long

as we don't do it anymore—not counting what he's putting
away tonight at the bar. That's bribery of a public official. Probably a felony."

"Do you want us to stop?"

"Hell no. I've got a case of whiskey invested in it now."

"What about your husband—"

"What about him?"

"Does he approve of our activities as well? He must've noticed—"

"William wouldn't notice you were stealing his brain if you
pulled it out through his eye sockets, and he sure as hell
wouldn't miss it after it was gone. *That's* my husband. And don't
get me wrong. I, personally, don't approve or disapprove of
what you're doing. All I know is that you're the first truly interesting thing to happen in this place for a good long while, and
I'm not ready to give up my entertainment. So I thought I'd help
you keep things going just a little while longer."

"And then what happens?"

She seems surprised at the question. "They fall apart. Things
like this always do." She looks at Shannon, still chatting and
smiling, then at Fred, sucking on a cherry, his eyes now on Shannon as well. "Fred and me will fuck them up one way or another
just by doing our jobs."

She stares sadly at this imagined future—as if she can see it
there on the other side of the looking glass—shuts the door, and
grinds out her cigarette. Several old butts escape over the sides
of the ashtray, and she swipes them into a trash can she pulls out
from under her desk. She picks up the ashtray, dumps it into the
trash can, and has them both back in place in a single, practiced
motion she must repeat several times a day.

I notice one of the photographs, visible now that the door is
closed. A young smiling woman poses with a scowling Doris beside a sphere easily a yard in diameter made from hundreds of
to-go cups, opening outward, joined together somehow and
mounted on a pedestal. Through some clever use of plastic, no
doubt, they all appear as if they contain varying amounts of
gravity-defying coffee—some with cream, some black. Stolen

stir sticks are immortalized in some of them, though the single prominent lipstick mark at ten o'clock is likely the artist's own. The unrepentant thief, her arm draped affectionately around her victim's shoulders, holds a blue ribbon.

Doris shakes a cigarette halfway out of her pack and points it at me. "You sure you don't want a cigarette?"

I pass on the cigarette but take a cup of coffee with me for the walk home. The house is empty, and I recall that the band is playing tonight. I take advantage of the solitude to take a longer, hotter shower than usual. No amount of organization will make my job any cleaner than a dive into a pig wallow, and tonight I possess the additional bouquet of Doris's cigarettes. I let the water beat down on my head hoping to drown out her voice matter-of-factly reminding me, *They fall apart. Things like this always do.*

Things like what? Compassion? Cooperation? Hope? I have no illusions about the good we're doing the hungry, but the difference in my soldiers, as Doris called them, is immeasurable, and perhaps not something that will just fall apart at the first gust of greed that hits their lives. At least they'll never look at a basket of bread in quite the same way again. And then there's Buster, no doubt a happier pooch for having started the whole thing.

The hot water runs out, and I'm startled out of my reverie and out of the shower. As I towel myself dry, the man in the glass is a murky blur, and I leave him that way. Whatever's bothering you, Kropotkin, I say to myself, will be easier to face if you just know *what* the hell you're going to say! Best get to work.

I return to the basement and my studies, and Mortimer—a plump orange Tabby who lately prefers my lap to the porch— soon joins me. The cats will occasionally station themselves in a variety of favorite haunts, periodically reuniting as if by some signal only audible to themselves from all corners of the house to lie in a heap and groom one another and discuss feline issues of the day. I have introduced myself to all of them, but Mortimer is particularly fond of my head-scratching style.

In addition to the bed, I have completed my furnishings with a desk made of an unused door atop a couple of low bookcases where I stow my growing wardrobe. I've decorated the dark walls with artwork donated by the resident artists to the Resident Alien. My favorite is Caitlin's six-foot-long rendering of a green sea turtle. Brad has set up a computer on my desk, one of his castoffs. Ringing it are books, a thick and growing wall of them. The reference librarian, inspired by my curiosity, quietly slipped me a card granting me checkout privileges, and I have taken full advantage of it, having discovered that for serious inquiry I still prefer the page to the screen, the thoughtful turn of a leaf to the clicking of links. Go, go, go is no more to my liking in studies than it is on the street. At the moment, Lao-tzu, Wilson, Thoreau, Bookchin, X, and Singer lie open in a shifting pile as we confer on the perennial question, *What is to be done?*

A creak on the stair startles me, and Mortimer and I look up to see Sondra standing halfway down the stairs, her hand on the banister. "I need to talk to you," she says, as if I've been avoiding this very thing, and I recall Wilde saying one evening that inside every poet lurks an actor—usually bad—offering himself as a perfect specimen.

"Why certainly," I say, enthusiastically inviting her into my quarters. I set Mortimer on the monitor—he likes the warmth— but a dangling paw bumps the balanced books and sends them sprawling, burying the keyboard in the process. I clear a chair of books and offer it to my guest. "This is the first time you've been down here, isn't it? Since Jonah and I moved in?"

"Yes." Her eyes search my jumbled quarters for significance but find none. "It's very nice." She sits slightly forward, her straight white hair flanking her long narrow face like curtains, curtains abruptly thrown back and secured behind her ears with a stretch of her neck and a pass of her hands. She looks me in the eye with disarming candor. "He knew you were coming," she says. "He knew it weeks before you came, maybe longer."

"And 'he' would be?"

"Come on. You know who. Mike."

"He told you I was coming?"

"No, but before you came, he was going totally crazy *anticipating* something for months. I'd catch him looking ahead in the calendar, counting the days. If I asked him about it, he said it was nothing, none of my business. How could it be both? I asked him, and we had a big fight, so I quit asking. But he kept looking, waiting for nothing, for whatever it was that was none of my business. That all stopped when you got here. The Big Day had finally arrived. Ever since he's been just plain weird. He's not *there* anymore. He's *always* someplace else. I mean, he's always been a space cadet, but he'd have his moments, you know? He'd let me in. He paid attention. Now I ask him what he's thinking, and he just gives me this creepy look and says, 'You'll see. You'll see *exactly* what I'm thinking.' What am I supposed to do with that?

"And you—you treat *him* different from everybody else. With the rest of us, you're laughing and friendly all the time. You two hardly speak, even though it seems like you'd have the most to talk about of anybody. So what's going on, Peter? What's happened to turn my terribly smart, full-of-himself boyfriend into this psycho-jerk?"

How do I tell her, *your boyfriend is a spy*? What would such a statement even mean to her? What does it mean to me for that matter? I have scrupulously avoided these very questions, leading as they do back to Anchee, and a plot I want no part of. I have a life that makes me happier than I have ever been. No mere youthful exuberance either—though I seem to have recovered that as well—but a mature joy in life such as all men desire. Why should I risk all that by confronting my young friend Mike, clearly my cue if Anchee's writing the script? I suspect Uncle Chaney of borrowing a sticky page from Uncle Remus, and Young Mike is the Wonderful Tar Baby in disguise. "All of this could be mere coincidence," I say. "You're sure he said nothing at all to hint at this 'nothing' he anticipated?"

"When he was in a good mood or really high, he'd say that

something *really* important was about to happen—something *revolutionary* was what he said—and everything was going to change—he'd be all cryptic and weird, but I'm used to that. I thought it was just him psyching himself up for the Providence gig. People think performing's easy for him because he's so laid-back, but he gets all stressed out for days before he goes on. Everything's so life and death for him.

"When he got back from Providence, he was like, 'I'm the greatest genius on the planet.' But when I talked to Brad, he said they totally bombed. It was a rich college kid bar, and they had no use for some weird anarchist punk band from Richmond. Brad and Dave can't figure out why Mike even booked them there in the first place. Brad said Mike acted like he couldn't care less that they were practically booed off the stage and didn't even play the last set. *Mike* doesn't care? I don't think so. But when I tried to ask him about it, all he could talk about was you coming to dinner, like the whole reason they went to Providence was to pick you up at the airport.

"I made the mistake of asking why it was such a big deal that you were coming to dinner—no offense, but you were just some stranger in a limo who had the same name as one of his heroes— and he got pissy about it—all defensive like he gets—saying he didn't want to talk about it, and I wouldn't understand anyway, and I was going to ruin everything by obsessing all the time. But *he's* the one obsessing." She stops to catch her breath and rein in her anger. "Anyway, we had a big fight about it right before you came. His dad came over in the middle of it, and that was that. The last thing he said was that if he had his way, you'd be moving in, and if I didn't like it, I could leave."

I don't ask her how he could know such a thing before I'd even thought of it, for I trust I likely know the answer to that question better than she does. I can imagine the pain his cruel remarks must have brought her. No wonder she's had mixed feelings about me. I resist the urge to lay out my own suspicions about Mike, for I don't trust her sufficiently to reveal the truth about myself—and one revelation pretty much leads to the other. The only course left to me is to persuade her of her folly. "This odd behavior, you say, began some months before my arrival, but I never laid eyes on Mike before I arrived in Richmond. I didn't even know I was coming here myself until the last minute." I tick off our crimes on my fingers. "He and Brad and Dave gave me a ride; he put my name forth for this lecture I'm to give at the university; he correctly surmised that a homeless fellow such as myself might move in: This is the sum total of our collusion—hardly a matter worthy of such a transformation as you describe. Perhaps Mike is upset about something else." Perhaps he's drunk with power. It's like Marx's "dictatorship of the proletariat": Once they're dictators they're no longer the proletariat but the bosses all over again.

"It has something to do with you. I know it does. And this speech you're about to give."

"Then it's a matter of his own imagining, for he hasn't brought me in on the secret. My own suspicions are that he might be involved in some bad business with the mysterious Uncle Chaney about whom I've heard so much." I cast a scowl at his immovable chenille-draped form.

She shakes her head. "I don't see how. He's been gone for a while now. He left before I moved in."

"Where did he go?"

"I don't know. I don't think anybody does. You could ask TJ. He's his uncle."

"But he and Mike were particularly close?"

"I guess so. Everybody liked Chaney. They all used to tell Chaney stories. I kind of got sick of hearing them, to tell you the truth. But if it weren't for him, there wouldn't be a house."

"What do you mean?"

"I mean this is Chaney's house."

I'm glad I'm sitting down. My magical host is full of surprises. "*Chaney's* house?"

"I thought you knew that. TJ usually tells the story to newcomers, how his long-lost uncle appeared out of the blue and bought this house and put up the money to fix it up for a 'communal living experiment' and then left about nine months ago saying he'd come back when the world had changed."

"He said those exact words?"

"That's what they all say he said. But he was always saying crazy things like that. Nobody takes it too seriously. I've always thought it was his way of saying he wasn't ever coming back, like when I say 'I'll get my poems published when pigs fly.' "

This poignant admission can't fail to touch my heart, and I rush to reassure her. "Then I shall look forward to flying swine," I say. "They are certain to be the next thing."

In spite of her troubles, she manages a smile. "You're too nice," she says. "I bet people have told you that before."

"Yes, they have."

"Will you talk to Mike and find out what's going on?"

"Since I'm such a nice fellow, I suppose I'll have to. But I make no promises. Insofar as he knows himself what's going on, and insofar as he'll tell me, I'll endeavor to discover the truth of the matter and share it with you at the first opportunity. And while I'm at it, I'll suggest that he should treat you with the kindness and respect you deserve."

"Don't tell him that. Don't tell him I talked to you at all. *Please.* He'd be really pissed."

"As you wish."

"Thanks, Peter," she says, hugging me around the neck, and I am moved by recollections of my Sasha's spontaneous embraces when her indulgent father would once again please her. Above our heads, the front door opens and there are footsteps in the hall. Sondra dashes up the stairs, calling out as she disappears into the kitchen, "Mike, is that you?"

As I listen for his reply, the young man in me would warn her off the scoundrel, but the old man knows it wouldn't do a bit of good, might even render him more attractive altogether. Mortimer, bearing down on my lap across shifting planes of books like a polar bear on treacherous ice, advises me in his dry, laconic yowl to ignore them both and scratch him behind his ears the way he likes.

17 ✎ Through the Looking Glass

New ways, new issues must be looked for: the past has lived
and will live no more.

—PETER KROPOTKIN, *Fields, Factories, and Workshops*

The question is, then, not so much how to avoid revolutions, as
how to attain the greatest results with the most limited amount
of civil war, the smallest number of victims, and a minimum of
mutual embitterment.

—PETER KROPOTKIN, *Memoirs of a Revolutionist*

The following evening, after a long day of speech
writing, speech-wadding-up, and speech-tossing-in-the-trash, I
join Rachel, Jonah, and Wendy for an exploration of the newly
restored canal downtown. A small portion of the canal system
that flourished before the railways has been resurrected as a
lovely if pointless waterway for electric pleasure boats,
flanked, not by towpaths, but an attractive promenade with
views of the city on the one hand and the river on the other, the
whole business to be dubbed the Canal Walk. It's in the last
days of construction—the boats shrouded in tarpaulins, lights
and other fixtures in various stages of installation, neat
mounds of debris yet to be hauled away, yellow plastic strips
stretched taut here and drooping there to no apparent purpose.
But the walkways are finished, the workers have gone home
for the day, and we are part of a tiny and scattered population
of trespassers. A boisterous group of lads circulates, taking this
last opportunity to violate wholesale the ban on bicycles and
lethal little vehicles known as skateboards, but most of us are

strollers in early twilight enjoying a leisurely ramble on a brisk, fine day.

April is a changeable month here it seems. Historically also. It was April that it rebelled; April that it fell.

I pass this on to Jonah, who laughs at me: "You are becoming a Richmonder for sure, Peter. Wendy says sooner or later the history be seeping into your brain if you stay here long. She told me a joke: "'How many Richmonders it take to screw in a light-bulb?' "

"A couple of weeks ago, you didn't know what a lightbulb *was*. Now, you're telling jokes about them. You amaze me."

"There is a whole kind of joke called the lightbulb joke. Do you know it?"

"Never heard of it. How does it work?"

"How many does it take to screw in the bulb—like, 'How many anarchists does it take to screw in a lightbulb?' "

"How many?"

"I don't know. I was just using that as an example."

"Hmmm. I'd say . . . all of them."

"But that's not funny."

"It's not, is it? How about. One—in solidarity with all the rest."

"That's better. Still too serious."

"I've got it: 'Comes the revolution' "—I assist my pun with a spiraling motion—" 'the lightbulb will be equitably screwed.' "

He laughs at that one, so I quit while I'm ahead. "How many Richmonders does it take?"

"I almost forgot. It takes four. One to screw it, and three to discuss its heritage. You can be one of those three."

"It has been a busy place."

This outing is the most ambitious yet in Jonah's remarkable convalescence I've witnessed largely around the dinner table. The salve Earl provided him seems to work miracles, or perhaps he is responding entirely to Wendy's good offices. Like most new lovers, they have kept much to themselves, as have Rachel and I. This double date, however, was Wendy's excellent sug-

gestion. Their unbridled fondness for each other is made manifest in word and touch and gaze, prompting me to speculate that
her teasing of me has been a stratagem to distract attention from
the equally cute Jonah and herself, who hardly receive any rib-
bing at all. This inequity may also be due to Jonah's lack of the
requisite red coloration everyone seems to find so damned
amusing.

Rachel and Wendy, who've only talked before in the context of
the tumultuous Kitchen Table, have a great deal to talk about, it
seems, in this quieter venue. They walk a dozen paces in front of
Jonah and me, Wendy recounting some adventure in confidential tones, a lively tale judging by her antic hands. The sound of
their laughter at the story's end drifts back to Jonah and me, and
we smile in unison at our great good fortunes.

We must appear quite the sinister, if cheerful, conspirators in
our matching long black coats, hand-me-downs from Brad and
Dave, walking along head to head, comparing notes on our new
lives, pausing to scrutinize every bit of machinery along the way.
And the machinery is, I confess, quite irresistible to the boy in
me—rows of great iron wheels controlling pumps and locks and
who-knows-what-all monitored by mysterious dials and gauges
that have me straining my memory to recall my meager store of
hydraulic knowledge.

Soon enough Rachel and Wendy have pulled ahead of us
some distance, and Jonah, to my surprise, loses all interest in the
apparatus and says he has a matter of great import he wishes to
discuss with me in private. The machinery attracts a steady
stream of curious trespassers, so we continue along the promenade in search of a greater measure of privacy. Canal and walkway pass under a wide low automobile bridge ahead of us.
Under the bridge appears a likely spot.

At the railing above, stands a man with a camera taking pictures of the canal. I look over my shoulder and see he's chosen a
fine perspective—even finer up where he is—with grand old
buildings in the foreground and glimpses of the falls of the
James in the distance. I make a mental note to have a look at a

modern camera when I get the chance to see what advances have been made. Though it would seem to me, that even now, the man's more important than the lens.

As we step under the cool shadows of the bridge, Jonah comes right to the point. "I told Wendy the truth."

He has been struggling with this decision for some time now, and we have talked about it more than once. "How did it go?"

"I tell her I be a slave my whole life, that I come from a different time, whole different world. I had to tell her. Can't lie to the woman for long. Not when we be feeling like we do. Can't be having her thinking me stupid all the time because of all the things I don't know. All day, every day, I be trying to figure things out, you know? *Everything* is different. Music in a little silver circle like this. Rubber bands. What you call it?—telephone. First time I heard it *chirp, chirp, chirp,* I hunted it down with my shoe in my hand. Wendy be laughing so hard couldn't even talk."

"Don't keep me in suspense, my friend. Did Wendy believe you or not?"

"Pretty much." He laughs, obviously amazed she believes him at all. "She wants to see the watch—so she knows for sure— and I said I'd show it to her. Do you still carry it?"

I see immediately where this is going, and I'm filled with misgivings. "Of course," I say. "I never had the good sense to throw it away."

He holds out his hand to me. "Can I have it?"

I know that he and Wendy don't merely mean to *see* the watch, but to see it strut its stuff—to play with time like a shuttlecock— a pastime I find foolish and dangerous in the extreme. I don't want to give it to him, but how can I deny him the opportunity to be believed? The watch is *mine* only to the extent that Anchee slipped it into my pocket and not Jonah's.

"Of course," I say. "It's yours as much as mine." I resist the urge to caution him to be careful. He can imagine the risks as well as I; perhaps, with his aptitude for things mechanical, better. "Spare us from demons," I say, as I place the watch in his palm, and we clasp hands around it.

He laughs. "You and me—we been invited to the demons' own house." He holds the watch between thumb and forefinger and wags it. "This here be the invitation." He drops it into the inside breast pocket of his coat and gives it a pat.

"Just out of curiosity, what exactly do you and Wendy intend to do with it?"

He grins his appreciation for their plan: "We going to take it down to Monument Avenue tonight. Wendy says she want me to show her a time before that statue of Lee be sitting there. She says she believe *anything* then." He chuckles at his lover's declaration.

"That's an admirable scheme," I say. "I can't imagine a more peaceful means of toppling a hated symbol of oppression than to *preexist* it, but don't you think . . ." I stop myself before I wax paternal. "Good luck," I say.

Rachel and Wendy have stopped to wait for us where the walkway emerges from beneath the bridge at the boundary between shadow and sun. We set out to catch up with them, and I notice that Jonah walks even at this quickened pace with complete ease. And yesterday he was helping Dave and Caitlin in the greenhouse. "How are your wounds?" I ask.

"Hardly bother me at all. No need for bandages anymore." He rolls his shoulders inside his coat and smiles. "Feels just fine, better than fine."

"Earl will be delighted to hear it. I went to see him yesterday. He asked after you."

"Maybe Wendy and me go see him tomorrow. He still the same?"

"Still the same."

"I thought about him the other day—about all three of us. Wendy and me, we went to see a movie the other day. You ever see one of them? All these pictures, very, very fast, a bright light shining through." He moves his hands to imitate a motion picture projector, his dark fingers portraying shafts of light; and I imagine him dragging Wendy up to the projectionist's booth so he could investigate how the magic was accomplished.

"Yes, I have, in my old life, though I wasn't quite up to the new one I saw on the airplane. But then, I didn't hear the sound. It came through these wires you put in your ears apparently. Since then, Rachel and I have watched videos."

"We saw one called *The Matrix.* Very strange. Very loud. Too many guns, I think. *Bang, bang, bang, bang, bang.* I don't understand a lot of it. But it made me think—I'm like the man in the movie—like you and Earl too—like him, I be living in a *magic world.*" We have reached Wendy and Rachel, and he puts his arm around Wendy's shoulders as they step into the sunlight, and without the grimace of pain such a motion would have cost him not so long ago, he sweeps his free arm across the spectacle of the towering city buildings. "Totally awesome, magic world."

I come up behind Rachel and wrap my arms around her waist, and she hugs them to her. "Jonah asked me for the watch," I say, "and I gave it to him."

"I figured you would," she says.

"You knew? Did Wendy tell you their plan?"

"Of course. What did you think we were talking about, baking cookies?"

"No such luck, I'm sure. Now that you mention it, I'm terrifically hungry." I nuzzle her neck and growl.

"Are you going to eat me up?"

"Just the ear, I think." I nibble her earlobe and she laughs and turns in my arms. I look into her smiling eyes.

"Don't worry, Peter. Everything will work out all right."

"Do you think so? Did I do the right thing with the watch? Is this really such a good idea?"

"We'll see for ourselves tonight, won't we?"

"We will? You mean we're invited?"

"Of course. I wouldn't miss it. To tell you the truth, I've been working up my nerve to ask for a demonstration of that watch myself. Faith is wonderful, Peter, but only an idiot completely turns her back on hard evidence."

"I agree. But you'll still need the faith, I'm afraid. Just because

I carry a time machine around in my pocket doesn't mean I am who I say I am."

"You're right," she muses. "But it certainly makes you more interesting." She gives me a quick kiss. "Don't pout, Peter. I know you're who you say you are because I know you wouldn't lie to me."

"A most convincing argument."

"Wendy thought so. She said Jonah was certain you would give him the watch, but you wouldn't like it."

"He was quite right."

"Where's the bold, young explorer?"

"Not so young anymore, perhaps."

"I know better."

"But what if our 'explorations' change things?"

"That might not be such a bad thing—as you often point out."

"*Touché.*"

When we catch up with Wendy and Jonah, he says over his shoulder, "Peter, I almost forgot—I learned the alphabet you gave me. Wendy told me all their names and sounds. And some—what you call them?—suffixes. I been practicing."

"He's scary," Wendy says. "We raced through the alphabet like twice one morning, and when I get home from work, there's a love letter waiting for me." She bumps him affectionately with her hip, and he's uncertain whether to be proud or embarrassed. "Meanwhile, he fixes my rocking chair, fixes the door to our room so it doesn't stick anymore and the old lock actually works. He even got my vacuum cleaner—that's been waiting to go to Goodwill for like a hundred years—to suck again."

"Just jammed up is all," he says. "I like to stay busy," he adds in defense of his industry, and I recognize a penned-up soul set loose. When the serfs were freed, many a foolish master had his prophecy of idleness disproved tenfold and wondered aloud why the deceitful wretches never worked so hard for him and his lash.

We take a flight of stairs back to street level, and Jonah points to the signs that line the curb. "No. Park -ing," he says slowly.

"No Parking. Any. Time?" (He looks to Wendy for confirmation, and she smiles adoringly.) "No Parking Any Time."

As if he knows I wish to speak with him, Mike has made himself scarce all day, and hasn't returned by the time we set out on our expedition to Monument Avenue at midnight. Rachel, whose enthusiasm for this adventure seems boundless, campaigns hard for bicycles as the mode of transportation, pointing out that if we should need to flee the area, we could easily elude pursuit in the alleys thereabout; but upon discovering that Jonah (though eager to learn) has never actually ridden a bicycle, she quickly relents and joins me in the backseat of Wendy's car.

"Put on your seat belt," she advises me, and has her own secured even before the motor is running.

Mine, obviously unused for some time, must be unearthed from the seat cushions and assorted debris—pens, candy wrappers, coins—an excavation which delays our departure some minutes. "Do I need to point out how ludicrous it is to worry about my safety in *this* machine," I inquire of my companions, "when we are about to throw caution to the winds with the other?"

"*No!*" they reply in unison, and thus chastened, I sullenly cinch myself in for the journey.

I've attempted to persuade the others of a more secluded site for this experiment, but they are resolute in their desire to outflank the General with a tactical retreat to the past. Reminding them of the kidnapped crow, I've managed to persuade them to travel to a time prior to the European and African settlement of the area, so as to reduce the risk of abducting persons from the past—not to mention frightening them half to death or invoking their ire. Wendy and Rachel, the historians for the expedition, settle upon a date of 1600 as being safe in that regard. Though neither one can speak with confidence on the matter, they believe the native population to have resided much closer to the river than we will be. Short of traveling to prehistory, where other haz-ards present themselves, there's no avoiding the risk altogether.

Several electric lights illuminate the monument at night, and it's only when we arrive and park a block away that Wendy al-lows that there have been acts of vandalism visited upon the stalwart soldier in the past, and police may be watchful of any suspicious activity in his vicinity. We sit in the car and wait out the pounding, puffing passage of a runner who apparently didn't have his fill when the sun was up. I wonder aloud if it's something in the food that causes this aimless dashing about even while at leisure, and Wendy says it's *endorphins* and prom-ises to explain later. When he's out of sight, we exit the car, clos-ing the doors as quietly as possible, and head for the tree-lined esplanade, walking the same path the runner used, cautiously approaching General Lee in a slow, single-file parade. It occurs to me we would be less suspicious if we all stripped down to our underwear and broke into a run.

We carry my old blanket to spread on Lee's lawn so that we might appear mere moonlight picnickers, though no one thought to bring food to complete the ruse. No matter. So anx-ious was I at dinner that I hardly ate a bite, and I still don't think I could. There's something about this whole business I don't like, but I can't quite put my finger on it.

We emerge from the trees, and there's Lee across the street all lit up, as stately a statesman as a State could wish for, and a very nice horse indeed. "We can see him perfectly well from here," I point out. "What's wrong with right here?"

"You don't understand. I want to be in his face," Wendy says. "I want to be standing in his front yard."

I look to Jonah for support, but he just shrugs as if to say, *if that's what the woman wants*, and I look to Rachel, who says, "Come on, Peter. This is Wendy's show. We're just having a harmless picnic. We're not breaking any laws."

"If we were, I might be more easily persuaded to see the good in it." Rachel indulges me with a smile, and I relent. "Very well," I say. "Let's get on with it."

The simple plan is that we will post ourselves before the statue, turn on the time machine, visit 1600 or thereabouts, be back in an instant, and quit the premises posthaste. An occasional car passes, but we should be able to time our journey so that no one sees us. It's not clear to me what a witness would observe in any event. Should someone in one of these grand houses nearby look out his window and see (or think he sees) a picnic glow briefly blue before it decamps, it's doubtful he would report this incident to the authorities or that they would care about it if he did. We've discussed all this before coming here and are certain we face no real danger. Still, I'm as nervous as a cat, a good deal more nervous than Mortimer, I trust, who likely snoozes atop my monitor as we speak.

We all agree that Wendy should have the honor of operating the watch. As Rachel and I spread the blanket on the ground, Jonah once more explains the controls to her, and she repeats his instructions back to him. We stand on the blanket, all huddled around Wendy, facing Lee. Wendy switches on the machine, and the blue light appears. She grasps the stem in her fingertips. "Ready?" she asks.

At that moment, a dark figure steps out from behind Lee's stone pedestal, and a gruff voice shouts, "Freeze! Police! Put your hands where I can see them!" At the periphery of the blue light, a policeman stands in a crouch, his gun and flashlight pointed at us. At Jonah, actually, whose brightly lit, defiant visage doesn't bode well for peaceful negotiations.

"Clockwise," I whisper urgently in Wendy's ear as a gentle reminder that our fate rests entirely in her hands. She understands me immediately, and the world turns reassuringly black, sans policeman and gun, and the blinding light in Jonah's face tumbles to his feet. I look with some apprehension to see if there's still a policeman's hand attached. There's not.

"That was close," Rachel says with a shudder.

"Telling me," Jonah exclaims.

"He's still there," I remind them. "*Then* and there."

"What in the fuck was he doing there in the first place?" Wendy demands. "He was like *waiting* for us."

"Maybe he was," Jonah says. "Maybe Anchee playing his tricks again."

"But what did the cop think we were going to *do?*" Wendy asks. "He was pointing a *gun* at us. That's like totally insane."

"Maybe Anchee whisper some lie in his ear," Jonah suggests.

"Enough Anchee," I say firmly. "We can't be bothered with his tomfoolery: We're on an expedition of our own."

Rachel hugs my arm. "That's the spirit," she says.

During this discussion we're all focused on the watch Wendy holds before her so we can witness the years counting backward with increasing rapidity. The blackout imposed by the machine's refusal or inability to conduct its passengers to a time and place where they might rendezvous with their earlier selves endures somewhat longer than with the journey Jonah and I took—since both Rachel and Wendy's lives began in this city some years ago—but it's still only a matter of seconds—just long enough to have conducted the conversation I've set down above. When the blackout lifts and Lee's statue pops into view on the spring day Rachel was born in a nearby hospital in 1965, we boo him roundly in the quickening flicker of days down to 1890 when he abruptly vanishes after a quarter of a minute or so. A scurry of soldiers lasts no more than a second as we accelerate through the centuries. We soon reach such a velocity in our movement through time that the world appears devoid of distinguishable objects and becomes a mere progression of colors.

We come to a stop amid a towering and fierce green. A great forest looms all around us, silent but for the faint twittering of birds, the chattering of squirrels. The trees are immense and widely spaced—chestnuts, white oaks, hickories. Most are four feet in diameter. I spot one of such a girth that the four of us might not be able to clasp hands around it. Vines as thick as a man's arm climb up into the lush, leafy crown of late spring, over a hundred feet above our heads. It is as if we have all

shrunk in a moment to half our former size. The thick canopy
lets little direct sunlight through and all is cool and dark and
smells like life.

"Awesome!" Wendy astutely whispers.

Rachel is squeezing my hand so hard I fear it will break. "Oh
my God," she says. "It's all true."

"I thought you had faith," I say.

"Nobody has this much faith. *Look* at it! Can we go into the
woods?"

Without hesitation, Wendy turns off the watch, and the blue
glow vanishes. Before I can stop her, she bounds into the woods
with Jonah willingly in tow. She flings her hands into the air and
dances around where a few centuries from now a bronze Lee
will stand. Jonah seizes her by the waist and hoists her into the
air laughing. "Come on!" she calls to us. "It's unbelievable!"

I've read accounts of what the first European visitors found
when they came to these shores, but they didn't quite prepare
me for the reality of this wilderness. By the time Jonah arrives in
a couple of centuries, most of this will have already fallen to the
axe. How did it ever come to pass—I ask myself for the thou-
sandth time since boyhood—that people ever thought they
could *own* this magnificence? Perhaps that's the very *arrogance*
that led them to conclude they could own their fellow creatures
body and soul.

"Shall we?" I ask Rachel, offering my arm.

"Why certainly," she says.

We step from Lee's manicured lawn onto the forest floor, littered with chestnut and acorn and bone-hard hickory (enough
foodstuff to sustain an incredible population of wildlife), and I
experience a sense of complete freedom such as I have longed
for all my life. Here we are in a timeless wood owned by no
one—lawless, churchless, copless—who could ask for anything
more?

"We'll be back in a little while," Wendy calls to us. She and
Jonah have been navigating a deer trail into the woods and now
disappear over a low rise.

I start to call after them, but Rachel says, "Let them alone."

"Where are they going?" I inquire.

"Oh Peter," Rachel replies. "Where do you think? We're in Eden, after all."

"Oh," I say, and Rachel and I soon discover a path of our own into the cool quiet depths of the dark green forest. My crimson countenance illuminates the way like Rudolph, another Christmas tale Rachel recounts to me in low tones as we contentedly lounge on a mossy stream bank idly chewing sprigs of watercress. A flock of wild turkey browse around us. Ground squirrels gleefully explore the folds of our discarded clothing.

After a time—and I honestly couldn't say how long, though long enough to regret the omission of a picnic basket—the four of us reunite in the highest of spirits to discuss our next move.

"We have to go back," I say, and everyone reluctantly agrees.

"What about the cop?" Wendy reminds us.

It doesn't take long to devise a plan, since we have all the time in the world to script our roles and rehearse them in advance. We take up our positions and head hell-bent for the future, appearing before the surprised constable on patrol practically on top of him. Jonah has the honor of blinding him with his own flashlight beam. It falls to me, with my low center of gravity and upper body strength, to sock him in the stomach. Wendy and Rachel relieve him of his gun, and we all throw the blanket over his head. A tap on the head with the flashlight silences his objections, and we roll him up in the blanket—carefully so that he can breathe—and cinch it with our belts. Then we run like hell to the car and drive slowly away. Wendy, in spite of her high spirits, possesses the presence of mind to drive moderately, even while bouncing up and down in her seat screaming, "That was so fucking *awesome!*"

Rachel and I cling to one another, our seat belts quite forgotten. She frees a sprig of watercress from my beard and brushes it back and forth across my nose. "Where have you been all my life?" she asks, and I can't imagine how to answer such a complex question.

I wake next morning to Zipper smiling down on Rachel and me in bed. I attempt to cover Rachel's bare shoulder with the sheet, but the combined weight of all the cats renders it unmovable. They showed up sometime in the middle of the night. Wendy once claimed they seek out postcoital afterglow—hence their fondness for my room when Rachel's here—but she may have only been teasing.

Zipper—whose nickname I've discovered is a refinement of ZipLoc, a variety of plastic bag in which he prefers to package the cannabis he sells—looks to have been sampling the goods already this morning. "Hey, guys. I'm cooking tonight, and I'm headed to the market. All the hard-core vegans have split with the band for Chapel Hill, and I was thinking—"

"Mike's gone?"

"Yeah. Some Free Somebody-or-other benefit concert thing. I don't know. I don't think they know what they're playing for half the time. He told me to tell you they'd be back for your thing at school. Anyway, I was thinking—"

"Did Sondra go with them?"

"Yeah. Everybody but you guys, Wendy and Jonah, TJ, me. I've talked to everybody else already. What do you say? Steak on the grill. We're all sworn to secrecy."

Rachel laughs softly on my shoulder as she stirs awake and rolls over onto her back, stretching her arms above her head. "Sounds delightful," she says.

I am eager to sit down to my own work, for I have finally arrived at a sense of what I want to say, but no sooner has Rachel pedaled out of sight than Wendy and Jonah ask to see me in the kitchen for some new revelation.

"When I learn something new," Jonah says, "I try to find it everywhere, read everything over again, looking for it. Wendy taught me about 'ch' like in 'church' and 'chains' and 'beach.' So I be looking for it all morning—'match' on the matchbox, 'Richmond' and 'Dispatch' on the newspaper, 'channel' on the TV control. 'Chapstick.' Cat 'Chow.' Then I come across this here— almost don't notice it cause it's in the middle of the word and the letters are so small." He holds up the tube of salve Earl gave us and reads: "*Doctor Anchee's Nano-Heal All.* Wendy says 'nano-' means there's little *machines* inside rebuilding everything the way it was." He offers the tube for my inspection, but I hold up my hands. "You keep it," I say.

"Don't need it anymore," he says. He turns around and shrugs his shirt off his back. Not only are his recent scars healed, but the old ones as well. He is as scarless as my reborn self.

"There's no medicine now that can do that," Wendy says. "Not even close. It must work at the molecular level."

"It's like magic," I admit.

She touches Jonah's scarless shoulders as if the scars were still there and kisses his back. "Why is Chaney doing all this?" she asks. "All that *pain*. Does he think it's okay now because it doesn't *show*?" She covers him with his shirt, and he turns and holds her in his arms. She lays her head on his chest. "Everybody *liked* Chaney. He was always so *nice* to everybody. Now it's like he was just lying to us, using us. For no reason."

"His intentions might be decent," I offer. "We don't know what they are."

"Don't matter," Jonah says. "They're not *my* intentions; they're not *your* intentions. Way I see it, the man beat me, now he comes along and heals my wounds. Okay. That's cool. We *even* now. This is as far as I go till I know where it is we be going."

I sigh wearily. "You're right. There's no point pretending any longer that Anchee will *ever* leave our lives alone. There's nothing for it but to get to the bottom of things."

"We *in* the bottom of things," Jonah says. "We need to be getting ourselves *out*."

After dinner, Zipper, TJ, Wendy, Jonah, Rachel, and I sit in a circle in the backyard like a pride of gorged lions recovering from a bloody repast. "I knew y'all were closet carnivores," our chef chuckles. "Even you, Wendy Lee."

"Don't call me that," she says.

"How did the commune come to be vegetarian?" I ask.

"It was Mike's idea," Zipper says.

"And a good one," TJ says. "It's healthier. It's more ethical."

"Whatever," Zipper says. "I just know when the moon gets full, I want to tear into some flesh. Like Chaney used to say, we are beasts in the jungle."

"Chaney used to say a lot of shit," TJ says, clearly amused by memories of Chaney's shit.

"Who is this Chaney I be hearing so much about?" Jonah asks, his face a mask of innocence. I've seen him use this face before. He calls it his slave face.

"He's my uncle," TJ says. "Or my half uncle I guess you say. My grandmother remarried after she left my grandfather, and she and her second husband had Chaney."

"So you know him your whole life?"

"Oh no. I didn't know anything about him. My father didn't even know him. I never even saw my grandmother—my dad and my granddad were pretty bitter about her leaving—and if they knew where she was or that she'd gotten married again, they never said a word about it. She didn't tell Chaney about my dad either. He only found out after she died and he was looking through her stuff that he had a half brother. He came looking for my dad, but my mom and dad had just died, and he found me instead."

"And you knew nothing about *none* of this before Uncle Chaney tell you the tale?" Jonah asks.

"I had no idea. But my parents were like that. They didn't tell me stuff. They certainly wouldn't tell me my grandmother married a black man. No offense, but that's how they were."

"Both your parents died right before he showed up?" I ask.

"They were in a car wreck. The cops said they were probably trying to avoid hitting a deer or something and lost control. My dad used to drive kind of fast."

Or perhaps, I think, the future appeared out of nowhere, and they couldn't outrun it. Wendy draws in a sharp breath and starts to speak but thinks better of it. The same suspicion is writ large on her face. And unlike me, she *knew* Chaney/Anchee. I recall her fond expression when she recounted those skinny-dipping outings. And yet here's the same man suspected of murder—how can that be? It must be the thousands of lies he would've had to tell, eliminating all possibility of trust.

TJ, however, speaks fondly of his long-lost uncle: "I was in the middle of my junior year. I didn't know what I was going to do. Chaney came along and set us up in this place. That's really how the commune got started. He sort of saved my life."

I'm rendered speechless by this testimonial. Wendy can scarcely contain herself. But Rachel thinks to ask, "Weren't he and Mike real close? He was talking about him the other night."

TJ laughs. "Close? It was like they were from the same planet. They were always talking this deep, deep shit. Nobody could understand a *word* they were saying."

"I could understand them," Zipper says.

"Only because you were stoned all the time."

"It helped."

TJ laughs, remembering his uncle. "What was the thing he used to say about the cats?" TJ prompts Zipper—known in the household as a consummate mimic.

Zipper holds up a hand and gets into character, pantomimes Chaney inhaling cannabis, and says in Anchee's unmistakable accent—'These cats are no ordinary cats; these cats have lived nine lives nine times over. These cats' "—he inhales again— " 'knew the fucking Pharaohs!' "

TJ applauds the performance and is surprised Wendy doesn't join in. If he were sitting where I'm sitting, he'd see that Wendy's eyes have filled with tears. Jonah reaches out and takes her hand.

"What about you, Wendy Lee?" Zipper asks. "Did you understand the Chaney-Mike Dialogues?"

"Don't call me that. Chaney used to call me that. Just to piss me off."

"I didn't notice him pissing you off just a whole whole lot when he was around," Zipper says.

"Well, he did. He did a *lot* to piss me off. He left, for one thing."

"He did that," Zipper acknowledges, holding up his hands, cutting his eyes back and forth, wondering what's up with Wendy. "You got me there. He did do that."

"He'll be back," TJ says.

"Why do you say that?" Rachel asks.

"I just think he will. It doesn't seem like him, you know. To just leave."

"Why not?" Wendy wants to know. "He just showed up, didn't he? Out of the blue, out of *nowhere*. Maybe that's where he belongs. How do you know what he's *like?*"

TJ is completely bewildered by Wendy's anger. But even if he knew our worst suspicions, it's doubtful he could begin to believe such things of his savior.

Zipper, never one to dwell on the negative, says, "I'll say one thing about Chaney. He knew more about growing plants than any man alive. And that's a fact."

"He knew stuff," TJ agrees.

"He knew *science*," Wendy says, and the three of them silently agree to stop at this point of seeming agreement, even if the young men are more than a little puzzled that Wendy, of all people, should speak of science in such a dismissive tone of voice.

"Hey, Peter," Zipper says after a while. "Aren't you giving some kind of talk at school tomorrow?"

"Yes."

"What's it about?"

"Anarchy," I say.

"Cool," says Zipper.

A loud crash comes from the house. "The cats!" TJ exclaims. "Where did you put the bones?" he asks Zipper.

"I put them in the trash can with that humongous cutting board on top to hold the lid on."

"Why didn't you just turn them over to begin with?" I ask. "I trust those cats could get into a bank vault if they put their minds to it."

Zipper shrugs. "I never cooked a steak here before."

18 § An Appeal to the Young and the Liberation of Richmond

> Ay, all of us together, we who suffer and are insulted daily, we are a multitude whom no man can number, we are the ocean that can embrace and swallow up all else.
>
> When we have but the will to do it, that very moment will Justice be done: that very instant the tyrants of the Earth shall bite the dust.
>
> —PETER KROPOTKIN, *An Appeal to the Young*

> We heard the very welkin ring with cheers as the United States forces reached Capitol Square, and then we turned and slowly rode on our way.
>
> —CAPT. CLEMENT SULIVANE, C.S.A., upon quitting Richmond. April 3, 1865

The band returns in the middle of the night as silent as thieves. I borrow a page from Zipper's book, and Mike awakens to find me sitting in his room like Marley's ghost, only we're well past midnight and approaching noon. In fact, the hour has grown so late that if there's going to be any time at all to have a few of my questions answered before one o'clock—the appointed hour of my lecture—Mike needs to stir from his slumbers, and so for the last ten or fifteen minutes—lacking chains to clank—I have been playing the "Internationale" (a grating song actually) on a D harmonica I found on the bedside. It's nice to know I remember how to play, at least as well as I always have, and I like to think my enthusiasm makes up for whatever deficiencies there might be in the performance.

His room is spare. Its neatness, legendary in the household, has not been exaggerated in the telling—Dave's *It's like nobody fucking lives there* being the most insightful, I believe. Except for the breathing lump in the bedclothes, this could be a furniture-store display. His father and mother share a picture frame on his desk. No one else is so honored. Keys and change and a pocket comb are the sole extent of his personal belongings left visible on dresser or bedside except for the aforementioned harmonica, an uncharacteristic lapse, I'm sure. His bags are still packed, sitting just inside the door, heightening the effect that this is a hotel he means to depart directly, next stop—who knows—the future perhaps. Whatever truce he and Sondra may have fashioned for the trip to North Carolina, he's sleeping alone this morning. I suspect he prefers it that way.

My reveille finally has its desired effect, and he sits up in bed. He rubs his eyes—a rather ordinary hazel this morning—gropes in a drawer for glasses I've never seen him wear before, and holds them up to his face so that he can identify his tormentor.

So this is what he actually looks like, I think. A rather ordinary chap.

"What time is it?" he asks.

In the process of attempting to set off his alarm clock, I caused it to commence flashing 12:00 12:00 12:00 12:00 12:00 with persistent frenzy without quite knowing how I accomplished this feat or why the silly machine is capable of it. "Noon," I lie, for it's really eleven-thirty, and he curses and hops right out of bed like a good lad and heads for the shower. I go down to the kitchen and wait for him there. It's not long before the hot water runs out, he's dressed, and downstairs, though I can tell by his unhurried pace he's apprised himself of the correct time since I saw him last.

He sits down with his usual breakfast of a Diet Coke and a Power Bar as if it were no bad repast. I've noticed he never cooks for just himself, but eats various packaged goods. Cooking is one of his several accomplishments not to be indulged for mere pleasure or survival, but reserved strictly for performance.

Singing is another one. You're as likely to hear him singing in the garden as to see a turtle dance.

"The big day is here," I say, fishing.

"Yes," he says, nodding in agreement, his smile scarcely ironic, given that all his expressions and mannerisms come touched, shaped, manhandled by irony, so that one must always settle for degrees of sincerity only, and never the thing itself. "The Big Day is here."

"What is it, exactly, you think is in the offing today of such great importance?"

"Why, you're going to speak in the Business Auditorium on 'anarchy,' of course." Even this literal statement gets the ironic sneer, the quotes around *anarchy,* the gratuitous "of course."

"Auditorium? I thought there were twenty or so students, a seminar. What do we need with an auditorium?"

"Some other classes have been invited—biology, philosophy, political science, history, economics—all Kropotkin's areas of expertise. Even some high-school classes."

"How about jailbird, do you have that covered?"

He laughs at my wit. "Oh yes. Criminal Justice will be there."

"I'm sure. How many then, altogether?"

"A couple hundred, maybe more. Not counting the newspeople. You're going to be on TV, Peter. With any luck you'll make the local news. Don't worry. It's a slow news day. They're just after a sound bite. It's PR for the university."

I'm familiar with the *sound bite*—a fragment of language torn from context and shaped to the needed sense. So that language, too, is just another "resource."

"How long have you known all this?"

"Sapworth called days ago. I thought you knew."

I push myself away from the table. "That's it: the last lie I listen to. Sapworth's a pawn as much as I. You knew *all* of this, I imagine, before you even introduced me to Sapworth, before you laid eyes on me at the airport. I am old. I'm new to all these relativistic paradoxes, having failed to understand Einstein's importance in my day. But I'm no fool, and I'm a quick study. So don't answer, if you must, but *no more lies,* or you will have seen the last of me in this or any other time. Do we understand each other?"

"Yes."

He's adopted the look of ironic amusement I've noted in his master at any display of my temper—as if I were a puppy on a rampage, no real threat except to itself and the furniture. It's all I can do not to fly at him, but whatever flaws I may yet possess, being too young isn't one of them.

"So let's try that again: How long have you known?"

"I knew you were coming for almost a year, the date and everything for a few months."

"'Everything' being everything that's happened so far."

"Yes."

"And when does your knowledge end?"

"When you speak."

"Why is this damn speech so important anyway?"

"I don't know exactly."

"What if I don't make the speech at all?"

A look of panic flits across his face, the first real reaction I've been able to provoke since rudely awakening him. It's Tim Binder all over again.

"What do you get for your services, a hundred dollars?"

"I don't do anything for money."

"For what then?"

"A just world. A better world."

"From one speech? Believe me, I'm not that good."

"Not just your speech. I don't know what else. I only know my part of it."

"But it's crucial, this speech. A prime mover, the first domino, something like that, correct?"

"I believe so. We are creating the future in which Anchee dwells."

He says this last bit rather solemnly, and I have to confess, it does have a ring to it. "Been there?" I ask.

"He said I couldn't—"

" '—possibly adapt.' I know. I got that line myself. It's quite a fatalistic little circle he's got you in here, isn't it? From out here it looks like nonsense. Does it make any difference what I actually *say* in this speech, or is it merely the event that matters?"

He's slow to answer, and I fear he's sworn to secrecy. But eventually he says, "I don't think so. I don't think it matters *what* you say. That would involve too many variables."

"Doesn't that bother you?"

That's not the question he expects, and he puffs up—offended that his conscience should be dragged into the matter! "No one listens anyway," he says petulantly.

"Perhaps they've listened, and you've bored them. Perhaps they don't imagine you've listened sufficiently to them to warrant an opinion on their lives. How could you? You've been too busy arranging things. Following orders. *I only know my part of it.* What a bloody fool you've turned out to be!"

He doesn't even bother to defend himself, just stares back at me defiantly. "Tell me," I ask, "who is it you think I am?"

"I think you're who you say you are."

"Now you're a solipsist. Very well. I submit to you that I am *not* who I say I am. I am, in fact, anyone *but* him. So now, I'm asking you. Who am I? You act as if you think you know."

He chews up the last of his bar and finishes his drink. He shrugs his indifference to the issue. "Anchee claims telling you won't make any difference in the outcome, so I might as well." He looks me in the eye. He's leveling with me: "You're a facsimile of Kropotkin. An android from the future."

"The future. Like Uncle Chaney's future."

"Yes. Like Anchee. But he's no android. Anchee is a posthuman."

I consider the terms. *Android.* Like Mary Shelley's Creature, I imagine, but descended from plastic instead of the churchyard. *Posthuman.* Unfortunately it only conjures a postman delivering cryptic letters up and down the streets of time, mostly advertisements. I think I'm supposed to perceive something grander. But even without their precise meanings, they leave a familiar stench in the air, and I understand a few things more clearly. "Let me guess—the lesser race, and the superior one. That's why you have no qualms about deceiving me: I'm not really human. I'm merely an android, and if you use me, then maybe you can be a posthuman someday, too, or at least live off their favor and sell your fellows down the river. I thought you were an anarchist! How could you fall for this racist drivel? I am *human*, I assure you, from the inside out—and I have seventy-eight years experience as the animal to know it when I live it!"

Brad comes through the back door with baskets of basil and cilantro from the greenhouse for the midday restaurant deliveries. ("Yuppie restaurants are the cornerstone of our economy," Wendy once explained to me.) Instead of his usual nose ring, Brad sports tiny Texas longhorns sprouting from each nostril as if a tiny bull were hiding inside his nose.

"I like the horns," I tell him.

"Thanks," he says warmly. He's such a sweet, good-natured fellow. I wonder if he's in on the Plot, whatever it is. I decide I'd rather not know. "Business Auditorium at one, right?" he asks.

"Right," Mike says. "Sapworth'll rattle on a while, so it won't get started till a quarter after." He delivers this opinion, if such it is, as if it were fact.

Brad, who trims and bundles herbs with the same amazing rapidity some women knit or crochet, nods like a contented bull. "I'll be there. I wouldn't miss it. Are Wendy and Jonah coming?" he asks me.

"Yes. They're visiting a friend this morning. They'll meet us there. Rachel's walking over from work."

As I speak these words, a great sadness descends over me. Mike's knowledge ends when I speak. My premonition shines its baleful, persistent light shortly afterward, slanting into a cold, dark cell. I run my hands along the kitchen table. I've enjoyed living here these few days. I could just stay here a few hours longer. An hour or two should do it. It's all just a stream of events. One merely diverts the flow . . .

No, I can't do it. I stand and put on my long black coat, for it suits my mood, I must speak. To fall silent would be to concede that it doesn't matter what I say. If you're still with me after all these pages, no doubt you know how likely I am to concede *that*!

"Come on," I say to my young, misguided friend. "Let's get this over with."

Soon enough we're all arranged. I'm seated on a stage with Mike and Sapworth and other luminaries. The auditorium is near full. Somehow my talk, according to the program and a poster in the lobby, has become the first in a series of talks on "Leadership" sponsored by the university as "part of its ongoing commitment to a meaningful presence in the community," a phrase I suspect means it doesn't usually give a damn about the community and this hastily arranged bit of business is a mere sop. From what I overhear among the dignitaries' gossip, its purpose is to "look good in the Self-Study," some sort of institutional narcissism I don't have the heart to pursue.

I find it amusing that "Anarchy," the title in plain view on program and poster outside, would be thought a suitable topic for a state-sponsored series on "Leadership," but such contradictions no longer surprised me in my old life and seem almost expected in this one. My sponsors must think I intend to denounce anarchy; or, more likely, use the term ironically; or, most likely, they haven't given it much thought. The whole thing's a sham in one way or another.

I suspect that this is how Anchee's entertained himself during his recent silence: He's been turning the molehill of my speech into this mountain of bull dung. There was a line of school buses outside the auditorium. Why all these young people? What *is* he up to?

As I sit in this boxlike theater it's hard not to think of the lot of us as puppets in a puppet box. The front rows are filled with friends from the house and the restaurant. Only Sondra is absent from the house crew. Dave and Caitlin look like Egyptian royalty and draw more attention than any of us onstage. TJ and Zipper unfurl a banner which reads ANARCHY RULES, and I can't help but smile. Even Deidre and Ahmed are here from the restaurant. I'm surprised to see they're holding hands—I had no idea. They are, I believe, the recruiting soldiers Doris spoke of. Doris herself returns to her seat beside them, after smoking a cigarette I assume. Wendy and Jonah are sitting in front of the podium half-turned in their seats keeping a watchful eye on the growing throng like a pair of spies on the lookout for the Other Side. I can't imagine who or what that might be in this instance.

I am doing reasonably well, all things considered, but for one overriding concern: *Rachel isn't here yet.* I put off taking my seat onstage for as long as I can, hoping to see her before my speech gets under way. And still, if she were to show up now in the midst of my lengthy and fallacious introduction, I would quit my seat and go to her, to warn her: *This is a trap. Do something different. Break the chain.*

But Rachel, it seems, is running late. What might it be? A wayward last-minute immigrant flown in on the midnight plane? A flood? A plague? A loquacious vendor? Whatever it is, she's not *meant* to be here, I'm not *meant* to speak to her before I address the crowd. That *meant* is a bitter pill to swallow, for I know who *means* in this world, and I am, like Mike's Tercera, just a symbol at his disposal.

As threatened, Sapworth is making his opening remarks. He's having a go at Nietzsche this time, and I can't bring myself to listen. The fellow next to me, introduced as Dean Fine—though I don't know whether that "Dean" is name or title—snickers at Sapworth's wit, and it's hard not to think of him as cued somehow, as if everyone has a script but me. He spoke earlier, in the vaguest possible terms, about Leadership, but I didn't listen to him either. I trust they'll let me know when I'm to be led on. I recall blind Samson and imagine myself Blind Peter, red beard flowing wildly, bringing down this plastic palace with a good hard tug on my chains, screaming, *where is she?*

As if to confirm my suspicions by signal, a back door opens

just as Sapworth concludes his remarks at precisely 1:15, and I take the podium to polite applause and the sight of Rachel waving her encouragement as the door closes noisily behind her. I return her wave and hope it's not good-bye.

And though he's not visible here, I am mindful of Anchee's presence—*we are creating the future in which Anchee dwells*, after all—a future in which he told me I was a famous man, but I foolishly didn't ask what for. Famous like Dickens, or famous like Jesus? The latter perhaps illustrating what befalls a storyteller who becomes the tale itself —beginning, middle, and end.

The TV crews flanking the stage turn on blinding lights that leave me blinking like a mole in sunshine for a few seconds, my vision filled with splotches of color. My audience, I have already observed, is a patchwork. With the younger students, it's not hard to see where one class starts and another begins. Uniforms both literal and figurative demarcate them by class, by race, by gender. I rather like the city kids, mostly black but not exclusively so, corkscrewing around in their seats, greeting each other. A row of private-school girls in pale blue uniforms (all, but one black girl, white) seem bred to purity, though gossip moves well enough up and down their ranks. The college students are a more varied bunch and scatter themselves more randomly about the hall, which is, after all, their territory. Some look ready to Lead tomorrow. Some look rather unlikely to follow.

As I look at all their faces—young, innocent (in spite of their affectations)—I decide, as I must, that Mike and Anchee notwithstanding, it matters what I say to them. As if they read my mind, they fall silent. They do not stir. Thus comforted, I begin:

"Good morning, young people of Richmond. I originally planned this talk for a much smaller group, so I hope you will forgive a certain informality—"

Sapworth reappears and grabs the microphone as if it were a serpent and wrestles it into submission with a racket the envy of any timber rattler, and leaves me to it with a smile, the microphone now on a level with my nose. Some find this episode amusing, and I egg them on with exaggerated grimaces at each rasping twist and turn of the recalcitrant mike. When I speak again, I startle myself it's so loud and clap my hands to my chest. That gets another laugh, so I go ahead and play to it, having a bit of hammy fun with the microphone as I continue, coming down on the sterner words with a godlike boom:

"I can only imagine the various pretenses under which most of you have been brought here. Perhaps something along these lines: 'There's a funny little Russian fellow who rants on about something or other terribly smart and trivial for your *betterment and edification*—attendance is *required*, *expect* a question on the exam, slackers will be *severely reprimanded.*' " This brings laughter and smiles of recognition from my audience. The faculty trade looks signifying—*one of those.*

"Professor Sapworth introduced me quite well, I'm sure. The Fine Dean had a few Fine words to say. I try not to listen to these things myself. I want you to imagine that everything they said about me, however outrageous, is indeed true: I am Truth, I am Justice, I am The American Way. I am Good For You. I'm an Expert. Follow me, and I'll make a Leader out of you."

I lean confidentially away from the mike, so that now the people in the lobby might not catch it all: "What if we're all lying to you? For all you know, I might be an android from the future come to take over your minds and foment revolution." This gets another laugh, and most of them have decided that I'm just crazy enough to be an improvement over their usual routines.

"Have no fear. Revolution foments itself, I believe. It's in the nature of things. Like evolution. Revolution, it has been said, is rapid evolution. But evolution itself, recent thinking has it, is not a smooth continuous process at all, but helter-skelter—or what is it you say, like a roller coaster?"

A thoughtful young woman in the third row nods yes, and I smile at her.

"What I want to talk about this morning is the imagination. This might seem a strange topic coming from a man of science such as myself. But there is not really any contradiction here at

all. Science and fiction are born in the same place—in the imagination. The scientific hypothesis and a novel's inspiration are
both *imagined* first—one to be tested scientifically and practically
by observation and experiment, the other to be tested aesthcti-
cally and ethically in the process of the story's unfolding. Fur-
thermore, the purpose of both, in large measure, is, in turn, the
education of our imaginations, so that we don't just respond
willy-nilly to whatever sensations come our way. But we, in effect, get good at it—imagining how it is the world works, imagining how it might be otherwise, imagining how, if the
conditions were made right, the one might become the other.
Out of the educated imagination, I believe, revolutions of all
sorts are born. What can I possibly mean by this? Allow me to illustrate by setting for your imaginations a few simple tasks.

"I have not been in Richmond long, only a few weeks. I came
here somewhat by chance, but I have found it quite delightful. As
you know one of the wonderful things about the city is the beautiful river that runs through it, the reason, in fact, why the city is
here in the first place, for this is wonderful habitat for humans.
The first task I'd like you to set your imaginations to this morning is to imagine you are animals. Not hard to imagine, since you
are animals. Imagine strolling down to the riverbank on a warm
pleasant day, a light breeze blowing. Imagine stripping naked
and diving into the river, swimming about, cavorting in the
water, playing with your companions, drying in the sun, putting
clean, dry clothes on—if you like—or not, if you'd rather. Each
one of those sensations is delicious beyond measure, is it not?
Feel free to add to this stock of sensations with your own imaginations and animal knowledge." They are pleasantly scandalized
and even the scattered faculty smile lazily like napping otters.

"Such imaginings, while pleasant fictions, can be quite instructive to the inquiring scientific mind as well, for they raise all
sorts of questions: Do you think these sensations feel any different for black or white humans? Do you think they were the same
for red before either black or white were here? Do you think
these sensations feel finer somehow for Bill Gates, let us say, or

for the Pope? Who's more likely to go skinny-dipping—you or them? Should any of these sensations be against the law? And if so, by whose authority? Such are a few of the questions imagining yourself a happy animal on the banks of a river might raise, and isn't that after all, here and now, exactly what you're striving to be? And if that is so, aren't these the very questions you should be asking yourself as you prepare for life on the shores of the world? Sometimes the hardest thing to imagine yourself to be is exactly what you are. It is often the most instructive."

They're not sure where I'm going with all this, and perhaps neither am I, but they look willing to stay the course with me, which brings me in mind of a story I decide to tell, for I'm afraid I've gotten a bit too heady for some. "You may be asking yourselves what all this has to do with *Leadership*, and so I'll tell you what I know on the subject. Once when I was transporting some goods in Siberia a steamer creeping slowly up the river overtook me, and when I boarded her, the passengers told me that the captain had drunk himself into a delirium and jumped overboard. He was saved, however, and was now lying ill in his cabin. They asked me to take command of the steamer, and I had to consent; but soon I found to my great astonishment that everything went on by itself in such an excellent routine way that, though I paraded all day on the bridge, I had almost nothing to do. Such you see is Leadership. Since everyone on board imagined they needed a leader, and they imagined me to be such a fellow, everything went well. But if they were to have imagined with equal conviction that they needed no leader, they would have managed just as well, better, I trust, for not having me strutting about distracting them from their own good sense."

As I pause for a drink of water, I can tell which faculty fancy themselves the captains of ships and which do not. I can't look at anyone close to the stage without blinding myself in the TV lights. Rachel is standing at the back of the hall beside a post looking quite proud of me, and the sight of her gives me encouragement. Maybe it will all turn out right; perhaps my fears are groundless. I shuffle my papers and find my place.

"Besides the James, another great river flows through Richmond, and that is the river of time. Perhaps it is an imaginary river. Perhaps it is real. The physics jury seems still to be out on that one. But time is real enough in the living of it, and like a torrent seems to carry us along. Sometimes we call that river history, and Richmond is said to be especially rich in that commodity. So the second thing I'd like you to imagine this morning is a journey to the headwaters of that river. Before this city, built by slaves, was imagined into existence by a white man named William Byrd, before . . ."

Doors at each side of the hall open noisily, and policemen step inside. One of them looks altogether too familiar. I would recognize him even without the bandage on his head—probably for show. We didn't hit him that hard. Our eyes meet, and he clearly disagrees. He's brought all his friends, it seems. There's not a blanket big enough for the lot of them, at least one policeman for each exit by my count. I brain a policeman with his own flashlight and wonder why I have the premonition that *somehow* I might possibly end up in jail. What a bloody fool *I've* turned out to be! But still, this isn't all my doing, there's entirely too many of them for that, and they all have their eyes on me. I wonder what lies Anchee has told them. Rachel sees them, too, and is working her way along the wall to one of the exits, perhaps to create a diversion, but the matter looks hopeless from my position.

I take another drink of water. "I don't know how much longer we'll have this morning, so allow me to set aside my prepared text and come right to the point. Look around you, what do you see? Humans, every one. The same species. Imagine yourself in Russia, let us say. Or Africa. It's easy for you, or so I'm told, with television and the Internet, to conjure up a roomful of humans there or anywhere. Now, or in the past, or in the future. Old, young. Gay, straight. Rich, poor. Black, white, yellow, red, brown. Get to know them. Don't forget them. They are the same as you: same species, same needs, same habitat. Educate your imaginations, so that you know that it is true. And if you want to be happy animals, live accordingly. Every injustice committed against one individual human on these shores, is experienced by humanity as a whole, and every wound thus inflicted must sooner or later be washed clean in that same river of time."

Sapworth has left the stage and is conferring with one of the policemen, and a couple more have filed in. The young, favorite targets of police harassment and justly nervous in their presence, spread the news that something's up. Some, fearing a drug raid, squirm to dispose of their contraband as discreetly as possible. The room is abuzz with rumors.

"The police—" I say, and in an instant I have everyone's undivided attention, even the police themselves. I begin again. "The police, I believe, are here for me. The rest of you can relax. But before I go, I would like to ask a favor of all of you here, two favors actually. The first is simply to speak up for the truth. Sound bites have a way of chewing up the sense. You'll no doubt hear all sorts of nonsense claimed about what I've said here today, and I would just like you to say it isn't so. Second, the next time you buy something—a shirt, a watch—here's one more task for your imaginations: Go to the room where the person who made it lives, imagine her life, imagine how much of the money you have just spent actually makes it into her pocket, if pockets she has. Imagine where the rest of it goes. Imagine where it could go. Imagine justice. Imagine equity.

"Darwin says that conscience 'looks backwards, and serves as a guide for the future.' Here in Richmond, which has seen more than its share of slavery, imprisonment, and inequity, let the past prompt you to imagine freedom, imagine justice, imagine *anarchy*!"

Ah! the word the cops were waiting for it seems, and they move down the aisles toward the stage. "Peter!" Jonah calls, and at first I don't see him, a few yards in front of me. He holds it up and throws it to me without giving me a chance to think whether I want to catch it or not, but catch it I do—the cursed watch— and dash backstage, so that when the police catch up with me I've vanished without a trace, and I'm sitting on a hillside, the city ablaze below me. There is a terrific explosion to the south-east that lights up the sky as if judgment has come. The earth trembles beneath me from the force of it, and hundreds of shells detonate in the air and rain sparks on a river that already seems made of fire. A lone bridge crosses the James down where the Canal Walk is—or will be. The explosions illuminate a stream of wagons and soldiers traversing it, heading south.

According to the watch, it's April 3, 1865.

I realize what I'm seeing. The Confederates—government and military—are evacuating the city. Without giving the matter further thought, I shut off the watch and pocket it, dashing down the hillside to join those streaming in from all directions to the docks, I assume to battle the blaze.

The city roars with flames, leaping from building to building, devouring everything. I waylay a bright-eyed fellow who says he's a newspaperman and hasn't got time for me, but I run alongside and persist in my questions, until I have the gist of the thing: The Confederates have set the torch to anything that might be of value to the advancing Federals—including tobacco and cotton warehouses and powder magazines. They could not have chosen a more cataclysmic policy if their deliberate intent had been to raze the city to the ground and leave the entire population dead or homeless. Even now can be heard the fresh explosions of shells, and the steady rush of spreading flames. My dashing informant darts into a residence where a pair of gray-clad soldiers block my way.

"The city's ablaze," I say to them, "whoever's within might be better served if you fellows battled flames instead of me."

"Who the hell are you?" one of them finally thinks to ask me.

"I'm the Russian Ambassador," I tell him, and turn a quick about-face, plunging once again into the street, now a river of humanity, or rather the poorer members of the species—black, white, men, women, children, old fellows on canes, young ones on crutches—all flowing in the same direction.

"Where are you headed?" I ask a white-haired old fellow pushing a wheelbarrow.

"The commissary on Fourteenth Street," he shouts in a German accent. "The guards be leaving soon. I hear plenty food inside."

The gauntness of his features is accentuated by the flickering light. I look around and see the same starved desperation on every face.

A black woman who has overheard our exchange, asks him, "What makes you think they let us have any of it?"

"They 'bout run outa wagons to haul it away," a young one-legged white boy says. "They ain't got no choice."

"He's right," another fellow says with a bit of Scottish brogue. "You can't buy a wagon in town for a sack of gold."

"Man offered me ten dollars in gold for my wheelbarrow!" my German informant exclaims. Most everyone is toting a bag or basket or tub or sack or pushing a wheelbarrow. I help the black woman tear loose an awning from the front of an abandoned shop with which to fashion a bundle.

"But they say Lee's boys is starving," a haggard white woman objects.

"They is," the one-legged boy says. "And so they'll be tonight. But you can bet Jeff Davis and them ain't. The government fellows that done skedaddled yesterday—they got plenty to eat."

The crowd swells around the commissary depot like a stormy sea, and watches with growing impatience and rage as the soldiers load wagon after wagon with bacon and hams and meal and flour and sugar and coffee and whiskey and drive them away as fast as they can. And still, there's more—even though the people in this crowd can't remember their last good meal. For some, the realization that this bounty was here all the time, kept under lock and key, is a terrible disillusionment; for others, it is the confirmation of their worst suspicions. All show remarkable restraint in not rushing the commissary *en masse*, though perhaps they are simply too starved and weak to make the attempt.

Finally, at dawn, when the last rickety wagon, commandeered no doubt from some dirt farmer, lurches toward the bridge, and the soldiers go with it, a group of men force open the depot doors, and the people surge forward and claim the bounty of the fallen State as if they imagine, by virtue of their sweat and toil and suffering, it is theirs for the taking.

It is a lawless mob, to be sure, with many drunk, and all starving—but I feel no great danger in the midst of it as we shuffle toward our share of the plunder. Only when the last fleeing gray-clad cavalrymen charge through the crowd on the way to the bridge, swords drawn in case any citizen should prove an obstacle, and many of us have to dive for the gutters to avoid being trampled—do I feel in any real danger—for the forces of Law and Order are passing through! And when the last of them has clattered across the bridge and out of sight, taking their Lost Cause with them, the populace turns back to the business of survival with almost an audible sigh of relief. These people don't yet know that the Confederates will be back, their cause with them—under the command of General Jim Crow—and I certainly don't have the heart to tell them.

When I reach the front of the jostling queue, I bundle up a hefty share of provisions in my coat, throw it over my shoulder, and stagger back out again. The air is thick with smoke, and soon the flames will envelop the commissary itself. I head for the tumbledown shanties along the canal where a row of children are sitting watching the last bridge burn. They are both black and white, the sons and daughters of watermen they tell me, and like Santa Claus I distribute the bounty among them.

Deafening hurrahs originating at some distance to the west resound even over the tumult around us, and one of the boys shouts, "It's the Union!" And they all grin ear to ear. One of the girls, rail thin and as pale as paper suggests, "Perhaps they'll want coffee," and holds up the packet I just gave her.

I leave them to their celebration and head toward the shouting and singing and dancing. I've never heard anything like it. Thousands of voices raised in exultation, and I haven't even reached the heart of it. The song I find most affecting issues from a crowd of black men and women who were slaves only yesterday:

Slavery chain done broke at last!
Broke at last! Broke at last!
Slavery chain done broke at last!
Gonna praise God till I die!

I come upon a detail of Union soldiers calling for the able-bodied to fight the blaze, and I lend my labor to the cause. Since we are totally without firefighting engines with which we might douse the blaze, our task consists of clearing flammables with axe and brute force from out of the conflagration's way. A Union engineer hits upon the happy stratagem of blowing up key houses in the fire's path, and thus the blaze is contained in a remarkably short time, though still a third of the city has been senselessly destroyed by the Slave Empire's violent withdrawal.

Exhausted and blackened with smoke, my hair singed to a fine frizz, I join my fellow firemen, mostly former slaves who are refugees from the countryside, in an evening celebration where I have another opportunity to practice my harmonica playing. They try to imagine the lives ahead of them, and I keep silent on the issue. The subject of Lincoln comes up often, and I clasp the watch in my hand, knowing what happens tomorrow, and I resolve to see it for myself.

I conceal myself in the boughs of a magnolia tree in Capitol Square and wait for everyone else but the Union sentries to fall asleep. I take out the watch and nudge myself forward in time less than a day when the Square is filled with an expectant crowd. He arrives in a coach, dressed in a long black coat and a high silk hat, and speaks from the steps of the capitol. He is quite a remarkable and odd-looking man, which none of the images of him have quite prepared me for—homely and awkward and gangly as a gnarled tree. He would look a fright on a TV screen, and what's more, I don't think he'd care. I have never witnessed another leader whom power seems to have corrupted less than he.

It's a remarkable speech, all the more remarkable by the throngs of property turned human overnight who make up the majority of his audience. One sentence sounds in my memory with particular force, as I'm sure it does for those to whom it is spoken:

Although you have been deprived of your God-given rights by your so-called masters, you are now as free as I am, and if those that claim to be your superiors do not know that you are free, take the sword and bayonet and teach them that you are.

It is all I can do to remain in hiding as he climbs into his carriage and rides away, for I would run after him and warn him that in eleven days a proslavery fanatic will murder him while he sits in a theater watching a play with his wife. And yet, he did get to see Richmond free before he died, and that must have been some consolation. He brought his twelve-year-old son Tad to Richmond with him. I'm sure he wanted the boy to see it, to remember it, to imagine the way it could be.

I climb down from my magnolia perch and hike to the edge of town and beyond to what I believe is the right place. I must be getting back to my own life, just as surely as Lincoln must sail back to his. I can't live in the past. And I'm not yet ready to abandon imagining a life for myself in the future. My present now, I suppose.

The watch performs flawlessly, though I'm a few dozen yards off the mark, and my appearance on the steps of the Business Auditorium causes something of a hubbub:

What's the blue light?
What blue light?
That's the anarchy guy isn't it?
Ooh gross! He's like burned or something!
He's over here! He's over here!

There's something familiar about this last voice, and I turn to see it's Sondra, but she melts into the crowd just as policemen fasten themselves on either arm and wrench me about, hauling me down the steps with TV cameramen racing all around us like swarming hornets. I can't imagine why I'm causing such a fuss. I spot Rachel at the edge of the crowd, and with a toss of her head she directs me to a bumbling homeless man loudly talking to himself, bearing down on the police and me, not watching where he's going. "The watch! The watch! The watch!" he cries, and so I'm ready for him. The police are outraged when he bumps right into their prisoner, and the two of us—both clearly insane—exchange a few words, calling each other crazy and falling into a bit of a tussle, as the one gives the other the time of day.

19 ⑨ Jailbird at Eleven

> But one who casts his lot with an advanced party must be prepared to spend a number of years in prison, and he need not grudge it. He feels that even during his imprisonment he remains not quite an inactive part of the movement which spreads and strengthens the ideas that are dear to him.
> —PETER KROPOTKIN, *Memoirs of a Revolutionist*

> It is impossible to see Kropotkin in the yard of the gaol and to exchange a greeting with him without asking oneself: "Why am I free? Is it perhaps because I am worth nothing more?"
> —ELIE RECLÚS

Allow me to describe my cell for you. It is six feet by twelve feet, the ceiling high, twelve feet at least, with a camera hanging like a bat in each corner. One long wall is bars, with a door of bars, opening onto a parallel gray hallway lit by fluorescent tubes twenty-four hours a day. For as far as I can see up and down the corridor, there are no other cells or doors of any kind. No one passes down this hallway unless they do it when I sleep. The other three windowless walls of the cell are hard concrete, painted concrete gray. There are several shades detectable, later rectangles added to obscure graffiti, thick in all the obvious places; but in the corner behind the cot, the censor with the bluest gray failed to completely obscure the words just visible through the paint—*TURN THEM OFF*—scrawled repeatedly in tiny block letters. My furnishings consist of the following: a steel toilet that gleams like a spaceship and reeks of disinfectant and replenishes itself from some vast disinfectant spring, a cold-water sink with a spring-loaded faucet and no plug, a steel cot, an acrylic blanket, a towel roughly half the size of a handkerchief with an abrasiveness not unlike the concrete floor, and a block of green soap or curdled disinfectant. On one of the narrow walls is a compartment, roughly eight by eleven inches, also gleaming steel, in which my meals are placed behind a sliding door. A buzzer sounds to announce the meal. The fare is simple but decent enough—a ham-biscuit for breakfast, a stew for lunch, a hamburger or pizza for dinner. Each evening with dinner I'm given a book or a pamphlet—always one of my own from the old life, as if I were a serial subscriber to *The Collected Works of Peter A. Kropotkin*. Some sort of cruel joke, I suppose, though I am not amused. Dead Peter is the last person I wish to hear from right about now. I let them stack up in the corner. The *In Russian and French Prisons* is an American edition of such a size that it serves as toilet lid to reduce the disinfectant stench. The others have yet to find a purpose, as I have been provided with adequate supplies of toilet paper for the foreseeable future.

"Foreseeable future." A silly phrase now that I've set it down. If it's foreseeable, how can it be the future anymore? How can it avoid being history as long as one person knows it with certainty? Ah well, let it stand. The foreseeable future is the future we live without surprises, I suppose. I don't know the time, the date with any certainty, or where in the world this prison might be. It could be anywhere, but most likely underground, for I've yet to see the light of day or any hint of it. I have only my conventional meals with which to regularly mark the passage of time. The kitchen, it occurs to me, could speed or slow my days at will, simply by varying the rate of meal service. My stomach wouldn't know the difference, for it grumbles all the time. When a roasted goose shows up behind the sliding door, I suppose I shall wish myself a Merry Christmas.

A week ago, or perhaps I should say seven ham-biscuits ago, I was relieved of my belongings, given prison duds (gray naturally), and brought here by pointedly silent officers. I have yet to be questioned, much less charged or brought before a magistrate. I have spoken with no one at all.

You may have noticed, in my description of this place, I've made no mention of sounds other than the meal buzzer. You may mistakenly assume I lead a near-silent life, with perhaps the hum of the fluorescent tubes or the whoosh of air-conditioning or the rumble of my own thoughts as the only breach of silence. Would that it were so.

Up the corridor—which is to say, in the direction my book/meal compartment lies—beyond where I can see, but close enough to hear quite clearly, a television plays at all hours. I assume someone watches it, for the channels change, sometimes in rapid succession for what seems hours on end splintering what information I might glean from it, like the time of day. My imagined watcher has a preference for sports and occasionally the news. I most often sleep during the sporting events. I don't recall the rules of the sports I know, and half I've never heard of, making it near impossible to imagine what I'm hearing described. Early on I tried to imagine some high divers—to picture them executing their controlled plummets into the water based solely on the nattering descriptions and critiques of the commentators—but the effort only saddened me, for the animal beauty of the thing was entirely absent. Though I always felt a thrill at the splash of entry when I could hear it over the chatter. One night I listened to a boxing match from beginning to brutal end that had my blood racing, my fists clenched and throwing punches—but have resolved to renounce that particular pleasure in future as unhealthy for my state of mind, overheated enough as it is.

The oddest thing, it seems to me, is that my watcher never makes a sound. Even when pandemonium issues from the television after some spectacular play or race or injury, and the announcer is screaming in delirium with the best of them, my watcher never makes a peep. If he is so neutral to the outcome, why does he watch so many competitions? Perhaps he is a connoisseur of conflict and will rouse himself only for the most exquisite. Or perhaps the silent bastard's not even there. If he is, however, he is most certainly blessed with evidence of me and my principal recreation, for I snore quite loudly during the two most tedious sports for listening, golf and auto-racing.

Occasionally, when my watcher can't find a contest to suit him, or when a story catches his interest in his flit from program to program, he'll take in a bit of the news. Fortunately or unfortunately, he seems particularly interested in my case—not surprising, I suppose, since we're neighbors.

At these times, I pace the bars and listen to the adventures of yet another Kropotkin—TV Peter this time—the most fantastical yet. I walk four paces up and four paces down, trying to stay fit but succeeding only in dizzying myself. Or perhaps it's the tale being spun that does that, to hear my life suspended in a web of lies, a plump and foolish anarchist fly:

As a stunned nation looks for answers in the wake of the Littleton tragedy—in which Eric Harris and Dylan Klebold senselessly gunned down thirteen victims in a rampage of terror before turning their weapons on themselves—many are pointing here, to Richmond, Virginia, and hints of a much wider, much more sinister conspiracy than previously imagined.

Most Americans first heard of Peter Kropotkin when this footage of his dramatic arrest, literally coinciding with the events in Littleton, was first broadcast in the wake of the high-school tragedy, and a possible connection between the two episodes was first suggested by investigators. But for the people of Richmond, this was only the climax in a series of troubling events.

Our story begins in early April when a mysterious man calling himself Peter Kropotkin arrived in this sleepy southern town steeped in history and tradition, and began to organize the local disaffected youth, preaching a vague, antigovernment philosophy, with violent overtones. Buddy Showalter vividly recalls the day Kropotkin showed up at his airport limousine stand:

We get all kinds now, but I knew there was something weird about this one from the get go. He's got no luggage for one thing. Says he comes all the way from Russia, and he's got no luggage? He tries to give me some story about the airlines losing it, but I didn't buy it. Then these three Trenchcoat Mafia types show up—with the black coats and the tattoos and all the rest of it—and they're downright rude to me— but that's the way these punks are these days. No surprise there. But then out of the blue they offer to share their limo with this Kropotkin guy. It didn't make sense.

It seemed pretty obvious to me that the three of them were meeting up with this Kropotkin character for some kind of deal, like they were in cahoots or something, but they were pretending not to know each other, like they just happened *to be heading the same place, and these punks are all of a sudden nicey-nice to some total stranger from nowhere. I didn't buy it. I figured drugs or something. I had no idea they were terrorists. They had these cases with them. Wouldn't let me touch 'em. Music cases supposedly, but my driver says they were awful heavy, and I'm thinking they were guns.*

The trail next leads here to this run-down house near Virginia Commonwealth University. After first dropping off Kropotkin in nearby Monroe Park, this is where driver George Stovall delivered the three young men who met Kropotkin at the airport:

That's right. I carried them here after I let off the Russian fellow. They had lots of heavy stuff, all right. But they tipped good. Don't know that any of it was guns though. I don't know if they knew the Russian before or not. They all seemed to get along pretty good back there, talking about stuff. The Russian fellow was especially nice, a real gentleman. The fellow with the tattoo on his head, he wrote something down and give it to the man, but I don't know what that was about.

Indeed, that's just one of the many unanswered questions surrounding Kropotkin. The house is empty now, sealed by police as part of the ongoing investigation, but apparently it was the residence of several known radicals and drug dealers. We spoke with one of the officers who made the initial search of the house:

They'd obviously all left in a hurry. It's safe to say there were people living in practically every room of the house. It's difficult to determine an exact number. Kropotkin and the black guy were apparently set up down in the basement. We found a bunch of books down there missing from the university library, radical in nature, and an acetylene torch. They had growing paraphernalia everywhere—pots and soil and lights and fertilizers. It was like a nursery. They had a greenhouse out back, and they were even growing stuff up on the roof. It seems to have been a moneymaking operation for them—they had a bank account and everything. They took all the plants, but we intend to examine the residence more thoroughly in that regard, and we are considering this a drug investigation at this time. There's not too many things you can grow in this small a space and turn a profit on it, if you know what I mean.

Police then attempted to locate the owner of the property only to discover that the owner of record is a company calling itself Mutual Aid Ltd., owned by Peter Kropotkin of Russia, and that the house was purchased in 1995 by an agent of his, one A.M. Chaney, a flamboyant figure in the local arts scene who left for parts unknown some nine months ago and hasn't been heard from since. So the three young men who met Kropotkin at the airport, as if by chance, were actually living in his house.

So just who is this mysterious Kropotkin now in custody? For a clue we might turn to the historical figure whose name he has assumed. Those of you with a knowledge of obscure figures in history may recall Peter Kropotkin as the Anarchist Prince who lived a life of privilege in czarist Russia, actually serving as the personal page to Alexander II at one point, as we see here in this old photograph of Kropotkin in uniform, only to turn his back on family and country and dedicate himself to revolutionary activities, serving at least two prison terms for his efforts before he died in 1921 at seventy-eight, shortly after the triumph of the Bolsheviks. Here we see a photograph of Emma Goldman, famed American radical often known as Red Emma, speaking at Kropotkin's funeral to a huge crowd of mourners, perhaps the largest assembly of anarchists in history.

The INS and the State Department have no record of this man under the name Peter Kropotkin or any other, and Russian officials report that they are equally baffled. Even the airline has no record of selling him a ticket, though the flight crews on both his flights recall him vividly, en-

thusiastically sharing George Stovall's judgment that he was an exceptionally nice fellow.

But as charming as he may be to limo drivers and flight attendants,
authorities find it a matter of grave concern that he would adopt the
alias of an infamous anarchist who advocated the abolition of the State
and the rule of law—in short, total anarchy. One immigration official
with whom we spoke described Kropotkin's bogus documents as quote,
undoubtedly the best forgeries we have ever seen, unquote, suggesting
perhaps that this is no simple case of immigration fraud but the work
of experts in the art of espionage.

Whoever he may prove to be, he faces several charges including as-
saulting a Richmond police officer and resisting arrest. The authorities
with whom we spoke were not at liberty to discuss the details of the
other possible charges pending against him and would only say that he
is the subject of an ongoing investigation by both the INS and the FBI.
Citing security concerns, they also declined to divulge the prisoner's
whereabouts except to say he is in a maximum-security facility. He is
generally thought to be somewhere in the city, but authorities would
neither confirm nor deny these rumors. Authorities stressed that the
American public would be kept informed of important developments in
the case just as soon as such disclosures would not jeopardize the ongoing investigation, or compromise agents in the field.

And now in Little—

In this photograph taken by an amateur photographer and released just
hours ago by authorities, we see the man who calls himself Kropotkin
on the left of your screen with a coconspirator known only by the code
name Jonah on the right. You'll notice they're both wearing the trademark black duster made infamous by the Trenchcoat Mafia. The photographer who snapped this shot just happened to spot these two
trespassing on the construction site of the new Canal Walk in downtown Richmond and thought they looked suspicious. Authorities refused to speculate as to what the pair may have been up to but would
not rule out the possibility that they were considering it as a potential

*target for another Littleton-style attack, perhaps during the opening
ceremonies for the Canal Walk slated for early June, where several state
and local dignitaries are expected to be in attendance.*

*As for the man called Jonah, while he has been the object of an ex-
tensive manhunt, so far, authorities concede, he seems to have vanished
without a trace.*

And now with the forecast—

*This morning, authorities released this videotape from a police under-
cover operation showing Kropotkin and his followers distributing food
stolen from several area restaurants to indigents and the hard-core
homeless, in an attempt, investigators believe, to recruit an Army of the
Disaffected from the city's underclass to create unrest and possibly engage in acts of violence. Police were tipped to the possibility of this ring
of young radicals by city health department employee Fred Spurlow
who claims that he was offered bribes and sexual favors to keep silent
about what he knew. He stumbled upon the conspiracy, he says, while
investigating a routine complaint at the restaurant where the shadowy
figure known as Kropotkin worked.*

*As for the mysterious figure at the heart of all this controversy—the
man called Kropotkin—authorities refused to speculate on the full extent of his underground activities. Aware that rumors are flying, they
nonetheless could not lend credence to—or deny—any of them at this
stage of the investigation.*

*Sources close to the investigation, however, did reveal to this re-
porter on condition of anonymity, that Kropotkin and his crew are suspected in a plot to blow up the famed, beloved, and often controversial
monuments of Monument Avenue which honor several heroes of the
American Civil War—including General Robert E. Lee, whose statue
you see behind me. It is believed that these attacks were planned as part
of a larger plot to create racial unrest in this usually peaceful city, and*

the opportunity for further acts of violence. It is known that several of Kropotkin's followers shave their heads after the fashion of skinhead white-supremacist groups advocating race warfare, although my sources did stress that no clear link between Kropotkin and those groups has yet to be established.

Whatever answers the investigation may yet provide, the city of Richmond must breathe easier tonight knowing that Kropotkin is behind bars—even though bizarre effects of his presence continue to be felt. Efforts to locate and question other possible conspirators have been severely hampered, police report, by active defiance among the city's youth, including, as shown here, the wearing of long black coats and phony beards by both males and females. And here I have the most popular T-shirt in town among young radicals. As you can see, it shows Kropotkin behind bars with the caption I AM KROPOTKIN.

Meanwhile, a local chapter of the Sons of Confederate Veterans has posted a security guard on the grounds of Lee's Monument. They are, as you can see, dressed in authentic Confederate uniforms as they solemnly stand watch over their former commander. Their presence has spawned fresh controversy with demonstrations and counterdemonstrations, and heated debate in the Richmond City Council. Confederates insist, however, they will not abandon their posts as long as this monument is potentially in danger. By the look of things here tonight— with Rebels and Radicals squaring off for another evening of dissension—they could be in for a very long vigil indeed.

As General Lee and his beloved horse Traveler look out over Monument Avenue tonight, they surely must be—

"Inanimate" is the word that comes to mind, but I'll never know. We've moved on to tennis, my watcher and I. *Thunk, thunk, thunk . . .* Rather a soothing sound. Was that a *sound* from my watcher, just now, right before we retreated from Lee? A disgusted grunt when the Confederates bravely took to the screen to protect their Bronze Commander of the Lost Cause—an image in my mind rather like the Children of Israel and the Golden Calf with a good deal less gaiety. I can't be sure. I may have unconsciously made the sound myself. I have no trouble at all picturing them, as I say, all gray and solemn as a smoldering city, and

the image is painful in the extreme. There was such a grand celebration when they left, and here they are back again.

*Just released by authorities is a portion of a videotape made of
Kropotkin's address at Virginia Commonwealth University in Richmond, Virginia, delivered on—as everyone must know by now—April
20, Hitler's birthday, at precisely the same time the Littleton tragedy
was taking place. Kropotkin's speech is entitled simply "Anarchy,"
which—when you see the videotape—you'll certainly agree seems to be
the intent of his remarks, and a good description of his thought
processes as well!*

*Joining us now to shed some light on the rather bizarre content of
this videotape are, in our Washington studios, Dr. Rudolph Klausner
of the Strickland Institute in Washington and an expert in Social Dys-
functionalism—I hope I have that right—and here with me in New
York, we have Barbara Blaine, author of several provocative books on
modern culture including her most recent volume you see there on your
screen—FREEDOM IS KILLING AMERICA, which USA Today
calls bold and incisive. Good evening to you both.*

Good evening, Jill.

*Before we view the videotape, a few lingering questions. First of all,
the mysterious person known only as Jonah—who has yet to be appre-
hended at this hour—some have found it odd, in light of recent indica-
tions that Kropotkin may be linked to various racist hate groups, that
he appears to be, in the only—admittedly blurred—photograph we have
of him, an African-American individual. Does that strike you as odd,
Dr. Klausner?*

*Not at all, I'm afraid. It is almost, shall we say, to be expected. As
you know, Jill, during the Nazi era, there were indeterminate numbers
of Jews who worked in willing collaboration with their oppressors. In
such situations, the minority internalizes the hatred directed at them
and transforms it into self-loathing, eventually directing this hatred
outward, and in the final stages, they themselves become the oppressors
of their own kind, their own worst nightmare, if you will. Much alleged*

discrimination in this country, my researches show, is actually of this type.

Fascinating. So for such misguided individuals it's as if black is white and white is black. What do you think of that assessment, Barbara?

I couldn't agree more. And just let me add that Dr. Klausner's brilliant analysis is further underscored by recent reports that this Jonah had a white girlfriend, perhaps several, who lived with him, and we may assume, since he had no visible means of support, who likely supported him as well. The employees of the movie theatre where the two of them saw a violent science-fiction cult film only days before the tragedy, report that the girl—who shaves her head and wears men's-clothing, by the way—paid for literally everything. All of this is symptomatic of the racial and gender identity fragmentation our all-too-free society actually fosters and encourages in our youth in a myriad of ways—as I discuss in my book at some length—in particular in the chapter I call Black Athletes and White Feminists: The New Miscegenation.

Hmmm. Really? That sounds like . . . pretty strong stuff there, Barbara. But getting back to Kropotkin—as evidence continues to mount, there are those who still claim there is nothing clearly linking this Kropotkin with either Eric Harris or Dylan Klebold and that the media and the police and the American People are simply rushing to judgment. What do you two think about that? Dr. Klausner?

(Masculine chuckle) Better to rush to judgment than no judgment at all! I have had the opportunity to view at some length the videotape that we are about to see of this man's address to a group of innocent high-school students, and I must tell you, it disturbs me. It disturbs me deeply! And of course, the man timed his remarks to coincide precisely with the incidents in Littleton, on Hitler's birthday, clad in the black coat of anarchy, exhorting his followers to be animals for God's sake! Coincidence? Perhaps. Perhaps not. But let us not forget that reports are flooding in from police departments throughout the country to suggest that other such vicious attacks were planned throughout the nation, but that authorities were able to nip them in the bud with some heads-up police work. No, rather than second-guessing the authorities,

I think we should be thanking them for averting what could have been a tragedy of major proportions.

I quite agree with Dr. Klausner, Jill. The price of freedom is eternal vigilance. There are those in our anything-goes society today who seem to think that freedom comes without this price, that we can simply allow this sort of self-styled demagoguery to go on unchecked right under our very noses without putting at risk the precious liberties for which our forefathers endured so many hardships and made so many sacrifices. As I explain in the opening chapter of my book, the first task of a truly free society is to accept limitations on its freedom.

With that in mind, let's watch the videotape, shall we?

(It is hard indeed to set this down. I have seen enough of Brad's wizardry to imagine how it might be done, that I might actually be made to appear to be uttering this gibberish. I can see it all too well. In fact, at this point—it's played repeatedly every hour it seems—I recall it better than what I actually said.)

Good morning, young people of Richmond. I am Truth, I am Justice, I am The American Way. I am Good For You. I'm an Expert. Follow me, and I'll make a Leader out of you. I am an android from the future come to foment revolution. Have no fear. Revolution is in the nature of things. Revolution foments revolution foments revolution foments revolution. Like helter-skelter. Imagine you are animals as Darwin says. Take command. . . . I don't know how much longer we'll have. Look around you, what do you see? Gays, blacks. Not human, not the same species. It's easy for you, with television and the Internet, to know you are the true animals washed clean in the river of time. Look to us. Imagine yourself in Germany. In Colorado. In Richmond. Everything I say is true! Here in Richmond imagine anarchy! For the betterment and edification of the race, blacks will be severely reprimanded!

Whooo! I must say. Pretty strong stuff. Dr. Klausner?

Well, it's a familiar pattern, isn't it? The use of pop icons, the appeals to the baser instincts, the helter-skelter reference to Charles Manson, as well as to the Beatles' song "Revolution," the clearly paranoid world vision full of androids and other antisocial images drawn from science fiction—such as the film Barbara astutely called our attention to a moment ago. The man's clearly demented. But let me stress that he's

merely part of the larger cultural dementia under which we labor. A
tradition of dementia, as it were. In which every sick twisted horror is
glorified in the name of freedom of expression and protected as a right.

Absolutely, Dr. Klausner. I couldn't agree more. In fact I devote an
entire chapter in my book to precisely this issue in relation to so-called
affirmative action and the NEA in a chapter I call The Myth of Mem-
ber Size and the Violation of the Virgin.

That sounds fascinating, Barbara.

That's quite a compliment coming from you, Dr. Klausner.

Rudolph, please.

Getting back to Kropotkin, Rudolph and Barbara, one last question.
Wouldn't you two agree that the specific mention of Colorado in this
inflammatory speech suggests rather strongly some foreknowledge on
Kropotkin's part of the events taking place in Littleton—innocent chil-
dren being gunned down at the very moment he was saying these hor-
rible things—possibly even complicity in these events himself; and not,
as some have maintained, some media rush to judgment?

Certainly, Jill.

Well I see we've run out of time. I'd like to thank you both for being
with us this evening. And Barbara, we'll certainly look for your book,
FREEDOM IS KILLING AMERICA, available from, Simon & Schus-
ter, is it? It can also be ordered on-line at our website, where you'll find
continuous, around-the-clock, in-depth coverage of our headline story
this hour, Kropotkin: America Invaded!

If I thought for a moment that such absurdities would be made
of my life and my words without Anchee's active hand in the
matter, I don't think I could bear it. To be transformed into
everything one loathes. But no one spends any significant time
in prison without contemplating suicide, both motive and
means, and I've already determined three ways to manage the
task here if it should come to that. Fortunately, then, I suppose, I
see Anchee's meddling hand in everything and feel more rage
than disillusion and despair. It occurs to me what a terrible fool

Samson would seem without God to pin the whole business on. And the woman, of course, who stole his strength with a haircut. Why is it the God lovers are always blaming the woman? I wonder what Freud would say? I'll have to ask Rachel when next I see her.

In a related incident, in which arson is strongly suspected, the restaurant in which Kropotkin and several of his followers ostensibly worked, burned to the ground in a mysterious predawn blaze. The restaurant was closed at that hour, and fortunately no one was injured. Firemen shown here battling the inferno, say the fire appears to have originated in a locked office where sensitive restaurant records were stored. Restaurant owner William Bates reportedly told authorities that he believes his wife Doris may have fallen under Kropotkin's influence and deliberately set the blaze to cover up their illegal dealings. An undisclosed amount of cash is missing as well. Police are seeking Mrs. Bates at this hour for questioning. Anyone with any knowledge of her whereabouts should contact local authorities.

Try Tuscany, I hope for her.

Rachel Pederson, shown here leaving police headquarters, was released after being held in connection with the bizarre case of the man calling himself Peter Kropotkin. Originally thought to be involved in Kropotkin's midnight raid on the statue of General Robert E. Lee, in which Richmond police officer Darin McArthur was viciously assaulted, Ms. Pederson was released when McArthur failed to positively identify her as a member of the gang, saying, I had my hands full with the two men, so I didn't get a good look at the women.

In remarks to reporters, Ms. Pederson claimed that Mr. Kropotkin is being victimized by a systematic tissue of lies and innuendo, and that time will eventually vindicate him. She offered no evidence, however, for her claims. Threatening massive demonstrations, she vowed that Kropotkin supporters would not rest until he is cleared of all charges and released. Meanwhile, the agency for which she works, the Refugee and Immigration Assistance Agency, has issued a statement maintaining that at no time did the agency knowingly provide any assistance to Kropotkin or his followers, and that Ms. Pederson is no longer an employee of the agency and is acting entirely on her own.

Local authorities pooh-poohed the idea of massive demonstrations, pointing out that there was little evidence to indicate that Kropotkin commanded the support of more than a few dozen disturbed individuals.

When asked about that, Ms. Pederson laughed and said, quote, Give us time, unquote, but declined to elaborate.

At least they didn't call her *Miss.* I have to imagine her laugh, her voice. They only report what she has to say in dismissive summaries while Buddy Showalter practically gets his own show. No matter. I can imagine her more vividly than they could ever show her—even with dozens of cameras, color commentators, and anchorpersons—and so that's what I do:

They ask her where she intends to dig up more than a few deranged anarchists in Richmond, and she imagines the legions the place must harbor just below the historical surface, and laughs out loud, I think, as her punning answer occurs to her, with the added bonus of a message in it for me. "Give us time," she says with the little stress on "time" in case I'm listening, and I know exactly what she means.

She intends to use the watch.

The watch! The watch! The watch!

Rachel's not one to make an empty boast. If she promises massive demonstrations, then massive they'll be. I consider the possibilities, and I can't help myself, I laugh out loud. It is delicious to imagine the downtrodden rising from their graves to new lives. That's what I always imagined the Christian resurrection of the dead on Judgment Day to be all about, though I never heard a preacher speak of it so. They all saw it as some massive summons to appear before the Headmaster.

So ebullient do my spirits become, that I begin singing for my watcher in hopes he'll tell me to shut up and we'll both be the happier for having had some human contact—but I tire of my singing before he does apparently—further proof he doesn't exist.

And so I fall into a fitful sleep and dream of Rachel in my arms on the banks of the river, making love, when we're shaken by a terrific explosion, and see the city in flames on the opposite shore. We run naked, no time to dress, as fast as we can, but when we reach the bridge, it is already ablaze. We clasp hands and run into the fire. I can feel the blistering heat from head to toe, and then miraculously, the flames retreat before us and we chase them from the bridge, from the city, into the sky, where they turn to clouds and drift away, and she and I are flying.

When I awaken, the tone of the television has changed somehow, not so smooth, not so scripted, perhaps even a little frightened, and it's as if I can actually hear the tide begin to turn.

For the benefit of our viewers at home, perhaps you could tell us what, exactly, we're seeing here, Stephanie.

Certainly, Dan. The footbridge you see behind me underneath Lee Bridge is usually the route used by joggers and cyclists and picnickers on their way to and from Belle Isle, part of the James River Park System here in the city of Richmond. At dawn this morning, the men you see passing by, suffering from exposure, malnutrition, frostbite, dysentery, and ailments too numerous to mention began to stream across this bridge into the city. No one seems to know where they came from, but there are literally thousands, and their numbers show no signs of abating. As you can see behind me, the city has mobilized every available ambulance and has even called for volunteers to help shuttle these men to hospitals downtown.

Have you been able to talk with any of these men, Stephanie?

As you can see, Dan, local police have set up barricades in order, they say, to facilitate the prompt evacuation of these men. But before the police put the barricades in place, we did manage to talk briefly with a few of the men. Most seem to be in shock and were unwilling or unable to talk to us about what they have been through, but there were a few who would, and they all claimed to have been held prisoner on the island without proper food and shelter for a number of months, even longer, though details were vague and contradictory. But as you can see even from here, these men look truly awful, like something out of a concentration camp. I've never seen anything like it.

Not too long ago, someone claiming to be a spokesman for the group, a Dr. Earl Hollander, claims that all these men, get this Dan, have come here in support of Peter Kropotkin and are demanding his immediate release! We have, however, not been able to confirm this claim or even Hollander's connection with these men. Hollander took off rather abruptly shortly after State Police arrived.

I understand that the governor of Virginia was actually on the scene.

That's right, Dan. Governor Jim Gilmore was here to survey the situation some moments ago but declined to speak with reporters, saying there were other pressing matters requiring his immediate attention.

To which, I take it, he was referring to the African-American men who began marching into the city as well.

That's quite right, Dan.

Do we have a visual on that? Who? We're going to Chan Rundgren in Richmond for the latest in a series of bizarre occurrences there. Chan?

Yes, Dan. Chan Rundgren here at Capitol Square in Richmond with a man who identifies himself merely as Gabriel and who claims to be the leader of this march. As near as we can determine, they began their trek about six miles north of the city sometime this morning. The original

group, some five hundred African-American men in old-fashioned at-
tire, have picked up quite a number of recruits or curiosity seekers along
the way. Their route took them through Virginia Union University, an
historically black college active in sit-in demonstrations in the sixties,
where it's reported that Gabriel made a speech that emptied out both the
classrooms and administrative offices. He was equally successful in en-
listing the residents of the traditionally African-American neighborhood
Jackson Ward. Reporters caught up with him here at the terminus of
their march, Capitol Square. Estimates of the numbers assembled here so
far range between two and three thousand, and more continue to arrive.
Mr. Gabriel, what is it your group hopes to accomplish here?

We have come across two centuries of time to see the city free, to set
it free, if it is not yet free. We welcome all men who love freedom to our
cause—both black and white, past and present.

Where is it your group is from exactly?

Here, the ground under your feet. Can I make it any plainer? Two
hundred years ago we were poised to strike here to free ourselves and
free this place. But we failed in the attempt. This time, instead, we have
traveled across time with Jonah, who rescued us from the gallows. In
return, we come to aid him in his efforts to set his friend Kropotkin free.

Excuse me, Chan, but we have word of yet another late-breaking
story in Richmond, and we go to Melanie Maples down by the river-
side. Melanie?

Uh, yes. Dan. I'm here in front of the Annabelle Lee, an excursion
riverboat that is the scene of what may be the most bizarre episode yet.
A short while ago, African-American men, women and children, many
in chains and leg irons, began disembarking from this vessel. Accord-
ing to the janitorial crew who showed up to ready the boat for a wed-
ding party scheduled for this morning, they found these people already
on the boat, every deck packed. No one can explain where they came
from, or how they managed to get so many on board. Hundreds have al-
ready disembarked, and as you can see, Dan, the boat is still packed to
the railings, and they continue to pour forth. As for why they're here,
the ones I talked to say they are slaves who've come here to be free.
They, too, claim to have been rescued by Jonah and demand the release
of Peter Kropotkin.

So this is, then, the same mysterious Jonah wanted in conjunction with the Kropotkin affair?

That's right, Dan. They say that he will come out of hiding when it is prudent to do so. It is believed he may be on board the boat, but so far no one has been able to gain access to the vessel to conduct a search. As you can see, the boat is awash with a blue light locals tell us is not normal. It is rumored that three city of Richmond police officers boarded the boat over an hour ago but haven't been heard from since, though we have not been able to get confirmation on that rumor. Police officials declined to comment other than to say the matter is under investigation.

And where is it these people are heading, Melanie?

They are going to Capitol Square, where they intend to meet up with Jonah's group and have the chains struck from them and to celebrate their freedom. What's that? We now go back to Chan in Capitol Square.

I'm having a little trouble hearing, Dan. As you can see, the crowd here continues to grow. At the center of it is a makeshift blacksmith shop where Gabriel, a blacksmith by trade, is striking the shackles from off the Annabelle Lee refugees who have begun arriving here. A short while ago the crowd was ordered to disperse and return to their homes, but Gabriel replied—We have no homes to return to, unless the governor would care to invite us into his—a reference to the Governor's Mansion, which is just a few hundred yards from where we're standing. Authorities didn't press the issue, for at this point this remains a peaceful, if illegal, demonstration. Any action by police could prove disastrous at this point, for despite repeated announcements discouraging people from coming here, more and more keep pouring in. I've spoken with many of them. Several seem actually to believe Gabriel's claims of time travel, believing him actually to be the charismatic young blacksmith who was the leader of an abortive slave uprising here in 1800, resulting in his execution along with many of his followers, an event whose memory is still kept alive in the African-American community here. Others say they don't care about the history, but that they find his message of equity and inclusion compelling. But I tell you, Dan, I've never seen anything like it in my life. I learned just moments ago that the wedding party that Melanie spoke of has moved the whole affair here, and they've invited all these people to help them celebrate. In fact,

the mood all around is as much celebration as demonstration. As one
elderly black gentleman said to me a little while ago, If this city wasn't
free before, it sure as hell is now! Excuse me? You're kidding!

I've just been informed that in the latest bizarre twist, the first so-
called Belle Isle refugees to be released from MCV hospital just across
the street have joined the assembled crowd in wheelchairs with IVs,
in the company of MCV medical students in I AM KROPOTKIN *T-shirts!*
The reports we have from MCV indicate that authorities there are con-
vinced that the men coming off Belle Isle are, in fact, prisoners escaped
from the Civil War prison camp there.

I've been asked by local authorities to continue to urge people to stay
away. Several downtown streets have been closed already. Don't even
try to get anywhere in the city in a car. And we have reports of traffic
backing up on all major arteries into the city. There are rumors that
black police actually refused to arrest the first wave of demonstrators
when they arrived in the city and that white police refused to arrest
their fellow officers. It does seem that the police have taken a hands-off
approach. There are also rumors that the governor has fled the city by
helicopter, while others claim to have seen the mayor and several city
council persons in the crowd. The rumor has also been circulating that
a huge march is planned for later this evening down Monument Av-
enue. None of these rumors are confirmed however. As for Peter
Kropotkin, so far authorities have refused to release his whereabouts,
and say they have no intention of negotiating with terrorists . . .

This goes on for a while, a great tumult from past and present,
rising up for my release like magma through the earth even
though they can't have a clue who I am. I wonder how many
weeks Jonah and Rachel and Earl spent laboring in the past to
persuade them I was a man they should help, and in so doing
they would help themselves. It wasn't difficult, I suppose. All
these thousands are free here and can hardly be sent back. That
achievement in itself makes me smile. But the means give me an
uneasy, nightmarish feel. It all happens too fast when cause and

effect go out the window, as if the floors of a high building were all to give way at once. I imagine the world ending, and me trapped here forever. I half listen, half doze to the murmuring voices, experts and politicians from everywhere now, even some poor soul standing in the cold—*I'm in the town of Dmitrov, Russia, northeast of Moscow, today a town of some seventy thousand people, where, on February 8, 1921 ...*

I drift off, only briefly I think, and when I wake, it is silent.

A chair scrapes.

A door opens and closes.

My watcher has departed.

Fortunately for me, the kitchen crew—perhaps they're androids or machines—stay on. Tonight, there's no book with dinner (fish and chips), but there's a pen instead, of the same design I gave to Jonah what seems so long ago. There's no paper with it, but I realize there's paper enough piled up in the corner. And so I commence to write.

Chapter One

I Am Reborn . . .

20 ⑨ Free Peter Kropotkin

I also read during this time [in prison] a great number of novels, and even arranged for myself a treat on Christmas Eve. My relatives managed to send me then the Christmas stories of Dickens, and I spent the festival laughing and crying over those beautiful creations of the great novelist.

—PETER KROPOTKIN, *Memoirs of a Revolutionist*

"But you were always a good man of business, Jacob," faltered Scrooge, who now began to apply this to himself.

"Business!" cried the Ghost, wringing its hands again. "Mankind was my business. The common welfare was my business; charity, mercy, forbearance, and benevolence, were all my business. The dealings of my trade were but a drop of water in the comprehensive ocean of my business!"

It held up its chain at arm's length, as if that were the cause of all its unavailing grief, and flung it heavily upon the ground again.

—CHARLES DICKENS, *A Christmas Carol*

I am not sure how long I've been writing these pages, or margins I should say, for the only paper I have is the *Collected Pile of Peter K.*, a modest Babel not even tall enough to reach halfway to the cameras that watch me write. Or not. Since my watcher quit the scene, perhaps all watchers have abandoned their posts, and reality is on its own, unobserved. These cameras, then, are mere artifacts for my observation. The only *life* to observe is me, and the only mirror is this pen and page. I would welcome a flea, a spider, or even a microscope with which I might observe the bacteria that surely must share my cell, though it would not surprise me to find it lifeless save myself and whatever resides in the vessel of my body, adrift on a disinfectant sea.

Lacking other lives, I've told my brief one in these margins. But now it nears an end—tale and life both most likely. Whenever a prisoner's narrative comes down to *About the same as yesterday* and *No change* for day after day—whether in pine box or on paper, the thing's coming to an end. I know this road. I've almost reached the end of it two or three times now. It's all downhill from here.

But enough dark thoughts. There is, after all, always light here. Relentless, humming, buzzing light. A cellmate who made such a noise without cease would drive one senseless. But not me. I'm as sound as the day I was reborn.

I embarked on this story of my life, thinking it a manageable journey given the singular shortness of it—singular at least for being able to speak of it, much less write about it, after only a few weeks existence. Still, brief as it is, I've left out more moments than I've included. Some of the most cherished I reserve for my dreams and my eventual madness. Most, though fine moments each one, are nonetheless unremarkable, unrecalled. Farewell, Time Forgotten. I can't properly say I'll miss you, but I've been glad to make your acquaintance.

But there are some moments—Wordsworth, I believe, calls them *spots of time*—wherein resides a great significance—sensed, if not always understood—whose recurrent and intertwining recollections shape one's life thereafter. Moments at which life changes. Evolutionary moments. It is by their lights new moments are experienced. They dominate one's so-called idle thoughts (all those not directly involved with getting to the grocer's or tightening a bolt) and grow in influence over time, as one's thoughts grow increasingly idle and reflective, like a still pool. These moments are the ripples, the fish darting beneath the surface, the glance of light refracting one's vision. The plot.

Sometimes evolutionary moments seem fraught with difficult choices like an unmarked crossroads in the mountains. To revisit them is to wander a maze of alternatives, to curse oneself for a thousand failures. Others seem fated, as if no amount of reliving could alter the slightest detail. These are the moments that bring men to their knees, like Oedipus, blinded, broken. A foolish old man. I try to avoid those. Wise old sage is a much overrated life.

I've chosen the present tense in order to understand these moments as I lived them; rather, I come up with this reason *after* I've written a chapter and there it is! (Of such rationalizations, I believe, most literary criticism is born, especially as practiced by authors—though their absurdities license those later dreamed up by the professional critic.) To put it simply, the present tense seems to help in the reliving of these moments; the reliving of them helps keep madness at bay. That's the theory, at least. Some days I feel as if I'm living in the demons' own house, summoning the very furies to drive me mad.

You come here with your own purposes, which, I'm aware, may not be altogether compatible with mine. You might enjoy an insane prisoner story, something after the manner of Dostoyevski, that pious reactionary, but I am loath to give it to you. Or perhaps your tastes are more romantic, and you would prefer a rattling good yarn about the imprisoned prince who makes a bold escape, but I've already written that one in the *Memoirs*. It was one of Rachel's favorite parts. You may read it on the Internet, if you like. It's in the fifth section of part five.

Yes, it's true: I've fancied for these words, an audience, somewhere outside this cell, sometime in the present. I've further fancied that somehow I'll smuggle these words into the world and into the hands of this fancied audience. If you're reading this, you can't imagine how incredible your existence seems to me. You're not the one who requires convincing on that score. Only on all others.

It was Coleridge, wasn't it, who made the distinction between the fancy and the imagination? I can't recall. What I'd give for books other than my own! In any event, if you exist, gentle reader, I thank you; for then I'm talking to you, not to myself. To this slender reed I've moored my craft, and keep writing. It's been a great comfort to me.

Still, I would dearly love something, anything, even a bread bag or a *People* magazine, to read. God, how I miss it!

I attempted reading a few of the introductions and commentaries in these volumes, but felt as if I were eavesdropping at my funeral. The more they admired me, the more I wanted to pick a fight with them. If I'm so damn *right*—I wanted to say—I who have such a high opinion of the human species—then how is it I'm in jail, *again*? An old conundrum, that one. Not worth bothering about. If you ask humanity whether I should be caged, I am confident a majority would say no, but humanity wasn't consulted, and the majority had no say in the matter. Who landed me here but myself? I knew the lay of the land, that I was walking into a trap, and yet I persisted in my folly. When Mike told me, *You're going to be on television, Peter,* did I think that was going to be a *good* thing? Complaining about landing in this jail is like jumping off a high cliff and blaming gravity for any resulting misfortune.

The truth is, I was suckered in. I just *had* to see what would happen next, as if I were somehow removed from the events, immune from their consequences, as if I could just change to another reality if I didn't like the way this one played out.

But I digress. The subject was reading, as I recall. For whatever reason, Dead Peter's commentators consistently put my teeth on edge. So it was with great reluctance, I tried reading Dead Peter's words themselves. After all, I'm working around them all day—across the top margin, down the side, along the bottom—and the eye wanders from time to time to that thicket of old sense in the middle of the page. I thought it might be interesting to have a look at it. So whenever I was written out, I started reading to pass the time. I feared, I suppose, bad writing, facile thinking, tedious stretches—the usual writer fears. And I found all those, more or less, but not so very many, for the words meant little to me in themselves but served only to cue some unwelcome memory every page or so, like visiting a place where one once lived.

The last such memory happened like this: A likely phrase recalls the night I came up with it, though now it strikes me as a
bit overblown. I remember reading it aloud to Sophie, who
smiled from the fireside, remember being flooded with a renewed sense of hope and purpose. We lay in bed that night and
watched thick, heavy snow fall beneath a moon we knew to be
full. And when it stopped, the most beautiful light I'd ever seen
streamed in through the windows—from the sky, from the
ground, from everywhere—and filled our room. It glowed on
the hills and valleys of our flesh.

But that was one of those moments I'd thought to keep to myself, and here I've blabbed it, though it's more properly Dead
Peter's moment—even though I still look after it—and the dead,
as any good scholar will tell you, are never afforded a moment's
privacy. Besides, you and I, imagined reader, have been cooped
up together in this cell for a long while now—trust me on this,
even though I've mercifully spared you the unchanging details—so a certain intimacy seems proper. How can I keep anything from you? Either you don't exist and I'm raving in an
empty hall, or you do, and you can indulge me a pleasant memory.

Not that its effect is pleasant for me, not under these circumstances—certainly not pleasant for the now-broken-spined volume that provoked it. The more cherished the memory, the
deeper the despair it can cast me into, for such moments seem
gone forever. *Are gone forever.* Meanwhile, dark memories don't
have the decency to abandon their grim influence, and continue
to ruin long stretches of time with their usual facility. Like Frol's
scars, the ones on his soul, they never fade. There's no justice or
peace for an imprisoned mind: Memories, good *and* bad, provoke despair. Thoughts of the "foreseeable" future provoke despair. *Time* provokes despair. Thus is imprisonment. Thus is
slavery.

That is why I write—because I choose to. It makes me feel free.
It cheers me up. (Can't you tell?) So I'll press on, for perhaps you
exist and want to know what happens next. There are a few

more episodes yet, a few more ghosts to come calling in the night when their appointed hour comes round, a bit of the future not yet foreseen.

I awaken thinking I've heard the door down the hall close, though there's no remaining evidence of the sound even in this echoing place. I listen intently, but there's only the buzz of light, the sound of my own breathing. "Is anyone there?" I call out, but only my echo answers, and I feel immediately the fool, tricked again by dreams, losing hold on reality.

And then commences an odd medley of sounds, clearly purposeful, but baffling in their complexity and rhythm, as if the perpetrator of them were severely palsied or multilimbed—a series of thumpings and clatterings and scratchings—that ends in a crash I would guess to be a drawer laden with coins and clutter falling to the floor. Something plastic bounces. Coins roll and fall. And then there's a rustling, bustling, burrowing sort of noise. A distinct jingle. A distinctive jingle.

Keys.

I imagine them vividly. In all that noise, of course, there must be some keys. But are they the keys I need to get out of here?

Now comes the tinkle of metal plowing through clutter, then along the concrete floor, ringing as they go, and I imagine I have somehow gained the power of telekinesis, and it is I who have thrown open the desk and found the keys and am dragging them to my cell by sheer force of will!

An embarrassing confession, that last train of thought. I can only offer in my defense that I've been locked up too long, that I've succumbed to the natural religion of solitary confinement—superstitious solipsism. I abandon my folly when my true deliverer walks briskly into view. It is Mortimer, wearing a large chromium key ring around his neck like an oversize halo, the keys—dozens of them on a smaller ring tethered on a chain—jingle merrily along behind him. Six of the other cats draw up the rear. I do a quick survey and determine that Zahra, a white Persian, is the missing one. Perhaps she serves as lookout somewhere.

Mortimer has no difficulty passing through the bars, rubbing himself against this bar then that one, springing onto my cot in a bounding leap that sends the keys catapulting into my outstretched hands. I free him of his halo and give his head a good scratch with promises of many more in the future, and set myself free. I make my way through the keys. It's the thirteenth one. In a cage, one's notions of freedom are greatly simplified: Outside the cage is freedom. One often discovers that the cage is inside another cage inside another and so on, and it's hard to know when one's reached the end, but for now, opening this door is freedom.

I step into the hallway and look up and down. There's a slight bend to it I wasn't aware of from inside the cell, so I can only see a dozen yards in either direction. I follow the cats in the former direction of TV. Around the bend, for it's all bend, we come to an anteroom where a desk stands, its single drawer dumped on the floor in a mess. There's a television hanging from the wall on an iron bracket. There's a photograph of a baseball team on the desk. Half the players are black; half are white; half are women; half are men. My watcher might be any one of them or their coach or a parent. There's a half-full Styrofoam cup of coffee with cream, no lipstick. A stir stick lies beside it, stuck to the calendar that covers the desk like a mat. April 1999. Sporting events, including the fight I heard, are written in the dates in neat script I'm pleased to see is not Anchee's. The only other entry is on the twentieth. *Kropotkin*, it says, nothing more. There's a newspaper with the photograph I heard about on television of me and Jonah on the canal. It's not quite as good an angle as I'd imagined, and Jonah's face is oddly blurred, oddly, for everything else is clear enough, and the camera has caught me in pontificating motion midsentence, my gesturing hand crisply frozen by the shutter. Yet his face is slightly blurred, making certain identification difficult. The story wrapped around the photo follows the same bent course as the TV version. Under the newspaper lies the remote control. I try it, but the TV remains dark.

There's a door with an altogether different-looking lock than the one on my cell. It looks like one of those money machines, with a keypad and a slot beside it for a plastic card. I start to search the dumped drawer for the card when Mortimer yowls and a furious scratching starts up on the other side of the door. I look down just as a plastic card slides into view; barely visible is the tip of the white paw pushing it. I scoop the card up, slide it in the machine, and try the door. Still locked. The little display says, ENTER ACCESS CODE.

I would prefer a bottle labeled DRINK ME. The chances of my stumbling upon the right number are too remote to contemplate. Again I start to sift through the debris, this time to see if my watcher was careless with the code and wrote it down somewhere. But I am blown off course by the cats, who begin racing about, scattering the mess to the four corners but for a box of paper clips they slice open and set upon in a frantic fit of batting and leaping and rolling about. I've seen them like this before when Brad lets them at the catnip. One night, thoroughly nipped, they played a goalless soccer game with a Ping-Pong ball that thumped and skittered for an hour or more.

Then as abruptly as their game started, it's over, and there's a space in the middle of the floor cleared of everything but four tiny piles of paper clips in a row about a foot apart. All seven of the cats on my side of the door stand behind the pile on my left, as if posed for a team photograph, and give me an encouraging look. They've taken leave of their senses.

"I'm sorry, my friends, but I don't have time to play right now."

They run to the door and back to that pile of paper clips. Ashanti, an Abyssinian who, if she knew the Pharaohs, no doubt ordered them to do her bidding and they did, lays a paw on the clips and looks me in the eye. If I could read her thoughts, I think they would be something along the lines of *you idiot!* And I must agree, for I finally got it and fall to my knees and count. There are nine clips in the first pile, three in the second, seven in the third, and six in the fourth. I stand up and punch 9376 into the keypad, swat ENTER with my paw, and the lock disengages. I hold the door open for the cats and pass through the second door. Zahra, looking like a pug-faced cloud, rams her head against my calf in greeting and congratulations.

The cats lead me to an elevator, and showing off or celebrating, pile themselves in front of the call button. Gawain the Havana Brown perches atop his comrades and pushes the button with a sinuous stretch. He's a rare and expensive breed of cat according to TJ and reminds me of one of the film stars Rachel introduced me to, the marvelous dancer with the pretty voice. Astaire, I believe his name was. When the elevator bell rings, the cats cascade to the carpet and into the elevator as if they have been riding in them all their lives, a time quite a bit before the thing was invented, I should think. I don't recall any elevators in the pyramids. They let me push the one button, marked G, having had their fun. The ride is a long one; I sit on the floor and pet the cats.

In addition to Mortimer, Zahra, Ashanti, and Gawain are Faustina, a calico; Pearl, a gray-and-white alley; Rashid, a Siamese mix; and Sylvester, a black-and-white longhair who looks exactly, I'm told, like the cartoon character after whom he is named. Rachel had plans to introduce me to his namesake some evening, an evening I've long assumed will never be. I look up at the elevator's ceiling. More buzzing lights. When I get to the surface, the first thing I must do is find Rachel. Everything else can wait. This is one of those moments, I believe, when a believer would pray, but, of course, I do not. The cats press up against me and purr from all sides, and it feels for all the world like an embrace.

The doors open onto what appears to be the austere lobby of a modern office building. It's a deserted glass-and-granite affair, a mere housing for the elevators, not even any chairs. The cats lead me to a revolving door. They pile into a single compartment and get the thing spinning—one, two, three revolutions—before tumbling like dice onto the sidewalk. From what I can tell through the heavily tinted glass, no one seems to notice. I give it a couple of revolutions to slow down, then step into the whirling door and am ejected into the heart of Richmond, free and unfettered. There's only one catch. I see it immediately in the sculpted plume of water that rises from the still fountain directly in front of me: Time is stopped here.

At first blush, everything, though motionless, appears normal. I'm embarrassed to confess that the first oddity I'm aware of is the scarcity of automobiles, especially with so many people out, for the sidewalk is unusually crowded, people spilling into the street. The buses are running. There's one headed up the hill stuffed with passengers. The few cars are likewise full, a rare occurrence from what I've seen.

It's only then I take a close look at the still inhabitants of the street. This isn't the usual crowd. That one there, clearly, though he has fresh clothes, is a slave recently escaped. His unblinking eyes are filled with wonder. That one, too, is still taking in a strange new world. He carries several fish in a drawstring bag over his shoulder. Once I look for them, they are everywhere. Richmond was a center for the slave trade, import and export. If they were all set free and brought here, they would outnumber the current residents at least two to one. The Belle Isle refugees are easy to spot, though they, too, have been outfitted, many of them wearing MCV T-shirts. Even modern medicine cannot completely erase the ravages of starvation and exposure, and they look like walking skeletons. But though scurvy has made of their smiles a grotesque grimace, many are smiling nonetheless. Like me, they were miraculously snatched from death. I know that joy. Free at last. I know that one, too.

The prosperous white people in business suits who usually dominate this vicinity are conspicuous by their absence. That's where all the cars have gone, carrying them out to the suburbs, to the airport and beyond. This must be Richmond after Rachel's "massive demonstrations." The city has been invaded by its past, invaded and taken over, by the look of things. Some modern residents have apparently fled, fearing the worst. Their version of history has treated them rather well. This new one might not be so kind. But not everyone here is from the past. A good number of modern residents, black and white, yellow and brown, remain in the city, welcoming perhaps, that most un-Richmond of occurrences, a *change*.

I reach these conclusions as I pass among them unremarked, trailing along behind the cats, who are enjoying their outing in a world without automobiles. (They usually avoid the streets; all four of their deceased companions were struck by cars.) They snake their way up the street, tails held high, like the banners of eight nations, in a game of follow the leader, rubbing up against as many legs as possible, as still as tree trunks, and not a single person moves. If time were to start up again, would these people know what lives brushed against them between moments?

I trail along behind, rubbing up against no one, but taking in the scene. A swank men's clothing store is filled with men trying on suits. They stand around in various stages of undress. Wives and girlfriends form an amused audience. Most of these men have probably never worn a suit in their lives. One wag has climbed into some elephantine trousers, puffing his cheeks and sticking out his stomach to evoke the man who might fill them, and his companions are laughing hysterically.

A restaurant with tables spilling onto the sidewalk is packed with refugees and freed slaves. The servers mostly come from their number as well, and all seem to be eating the same hearty soup, the same coarse bread. I can only assume this fashionable spot is no longer a profitable enterprise. Judging by the faces of its new clientele, it has become one huge Kitchen Table. Deep in the dining room I can see Zipper, the famous mimic, holding a glass aloft. Is that supposed to be me, I wonder?

An expensive hotel looks full, the lobby crowded, though the doormen and bellhops, their jackets unbuttoned, sit out front with the new residents and talk and smoke. Clothes hang from the balconies. Children play a game of baseball in the valet parking lot with brand-new equipment. The gloves, price tags still dangling from some of them, look enormous on their little hands. A group of Hispanic women, most likely the former housekeeping staff, have shed their uniforms for jeans and are digging up the flower beds and putting in a kitchen garden.

Most stores are open, wide-open, but no one seems to be exchanging money or plastic. The glowing numbers that usually grace cash registers are dark. Some stores are quite busy, like the shoe store; while others, like the jeweler's, are near empty.

There's a huge truck—UKROP'S GROCERY STORES it says on the side—stopped in the street, its back doors open, a queue at the rear. A crew inside is handing out boxes of foodstuffs. I recognize the man I called Gray in their number, Pierce from the restaurant, and Caitlin. I seriously doubt Mr. Ukrop knows about this.

Oh yes, I suppose I must tell you that I'm not the only observer. All along my route, and subject to their fair share of cat slinking, are journalists with microphones, cameramen, mysterious technicians, trucks, wires—an entire industry, in short. It would seem that the whole world is watching.

We turn up a steep hill. I have walked this route in earlier times and I've guessed where the cats are taking me. Capitol Square. I'm not surprised to find there a tent community a good deal more civilized than the one on Belle Isle during the war. The tree-shaded south side of the square, sloping away from the high building, is filled with tents in neat rows. At the center of it is a three-tiered fountain of black iron ringed with shrubbery and flowers. Redbrick walkways lined with park benches radiate out from it, and the cats lead me on a circuitous journey through this new community. I'm struck by how young it is on the whole. It's the young who are enslaved; it's the young who fight wars; it's the young who rise up in rebellion. Some people from the present are helping out, including several in medical garb, police who aren't wearing guns, and many of the homeless who were already here. Human sympathy can be as great a motivator as greed if it's given the chance, if people aren't constantly set at each other's throats like dogs trained to fight.

The stairs to the capitol are filled with the comings and goings of the tent-city residents. At last they have access to the seat of power, though I would guess, even though plastic portable toilets have been brought to the site, the water closets are currently the main attraction. The Governor's Mansion of which Gabriel spoke is on the other side of the capitol from me and is blocked from view. I imagine it equally busy. Somehow, I doubt the good governor has returned. I laugh to recall that he declared April to be Confederate History Month. It looks like he got more history than he bargained for.

I'm stopped in my tracks when I see who it is I've been brought here to meet. She moves, taking an awkward sideways step so that I will see her. The cats scatter like smoke. She's beside a statue of Edgar Allan Poe, the cats' idea perhaps. She looks exactly as I remember her when first we met, when I fell in love with her straightaway. I crush her in my arms, and her hair smells the same, feels the same. Her eyes are Sophie's dark almonds that could thrill me with a glance. She is young, and she is beautiful. But when she speaks, I know that like me, she carries the full measure of old life with her, however young she might appear. She disengages herself from my arms, nods to a park bench, and we sit stiffly like an old married couple when a fight's in the air.

"I cannot stay," she says. "I have come to persuade you of something. Please don't think ill of me for it. I couldn't bear that. I never felt as if I were quite as good as you thought I was."

"No, that's not true. Don't say such a thing."

"But it *is*, Petya. I know. It's why you left me behind. It's just as well. I don't think I could bear this life again. You in jail, and me keeping up a brave face for you. What good is it, my darling, if nothing ever changes? You have tried the old way. It doesn't work."

"Look around you," I say. "Something is certainly going on here."

"This time you see won't just happen. But he can make it happen, if you wish. You must speak with him, with an open mind."

"Anchee you mean. That's why you've come here? To plead *his* case?"

"I have come here because I want to help. What of you, Petya? Why did you come here? You come here in this unnatural way, and now you have the chance to make something beautiful of it, to have the world of which you have always dreamed! You see the beginnings of it here and now. Don't let your quibbling principles stand in your way. Just give the word, and it will be so." She lays her hand on mine. "My prince."

"I am not your prince, Sophie, nor anyone's." I tap my head. "Up here there are no princes. No kings. No presidents. No slaves. No masters. No puppets. No strings. I cannot endorse this madness. This isn't revolution; it's puppetry."

She withdraws her hand and hangs her head in sadness, a look that never failed to pierce my heart. "I know," she says. "That's what I told him, but we hoped . . . He admires you, I think, almost as much as I. Please, just talk to him. That is all I ask. You owe me that much, Petya, for leaving me behind. He says you've threatened to murder him."

In spite of everything, I have to laugh. Did he take my threat seriously? "It's a little late for that, unfortunately. He's perfectly safe from me."

"So you'll speak to him, and hear him out?"

"Yes."

"It's not like you think. He only asks you to do *one* little thing."

"I *told* you I would speak with him."

"You could finally be happy, Petya."

"I have *always* been happy," I snap, and feel immediately ridiculous.

She smiles sadly and shakes her head. "I know better. This revolution you gave your life to, it only broke your heart over and over again. Your funeral was the end of it, Petya. There was no hope after that. It was finished."

"That's not true. There were anarchists in the Spanish Civil War years later. I read about it. In Barcelona, they actually—"

"Did they win, Petya? Did they *win?*"

"No, but—"

"Then what good are they?" Her eyes blaze with anger, and she is on the verge of tears. "Talk to him, Petya. Just talk to him. Don't be so damned stubborn. He's up there, waiting for you." She points to the capitol, the great government temple, Jefferson's design, I believe, cribbed from a Roman temple in Nîmes. I'd feel better if it were still in the service of some pagan deity instead of the State.

Perhaps my question is cruel, but she seems well informed, has glimpsed more of the script than I have, and is working for my enemy—might even be a counterfeit created *by my enemy*, and not Sophie at all: "Where's Rachel?" I ask.

She stiffens. "How should I know?"

"You know *who* she is. I can tell that much by your tone. So why is it unreasonable to think you know *where* she is?"

"There's no point. She won't know you're here. She's stopped in this moment."

"Then start it up again."

"You'll have to take that up with Anchee."

She says it as if playing a trump, and in that moment I loathe her. "Ah, a hostage. Worthy of a Lenin. You're not really Sophie, are you?"

She winces at that, cut to the quick. "You'll never know will you? She's over there, if you must know. Plotting." Her voice is filled with jealousy and scorn. She points to a large tent at the foot of the steps.

This is not my Sophie; I can't believe it. "Good-bye," I say to her, whoever she is.

"Good-bye," she says, calling after me, "Listen to him. Please."

I don't turn back, sprinting the last few yards to the tent. Inside, a group I take to be the core conspirators—Rachel, Jonah, Earl, Wendy, and a towering man who must be Gabriel—are conferring over a map of the city. Rachel is making a point, her hand hovering over the heart of the city. She looks weary and beautiful. She—they all—wear shirts that say FREE PETER

KROPOTKIN. I circle the table so that I look into her unseeing eyes. If time were a wall, I would batter it down with my bare hands. I lean across the table and kiss her cheek, leaving a tear there. Perhaps, since time is stopped, it won't evaporate, but will be there still when time resumes. "I'll be back," I say, "as soon as possible." Sophie's right. There's no point conferring with Rachel's statue.

I find Anchee easily enough. He stands in the Rotunda in front of the life-size statue of George Washington on a pedestal. Washington's fenced, of course, wouldn't want the revolutionary general to escape. I've seen reproductions of this statue and rather like it. The sculptor gave us the real man, grown a bit plump and straining at the buttons of his old revolutionary uniform. A couple of buttons are missing altogether from the lapel of his coat. Why sew them on? The war's over, his sword's hung up. He's gotten down off his horse and welcomed peace.

"What now?" I ask Anchee.

"You anticipate my question exactly. Only I'm asking you. I told you from the beginning this was your life, and I meant it. As you probably suspect, I've undertaken a good deal of work on your behalf, but it's still your life, and I want you to accept it, embrace it. Or deny it, if that's your choice."

He reminds me of someone running for office, the most insidious means of robbing one's neighbors of their freedom. I want none of his "choices," like choosing the fabric to line one's coffin. "I want to see Rachel. I want to speak with her. Start time going again."

The mention of Rachel lights him up. I reconsider my promise to do him no harm. "Yes, Rachel. Remarkable isn't she? You two have met many times, in a sense, under all different circumstances, and you fall *every* time. And she for you. That was one variable I could always count on. Terribly romantic. Have you ever heard of pheromones, Peter?"

"Yes," I say icily.

"Oh I don't mean to suggest that's all there is to it. The ideal loved one embodies the ideal. Pheromones do the rest. You love her body and soul, and she you. How can you bear to give her up?"

"I don't intend to give her up."

"She's in *this* life, you know."

"And from what I've seen she's doing a splendid job of it. Sophie, or whoever that was, said you had something to ask me. Ask it, and let's be done with it."

"Don't you want to know what Rachel is in the process of accomplishing?"

"I'll discover that from her. I want to speak with you as little as possible."

"What have I done that's so horrible? I introduced you to Rachel. I'd say, judging by your actions, you don't have a problem with that. I brought together a remarkable group of young people, some like-minded folks. Is there anything wrong with that? Doing a little organizing? Isn't that what radicals *do*? Educate and organize? I didn't use any mind control or space rays. They all made their own choices. I harmed no one."

"Did TJ *choose* for his parents to die?"

"Certainly not. What kind of monster do you think I am? I suppose you could call me a vulture, because I knew his parents' death and his family history made him wide-open to the idea of a long-lost uncle. But I didn't prey on anyone. I bought him a house, dragged him out of his depression, got him to start taking his painting seriously.

"But that's all water under the bridge, as they say. I brought like-minded people here. Then I resurrected you as a catalyst or a protagonist—those terms are as close as I can come—but that's right—you're not interested in aesthetics. You've seen the results. All they have to do, you see, out there in that tent, is figure out how to hold the city for ten more days. That's how long it takes with the most intense media coverage in history going on all over the world, for things to evolve to the next level, and the revolution starts to spread—ten days from the day *you* are set free, that is. The media fall in love with you, I think."

"Am I set free then? Is this the end of it?"

"In *this* life. But this is your life, as I said, and I must know if you approve of it before I start it up and let it go, if it's a life you *choose* to live."

"Choose! How can you speak of choose? You and your spy manipulating me, linking me to that insane business in Colorado I had nothing whatsoever to do with."

"It was important to get you on television, on T-shirts, on the Internet."

"In jail."

"Exactly! That goes without saying. Some things never change. But for those things that have, we gave you a little push. When the details of your frame-up are brought to light, the resulting scandal works wonders, topples tyrants, changes things. It was my spy's idea, as you call her. She has an exceptional grasp of these things."

" 'She'? I thought Mike—"

Anchee snorts his disgust. "Mike's an idiot. Show him a philosopher's stone, and he jumps at it. He's in it for the magic, the imagined power and glory. There was no end of the nonsense he would swallow. Too much Nietzsche, I think. But he was just a red herring. No, Sondra was the one, drawing you in, keeping you focused on Mike, making a chivalric duty of it or some such nonsense, so that you didn't hesitate to rush in and face down the lion in its den; unfortunately, you had the wrong lion, the wrong den."

"Sondra? But why? She scarcely seems to care about political matters. Why would she do such a thing?"

He holds up a small magazine. The something-or-other Review. He opens it to a dog-eared page. "Here's her first published poem, if you'd like to read it." He frowns at it."It's not very good, I'm afraid." He confides in a stage whisper, "I'm a friend of the editor, helped get him tenure."

I read it through. It's short. "Momentary Freedom," it's called, and it's about herself, or seems to be. I can't really make it out. "She betrayed me for a *poem?*"

"Several actually. All she's written so far, prestigiously placed. All for art, Peter. And contributor's copies. There'll be a book next year. A few prizes. Without me she was going to end up a tech writer for Radio Shack. I showed her the future, and it gave her pause, shall we say.

"But you've known all along there were spies, as you call them—supporting roles. You were only wrong about who they were. How does that change things? The question is whether you want me to start this time again with you in it or not."

I feel a bit dizzy. I'm being asked to play God. That has to be wrong. But still I find myself wavering. "I've acted in good faith. From what you say, everyone else acted in good faith and conscience."

"That's quite correct," Anchee says. "Before you decide, I want to show you something." He leads me around Washington and into the north room. "This is the old House of Delegates." There's a bronze statue standing with its back to us, a half dozen paces into the room. It, too, is life-size on a pedestal in military uniform. He has a circled A—the anarchist symbol—painted in white on his back. A few drips testify to the artist's amateur status. I have a good idea who it will be even before I see his face. I'm getting to the point where I can recognize him coming and going. Here's Lee again.

Anchee plays tour guide. "This Lee is here to commemorate where he stood when he accepted command of the Confederate forces of Virginia, in April naturally. A busy month around here. Over there you see a bust of Davis, there's Stephens. The place is stuffed with the Confederacy. You could put it out of its misery."

"I'm not sure I approve of your tactics."

"Revolution is a state of mind, right? I just nudge people along, so that they have a revolutionary state of mind, your mind actually. What do you say? Just give me the word, and the revolution is yours."

"What do you mean, 'nudge people along'? Do you force them? Deceive them? How do you do it?"

"It's a good deal of work to motivate so many, as you can appreciate. But as you know from the primitive propaganda you employed that one true believer begets others, so that once you reach a critical mass it takes on a life of its own."

I nod my agreement. True enough.

"And then there are those whose contribution is simply immeasurable without whom nothing of significance is likely to come of even the best efforts. They are the ones with the flashes of insight, the intuitive sense of what is to be done."

I nod again, foolishly innocent of where he's going with this.

"Rachel is one of those," he says. "None of this would've happened without her. She came up with the idea for the demonstrations when she was in jail, worked out the whole thing, spent *weeks* in the past setting it all up. All to spring her man from the hoosegow."

As he tells this story, in spite of my pride at her accomplishments and devotion, I have a growing sense of uneasiness. "So she achieved all that by her own will, her own powers of persuasion, her own hard work. She forced no one, deceived no one."

"That is true. Deception's more in my line, actually."

He hands me a letter, and I open it. There's a newspaper clipping inside. It's an advertisement for a position in Richmond, dated some years ago, Rachel's position until recently. The letter doesn't say much. *I saw this and thought it sounded perfect for you, Love, Dad.* A chill goes down my spine.

"Unfortunately, you see, Rachel's father never actually saw this ad or wrote this note, or mailed it to his daughter. But when she called to tell him she was moving back home hours after he'd gotten a death sentence from his doctor, he wasn't about to argue with her. So here it is, Peter, the deal: You hold it there in your hand, the, how was it you put it? *The string to make her dance.*" He dances his hands in the air like a puppeteer. "Tear it up, and I never mail it. No one—including your precious loved one—is deceived or manipulated. Or you give it back to me, I mail it, and she reads it one cold drizzly morning in Seattle and sits waiting for you when you come to town, waiting for you at the foot of the stairs as we speak. It will be our little secret.

"So which is it? The time that you would be living if I hadn't interfered at all? Or an anarchist revolution in full swing?"

"This isn't a revolution! The *people* make a revolution, not some tinhorn god from the future."

"The people are greedy swine."

He's shown his true stripes with that line, or at least the role he's playing. The revolution means nothing without faith in the people. I tear the letter once, twice, three times, and throw it in his face. The pieces flutter to the floor, and he smiles.

"You didn't even *ask* what your life will be. You're a remarkable man, Peter Kropotkin. It's jail, of course. But you probably guessed that."

"You knew this is how it would end."

"I did indeed."

"Why bother bringing me to life, then?"

"I tell stories, Peter. I just tell stories. You're the revolutionist. Any parting requests?"

I think I finally understand him. It's a curious symmetry, I suppose, but the story of Sondra's poems gives me the idea for the one scrap I might snatch from this life. Anchee will be my smuggler. "I want you to see that the book I wrote in the margins gets into print. Surely you have other friends as convenient as Sondra's editor."

"There's a fellow here in town who might do it, pass it off as his work. But he's a *science-fiction* writer. No one would take it seriously."

He uses the term "science fiction," a most intriguing union, with the same sneer Sapworth had applied to "anarchist," and I immediately like the fellow, whoever he may be. "He'll do," I say. "I'll finish it up tonight."

"I'll come round to fetch it. You'll be changing cells. I'll see you have some paper for your final thoughts. This is a terribly unhappy ending for you I'm afraid. So hopeless."

"You're not the only one who can spring people from jail."

"Oh yes, 'the people.' If you leave it to them, you know how it ends."

"And how is that?"

"You stay in jail for the rest of your life."

I don't really notice when the still life around us changes population. He's been backing up as he talks, leading me around behind Lee's back. He hands me a can. Spray paint. White. "It's a revolutionary tool these days, Peter." He pats me on the shoulder. "Good luck." Time starts up again, and you can imagine the rest.

I'm in a different cell, awaiting transfer in the morning to I know not where. After my arrest, spray can in hand, justice was swift. Even though in this reality I'm not linked with that madness in Colorado, when the police checked my documents, they found soon enough that I'm a human without a State, an intolerable condition apparently for someone caught committing "terrorist acts," so I must be locked up until a State claims me or Hell freezes over, whichever comes first. Anchee showed up in the guise of a guard, bringing paper as promised. He talks to me incessantly as I write. He says my new prison is filled with Arabs and Cubans with equally indefinite crimes and sentences as I. I look forward to the companionship and the opportunity to learn some new languages, new perspectives. I can survive anything but solitude.

Outside, there is literally no one who knows me. Anchee delights in recounting the whereabouts of my friends, all strangers here: Rachel is in Seattle riding her bicycle to a job she hates. Brad is living with his mother. Doris is smoking a cigarette, watching her life being stolen bit by bit. Zipper is in jail in Florida. Alicia is taking in strays. Caitlin is studying art in Rhode Island. Dave is a busker in Los Angeles. Clement Arthur is a garbageman. TJ shot himself three years ago. Jonah and Earl are dead and forgotten.

So it comes down to you, gentle reader. You're the only one who knows me. The only one who can set me free. You may wish to discount all of this as just another fanciful story. But believe me—it's true, every word—and be it novel or Bible, the only authority a text can claim is itself and its readers.

But even if you believe me, how will you ever find me? Where is *here*, you may well ask? It's not hard to find a prison these days. It's a booming enterprise. Strike out in any direction. You'll find prisons and prisoners everywhere you turn. If you want to set me free, set all us jailbirds free. I'll be in there somewhere.

Acknowledgments

There is not even a thought, or an invention, which is not common property, born of the past and the present . . . every new invention is a synthesis, the resultant of innumerable inventions which have preceded it in the vast field of mechanics and industry.

—PETER KROPOTKIN, *The Conquest of Bread*

All these people significantly contributed to this book, though many of them don't know it, and some of them aren't real. There are numerous omissions I'm sure:

Anonymous, Patricia Anthony, Ludovico Ariosto, Paul Avrich, Antigone Barton, Afred Bester, Jesse Bohl, Luis Borges, Jennifer Brehl, Katia Brock, Marina Brock, John Brown, Byron, John Carroll, Lewis Carroll, Karen Chandler, Raymond Chandler, Charlie Chaplin, Arthur C. Clarke, John Clute, Samuel Taylor Coleridge, Cotton, Betsy Daniel, David Danvers, Liz Darhansoff, Santa De Haven, Tom De Haven, Morris Denmark, Charles Dickens, Daphne Du Maurier, Bob Dylan, Trebor E. Eel, Sa'ad El-Amin, Douglas R. Egerton, Debra Farrell, Suzanne Feldman, Dick Fine, Jeffrey Ford, Jimmy Ghaphery, Goethe, Kenneth Grahame, John Harvey, Andy Heidel, Steve Jobs, Randy Jones, Franz Kafka, Agymah Kamau, Steve Krause, Suzanne Langer, Lenore Langsdorf, Mei Leng Lau, Ursula Le Guin, John Lennon, Jonathan Lethem, Jeff Lodge, James W. Loewen, Aimee Mann, Paule Marshall, Maureen McHugh, John Morris, Howard Owen, Karen Owen, Parzival, Alice Irene Potatoes, Tom Ryan, Page St. John, Samson, William Shakespeare, Mary Shelley, Leslie Shiel, Peter Singer, Luke Skywalker, Lee Smith, Neal Stephenson,

Oscar Stovall, Henry David Thoreau, Leo Tolstoi, Patrick Tompkins, Traditional, Kilgore Trout, Simone Turbeville, John Weisiger, Minor Weisiger, H. G. Wells, Randall Williams, Tina Ennulat Wilson, George Woodcock, William Wordsworth, W. B. Yeats, Emiliano Zapata.

Also, James River Park, Richmond City Parks, Richmond Sanitation workers, GRTC, Richmond Battlefield Park, Food-Not Bombs, Carytown Books, the VCU Library, Virginia State Library, Valentine Museum, Richmond Free Press, and the Anarchy Archives at http://dwardmac.pitzer.edu/anar chist_archives/archivehome.html

A special thanks to Sarah Weisiger, inventor of the Weisiger interface, who makes all things possible.